About the

Scarlet Wilson wrote her first story aged eight and has never stopped. She's worked in the health service for twenty years, trained as a nurse and a health visitor. Scarlet now works in public health and lives on the West Coast of Scotland with her fiancé and their two sons. Writing medical romances and contemporary romances is a dream come true for her.

Danica Winters is a bestselling author who has won multiple awards for writing books that grip readers with their ability to drive emotion through suspense and occasionally a touch of magic. When she's not working, she can be found in the wilds of Montana testing her patience while she tries to hone her skills at various crafts (quilting, pottery, and painting are not her areas of expertise). She always believes the cup is neither half full nor half empty, but it better be filled with wine.

Rebecca Hunter is the award-winning author of sensual, emotional adventures of the heart. She writes sexy stories about alpha men and spirited women for Mills & Boon, and her books reflect her love of travel. To find out more or to join her newsletter, please visit rebeccahunterwriter.com

European Escapes

July 2023 **Madrid**	February 2024 **Prague**
August 2023 **Sicily**	March 2024 **Athens**
September 2023 **Sweden**	April 2024 **London**
January 2024 **Paris**	May 2024 **Berlin**

European Escapes:
Sweden

SCARLET WILSON

DANICA WINTERS

REBECCA HUNTER

MILLS & BOON

First Published in Great Britain 2023
by Mills & Boon, an imprint of HarperCollins*Publishers* Ltd,
1 London Bridge Street, London, SE1 9GF

www.harpercollins.co.uk

HarperCollins*Publishers*
Macken House, 39/40 Mayor Street Upper,
Dublin 1, D01 C9W8, Ireland

European Escapes: Sweden © 2023 Harlequin Enterprises ULC.

A Festive Fling in Stockholm © 2021 Harlequin Enterprises ULC.
In His Sights © 2019 Danica Winters
Hotter on Ice © 2020 Rebecca Hunter

Special thanks and acknowledgement are given to Scarlet Wilson for her contribution to *The Christmas Project* series.

ISBN: 978-0-263-31975-0

A FESTIVE FLING IN STOCKHOLM

SCARLET WILSON

This Christmas story is dedicated to my two weddings of 2021,

Dillon and Megan Glencross, and Stuart and Carly Walker.

Two beautiful brides and two gorgeous grooms.

Wishing you all the love in the world.

CHAPTER ONE

CORA CAMPBELL WALKED briskly down the long corridor of the Royal Kensington Hospital, wondering if biting her nails might be an option. Her pager had already sounded twice.

As a neonatologist she'd spent the last twelve years of her life listening to the sound of a pager—at some stages it had almost dictated her life. Usually she welcomed it. It meant she was needed. She would be busy. She would be serving the tiny patients to whom she'd dedicated her life. But this time was different. This time it was Chris Taylor, the chief executive of her hospital, paging her, and her stomach was doing uncomfortable flip-flops.

She had to be in trouble.

The long walk wasn't helping. It was giving her lots of time to contemplate all the trouble she could be in. She'd signed for new state-of-the-art incubators last week. She'd authorised two extra staff to work over Christmas, because the same old faces went 'off sick' every year at that time. She promised one remote teaching session a week with a prestigious US hospital. She'd just had her fifth professional paper published on a new pioneering technique she'd introduced last year for neonates between thirty-one and thirty-three weeks. The before and after was quite astonishing, and right now she was wondering if the before had unintentionally shown the hospital in a bad light.

She glanced down as she neared the office. Maybe she should have gone back to her locker and put some heels on for a more professional look? Cora always tried to be dressed in a presentable manner at work, comfortable black trousers, a short-sleeved unfussy red top and her trademark shoes. A fellow doctor had introduced her to them at the conference in the US: flat, and completely machine washable, they were as comfortable as slippers and came in a rainbow of colours—all of which Cora had promptly purchased. They were also a dream when running the miles of corridors to an emergency page.

'Hey, Cora.'

Lucy, the chief executive's PA, was sitting behind her desk beaming like the Cheshire Cat. This didn't look like the sign of trouble.

'How's Louie?' Cora asked automatically. 'Can I see a photo of my favourite boy?'

Lucy grabbed her phone from her bag and immediately turned it to face Cora. Her son Louie had been born at twenty-six weeks, two years previously. Cora had looked after him, and always liked to check on his progress.

A sticky face and wide smile beamed up at her. Louie had a shock of blond hair, and a twinkle in his eye. He was also holding a crayon and had clearly just drawn on a white wall.

'Oh, no! The cheeky wee devil. When was that?'

'Sunday,' Lucy said with a smile as she stuffed the phone back in her bag. 'The decorator had just finished the hallway, and Louie decided he wanted to decorate too.' She shook her head. 'I swear, I just turned my back for second. He'd been sitting right next to me eating a yoghurt.'

Cora laughed and nodded. 'What can I say? He's just trying to keep you on your toes.' She winked at her. 'We teach them lots of tricks in NICU.'

She knew Lucy had worried endlessly about her early arrival. But although Louie was still a little small, he was meeting all his milestones with bells on. Cora shifted on her feet and glanced at the closed door. 'So, spill, am I in trouble?'

Lucy widened her eyes, in the way that only a person who knew everyone's secrets could. 'Dr Campbell, what on earth could you be in trouble for?' There was an edge of humour to her mocking tone.

Cora shrugged. 'I thought of nearly half a dozen reasons on the way down the corridor. You really should persuade him to move office. It would be much better for my fear factor if he were situated right next to the stairs.'

Lucy laughed and shook her head as the intercom on her desk sounded. 'That's for you.' She gave her a wink. 'And I don't think you've got anything to worry about.'

Cora sucked in a deep breath and walked over to the door, giving it two knocks before she pushed it open and stepped inside.

Chris Taylor rose to his feet and extended his hand towards her. Cora was immediately struck by the enormous window and the view of London outside. Even though she'd worked at the Royal Kensington for years she'd only ever been in this office on a few occasions. She smiled nervously and shook his hand. 'I would never get any work done in here. I'd be too busy people watching.'

His normally serious face broke into a smile as he

shook his head. 'I don't believe that for a second. You never stop working, Dr Campbell.' He lifted something from his desk. 'As your newly published peer-reviewed paper demonstrates.'

Darn. He'd read it. That must be why she was here. 'Oh, about that. I don't think you should concentrate too much on the before. The Royal Kensington still demonstrated an excellent level of care.'

One eyebrow arched. 'As I would expect,' he said smoothly.

Cora fought the urge to clear her throat and shift in her seat, conscious it would make her look guilty of something. Chris Taylor placed the medical journal back on his desk and clasped his hands in front of him. This was it. This was the position he frequently assumed in press conferences when he was about to deliver news.

'Dr Campbell, I invited you here today in part—' he nodded his head at the journal '—because of your latest publication, and in part, because of an offer I'd like to make to you.'

An offer? Cora immediately straightened in her chair, every cell of her body on alert. An offer was good—right?

'You've been with us a while, so I take it you've heard of the Kensington Project?'

Cora almost choked. 'Yes, of course.' Everyone who worked at the Royal Kensington knew about the Kensington Project.

It was obviously the correct answer because Chris gave a gracious smile. 'You know that we think of ourselves as being home to the best and brightest in the world. Every year we send four of our pioneering team members out to train staff in other hospitals across the world. This year, we'd like you to be one of those members.'

Something was wrong. Her skin was tingling as if a million centipedes were marching over it. Her mouth had just decided she was stuck in the Sahara Desert, and the thirty-three years of knowledge and experience her brain stored had just vanished in a puff of a magician's wand.

Chris was obviously waiting for some kind of response.

She'd wanted this. She'd wanted this for the last few years, and last year had been sadly disappointed when she'd heard that four others had been selected. She'd gone to a nearby bar with her good friend Chloe and they'd both had a glass of wine to commiserate.

This year though, between her teaching, her research paper, and the maternity leave of a colleague, she hadn't even had a chance to watch the calendar and wonder when the announcements might be made.

Chris was still patiently looking at her, as red London buses and black cabs whizzed by outside.

'Fabulous.' It came out almost as a squeak.

Satisfied, he continued. 'We've had a request from...' he consulted a list on his desk '... Stockholm City Hospital in Sweden. They'd like you to train a wide range of their neonatal staff on the pioneering techniques you developed while working at the Royal Kensington.'

She heard the hidden unspoken message. They might be her techniques, but credit would always have to be given to the hospital that had supported her. Cora didn't mind. The Royal Kensington had frequently put their money and trust in her over the last few years, when she'd outlined plans for improvement, both small and large. Her success rate was good. And even when a few things hadn't quite achieved their goal, there had always been learning for all those involved.

Excitement fizzed down inside her. This was an honour. A privilege to visit another country and teach them first-hand all the techniques she'd learned. Stockholm. Sweden. She'd never been to either before and that added even more to the excitement.

Chris kept talking. 'If you choose to accept, then you'll leave in three days' time—the first of November.'

'Three days?' If he heard the note of alarm in her voice, Chris Taylor showed no sign of acknowledgement.

'The arrangements are in place. You'll be flying into Arlanda Airport and we've arranged for you to be picked up and taken to your accommodation. You'll be there for just over seven weeks, flying home on Christmas Eve. I trust these arrangements will be suitable?'

Cora nodded. Her brain was kicking back into gear and she had a million questions.

'Who will I be working with? Do I get to take any of my equipment?' She frowned. 'How do I transport hospital equipment? Where will I be staying? Who are the others involved in the Kensington Project this year?' She paused to catch her breath. 'You said they requested me? Is that usual? Is that how this normally works?'

She caught the gleam in Chris Taylor's eyes and realised exactly how she must sound.

She gave a short laugh and a shrug. 'What's the weather like in Stockholm?'

There was silence for a few moments and Chris tilted his head to one side. 'Is that a yes, Dr Campbell?'

She jumped to her feet as he stood and held out his hand again. 'Yes!' she said, shaking his hand with an overenthusiastic grip. 'That's definitely a yes.'

He smiled. 'In that case, Lucy has a number of details for you that she prepared earlier. I think it's safe to say you're in very good hands.'

Cora didn't doubt it for a second. Lucy was meticulous with her work.

She let his hand go and moved back to the door. 'Thank you. Thank you. I'll check the rota. I'll need to make sure there's enough cover at short notice. I'll speak to Ron in Medical Physics about the transport and review all my patients.'

As her hand closed on the door handle she realised she was babbling again.

'Dr Campbell?'

Chris's amused voice came from behind her. She looked over her shoulder. 'Yes?'

He glanced at her red flats. 'Buy some winter boots.'

'I have wonderful news!' The door to Jonas Nilsson's office burst open with a bang and Elias Johansson came into the room, his eyes sparkling and his smile wide.

Jonas looked at the mark on the wall and shook his head. Elias's enthusiasm for work had never changed in the ten years that he'd known him.

He was seventy and should have retired years ago, but Stockholm City Hospital's Head of Neonatal Intensive Care was showing no signs of slowing down.

Jonas nodded to the chair across from him. 'What have you been up to now, Elias?' he asked.

Elias gave a hearty laugh as he flopped onto the chair. 'What makes you think I've been up to something?'

Elias glanced at the calendar. 'Because it's... Wednesday? And on any weekday, and on some weekends, you're usually up to something within this hospital.'

'Don't ask permission, proceed until apprehended.' Elias smiled, with a wave of his hand.

Jonas put down his pen and leaned forward. This was a favourite quote of Elias's and generally meant trouble.

'I'll ask again,' he said with one eyebrow rising, 'what have you been up to?'

'You've heard of the Kensington Project?' Elias continued without waiting for a reply. 'I put in a request for a doctor from the Royal Kensington Hospital in London to come to Stockholm City to teach us some of her new pioneering techniques in NICU, and I found out earlier today that my request has been successful. I'll be picking Cora Campbell up at the airport in a few days' time.'

Jonas opened his mouth and closed it again, trying to formulate his words carefully. 'What? Who? And no, I've never heard of the Kensington Project—what on earth is it?'

Elias's eyes twinkled. 'An opportunity. That's what it is. An opportunity for us to borrow one of their best— and most published—neonatal experts to come and share her expertise and knowledge with us. What's better, she'll be here right up until Christmas. Can you imagine how much we can learn from her?'

Jonas frowned. 'I have no idea who this woman is. Do we want to learn from her?' He could feel himself getting angry. He was very fond of Elias, but the older he got, the more he meddled.

'Of course, we do!' He winked at Jonas. 'And who knows? Maybe she'll learn something from us. She might even want to do some joint research projects. Now, that *would* be exciting.'

Jonas took a deep breath. As he was Head of Midwifery this new arrival would affect his work schedule for the next seven weeks. He was in charge of the nursing and midwifery staff attached to the NICU. A new doctor might want to teach new techniques. Coming from London, she would be unfamiliar with the standards and guidelines, procedure manuals and cross-check of training that Jonas insisted was adhered to within *his* NICU—because that was how he thought of it.

Jonas was a stickler for regulations and paperwork. Having been burned early on in his career, he wanted to protect both his staff and their patients. He knew just how important that was. Every t was crossed, and every i was dotted. He had high expectations of his staff and they all knew it. Woe betide anyone who fell below his standards.

But Jonas had good reason for feeling as he did. A harsh lesson had made him realise how important rules were, as well as listening to instincts. That was what he'd done years ago when treating a patient in the final stages of labour. She'd been insistent in her birth plan that she did not want a Caesarean section unless there was no other option. Surgery as a teenager had left her feeling traumatised and she didn't want to feel that way again. Having a natural birth would mean she would feel in control and Jonas had been with her all the way. Jonas always promised his patients he would do his absolute best to help them stick to their wishes. But when the condition of her baby had deteriorated rapidly, he'd had to move quickly and follow his instincts, advising her that she needed to undergo a Caesarean section. His instincts had been right. All other professionals had agreed.

But when the woman had been diagnosed with postnatal depression following her delivery and made a complaint that he had let her down, Jonas had been overwhelmed with guilt. His actions had saved the lives of both mother and baby. But he still felt responsible for letting his patient down. His emotions got in the way.

The investigation had shown he'd made the right call. And even though he'd acted on instinct, the hospital policies and his rapid note-taking of all events had saved him. From the first time the baby's heart rate had dipped, Jonas had followed every rule to the letter.

That was why he was now the way he was. Rules, policies and standards protected staff against any complaint—if they followed them to the letter. He also tried to ensure staff weren't ruled by their emotions. He knew how deeply he'd been affected by his own, and had always done his best to stay detached from his patients ever since. He could listen to them, treat them well, and be an utter professional, ensuring a high standard of care, but he couldn't ever let his emotions get in the way. 'You should have discussed this with me first.'

'Maybe.' Elias gave a careless shrug. 'But I've put in a request to the Kensington Project for the last ten years.' He wrinkled his nose and looked thoughtful. 'I'm not quite sure what tipped the balance in our favour this time around.' He smiled again. 'But I did write five thousand words about why I specifically wanted Cora Campbell.'

Jonas groaned. This was always going to be a losing battle. He knew exactly what would happen. Elias would happily entertain Dr Campbell every morning, but by mid-afternoon he'd start to flag and arrange for other people to keep Dr Campbell entertained.

Jonas didn't have time to entertain anyone. His job was busy enough, and one of his senior staff was starting early maternity leave in the next few days due to some complications. They hadn't found a suitable replacement.

'Where is she staying?'

He was asking the question, but Jonas had a creeping sensation that he knew the answer.

'With me, of course!' said Elias. I have plenty of space and I'll get the opportunity to show her the festive activities of Stockholm.' He rubbed his hands together. 'I'm quite looking forward to it—the opportunity to see our own city through someone else's eyes. I think it will be good for me.'

Suspicions confirmed. Somehow, he'd known that Elias would offer to host the visiting doctor. He'd rambled around his large home on the outskirts of Stockholm for the last few years, ever since his wife had died. Both of Elias's children were married with children of their own, and lived in other parts of Sweden. Jonas knew that Elias was lonely. He was sure it was part of the reason that Elias refused to retire.

Jonas sighed. 'Tell me again, when does she arrive?'

'November the first. I'm picking her up at Arlanda airport at two p.m.'

'Are you bringing her straight to the hospital to show her around, or taking her home first?'

'Oh, taking her home first. Give her some time to settle in, then probably take her out to dinner in one of the restaurants at night. You'll join us, of course?'

Jonas shook his head, an automatic reaction. He wasn't entirely comfortable with the idea of some new doctor coming into his unit to teach them 'new' things. The last thing he wanted to do was make small talk with the woman.

No. He'd rather meet her on his terms, in his professional setting. That way, he could be clear about boundaries, and the fact that anything that happened in the

NICU involving any of the nursing or midwifery staff, had to be run past him. There. He felt better already.

'I'd prefer to meet her the next day. When she's had a chance to relax and get her bearings. She'll probably be tired after travelling.'

Elias wagged his fingers at him. 'Excuses, excuses. All work and no play makes you a very dull boy, Jonas. When was the last time you went out for dinner? Threw a party?'

Jonas laughed and leaned back in his chair. 'There are enough people in this hospital already throwing parties without me joining in. Did you see the state of some of the medical and nursing students last week? I sent three of them home.'

Elias tutted. 'Finest days of my life. I love a good party,' he said wistfully.

'I'll meet her the day after,' Jonas said, in the vain hope it might lodge somewhere in Elias's brain.

Elias's page sounded and he glanced down. 'I have a patient. Here.' He pushed forward the pile of papers he'd been carrying. 'Read up on our visiting guest. You might find something interesting. We can talk later.'

Jonas smiled and shook his head as Elias left. He knew exactly what the old scoundrel was up to. Every six months or so, he got it in his head to play matchmaker between Jonas and whoever he thought might be a suitable companion.

Most of his matchmaking attempts had been in vain. Two or three had lasted more than a few dates, maybe even lasting for a couple of months. But Jonas was too involved at work to invest in a relationship and all of the not-quite-right women had grown frustrated and drifted off.

He pushed the papers to the side, instead pulling up the rota for the NICU on his computer.

He wanted to check who would be on duty at the start of November. He trusted his experienced staff to be able to deal with the new doctor in a polite but efficient way. He might have a quiet word in the ear of some of the other physicians. As he glanced to the side, he caught the title of a research paper: *The Basis of Hypothermic Rescue in Twenty-Six-Week-Old Neonates*. Interesting. He was just about to pull it out when he heard a yell.

'Help! Someone, help!'

Jonas was out of his seat in an instant. As he ran out of the door, he could see a nurse kneeling at the site of a collapsed body in the corridor.

No. No. He recognised the familiar shape instantly.

The nurse was relatively newly qualified. 'Good work,' he said quietly as he bent over the body. The nurse had put him into the recovery position, but it was clear it was Elias. Jonas checked his airway, breathing and circulation. He looked up at the nurse, putting a hand on her shaking arm. 'Maja, put out a treble two call.' There was a phone at the end of the corridor and she blinked and then got to her feet and started running.

Jonas stayed leaning over Elias. 'It's okay, Elias. I've got you. Just take some nice, deep breaths for me.'

He noticed the slight sag of one side of Elias's face immediately and his stomach gave a horrible ache.

Moments later there were thudding footsteps next to him, a portable monitor and trolley, along with a sliding sheet. Eight people moved Elias easily onto the trolley and Jonas walked alongside as they headed to the emergency department.

His head was already spinning. He knew both Elias's son and daughter. He'd make sure he was the one to phone them.

Seven hours later he was still in the hospital sitting by Elias's bedside. Initially, the emergency physician had suspected a stroke, but over the last few hours Elias had gradually regained consciousness and movement in his arm and leg. He was still groggy, his eyes were heavy and his mouth still drooping. His oxygen levels had also dropped slightly.

Elias's son, Axel, burst into the room, much in the way that Elias had burst into Jonas's office earlier. Jonas stood quickly and put his hand on his arm. 'He's okay. It looks as if he's had a transient ischaemic attack. They're going to keep him in and do a few more tests.'

Axel moved straight over to the bed and put his hand on his father's cheek. 'Pappa,' he said softly. 'I'm here.'

Elias's eyes fluttered open and he gave a soft smile, before they closed again.

Axel looked at Jonas. 'He has regained consciousness, but is very sleepy. It's the body's way of letting him heal. They are doing his neuro obs every hour and he's making gradual improvements.'

Axel finally seemed to take a breath. His coat was dotted with snowflakes and was damp in patches. 'Thank you, Jonas. Thank you for staying with him until I got here.'

'Of course. I would never have left him. Now you're here, I'll check and see if his doctor is around to talk to you.'

Axel looked around. He was an engineer by trade but knew his father well. 'What about this place? What about work?'

Jonas shook his head. 'Don't worry about a single thing. I can sort all of that out. If they think he's well enough in a few days, I can help you make arrangements to get him home and see if he needs anything.'

Something flitted across Axel's eyes. 'He was on the phone to me earlier, telling me about some doctor who is coming to stay with him. He was so excited about it. Will you be able to sort some alternative arrangements for that? I don't even know their name.'

'Leave it all to me.' The words came out instantly, even though Jonas was inwardly groaning. Getting cover for their head of NICU would be difficult enough, without the added responsibility of their international guest. Several of the other physicians had extended holidays before they hit the festive period, which was traditionally busy at Christmas. They still had strong staff numbers, but Elias's presence would definitely be missed.

'Thank you so much,' said Axel in obvious relief. He looked at his father with affection. 'I keep telling him he's too old for all this but he won't listen.' His face fell. 'Maybe he will now. I appreciate your help, Jonas.'

Jonas held out his hand. 'Let me know if you need anything.' He pulled a set of keys from his pocket. 'Here are the keys to your dad's house. I wasn't sure if you had a set, so I got them from his office. I'll find that doctor for you.'

The events weighed heavily on Jonas's shoulders as he left. He had complete confidence in the doctors and nurses looking after Elias. He just hoped the situation wouldn't become more serious. Elias was a mentor to him, as well as a verbal sparring partner. He enjoyed his company and respected his work.

As with any hospital, news would spread quickly and

Jonas would need to focus his efforts on making his staff feel supported within their working environment.

He collected his jacket from the locker room, pulled his hood over his head and walked out into the falling snow.

CHAPTER TWO

CORA HADN'T SLEPT a wink for more than twenty-four hours. After her initial news she'd dashed off to phone her friend Chloe, a neurologist who worked at the Kensington too. But Chloe had been in a meeting and phoned her back squealing with the news that she too was part of the Kensington Project and was on her way to Kingston in Jamaica.

Both were delighted and numerous calls of varying length happened over the next few days as they both tried to complete their workloads before leaving.

Cora had left lengthy instructions on the care of some of her babies, including follow-up plans if they were ready for discharge in her absence. She was meticulous about her work, and wanted to make sure nothing was left to chance.

There had barely been time to pack her case, and it had been as she was grabbing some jeans and a jumper to travel in that she'd looked down at one of her pairs of colourful shoes and realised they were totally inappropriate for Stockholm's potential snow and ice.

'Too late,' she sighed as she remembered Chris Taylor's words about winter boots. Running on adrenaline, she caught a cab to the airport. By the time she was checked in, she grabbed the latest crime thriller from the airport shop and a glass of wine from the bar, sipping nervously as she waited for her flight to be called.

Elias Johansson was Head of Neonatal Intensive Care at Stockholm City Hospital and had generously offered to pick her up at the airport and to host her for the next seven weeks.

Initially she'd been taken aback by his offer, but after looking him up online, and reading reports about him, then speaking to him briefly on the phone an hour after Chris had told her about Stockholm, she'd known she'd be in safe hands. He was so enthusiastic about her work. He'd read all her research papers and wanted his staff to learn from her. She couldn't help but be flattered by the experienced doctor's praise. By the time her flight was called, Cora was almost jittery with nerves. The flight was bumpy, with turbulence just outside Arlanda airport. It was a short flight, only two and a half hours from London, and she skidded as she walked from the plane to the terminal.

'I must buy boots,' she muttered to herself, wondering if there might be a clothing shop in the airport. She was shivering too, the temperature drop noticeable from the mediocre winter season that had just started in London. What she really wanted right now was a big fur-lined parka, rather than her loose green raincoat.

As she collected her luggage and walked through passport control and customs, she scanned the waiting faces, trying to pick out Elias from the crowd.

That was odd. She'd thought she would recognise his cheerful face. She pulled her phone from her pocket and checked she was getting a signal. Yip, she'd connected, just as her phone operator had promised, but there were no messages.

She looked around. Maybe she should have a coffee.

There was a good chance that Elias had been delayed at the hospital. The airport was more than thirty kilometres from Stockholm, so there could be a whole range of reasons for him being late.

'Dr Campbell?'

She jumped at the deep voice, then jumped again as she turned around and was met by the broad chest of a Viking.

'Y-yes,' she stuttered, looking up cautiously.

Okay, so she must be dreaming because this was clearly some kind of romance movie. This guy was too good-looking to be real.

'I'm Jonas Nilsson. I'm afraid I have some bad news.'

Well, that stopped the movie dream in its tracks.

'What do you mean?' She was confused, and, even though it was the middle of the afternoon, tiredness was hitting her in waves. What was it about even the shortest of journeys that could do that to a person? 'Where's Elias? He told me he would meet me here.'

A pained expression shot across the man's eyes. He really was a traditional Viking with bright blond hair and blue eyes. 'Unfortunately, Elias had a TIA a couple of days ago. He's just been discharged from hospital and will take some time to recover.'

'Oh, no.' She was a doctor. She knew instantly what a TIA was, and she was thankful that this man's English was impeccable, because the few words of Swedish she'd learned would be entirely inappropriate.

'Is he going to be okay?'

The man nodded solemnly. She could see the concern in his eyes and darned if it didn't make him even more attractive. 'We hope so. His son has come to stay with him. But in the meantime, your visit might not be how you intended. Would you consider rearranging?'

She blinked. She'd just travelled from London to Stockholm and was standing in Arlanda airport. Did he honestly expect her to rearrange?

'Who did you say you were again?'

He put his hand on his chest. 'Jonas Nilsson, Head of Midwifery at Stockholm City Hospital. Elias is a colleague of mine.'

She gave a thoughtful nod and looked Jonas in the eye. Head of Midwifery. It was likely that the Viking hunk would hang around the NICU frequently. Right now, she wasn't quite sure how well she could concentrate on work issues with this guy by her side. 'Well, Jonas, I'm assuming that, even though Elias is currently sick, the unit is still functioning at its usual high standard?'

It was a pointed question and she knew it. His response would be telling.

Sure enough, Jonas Nilsson bristled. 'Our neonatal intensive care unit is one of the finest in the country. We have a broad range of highly skilled staff.' Good. She'd annoyed him. She even liked the little spark of anger she'd seen flash across his eyes.

'Perfect,' she interrupted before he could continue. 'Then I'll do the job that Elias requested. I'll share my skills and train some of your staff in my techniques.'

It seemed that this statement caused an even deeper reaction than the last one.

Which was a pity. Because as he inhaled a deep breath, a waft of his aftershave drifted towards her, like a warm sea breeze. A sea breeze in which any easily distracted female could get lost.

'My staff are already highly trained, extremely conscientious individuals.'

She smiled. 'I'm sure they are. But Elias requested

my presence to share my expertise. I didn't come here for a holiday. I came here to work.'

It was a stand-off. And as she was a feisty Highland girl, this wasn't Cora's first rodeo. She'd dealt with more than one guy like this. A guy who seemed to think he could tell her what to do. Not a chance.

Jonas blinked his extraordinarily long eyelashes and had the good grace to remember she was, indeed, a guest.

He reached his long arm over and grabbed her case. 'Let me get you back into Stockholm. It takes around forty-five minutes. And we'll need to sort somewhere for you to stay.'

'Oh.' The word came out before she even had a chance to think. Of course. Staying with Elias would be out of the question. Jonas gave her a sideways glance as they reached the doors. It was a long walk to the car with very little conversation. Cora had the distinct impression that Jonas already thought of her as a nuisance.

She'd been so excited about coming here, seeing around the unit and training the staff. Getting introduced to a whole new country and city had made the whole project seem even more fabulous. She'd already searched and seen the pictures of Stockholm in the Christmas season. Christmas wasn't her favourite time of year, and she was glad to be away from London and be distracted by a new city. She'd expected the next few weeks to be amazing, but right now her hopes and expectations were sitting like a deflated balloon left behind when the party was over.

Part of the reason she'd dug her heels in so hard when he'd suggested she go back home was that she liked to avoid Christmas at home as much as possible. It brought back too many bad memories. The first, of being the child placed in the foster system two days before Christmas because there was no immediate placement available. No one wanted an extra unknown child at Christmas. It brought back painful memories of sitting in a quiet dormitory with a large decorated Christmas tree. And it was an agonising reminder that she was alone, and essentially unwanted. She had finally been adopted by wonderful parents, but had lost them both years later, so close to Christmas again. This time of year felt almost cursed to her. So the chances of her getting back on a plane and flying home were less than zero.

Jonas had a large four-by-four and he lifted her bright red suitcase into the back easily.

As they moved along the airport roads, she tried her best to fill the silence.

A male midwife. Interesting. And Head of Midwifery at one of the best hospitals in Sweden? No matter how grumpy this guy was, he must be good. Just a pity he was so darn attractive too.

'Can you tell me a bit about the unit?'

His eyes remained fixed on the road. 'We have twenty-five single rooms where families are encouraged to stay with their baby. The layout of all rooms is standardised so staff know exactly where everything is that they will require. Each neonate has their own team to provide consistent care. We have thirty doctors, and one hundred and ninety nurses and midwives. We use a colour-coded system to signify level of acuteness of our babies.' He gave her a sideways glance. 'As you know, Elias is our Head of Neonatal Care. He's responsible for the medical staff in the unit, and I'm in charge of the nurses and midwives.'

Ah…now she understood. When Elias had spoken

to her, he'd very much emphasised how it was a team approach to training in NICU—a principle that Cora had always agreed with. There was no point just training doctors in the techniques. In many units there were advanced neonatal practitioners who were often responsible for caring for the sickest neonates. Some of the experienced nurses she'd worked with over the years had more knowledge and skill in their pinkies than some of the doctors.

'I'm really looking forward to meeting the teams. Do you work much in the unit yourself?'

'Usually I'm in there two days a week. I like to make sure staff keep standards high.'

Cora shifted in her seat. Did he mean he spied on his staff?

He kept talking. 'My predecessor line-managed the staff in the unit with no supervision. It created...problems. I decided to be more hands-on. It also gives my senior staff a chance to fulfil their personal development plans and get study days if I'm there to be the supervisor on that shift.'

Ah. That sounded better. Cora nodded her head. 'I've worked with too many staff who miss out on some of the training opportunities they've wanted because units are short and they can't get time off.'

Did she imagine that, or was it a look of approval?

'Can you take me to a hotel somewhere in Stockholm, close to the hospital?'

He gave a nod. 'If you want, I could try and find you accommodation at the hospital. We have rooms for locum staff.'

She shook her head. 'But then I'm taking up a space you might need. As long as there are transport links to and from the hospital, any hotel will be fine.' She gave him a wary smile. 'You might need to let me take a few notes about the transport links before you leave.'

'What kind of place do you like?' he asked. 'Modern, traditional, boutique, luxury, or hidden away? Obviously, the hospital is picking up the bill, so price won't be a problem.'

There was obviously a correct answer to this question but Cora wasn't sure what it might be. She was here for seven weeks. She didn't want to end up in a youth hostel kind of place, or those very trendy places where you basically slept in a capsule that resembled a coffin with lights.

'Somewhere central,' she said promptly. 'I want to take the chance to see some of Stockholm. See the shops, eat in the restaurants. I've heard it's magical at Christmas and I'd like the chance to see some of that. Oh, and a comfortable bed. I definitely need a comfortable bed.'

For the tiniest second Jonas's eyebrow arched, and heat rushed into her cheeks. 'Oh!' She laughed self-consciously. 'I'm just tired. I've been awake for the last twenty-four hours. I was too excited to sleep last night. I keep leaving notes about some of my patients.'

The expression on his face softened. Finally. She'd said something that met with his approval. Thank goodness. She didn't want to spend the next seven weeks tiptoeing around this uptight guy. He was so hard to read. There had barely been a trace of emotion.

They were starting to move through the city now and Cora stared out of the window at the passing buildings and people. Everywhere was covered in a light dusting of snow. It really was a beautiful place.

Most people were wrapped much more warmly than she was. Before she even had a chance to think about the appropriateness of the question it was out of her mouth. 'Can you tell me somewhere I can buy boots and a new jacket? I didn't really have time to get equipped for the cold.'

'You want me to take you shopping?' His voice practically dripped with disdain and all of a sudden Cora was immensely annoyed. She'd had it with this guy. Cora had always been a girl with a tipping point. She could only grin and bear so much, and then her patience left the room and she let rip. Trouble was, the more annoyed she became, the thicker her Scottish accent got, and it was bad enough in London. Last time she'd lost it there, people had looked at her as if she needed subtitles.

She turned towards him. 'No. I don't want you to take me shopping. Just like I don't want to be treated like a major annoyance. Has anyone ever told you that it's time to work on your people skills? I'm truly sorry that Elias is sick, and you obviously feel you've been lumbered with me, but, funnily enough, I'm a fellow professional and I expect a little courtesy. If this is the way you treat all visitors to your unit, I'm surprised you have any visitors at all.'

The car came to an abrupt halt. She was still fuming. But after a few seconds, Cora wondered if he was about to throw her out of the car. He gave her a hard stare with those blue eyes. Finally, he spoke. 'Your hotel,' he said in a low voice, as if she should have known why they'd stopped.

She turned her head to the pavement and saw a uniformed man walking towards her car door. He opened it and spoke in rapid Swedish that went straight over Cora's head. 'Hi.' She smiled. 'Thanks so much.'

The man dropped into English easily. 'Welcome, madam, checking in?'

She glanced over his shoulder. The boutique-style hotel had glass-fronted doors and a dark carpet running over a light wooden floor. A warm glow came from the reception area, and there were a few large pink chairs scattered around, making it look welcoming. 'Yes, please,' said Cora.

'You have bags?'

Cora nodded and the man opened the boot of the car, pulled out her case and turned towards her. He gave her a wide grin and gestured his other elbow to her.

How charming. She threw a glance back at Jonas. 'Appreciate the lift. Sorry to be such a bother to you. But that—' she nodded towards the doorman '—is what I call a welcome.'

She got out of the car and slid her arm into the doorman's. 'Lead the way,' she said with a smile.

Jonas was stunned. By her rudeness. By her abruptness. By the sharpness of her tongue. By the glint in her green eyes. By the way the second he'd seen her at the airport, his breath had caught in the back of his throat. And by the way he'd treated her since he'd met her.

Cora Campbell was more than a little attractive. She was stunning. He'd never met a woman before who literally took his breath away. What was wrong with him? Elias would be ashamed of him. He knew how excited Elias had been about Cora coming here, and he had been annoyed at only finding out at short notice. But that wasn't Cora's fault. She'd travelled from London to a strange country, to be met by someone other than she had expected, only to find out her accommodation was no longer available.

He'd obviously added to the problem with his brusque manner. What was worse, he'd been completely aware he'd been doing it. He used to be a happy-go-lucky kind of guy, but now he was a by-the-book practitioner. He could count on one hand the number of people at Stockholm City Hospital who'd known him in the early days, so everyone now just accepted him for who he was. He knew he was uptight, but with Cora he'd just gone into overdrive. It was clear she was excited to be here, but he had the distinct impression she could wreak havoc on his orderly unit, with her brimming enthusiasm and plans to teach his staff.

But he was also completely conscious of her immediate impact on him. He was distinctly aware that he'd noticed every single thing about her—the few freckles across the bridge of her nose, the way she kept sweeping one piece of hair behind her left ear. The way her accent got thicker the angrier she got—or the more excited she got. Cora Campbell was *way* too attractive. Jonas had spent years keeping his emotions in check. Spending time around her would be difficult. What if his strong attraction to her distracted him from his job? He'd never dated anyone at work—and it was a rule he meant to stick to.

Truth was, if he'd known about her more in advance, he would have probably looked at the rota and scheduled sessions for her when staff would be free to learn and take part. But someone like Cora, with only a few days' notice, at one of their busier times, could cause disruption in a unit where calm and controlled were the order of the day. It looked as if he hadn't done too well with keeping his emotions in check this time, and his anxieties and annoyance had spilled over towards Cora.

He sighed. It was his duty, as a hospital representative, to make it up to her. He looked at the crowded streets. At four p.m. it was already starting to get dark.

He knew that Elias had booked a nearby restaurant to take her out to dinner on her arrival—he'd found the details amongst the papers Elias had left at his desk.

It was time to put this right.

The hotel was quite literally a dream and Cora couldn't have been happier as she lay in the middle of the deliciously comfortable, huge bed, wrapped in the snuggly dressing gown that had been on the back of her door.

Although the room wasn't oversized, its quirkiness appealed to her. There was a pink chaise longue under the window that looked out onto the busy streets. Thick curtains framed the window. Her bed was made up in rich white cotton sheets, but the duvet was thick, and a giant red comforter adorned the top of it.

Her suitcase was unpacked. The doorman had been great and given her a map of the surrounding area, a list of Christmas experiences to sample in Stockholm, a handwritten note of shops she might like, and restaurants to try. She couldn't have asked for more.

Well. Yes, she could. A warmer welcome might have been a bit better.

She wiggled her toes. Socks. Another thing to add to her list. Thicker socks. The wind had whistled past on the few short steps into the hotel and her feet were instantly cold. As were her arms in her green raincoat.

She rolled off the bed and moved to the chaise longue, staring at the street outside as she nibbled the plate of complimentary chocolates that the receptionist had given her during her unplanned check-in. It was such a nice touch.

There was a large store in the distance, with a variety of mannequins wearing thick jackets in the window. It might be a good place to start.

She was just contemplating what clothes to put on when there was a knock at her door. Cora frowned, and then brightened; this place had been so welcoming so far, maybe it was complimentary wine!

She opened the door and stared into a familiar broad chest.

Jonas took a step back and held up a large bag. 'Peace offering?'

'What?'

He held the bag out to her again and she reluctantly took it, putting a hand consciously to the top of her dressing gown as she bent down to look inside.

Green. Something green. She pulled out the item and her eyes widened in surprise. It was a thick green parka with a grey fur-edged hood. It took only a few seconds to realise this was a good quality item. It was lightweight, even though it was thick.

'You said you needed a jacket. I guessed your size. Sorry, couldn't do the same for boots, but I can take you to a shop if you want so you can get some for tomorrow.'

He was still standing in the doorway, filling most of the space. For some reason, she was reluctant to invite the man who seemed to exude sex appeal from his very pores into her room, worried about how she might actually react. Jet lag could do weird things to a person. In a flash in her head, she saw herself grabbing him by the jacket and throwing him down on her very comfortable bed.

'Elias had booked a restaurant to take you out to dinner tonight. The reservation still stands and it's only a few minutes' walk from here. I take it you haven't eaten yet?'

She was still holding her hand at the top of the hotel dressing gown, conscious of the fact she only had her underwear on. Her head was still in that other place where he was lying across her bed. She finally found her voice again. 'I was just thinking about it.'

He gave a nod of his head. 'Then why don't I wait for you downstairs and, when you're ready, I'll show you where to buy some boots and tell you a bit about the hospital over dinner?'

Cora swallowed, her throat a little scratchy. Now she'd seen her room, she kind of wanted to spend the rest of the night here in complete comfort, watching the world go by—obviously with room service too.

But Mr Antisocial was apparently making an effort. It seemed her earlier outburst had awakened his hospitable side. Thank goodness.

She took a deep breath and nodded her head. 'Give me five minutes.'

Jonas still wasn't sure about this. He actually wondered if she might just leave him sitting in the reception area for the rest of the night. But ten minutes later, Cora Campbell appeared in a pair of black trousers, a jumper and her new green parka.

Green was definitely her colour. It made her eyes sparkle. And he'd been right about the size. She looked perfect in it.

Cora was chatting to an older woman she'd met in the lift. It seemed that Cora was a people person, and they walked towards him talking like old friends.

He got up from his seat and nodded at the older woman as she left the hotel. 'Ready?' he asked Cora.

She gave a small nod and he could sense her hesitation. 'Thanks for the jacket. You shouldn't have done that. You have to let me pay you back. The doorman had given me a list of shops to try later.'

He shook his head. 'Take it as an apology and a welcome to Stockholm.' He gave a half-smile. 'But don't worry, I'll let you buy your own boots. They can cost the same as a small house.'

Cora's face brightened and as they walked outside she lifted the hood of her jacket. For a second, he was almost sorry he couldn't see her face properly now, but he gave himself a shake and guided her towards a crossing to reach the other side of the square.

As they walked around the edges and past a number of shops, he gave her a running commentary. 'Yes, no, maybe, definitely not, only for tourists, and the best bakery around.' He gave a non-committal shrug as they passed another.

Cora stopped and put her hands on her hips. 'Jonas Nilsson, you gave me the distinct impression earlier that you weren't much of a shopper.'

'I'm not. But I've lived here long enough to know where to go and where to avoid.'

He stopped at a shop with a large front window made of tiny panes of glass. It looked like something from the last century. 'This place is pretty unique if you're looking for a gift. Some carvings. Some glasswork. Paintings the size of the palm of your hand. And some unique jewellery. All done by local artists. Come back when you have some time.'

Cora nodded eagerly at the packed shop. 'I'll come back later in the week,' she murmured. 'It's the kind of place I could get lost in.'

They arrived at the boot shop and Jonas held open the door for her. 'This is the place that Nils, the doorman, recommended to me,' she said as they walked inside.

'I'm glad I'm managing to keep to his standards.' Jonas smiled.

Cora walked over to a wide range of boots and immediately started asking the saleswoman some questions. Jonas was happy to wait. At least she wouldn't fall over on her way to work the next day.

And that was what he kept telling himself as he watched her try on a few pairs of boots, before finally selecting a grey pair, fur-lined with suitably sturdy soles for walking in the freezing temperatures.

Cora was animated in all she said and did. The saleswoman was laughing and giving advice as they chatted easily. At one point, she nodded in his direction and Jonas felt a flush of embarrassment, wondering what had been said.

Finally, Cora gave him a bright smile before putting her own very flat and brightly coloured shoes in the large box that was meant for the boots and going to the cash register to pay.

She waved her card, then put her bags over her arm and dug her fingers deep in her pockets as they made their way outside.

'We should have got you a hat and gloves too,' he said.

She shook her head. 'I know how much you love shopping, Jonas. I think you've suffered enough for one day. Shall we go to the restaurant you mentioned?'

He took her to the restaurant, which was near the shipyard and had an interesting view of ships both young and old.

He could see her studying the menu. 'Would you like some recommendations?' he asked, knowing that Elias would have relished this kind of chat. It was something he wasn't generally used to. Jonas was perfectly capable of being a charming date if the desire was there, but he wasn't a man normally assigned the role of trying to charm a foreign visitor. He wasn't even entirely sure he could, when he didn't know exactly what Cora's role would be while she was here, and he still had that underlying feeling that she could disrupt the standards in his unit.

He pointed at two items on the menu. 'Depending on how you're feeling after your journey, I'd recommend this one. It's deep-fried smoked pork belly with turnip, chilli mayonnaise, crushed potatoes and sauerkraut. Or there's this one—herring with brown butter, chopped egg, potato salad, and pickled yellow beetroot and hazelnuts. Or, if you're feeling a bit delicate, I'd go for the grilled Arctic char with pine and butter sauce; you could have a side of smoked pumpkin with that if you wished.'

Cora leaned back in her chair and sighed. 'They all sound wonderful, and to be honest I'd like to try all three.' She took a sip of the white wine that she'd ordered. 'I'm here for seven weeks. I guess I'll get to try a bit of everything.'

The waiter appeared and Jonas waited until she'd ordered the herring, then ordered the pork belly and requested an extra plate. He could let her taste a little. And it was the kind of thing Elias might have done.

It was almost as if she'd read his mind. 'Have you heard any more about how Elias is?'

Jonas gave a nod and sipped his beer. 'I heard from his son this afternoon. Even though he's home, he's still very tired. A TIA for most people is a sign to slow down. He's been running on adrenaline for as long as I've known him. Apparently he was furious that his physician said he couldn't come back to work for at least six weeks—and then promptly fell asleep again.'

Cora drummed her fingers thoughtfully on the table.

He could see her thinking. 'What does that mean for the unit, if Elias couldn't come back?'

Jonas gave a wry laugh as his stomach twisted over. 'I can't imagine the unit without Elias at the helm.' He looked out over the water. 'But I guess I'll need to start. None of us are irreplaceable, no matter how much we think we are. And both Elias's son and daughter are married with families of their own. They don't stay in Stockholm any more, and I have a feeling that both will want him to move somewhere closer to them. Although they live apart, they're a very close family. Elias's wife died of cancer more than twenty years ago, and ever since then, his work and his children have been his obsessions.'

Cora drew in a kind of hitched breath. 'Family is what shapes us all,' she said with a tired smile.

Jonas nodded. 'For the last ten years, he's been like family to me too. But I know I have to step back and let his son and daughter be the ones to persuade him it might be time to rethink. If I said it—' he gave a small laugh '—he'd just be angry with me and give me a list of everything that currently needs sorting at work.'

'Can I help with that?'

Jonas drew back in his chair. It had just been a throwaway comment. 'Oh, no, sorry, I didn't mean anything by that. I wasn't trying to hint. I can assure you, the unit is run to impeccably high standards. You won't find anything lacking.'

He could feel his defences automatically coming down.

Cora gave him a look. The kind of look that told him that this woman could read him better than he thought.

'As you've guessed from the accent, I'm from Scotland,' she said, setting her wine glass firmly on the table. 'So, this isn't my first Highland Fling—so to speak. What I'm saying to you is—' she put her hand on her chest '—I'm a doctor. It doesn't matter what I'm here to teach, or to learn. I'm here for seven weeks. I'm not the kind of person to stand on the sidelines and watch, if I can help. In fact, I've *never* been that person. So, if you need help, rotas, supervision, teaching new medical staff the basic procedures in NICU, then use me.' Her fingers closed around the stem of the glass and the corners of her lips turned upwards. 'In fact, be warned: if you don't use me, I might just step in anyway.'

Talk about putting her cards on the table. 'You like to be frank?'

'It should have been my middle name.'

Jonas took a long drink of his beer. The smell of delicious food started wafting towards them.

'I only found out about you a few days ago. I had no idea Elias had asked for a visiting doctor to come to our hospital.'

He could see her taking stock of those words. If she was as good at reading people as he suspected, she would know there was a little resentment in there.

'I only found out a few days ago myself,' she answered in a slightly teasing tone. 'And I'm not a visiting doctor. I'm a specialist neonatologist, practising pioneering techniques.' The words rolled off her tongue and he wasn't sure if she was putting him in his place or taunting him further. No matter.

'It didn't help,' he added, 'that Elias has apparently requested you before through the Kensington Project. More than once, in fact.'

Now that clearly surprised her. Cora tilted her head to one side. The flickering candlelight in the restaurant made her all the more alluring—in a really annoying kind of way.

'I had no idea,' she said curiously. 'My research papers have only been published in the last few years. I mean, neonatology can be a small world. Everyone generally knows what everyone else is doing. I suppose he could have heard through one of my supervising professors.'

Jonas gave a small smile as the waiter approached with the plates. 'I sometimes wondered if the man ever slept.'

She gave a small smile. 'I spoke to him a few times by video chat. He was fun. So interested. Full of questions. I liked him.'

'And he clearly liked you too.'

Cora's eyes lit up at the plate crammed full of food. He took a few moments to slide some of his food onto a side plate and held it out to her. 'You said you wanted all three. Let's start with two.'

He thought she might refuse. Some women would have. But Cora grinned widely. 'Perfect,' she said as she accepted the small plate. 'Now at least I'll have to behave and not stick my fork into someone else's food.'

Jonas raised his eyebrows. 'Is that how things normally are?'

She'd already taken a small forkful of her herring. 'Delicious,' she sighed, then looked at him with laughter in her eyes. 'What, you were never a medical student, sharing a house with people who ate every item of your food anonymously? Or were the junior in a ward area where you're last to the canteen and only get the old withered leftovers?'

Now it was his turn to smile and nod. 'Actually,' he

admitted as he started on his pork, 'I was probably the food stealer.'

'I might have known that.' She shook her head, then waved her fork at him. 'You have that look about you. At least I'm...' she gestured to the small plate to her left '...upfront about it.'

She was obviously more relaxed now, but as their meal continued he could see she was clearly tired. It was odd. Sometimes he felt completely at ease around her, then she'd say one small thing, one throwaway comment, about teaching, or training, and he could feel every little hair on the back of his neck stand in protest.

'We should get you back to the hotel,' he said. 'Can you be at the hospital for eight tomorrow morning?'

She nodded. 'That's no problem.'

He raised one eyebrow. 'Just a tip, although the hospital food is fine, you might want to eat breakfast at the hotel. Their coffee is definitely better.'

'Noted. And what about tomorrow? Obviously I thought I was meeting Elias. Will I just meet with you, or is there someone else you want me to meet with?'

Jonas frowned. He hadn't really had time to think about it. 'Let's work on the assumption that our chief executive will want to see you at some point. Tomorrow will likely be introductions to the hospital, and its department and staff.'

'And who will help me with the training schedule?' She took the last sip of her wine. 'I'll need to see a list of the staff disciplines to work out who is most appropriate for what session.'

'No.' The word came out of nowhere.

Cora looked up in surprise. 'What do you mean, no? That's exactly why I'm here.'

Jonas was bristling again. 'I think we should discuss

the training elements once you've had your feet on the ground for a few days. Give yourself time to get a feel for Stockholm City Hospital. For the way things run in our NICU. For the staff, patients and parents.'

'You don't want me to upset the apple cart, do you?'

'Excuse me?'

She gave a wave of her hand. 'Sorry, it's a British expression. Probably doesn't translate well.' She folded her arms across her chest. 'Are you averse to change, Jonas? You don't look like a dinosaur. Do you think everything in medicine should stay the same?'

'Of course not,' he said quickly. 'I've been a midwife for fifteen years. There have been changes in practice throughout my career.'

Cora gave a knowing nod. It was maddening. 'Ah, I get it, you're a control freak. It's good to know. At least I know what I'm dealing with.'

She made the words sound so light, so flippant. As the waiter appeared with their coats, she slid her arms into the jacket that he'd bought her earlier.

She tapped the front of it. 'You picked the right colour. Green for go. That's how I am, and that's how I work. If you want to stop me doing the job that I came here to do, you'll have to be quick. And believe me, I can sprint like no other.'

She patted his arm in a way that made him seem like a child. 'Thanks for dinner. I think it's done both of us good. See you at eight.' Then she raised her eyebrows. 'Or maybe I'll get there before you…'

And before he had a chance to respond, Cora Campbell disappeared out through the doors of the restaurant and into the icy night of Stockholm.

CHAPTER THREE

JONAS HAD BEEN in the hospital since five-thirty a.m., but everything had gone against him. While everything was peaceful in the NICU, the labour suite had gone into full meltdown and, as senior manager on call, he had to assist.

Four midwives had come down with some kind of bug, meaning the staffing level was low. Six women had been in full labour, with another ten being observed. He'd had to pull midwives from other parts of the hospital to assist. Six of the staff on duty were newly qualified, and, having been there himself, he was careful to make sure there was enough supervision to keep them confident in their roles.

He'd already delivered two babies this morning, when he'd been called to assist with another; thankfully, all had gone well.

He snapped off a pair of gloves and washed his hands in the treatment room as Linnea, one of the newly qualified staff, came through, eyes sparkling and cheeks flushed. 'Oh, thank you, Jonas. I am so happy that things worked out.'

He gave a nod of his head. He'd stepped in to help when she'd asked for assistance. She'd been right. The baby's heart rate had started to fall slightly as labour progressed, which usually signified problems with the cord. Jonas had allowed Linnea to continue to be in charge of the delivery, while giving her the monitoring support and professional advice she needed to proceed. The cord had been longer than normal and had been wound around the baby's neck. The obstetrician had been alerted and agreed with the decision to continue as the heart rate drop was minimal during contractions. Linnea had been able to deliver the baby's head and gently slip the cord back over, before a healthy baby boy was finally introduced to the world.

'You did well,' praised Jonas. 'It was a difficult situation. You'll come across this again, and you have to judge each one based on the circumstances presenting.'

She gave him a knowing glance. 'I was tempted to ask you to take over when you appeared.'

He shook his head. 'We're all tempted in these situations, and, believe me, if I'd thought it was necessary, I would have stepped in. But there was no need. You're a good midwife. Congratulations on another delivery.'

He could see the clock on the back wall and his heart skipped a beat. It was nearly ten o'clock. Time had slipped away from him.

Things hadn't exactly gone as she'd expected. Cora had arrived at the hospital at eight. She'd taken Jonas's advice and had breakfast at the hotel, bringing them both takeaway coffees. But Jonas had been nowhere in sight.

Instead, she'd found her own way to NICU and introduced herself to the staff, standing awkwardly for a few moments with her coat. Alice, one of the sisters, had taken pity on her and showed her to the cloakroom to get changed and store her gear in a locker. Once she'd changed out of her boots into her more comfortable flat, bright blue shoes and tied her hair up, she'd been ready to start work.

But there was still no sign of Jonas. This time, Alice had directed one of the interns to take Cora on a tour around the hospital to get her bearings. Unfortunately, Hugo, one of the doctors, found himself entirely too charming for words.

Although he asked questions, it was clear he didn't listen, so he didn't realise just how experienced and senior Cora was. It might have been amusing, if she hadn't been stuck with him for more than an hour.

When Jonas finally appeared, clearly looking harassed, he came up on the tail end of a conversation.

'Twenty-four weeks is usually when babies are considered viable, but some babies at twenty-two and twenty-three weeks have survived here at Stockholm City NICU.'

Jonas ran his hand through his blond hair. She recognised the signs of someone who'd just been wearing a theatre cap.

He gave her a sideways glance. 'You haven't told him, have you?'

Hugo had the continued nerve to keep his haughty demeanour. 'Told me what?'

Jonas gave him a stare, and Cora completely understood why. Hugo's manner and tone were clearly lacking.

She bent around him and sighed. 'I have, actually. Twice. But listening is a skill that needs to be developed.'

'What are you both talking about?'

Cora smiled. 'I'm Cora Campbell, visiting specialist neonatologist. I'm here to teach members of Stock-

holm City Hospital about new techniques and carry
out training.'

'I'll take over.' It was clear Jonas was cross.

'But—' began Hugo.

'*But*,' emphasised Jonas, 'Dr Campbell specialises
in early neonates. She doesn't need you to define that
for her.'

Hugo straightened his white coat. 'Well, I was only—'

'Go back to the unit, Dr Sper. You and I will talk
later.'

Cora waited a few moments as they both watched
Hugo strut back down the corridor with his head held
high and his hands in his pockets.

'You owe me twice now,' said Cora succinctly.

Jonas turned with puzzled eyes. 'Twice?'

'Actually, make that three.'

His frown deepened. She counted off on her fingers.
'One, you were late. Two, I brought you coffee. Three,
you left me with Mr Arrogant and Insufferable for more
than an hour. So—' she gave a nod of her head '—Jonas
Nilsson, you definitely owe me.'

He turned to face her. 'Okay.' He followed her lead
and counted off on his fingers. 'One, I was here from
five-thirty a.m., but there's some kind of stomach flu
going around in the labour ward and I helped deliver
three babies this morning, then I had to go in and assist
at a potential emergency section. Three, I can only assume it was Alice who told Hugo to give you the tour?'
He shook his head. 'She's had enough of him and I appreciate why. I'll deal with him later. He's not a good
fit. Elias would have dealt with him, but that's down to
me now.' He took another breath but before she could
mention his odd counting he spoke again. 'And two, I

concede. Did you keep it? I'll heat it up in the microwave. I would kill for a coffee right now.'

Cora shook her head and gave a knowing smile. 'Sorry, no. I know who to keep happy. I gave it to Alice.'

A smile spread across his face. He knew exactly what she meant. The sister of the unit was a key partner. Cora was right. And he hated that right now.

He leaned against the wall of the corridor they were still standing in. 'How did your tour go?'

She nodded. 'The only place I've not been yet is the labour suite. But that's the last place you'll want to go back to.' She gave him a careful stare. 'But I need to know how to get there if there's an emergency page for a new delivery—a neonate.'

Jonas shook his head. 'You won't need to answer any emergency pages.'

She folded her arms. 'I warned you last night you'd have to be quick to catch me. I told Alice if she needed shifts covered, I was willing. She gave me a few provisional dates until she checked with you.'

His eyes narrowed. Then he shook his head slowly. He looked half impressed and half annoyed. 'This is my unit. My staff.'

She held up both hands in front of her. 'I know, I know.' She gave him her brightest smile, knowing that he wasn't convinced at all.

One hospital tour later and Jonas still wasn't at all sure about Cora Campbell. She was clearly smart and very sassy. But the underlying suspicions of 'disruptive' seemed to glow like a neon banner above her head.

She was looking him clear in the eye and telling him that, absolutely, it was his unit, and she would follow his rules, but the gleam in her eye made him suspect she had plans entirely of her own.

Although on the outside Stockholm City Hospital appeared calm, on the inside it was chaos. And Jonas appeared to be the only person whose job it was to deal with it.

The stomach bug that had affected the labour ward earlier seemed to be travelling at rapid speed throughout many of the staff groups in the hospital. He was beginning to suspect a nasty strain of norovirus, which was notorious for appearing in the winter months.

It also meant he was eight doctors down, three senior managers, around fifteen nurses and midwives, and many other ancillary services. Each time his page sounded, he cringed, knowing he was being notified of another staff shortage. He was lucky that there didn't seem to be any patients affected as yet.

He strode back to the NICU where Cora was standing with Alice, the sister. 'Alice, we've had multiple notifications of staff sickness. Sounds like norovirus. I'm going to contact Infection Prevention and Control. Let's start taking extra safety precautions in the unit. Last thing we need is any of our babies getting sick.'

Alice didn't need to be told twice. Staff were briefed, safety messages reinforced, and even more hand sanitiser sourced, along with additional protective equipment. She also placed a ban on any additional staff entering the NICU.

Sometimes, some of the junior doctors from other areas would come to observe specific procedures. The sonographers frequently had students, as did the physios.

Jonas had half expected Cora to object. This would thwart her plans to teach over the next few days. But instead of creating a fuss, she disappeared off into one of the offices to go through some of the babies' files.

She appeared a few hours later with a clipboard in her hand. She smiled at Jonas. 'I've made a list. You have a number of pregnancies that are being carefully monitored right now. If any of these women deliver early, I think we should look at some of the techniques I've been using back at the Kensington.'

He glanced over the list, recognising several names. 'You won't have time to train our staff—or get consent from parents to try something new.'

She gave a small shrug. 'The staff won't need to be trained in advance. I'll be here. I can start the procedures, speak to the parents, gain consent, and monitor the babies.'

Alice had walked over to listen to the conversation too. 'Sounds good to me. I've read your research. I liked it.'

'You have?' Cora brightened instantly.

'Of course, I have. Elias spoke about you frequently. I thought I'd better keep up to date on what Pioneer Woman was up to.'

Cora blinked, then her cheeks reddened. 'What?'

Alice laughed. 'That's what he used to call you. He was very impressed by your work. I think he secretly hoped to take part in whatever your next research might be.'

Jonas was stunned. 'He never mentioned you to me.'

The comment was unintentional. And entirely thoughtless. Once it was out of his mouth, he realised exactly how it sounded.

Cora instantly looked wounded, pulling back, her eyes darting in another direction. Alice looked at him reproachfully, as if she were an elderly aunt, and rolled her eyes. Her voice stayed calm. 'Well, he wouldn't, would he? Everything here has to go through our ethics committee and you know how long they take. Elias would only have spoken to you once all those agreements were in place.'

She nudged Cora. 'They turned down an application once because they didn't like the colour of the flow-chart.'

Jonas tried to do some damage control. 'Oh, of course, okay. Yes, our ethics committee are strangely unique. They tend to get stuck on some tiny detail instead of looking at the big picture. I'm sure that's why we hadn't discussed you yet.'

Cora gave him a sideways glance as his page sounded again. 'Give me a sec,' he said as he ducked to the phone.

By the time he came back he could see from the electronic notes that Cora had performed one troubleshooting procedure after another. He watched as she put a central line into one twenty-six-week-old baby, and a tricky feeding tube into a twenty-seven-week-old baby who continued to struggle with its sucking reflex. Before he'd had a chance to speak to her she'd moved on, next to one of the doctors from the unit. It was clear he was having some difficulty re-siting a line in a premature baby. She had gloved, masked and gowned up, and was positioning the baby's arm in another way, demonstrating the angle he should use to get the vein.

She was kind and encouraging, giving clear instructions. There was no bossiness to her tone, but he didn't doubt she would take over if required. Her eyes looked over her mask and met his for a few seconds. It was hard to read her. He couldn't see the expression on the rest of her face. He wasn't quite sure what the message was that she was trying to send.

Half an hour later, line inserted and baby settled, she joined him back at the nurses' station as he replaced the phone. 'Go on then, ask.'

'What?'

'The call you got earlier. It was another doctor off sick, wasn't it?'

He gave her a suspicious look. 'Any more of this and I'll suspect you had something to do with all this.'

She shook her head and patted her stomach. 'Not me. I'm fit as a flea. Now, do you need me to cover shifts?'

Jonas couldn't help it. He would have to go against his instincts. It was ridiculous to use a visiting doctor to cover regular shifts. It was even more ridiculous to have a visiting doctor who was a research fellow and actually here to teach his staff, cover those shifts.

'Jonas, don't make me beg.'

As quick as a flash, a thought instantly entered his brain. *Go on, then.* Where on earth had that come from?

He gave a half-laugh, which he did his best to disguise as a cough, and shook his head as he stared at the staff rota. 'We need cover on Wednesday night—and on Friday, during the day.'

'Done.'

Simple as that.

She was looking at him with those green eyes, expecting him to say thank you. And, of course, he should. But Cora had a glint in her eye as if she'd just won something, and saying thank you somehow stuck in his throat.

He leaned one elbow on the counter. 'Earlier, you didn't step in and take over. You just talked him through it. Why?'

She gave him an odd look. 'Because he's a good doctor. He just needs to build his confidence. He could do that procedure.'

'But you didn't know that. You'd never seen him do one.'

Cora pulled back and looked at Jonas in surprise. 'You've worked as a hands-on midwife. Trusting your instincts is everything. You must know that.'

His insides clenched. She couldn't possibly know about how that had affected him in the past. One incident had scarred him for life. He'd trusted his instincts, and hated every second, because he'd had to go against a patient's wishes to save her life, and the life of her child. There had been consequences for those actions. She'd complained about him. And even though the complaint hadn't been upheld, Jonas had never forgotten it. He still felt guilty—as if he had let his patient down. It had impacted on him in so many ways. Instincts were good. But rules were better. Rules were what protected staff.

'But you had no idea about his capabilities.' He could feel himself starting to get defensive.

She gave him the most open look and put her hand up to her chest. 'But I know me. I sense if someone is good at their job. Always have. Always will. I would never have let him carry on with the procedure if I'd had the slightest doubt.' Her forehead creased in a small frown as she looked at him. 'This is a teaching hospital, isn't it? All he needed was a hand on his back, literally, along with a whisper in his ear.' She smiled as she said those words, and it struck Jonas that he wasn't entirely happy at the thought of her whispering in some man's ear.

He didn't want her whispering in anyone's ear except his, and it washed over him as if he were some ancient prehistoric man.

He gritted his teeth and pushed his emotions away. This was exactly what he'd wanted to avoid. Cora Campbell was affecting him in ways he didn't like— not at work anyway.

'I would have taken over in a heartbeat had I any worries,' she said steadily, then she gave him a wide smile. 'I'm good at my job, you know. I'm good at lots of things. You just have to learn to trust me.'

For a few moments, neither of them said anything. Jonas was frozen by her gaze and the way she was looking at him as though she could see parts he didn't want her to see. Who was this woman? And why did it feel as if she were getting under his skin?

One of the paediatric nurses walked past and glanced at them both, slowing and tapping Cora on the shoulder. 'Just to let you know, we start our annual Christmas traditions this weekend. You should come along.'

The spell was broken. For a second he saw a wave of momentary panic in her eyes. Curious. She'd just performed a tricky procedure on a tiny baby with the utmost confidence.

'I think I've just agreed to cover some shifts,' she said swiftly.

'No, you haven't. You're free on Saturday night. You can go ice skating at Kungsträdgården Park.' He knew exactly what tradition his colleague was talking about. Even though it was November, it was sort of an inbuilt tradition for the staff here. They all gathered at Kungsträdgården—the King's Garden—ice rink on the first weekend it opened in November. It was almost like the start of the Christmas season for everyone.

She blinked. 'Where?'

The nurse waved her hand. 'It's right in the city centre. You'll have no problem finding it. And if you do, we'll send Jonas to find you.'

This time it was Cora who waved her hand. 'You know, I'm not that great at ice skating. I'll maybe give it a pass this time.'

Jonas lowered his head. He couldn't help the mischief in his voice. 'Dr Campbell? Something you're not good at? I'll need to see it to believe it.'

She sighed, clearly realising that he had her.

It seemed as though this was a game of tit for tat.

'Fine, I'll go.' But there was something in her eyes. Something he didn't understand.

He put a hand on her shoulder. 'It will be fine, I promise you. We normally meet around six p.m. I'll pick you up at the hotel.'

Then, before she had a chance to find a reason to say no, he left the unit and went to answer another page.

Cora had spent most of the day trying to find a reasonable excuse to back out of ice skating with her new colleagues.

How could she explain to people she'd just met that Christmas was a bit of a black hole for her? She didn't need to do that back home. People knew her. They knew her background and didn't ask questions. When Cora volunteered to work Christmas, most other doctors just accepted the offer gratefully and for that she was thankful. Here, she really didn't want to have those conversations with people she barely knew. Trouble was, from what she'd heard around about her today, this was just the start of Christmas events in Stockholm City Hospital. It seems they celebrated from this weekend, right up until the actual day.

For Cora, it was a bit like being in her own special horror movie.

It hadn't always been like this. Once she'd settled with her adoptive family, Cora used to love Christmas just as much as the next person. She hadn't just loved it. She'd loved it, adored it, revelled in it, and planned a million Christmas activities. But after a clash of terrible luck over a few years, all during the festive season, her Christmas spirit had been well and truly drained dry.

First, her beloved adoptive mum had died unexpectedly on the twenty-third of December after being admitted to hospital with back pain. It didn't matter that Cora was a neonatologist. She still had an overwhelming surge of guilt that she hadn't seen any tiny signs of the aortic aneurysm that had killed her mum in minutes. It was known as the silent killer for a reason. Almost no warning, and, unless detected through a scan, very often deadly.

The following year, her adoptive dad had died after fighting cancer. The light had finally gone out of his eyes on Christmas Eve. Cora knew the true reason that he'd died: he'd lost the will to live after the death of his wife.

So, the time of year that she used to share with the two people she'd loved most—the people who'd completely turned her life around, and given her the reason, will and determination to be a doctor—had been tainted.

Christmas had started to feel like a cruel reminder. Her rational brain told her that was ridiculous. But she was a doctor. She'd seen enough in this lifetime to know that Christmas wasn't a joyful time of year for everyone. Lots of others had painful memories too, and Cora had learned to cope by throwing herself into her work, and by allowing others to enjoy the season the way she'd used to, and giving them the gift of time to spend with their families.

Both of her parents had finally died in the Royal Kensington, so some of her colleagues there knew her circumstances.

Although Cora was usually a positive and encouraging person, this time of year just seemed to cast a shade over her mood. As she pulled her green coat on, and grabbed the snuggly red hat she'd bought in a shop nearby, she tried to push those thoughts from her head. She could put her game face on for a few hours. That was all it would be.

Then she could come back to her hotel room and snuggle up in bed. As she grabbed her gloves, her eyes couldn't help but glance at the square outside. Everyone had been so warm and friendly these last few days at the hospital. Jonas had been there, but not too much. If she hadn't known better, she'd think he was avoiding her, but she'd been too busy at work to pay attention to that little gnawing feeling that he hadn't been around much. Tonight would be different. Tonight, he was picking her up.

Dusk had already fallen and now she could see glistening white lights were everywhere. It really was pretty. The lights were twisted together in a variety of ways, and giant snowflakes were strung between the normal lights. There was a scene in the centre of the square with white reindeer and Santa's sleigh. People were already gathered around it and posing for pictures. All the lights had literally appeared overnight. Last night, there had been none. Then, today?

She pulled the curtains, letting out a wry laugh at herself and her Christmas Grouch behaviour. As much as she'd loved the view from the window of her room, this might be a bit much to see, night after night.

She sighed as she made her way down to the lobby. Again, it was now filled with Christmas trees, and boughs. She fingered the bright pink and purple decorations threaded next to the bright green foliage. Alongside the pink and purple were straw wreaths and small straw goat decorations. How unusual. She'd need to ask someone about those.

Jonas walked through the front door of the reception area, dusting the snow from his uncovered blond hair. Cora saw several of the female staff members take a second look.

She watched them, oddly suspicious as one nudged the other, and they both clearly murmured about Jonas under their breath. Of course other women would look at Jonas. He was tall, handsome, and clearly quite commanding.

But that didn't stop her quickening her steps and giving him a broad smile, along with a loud, 'Hey.' Okay, so he might not have a flashing sign above his head saying *This one's mine*, but she hoped she'd made her point. Taken. Look, but don't touch.

'You ready for this?' His voice had a hint of wariness.

'Of course,' she said without thinking.

'Really?' His brow had the slightest frown. 'I thought you were trying to get out of it earlier.'

She gave a half-shrug. 'Not the greatest lover of the festive season,' she said, not wanting to make up some elaborate lie.

Jonas gave a thoughtful nod. 'Okay.' She wondered if he would ask more, but he didn't, and that actually helped a little. He held his elbow towards her. 'But you can put up with a bit of ice skating, I presume?'

She nodded and smiled as she slid her arm inside his elbow as they walked outside.

'It's only around a ten-minute walk,' he said. 'The park really is in the heart of the city.' As they dodged around a few people on the crowded street, he gave her a sideways look. 'We celebrate the season pretty hard here—just a word of warning that you'll probably get invited to more events.'

She bit her lip and nodded. He still wasn't asking the personal questions.

'And, as another hint, there is a really good word for the hire skates at the park.'

She looked up at him, half smiling. 'What?'

He laughed. 'I heard it in a Sherlock Holmes movie and always wanted to use it.' He leaned down towards her ear, his warm breath tickling her cheek. 'They're dastardly.'

Now it was Cora's turn to burst out laughing.

But Jonas nodded sincerely. 'I'm telling you. They look like skates, but—' he shook his head '—as soon as you hit the ice you'll realise it's all been some kind of sly scheme.'

'You're not selling this,' Cora admitted as they kept walking.

He shrugged. 'Don't say I didn't warn you.'

'So, if they're that bad, why didn't you bring your own?'

'Yeah, I thought about that, but decided that might be a bit mean.'

Cora laughed. 'For who? Me?'

He was still half laughing as he looked at her again. 'It might be a bit much to invite you skating, leave you in the old hire skates, then bring out my professional skates and strand you in the middle of the rink.'

Now Cora was really laughing. 'Why, Jonas, I didn't know you cared.'

'Don't take it that far,' he said quickly. 'I might hire skates with you, but I still expect you to buy the hot chocolate.'

'There's hot chocolate?' She could almost feel her ears prick up.

'Of course, there is.'

They crossed a busy road and Jonas pointed. 'Look, there's the Royal Palace, and Gamla Stan.'

'Does the King actually stay there?' Cora asked, looking at the immense and beautifully lit building.

'It's his official residence.'

'And what's Gamla Stan?'

'Our old town, and one of our most popular tourist destinations. Cobbled streets and colourful buildings, it's all seventeenth and eighteenth century and is one of the best-preserved medieval city centres in Europe.'

Cora stared in wonder. She immediately planned to come back here some time during the day.

They crossed through the park entrance. The layout was impressive. The park connected the harbour with the main shopping district. There was an elaborate fountain, a stage, a lawn area, and, of course, a large skating rink.

The rink was already busy. 'What's that in the middle?' asked Cora. She pointed at the enormous statue, with iron lions around it, around which the skaters were circling.

'Oh, that's Karl the XIII. He was King of Sweden.'

They walked closer to the rink. There was a barrier surrounding it that was topped with a wooden fence on which people were leaning as they watched others skating. 'What are the tents?' asked Cora.

'They're warming tepees,' said Jonas. 'A place to huddle when you get too cold. That's where you'll find the hot chocolate, the lingonberry or the *glögg*.'

'Okay, you got me. What's that?'

Jonas smiled. 'It's good. *Glögg* is mulled wine. It's sweet, warm and spicy. Just the perfect thing for a winter's night.' He waved as they spotted other members of staff gathered near the skate-hire booth. 'Come on, then.'

As they approached Cora realised most of the staff had brought their own skates. She waited while Jonas hired them both skates, and strapped them to her feet. He was right, of course. They looked distinctly un-skate-like. And as the other staff stepped on the rink and started spinning off in various directions, she realised just what a big sacrifice he'd made on her behalf.

He held out his hand towards her. 'Don't worry, I'll catch you if you fall.'

'The first time, or all the times?' she asked as she grasped his hand and nearly landed flat on her back with her first step on the ice.

He put his other hand at her back and, since her feet seemed frozen in one spot, gave her a gentle push in the right direction.

Cora wobbled immediately and held out her other hand in a desperate attempt to regain her balance. Jonas just laughed and stayed behind her, putting his hands on either side of her hips and almost pushing her along.

At first, Cora couldn't pretend her legs weren't shaking, but after halfway around the rink, she started to relax a little and leaned back against Jonas.

'Is this okay?' he asked, his voice above her shoulder.

'Is this?' she asked, leaning back a little more. 'You're doing all the work.'

'Just enjoy the view,' he said as they continued around the rink. Other members of staff kept whizzing past them, laughing and shouting and waving.

After a few minutes, several of the girls from the unit came along on either side of Cora and took her hands, pulling her along. She let out a scream, half fear, half laughter as they continued dragging her around the rink. The air was crisp, cold enough to make her want to keep moving, but bearable enough that she wasn't freezing and desperate to get back to the hotel.

She finally collided into the back of another staff member, as the girls decided to stop at one of the tents for refreshments. It seemed to have been pre-planned as she recognised the faces all around her. She'd barely had time to think before something was pressed into her hands. 'I made an executive decision on your behalf,' said Jonas.

She looked down and inhaled. The scent of sweet, warm chocolate filled the air. He handed her a spoon and she tackled the cream on the top first.

'What if I'd decided to opt for the mulled wine, or the lingonberry?' she queried as she savoured the sweet taste on her tongue.

'I figure you'll be back here enough to sample them all. And it was hot chocolate you mentioned first.'

'It was.' She nodded as she took a sip. 'Oh, that's nice. It's different from what I expected. What is it?'

'White hot chocolate. It's their bestseller.' He handed his cup to her. 'But if you want to taste the mulled wine you can try some of mine.'

She gave him a surprised glance. 'So, you *do* share. I'm surprised.'

'What do you mean I do share?' His voice was distinctly puzzled.

She took a step closer, her arm brushing against his. 'I got the general impression that you weren't particularly keen on sharing your NICU with me.'

'Why would I share what's mine?' he shot back, a smile in his eyes.

He knew she was teasing him, and it seemed he would give as good as he got.

'I thought you might make an exception for someone that you'd invited here.'

'Elias did the inviting—without consultation, I might add.'

'But you watched me today. Don't think I didn't notice. I'm an asset to the unit. Particularly when your staff numbers have been hit.'

He gave a slow, thoughtful nod. 'A senior pair of eyes is useful right now. But...' he raised his eyebrows '...you seem like the type that—what's the expression?—if I give you an inch, you'll take a mile.'

'Ouch!' She feigned a wound to her chest as she smiled. Then her expression turned serious. 'I don't want to run out of time to teach your staff what Elias asked me here to teach.'

She watched the tiny twitch at the corner of his blue eyes as she said the name. She got that Jonas was trying to do two jobs right now—be Head of Midwifery and run the NICU in Elias's absence. Maybe holding onto rules and regular practice was his way of ensuring a steadying hand in a time of uncertainty for staff while their regular head was off sick.

She decided to press on. 'I'm here to do a job. Why don't you let me do it? There's a full rota of staff tomorrow. I could start with explaining the science behind hypothermic neural rescue. It's one of my most important pieces of research. I understand that, at first, it can be confusing for staff. One of our natural instincts the second a pre-term baby is born is to get them into a warming cot. If I can get a chance to explain the science, then I can teach and explain the techniques.'

She could swear that right now she could hear him tutting internally.

She gave him her best smile. Boy, Jonas Nilsson was hard work to win around. Part of her was curious enough to want to know why, and the other part of her knew it was absolutely none of her business.

But Cora had always been curious about people and what made them tick. She was open with her close friends. They all knew why she'd become a neonatologist, which was because she'd assisted at her mum's unexpected early labour, and helped to deliver her little sister, Isla. They also all knew she'd then had to intervene when her mum had suffered a postpartum haemorrhage. It had been a scary, terrifying and exhilarating time all at once, and had cemented Cora's career path in her brain. When her parents had died, she'd tried to persuade Isla to come and live with her in London. But Isla had no intention of leaving the Scottish Highlands where she'd grown up, and had insisted on moving to stay with their aunt while finishing school. Now she was attending Edinburgh University, just as Cora had, but was studying physics instead of medicine. The two were still close and spoke every other day. Cora's close friends knew the moments that had impacted on her life, but it wasn't something she'd share with a casual acquaintance. Yet something was plucking at all the curious senses in her brain and making her wonder about Jonas.

She'd only known him a few days. He could be grumpy. He could be funny. He could be cheeky, and he could be deadly serious. She might only be here until just before Christmas, but she had to work well with this guy in order to meet the rigorous demands of the Kensington Project. She had to recognise which buttons she shouldn't push. At times, Jonas appeared like a closed book. At other times, she felt as if there were so many more layers beneath the surface.

As if he were reading her thoughts, he gave a conciliatory nod. 'A teaching session on research and knowledge seems reasonable. As long as there aren't any emergencies in the unit tomorrow.'

'Of course,' she agreed quickly with a nod. She held out her hand towards him.

He looked at her as if she were crazy.

'Shake on it,' she insisted.

'Why? I just told you that you can schedule it.'

She gave a shrug. 'Call me old-fashioned, but I like to shake on things.'

He put his gloved hand in hers and she gripped firmly, looking him straight in the eye. 'See, that's better. I always find it's harder for people to go back on their word, if they've had to look you in the eye and shake on it.'

'I don't go back on my word,' he said, shaking his head at her.

'But I don't know you that well,' she insisted as she finally let go of his hand.

As they dropped hands she raised one eyebrow, then winked. 'Yet,' she added.

CHAPTER FOUR

FOR SOME STRANGE REASON, Jonas had a spring in his step the next morning. He wasn't quite sure why. He was always happy at his work but today felt different.

His footsteps slowed as he realised when the last time was that he'd been this happy at work: the day he'd decided to propose to Kristina—the last time he'd told a woman that he loved her.

That day hadn't been so good. He'd been dating Kristina for a few months. It had been a kind of whirlwind romance. One in which Jonas had finally let his guard down. He'd been guarded with his emotions since the event at work. When he'd finally got up the courage to put his heart on his sleeve and tell Kristina that he loved her, it had seemed like the start of a new life for him.

But things had proved disastrous. He'd gone home early the next day, to collect the ring he'd had resized, and found a stack of bills in his post box. The bills were all for his credit cards, all of them run up to their maximum limits in the space of a month—the amount of time that Kristina had been staying with him.

He'd been short and swift with his actions. The ring had been hidden and he'd had a long conversation with Kristina when she'd arrived back at his apartment complete with numerous shopping bags. He'd wanted to give her the benefit of the doubt. Perhaps she had money troubles, medical bills, family debt, or some other reasonable issue that would have meant she'd had to use all of his credit cards, without permission, at short notice. But, no. Nothing that could excuse her behaviour. There had been tears, a bit of a tantrum, then she'd stuffed her belongings into a designer suitcase, grabbed the new shopping bags and left with a flurry of colourful language. Her last remark, a laugh, had been that Jonas was clearly a poor judge of women, and it had cut deep. A short conversation with the police had revealed Kristina was known to them for this kind of behaviour, but it hadn't made him feel any less of a fool.

Wearing his heart on his sleeve, sharing his history, his vulnerabilities, with a woman he'd thought he'd fallen in love with, had been a disaster. He'd learned the lesson hard. The last three women in his life hadn't stuck around for more than six months. The acute stumbling block of not actually being able to say the 'I love you' words again had proved a major hurdle for any relationship. He wasn't quite sure he ever would again.

Four years on, he tried not to waste any thoughts on Kristina. But something about his mood today had triggered the memories in his brain.

By the time he reached the NICU the spring in his step had disappeared. It was early, but, while everything in the unit seemed to be going smoothly, he was struck by the lack of visible staff. He moved instantly to Alice's side; the sister of the unit was calmly taking a reading from a pump and recording it in the baby's notes.

'What's going on?' he asked in a whispered voice.

'Nothing,' she answered.

'Exactly,' he replied. 'This place is usually a hive of activity. What on earth has happened?'

Alice nodded over her shoulder to the small teaching room in the unit. 'What's happened is, everyone heard about the hypothermic neural rescue research that Cora is presenting this morning. All the babies have had their care delivered, medicines given, recordings taken, and I—as the old girl on duty, am doing the observations while the staff listen in.'

Jonas couldn't hide his horror. 'They can't leave you out here alone while they listen to a presentation.' He could feel his fury building, but Alice could read him like a book.

'Dr Campbell is doing her sessions in twenty-minute bursts. Anyone would think this girl had worked in a NICU before. And you and I both know if I raise my voice above a whisper, I can have every member of staff next to me in less than twenty steps. Anyway—' she held out her hands '—look around. Even though it's seven-thirty a.m., it feels like four in the morning. This place is so peaceful. Isn't it a nice change?' She didn't give him a chance to answer. 'We also have three sets of parents with their babies, and now—' she changed her position so she could point at his chest '—I have you!' She said it as if he were some kind of Christmas gift. 'So, Jonas, you start on that side and I'll do this side. Record all observations and check all pumps. I think Baby Raff might be due for his tube feed.'

She moved off to her side quickly and Jonas spoke a little louder. 'I'm not sure I agreed to this.' He looked over at the training room and, seeing all the rapt faces, had to stop his feet from automatically moving in that direction. He really, really wanted to hear what Cora was saying that was enthralling his usually sceptical staff.

'You didn't,' Alice said over her shoulder with a laugh, 'but you're a good boy, you never let me down.'

He rolled his eyes. Alice was one of the most experienced and most senior of his staff. He sighed and picked up the nearest chart, having a quick check over the twenty-seven-week baby girl who was doing better every day.

It didn't take him long to remember how much he missed working hands-on every day. When he'd stepped in to assist in the labour suite the other day, there hadn't been time to think, let alone enjoy it. Here, things were quieter, and he took time to talk to each of the babies he was monitoring. Gently handling some, feeding another, changing two and saying a few quiet words to the sicker babies while gently stroking their hands.

A little boy, Samuel, was irritable and Jonas took him from his crib and placed him next to his chest and sat down on one of the rockers. He'd just managed to settle him when he caught scent of something light and floral behind him.

'Aw, look at you,' said Cora. 'Now I see the real Jonas.'

He shot her a frown of annoyance. 'I'm a midwife. Of course, I like babies. And when it comes to settling a disturbed preemie, I'm an expert.'

She walked around, gently touched the top of Samuel's head, then moved in front of Jonas, sitting in the seat opposite and scanning Samuel's chart.

When she looked back up, she tilted her head to one side. 'So, tell me, why did you become a midwife?'

He gave an exaggerated eye roll. It was a question he'd been asked time and time again—hardly surprising when only half a per cent of midwives in Sweden were male. He gave her his truthful standard answer.

'I love the idea of bringing new life into the world. Simple as that.'

She leaned forward and put her head on her hand. 'What, no family story of inspiration, or childhood experience of delivering a baby in a field or something?' She said it in a jokey tone but her eyes were staring straight at him.

'Is that what you expect from me?' His tone was a little harsher than he meant.

She sat back. 'It's just an unusual career choice for a young man. I guess I'm interested. Only half a per cent of midwives in the UK are male.'

'Same in Sweden,' he countered. Then he gave a small shrug, which Samuel didn't appreciate. 'Maybe I just wanted to rush up the ranks in the health service and decided midwifery was the easy route.'

She folded her arms across her chest. 'Not a chance,' she said as she looked at him in interest. 'I've heard the same tales. That in a profession mainly dominated by women, males in nursing, midwifery and mental health all seem to be promoted quicker than females. I don't think for one second that you came into this job to claw your way to the top.'

'Claw? Interesting expression.'

'It is, isn't it?' she agreed. Her gaze narrowed slightly. 'You didn't come and listen to my first session. You were here. I could see you.'

He held out one hand. 'Have you met Alice? Also known as Attila. As soon as she saw me, she put me to work, because apparently all my staff were listening to your research instead of taking care of their charges.'

She leaned back her head and laughed. 'Oh, no, you don't. There's no way you wouldn't have dragged out every single member of staff if you thought for one second that your charges were being neglected.'

'True.' He really was beginning to appreciate just how well Cora seemed to read him. 'Actually, I *was* quite interested. Can I read the notes?'

She grinned from ear to ear. 'Read the notes? Sacrilege. It's never the same as listening to the real-life presentation. You know, where you can look the researcher in the eye, see their passion for their project and ask the questions that dance through your brain as they inspire you.'

He tried to hold in the laugh that was building in his chest, desperately trying not to disturb the little sleeping form against him. He shook his head, and stood up, settling Samuel back in his crib.

He gave an enormous sigh and turned to Cora, who was right by his side. 'I'd hate anyone to think you're short of confidence.'

But Cora was glancing again at Samuel's chart. 'He would have been a good one to try my technique on. There's a note in his chart about birth asphyxia. Who knows how long it will be before his parents know if there is any permanent damage?' Her expression was sad, her voice melancholic.

'Samuel has done well since he's been in the NICU. He's starting to suck and he's managing without any additional oxygen now.'

Cora nodded, her eyes fixed on the little boy. She looked up. 'But you still won't know for sure until he's much older. Let's try my therapy on the next preterm baby. Let's not wait.'

Every muscle in Jonas's body tensed. But Cora had started talking again. 'You know that research has proved that hypothermia reduces neurological damage in infants who've suffered asphyxia during delivery. The next time you get a baby in the unit that meets the criteria, we'll both speak to the parents, get their consent and start the procedure.'

He didn't have a chance to answer before she'd put both hands on his bare arms. 'Just think, Jonas, we might actually save a baby from damage. Think of what a difference that could make to one tiny life? Isn't it worth a chance? If you've kept up with my research, you'll know we won't be doing any harm. But we could actually change the life course for a child.'

Boy, Cora was right. Watching her talk about the subject she loved with passion and commitment was mesmerising. Every cell in his body wanted to scream yes. He already knew that this had been Elias's intention.

He pressed his lips together for a second, trying to word things carefully. 'If I can, I'll come to your next few sessions. Once I've heard all your research, *then* I'll make a decision.'

She sucked in a deep breath. He could tell she wanted to argue with him, petition harder for her cause. But something made her take a step back and give a small nod. 'Okay.'

As his pager sounded and he went to move away, she put her hand back on his arm. '*But*, if you don't attend the sessions, if you get called away with work, you'll let me deliver the sessions to you later—after work. So we can still have this conversation later—no excuses.'

He paused for a moment and gave her a brief smile. 'You've clearly been taking lessons from Alice.'

Jonas could tell she was trying really hard not to smile. 'Maybe,' she admitted. 'Again.'

'Do you both just like to join forces against me?'

Cora gave him a soft look and leaned against the

nearest wall. 'That's what it is.' She said the words as if she'd just made some kind of amazing discovery.

'What are you talking about?'

'You,' said Cora. 'I'm talking about you. I couldn't quite put my finger on it, but that's it. You always seem to think that people are out to get you.'

'Don't be ridiculous.' He could feel every one of his defences closing like a steel trap.

But Cora wasn't matching his defensive posture— quite the opposite. She was still just smiling at him, staring with those green eyes and giving a little shake of her head. 'You get so defensive. So protective. I get it, I do. But sometimes I feel as if you're constantly looking over your shoulder, waiting for someone to grab you.'

His skin chilled. She had no idea what she was saying, but she was striking every chord in his body. Was he always this obvious? Had the rest of the staff just been more cautious around him?

But if Cora was generally good about reading people, it seemed that her enthusiasm had taken hold. 'Do you ever relax?'

'What do you mean?'

'You always seem on guard. As if you're waiting for something to happen. Don't you ever just kick back and go with the flow?'

Another baby started to make small sounds behind them and Jonas quickly moved next to the crib.

It only took him a few seconds to assess the situation. This little girl, Elsa, had respiratory issues. Most premature babies were vulnerable to infection and this little one had picked up a chest infection soon after delivery.

He moved as the oxygen saturation monitor started to sound. The little girl's colour was slightly dusky as her noises, which resembled mewing now, continued.

Cora turned to the wall and automatically handed him a suction catheter as Jonas lifted the protective shield around the crib and positioned himself at the top of Elsa's head.

Suctioning on premature babies had to be done gently, and with caution, but Jonas had years of expertise. Within a few seconds, he withdrew the catheter as Elsa coughed, pulling it back with a tiny lump of mucus that must have been blocking her airway.

He signalled to one of the NICU nurses. 'Roz, can you speak to one of our physios? See if they can make time to come and assess her again?'

Roz nodded and walked swiftly to the phone, as Jonas changed Elsa's position in the crib for a few minutes, keeping a light hand on her little rasping chest.

Cora thankfully didn't speak again, leaving their previous conversation forgotten. They hadn't even needed to speak about what to do for the baby. Both had read the situation and acted appropriately. There had been no panic, no raising of voices, just two experienced practitioners working together.

He tried to push down the momentary resentment that had flared at her words. She had no idea why he was a stickler for rules. Jonas didn't want any other person on his staff to go through the same experience. Rules and protocols supported staff to practise safely and he firmly believed that.

Just then Mary, one of the physios, walked through the door. She immediately came over to Cora and Jonas. 'You called?'

He nodded. 'Elsa just had an episode where her sats dropped and she had mucus blocking her airway. Can you assess her, please?'

'Of course.' Mary nodded. 'And if she needs it, I can

put her on our rounds for chest physio. Leave it with me.' Her eyes drifted to Cora. 'Heard the first session went well. I'll try and get to one of your others if I'm close by. I'm interested in getting involved.'

He could hear the intake of breath from Cora as she smiled and straightened up, immediately launching into her favourite topic of conversation. Jonas, satisfied that Elsa was in safe hands, moved away.

'Don't forget,' came the voice behind him. 'If you get called to other areas, I'll find you later so we can play catch up.'

Heads turned in the unit. There was a rapid exchange of glances and Jonas groaned inwardly. He knew exactly what Cora meant, but it seemed that others were interpreting a whole different meaning in those simple words.

That was the last thing he wanted. People getting ideas about him and the visiting doc.

As he pushed his way through the doors to the open corridor, his tense shoulders relaxed a little. If Elias were here right now, he'd be roaring with laughter.

As Jonas picked up the nearest phone and dialled the number on his pager, he made a mental note to call his friend later.

'It's Jonas,' he said when the phone was answered.

'How soon can you get here?' came the reply.

And all other thoughts were lost.

CHAPTER FIVE

CORA STARED DOWN at the pdf map she'd printed in a few hurried moments at work earlier. It still didn't make sense to her, but then, she'd never really been a map reader. When she'd first arrived in London, the underground had seemed to mock her.

But another week had slipped past, and this was the second staff event she'd been talked into. Maybe they wouldn't notice if she didn't turn up?

'Ready for the Christmas lights tour?' asked Jonas as he walked up alongside her wearing thick boots and a black fur-lined parka.

She glanced up and nodded. 'To be honest, I'm looking forward to getting my bearings in the streets around here. I never seem to know where I am.'

He looked at her, frowned and pointed. 'But you've got a map.'

She laughed and tapped the side of her head. 'I also don't appear to have the part of the brain that was designed for map reading. It's just a skill I've yet to accomplish.'

'Would it help if I give you a hint?'

She sighed. 'If your hint is pointing at the map and doing your best to explain to me in terms a five-year-old should understand how obvious the map is, please don't.'

'Anyone would think you take these things personally. No, I was just going to give you the tip of—' he
held up his hand in the air '—following the lights. Believe it or not, that's what most people do.'

He gave her a nudge as she glared at him for stat-
ing the obvious, 'Then there's the other hint, that
we're starting at the place we were at last week, Kungsträdgården Park.'

She wrinkled her nose. 'Does everything happen
there?'

He gave a half-shrug. 'More or less. Gamla Stan really is the heart of the city. Tried the coffee shops and
cakes there yet?'

Cora shook her head. 'Like I said, I'm lucky I can
walk between the hotel and the hospital. My sense of
direction has never been great.'

Once the rest of the hospital staff had gathered
around them, there was a consensus that everyone
should start by getting something to drink. This time
Cora nudged Jonas out of the way. 'Ladies pick.' She
smiled. 'And I'm paying.'

She returned moments later with some mulled wine.
'Hope this meets your approval,' she said as she handed
it over.

The first sip took her by surprise as the hit of cinnamon, cloves, ginger and alcohol assaulted her senses all
at once. 'Well, that certainly reaches places.'

Jonas let out a loud laugh and a few others turned
to stare at them in surprise. Heat rushed into Cora's
cheeks and she held up her steaming cup. 'First sample of *glögg*.'

She turned back to Jonas. 'I think my eyes actually
just watered,' she whispered.

'Novice,' he joked, taking another sip of his.

'Show off,' she muttered as she leaned over her cup and inhaled. She pretended to sway. 'Wow, I think this could make me drunk by inhalation alone.'

He shook his head. 'That's why you're only allowed one. And why we recommend the Christmas Lights Tour. By the time you've walked four kilometres, you'll have forgotten all about the *glögg*.'

'Don't bet on it,' she murmured as the group started to move out into the streets.

They started walking down streets between rows of festooned shops. Above them were gold, green and red garlands. Every now and then they stopped to admire the displays in the shop windows, some intricate, some bold, but it seemed that nowhere in Stockholm hadn't been struck by the Christmas bug. And it was still only November!

There was a large department store, and every window had a different Christmas scene. By the time they'd worked their way along all of the scenes, the *glögg* had been finished.

When they reached a public square, Jonas turned towards her. 'This is the *svampen*—known as the mushroom. You can see it's a popular meeting place.' Cora tilted her head at the strange structure. A mushroom was exactly what it looked like, right in the middle of the square, with several groups of people gathered underneath and chatting together. Next to the mushroom was a huge lit tree. She stared at some of the designer shops surrounding the square, and the names of a few restaurants. 'I take it this is the posh bit?' she asked,

Jonas looked confused.

'The more expensive area—the place where the great and the good come to shop?'

He was smiling broadly as he shook his head. 'You

have some strange expressions. Sometimes I can hardly make out a word you are saying.' Now, he nodded. 'But, yes. I get it. If you want to eat or shop around here, bring your credit card. And make sure you've raised the limit on it.'

He glanced at some of the shops and for the briefest of pauses, Cora thought she saw something odd flit across his eyes. But a few seconds later, he was chatting to one of the nurses from Paediatrics.

They continued along the streets, which were all decorated in turn. Some had hearts in the centre of their strung garlands, others had stars. The lights tour wasn't for the faint-hearted. They had already covered half the route and Cora was very glad she had her comfortable walking boots on. She chatted to two of the staff from the NICU, and two surgical interns that had joined them.

At various points on the tour they stopped. The garlands changed to snowballs in the middle, and then to pinecones, and then frolicking angels. Near the palace were brightly lit royal deer. Cora stopped to admire the palace again. 'It's enormous,' she breathed.

Ana, one of the NICU nurses, nodded. 'I'm a history buff.' She smiled. 'And a bit of a data geek. Built in the thirteenth century, it has one thousand four hundred and thirty rooms. The national library is housed inside, and Parliament House is to the left.'

Cora laughed and put her hand on Ana's arm. 'I love that you know that.'

Ana tapped the side of her head. 'You have no idea the useless general knowledge I have in here.' She gave Cora a nudge and looked in the direction of one of the surgical interns. 'Think he'll like a bit of useless knowledge?'

Cora smiled. 'There's only one way to find out.'

Ana's eyes gleamed. 'True,' she agreed as she moved in that direction.

'What are you up to?' came the deep voice from behind her.

Cora jumped a little, then give him an appreciative smile as she continued to watch Ana. 'I'm playing matchmaker,' she said. 'And I'm just waiting to find out if I'm any good.'

Jonas followed her gaze and sighed. 'Oh, no. Not Rueben.'

Cora turned swiftly. 'What? Is he a chancer?'

'A what?' Jonas looked entirely baffled.

She threw up one hand. 'You know, a guy about town, someone who goes out with lots of women.'

Jonas was clearly holding back laughter again as he shook his head. 'No, he's an easily distracted intern, who needs to study a bit harder. Last thing I want is for him to fall in love and float off somewhere in the midst of his studies.'

'Oh.' Cora was almost disappointed.

Jonas took her by the shoulders and spun her around to where several members of staff had started walking again. 'And you seem to be easily distracted too. Come on, you don't want to get left behind.'

'No, I don't.' She cast another glance over her shoulder to where Rueben and Ana were clearly hitting it off and smiled again.

Jonas was right about one thing. This walk had certainly proved a distraction. The temptation had been high to snuggle up in her room with some chocolate and an old movie. But this was much better. The air might be stinging her cheeks, and she had to keep wiggling her toes, but just being in the company of all the other staff from the hospital, and with Jonas, was lifting her spirits in a way she truly appreciated.

These people didn't need to know about her past and her hang-ups with Christmas. She was just glad that they kept inviting her to all the activities.

'What are you smiling about now?' Jonas had fallen into step alongside her.

She gave him a sideways glance. 'What do you mean?'

'You always have that look about you—as if you're either keeping secrets or plotting something.'

Cora grinned. 'I quite like that description.' She pointed her finger at him. 'Okay, that's exactly the way I want you to think of me, at all times—as if I'm keeping secrets or plotting something. That way, I might get away with more and more.'

He rolled his eyes. 'I'm going to need eyes in the back of my head, aren't I?'

'I thought you already had them.' She pointed again. 'By the way, I tried to find you the other night to go over my research with you.' She blew on her gloved hand. 'But you'd vanished in a puff of smoke. There are three women in the antenatal ward who could go into labour imminently. All three of these babies would be pre-term—around the thirty-six-week mark. All three would fit the criteria for hypothermic neural rescue therapy.'

'You've read the mothers' notes?'

She nodded.

'Which one is your preferred candidate?'

Her eyes widened. 'Why, all three of them.' She kept talking. 'We have the chance to potentially improve the lives of three pre-term babies.'

'They're not born yet,' cut in Jonas.

But it didn't faze Cora in the slightest. 'Of course not, and I hope that all three stay safely inside their mothers for at least another three weeks. But, if they don't, I'd like us to be prepared.' She licked her lips, and caught his blue gaze. 'Most of your staff are prepared. It seems like you are the only sticking point.'

Was she being too direct? Probably. But Cora wasn't going to waste an opportunity. 'We can go over things tonight if you wish.'

For a second she thought he might agree. But, as his shoulders tensed and his back straightened, she knew she'd lost him.

'Let's talk tomorrow. Once we're both back at work.'

She knew it wasn't the time to push. But she really, really wanted to.

Someone handed her a piece of chocolate they'd just bought from one of the market stalls. 'Thanks,' she said, and popped it in her mouth to stop herself pushing him too far.

They moved back through the streets. The early evening crowds were starting to thin a little, but by the time they got back to Kungsträdgården Park and made their way past the skating rink, she noticed the large amount of people crowded around the herd of giant lit reindeer. Phones were flashing constantly as people posed next to the large structures, grinning and laughing.

'Go on, then,' urged Jonas.

Cora shook her head. 'No, not for me.'

He gave her a strange look and she shifted uncomfortably, hoping he wouldn't ask questions she didn't want to answer.

Several other of the staff members ran over and took their photos next to some of the reindeer. But Cora's stomach started to turn over. It was too much. She'd spent a whole night walking and admiring Christmas lights, and, while that had seemed fine, now, being here, back in the park, where everything was so concentrated, it all suddenly seemed claustrophobic.

Her breath was caught somewhere in her throat. Years of pent-up memories rushed up out of nowhere, and suddenly, the only place she wanted to be was back at the hotel and under her bedcovers.

'Cora, what's wrong?' Jonas was crouched down in front of her, his hands on both of her shoulders and staring her in the face. When she tried to breathe in, she caught a whiff of his pine aftershave. Concern was laced all over his face.

But the words just wouldn't come out. She wasn't ready to say them. She didn't know Jonas well enough to confide in him—not when she knew as soon as she started to tell her story, she'd get upset. She shook her head and pulled the hood up on her jacket in an attempt to try and hide part of her face. She didn't want him to see the unexplained tears brimming in her eyes.

Cora took a deep breath. 'Sorry, sudden headache. I'll go back to the hotel.' She was aware her voice was shaking. She tried to spin away, but he caught her.

'Let me help you,' he said.

She paused for a second as he moved his hand from her shoulder and for the briefest of moments his gloved finger touched her cheek.

She froze, not quite sure how to react. She wanted to grab his hand. She wanted to press his gloved hand next to her whole cheek just for a few fleeting seconds of momentary comfort. Although these warm, friendly people were new workmates, none of them really knew her.

She braced herself and blinked back her tears. 'I'm

fine,' she said quickly. 'Fine. Just need a few head-ache tablets.'

'Do you need a pharmacy? I can take you to one?'

She could see the concern in his eyes and for the odd-est reason it felt like a hand clasped around her heart. He was being nice to her. He was worried about her. And as much as she wanted comfort, she didn't want this.

She didn't want him to feel sorry for her—and that was exactly what would happen if she broke down right now and told him precisely how Christmas conjured memories she tried to forget and how painful she ac-tually found things.

Now it was her turn to straighten her shoulders. She ignored the way her stomach clenched and pasted a false smile on her face. 'Thanks, Jonas, but I have some back at the hotel. I'm sure a good night's sleep will do me the world of good. See you tomorrow.'

'You'll find your way?'

Boy, this guy was persistent.

'It's not too far. I'm sure I'll remember. I need to find my way at some point.'

It seemed he'd finally conceded. He gave her a nod. 'If you're sure, I'll see you tomorrow.'

He was staring at her with those blue eyes. And for some reason it seemed as if he could see further than he should.

So, Cora did the only thing she could do. She stuck her hands deep in her pockets, turned around and strode away as quickly as she could, ignoring the tears that started to stream down her cheeks.

CHAPTER SIX

HE'D SPENT MOST of last night worrying about her. There had been something in Cora Campbell's eyes. Something infinitely sad. It was almost as if he'd watched her retreating inside herself, even though he knew that was a completely melodramatic thought and he should probably just get over himself.

Over the last few years he'd lost a few members of staff who'd been burnt out by their emotional involvement in the sometimes heartbreaking cases they had to deal with. Hospitals were full of life and death, and the mental well-being of all his staff was a huge part of his responsibility.

Should he be concerned about Cora's mental well-being? She appeared capable and competent at work, but he had no idea what lay beneath.

His page sounded for the labour ward and he hurried down the stairs. Cora met him in the corridor outside Theatre, wearing a blue gown. 'Good. One of our ladies has delivered. Baby is born right on the thirty-six-week mark and meets all the criteria.' She counted off on her fingers, 'Less than six hours old, required prolonged resuscitation at delivery, and shows neonatal encephalopathy in a clinical exam.'

'I haven't had a chance to review the evidence.'

Cora looked him dead in the eye. 'No, but you did have the opportunity. And that's on you. What's on me is that I'm the doctor brought here to train your staff in these techniques. This baby has—' she pulled her watch from the pocket of her scrubs '—five hours and twenty minutes left to start treatment. Do you want us to sit in a corner and wait for you to catch up?'

His jaw clenched. They weren't alone. He wouldn't lose his cool. He kept his professional head firmly in place. ''Dr Campbell, these new procedures have to go to our ethics committee and governance forums for agreement.'

'Check your emails. Or, check Elias's emails. Because he did all that before I got here. Your paperwork is done, Jonas. The only person stopping this ground-breaking work starting is you.'

Every hair on his body bristled. He glanced at the clock on the wall next to him. 'Well, since I do have some time left, let me check. If I find the correct procedures have been followed, and my staff are safe to use these techniques, then I'll allow you to start.'

It was Cora's turn to look mad.

But he didn't wait for her response, he just turned around and headed into the nearest office.

He'd been given emergency access to Elias's emails, but had actually only put an out-of-office message on the account, notifying all people to send their emails on to him. He hadn't gone back through any existing emails on Elias's account—partly because it felt intrusive. But as he scanned backwards he found notifications from both the ethics and governance committees approving of Elias's proposals, along with safety protocols and guidelines for staff to follow. They'd arrived after Elias's collapse, which meant he'd put the applications in on the twenty-ninth of October—the day he'd found out Cora was coming, and just before he'd been taken unwell.

Part of Jonas wanted to be annoyed, but it looked as though Elias had just been laying the groundwork for Cora's visit—which was nothing less than he would expect from Elias. He just wished Elias had told him beforehand.

He printed out the documents, glanced over them to make sure he approved, then sent out emails to appropriate staff with the guidelines and protocols attached, asking them to read, sign and return, and to come back to him with any queries.

He tapped his fingers on the desk, moving to the coffee pot in the corner of the room and pouring himself a cup of the semi-warm liquid. It had only taken fifteen minutes. There were still five hours to start the new treatment with the baby—if the parents agreed.

He took one drink, then dumped the rest of the coffee down the sink before going back to find Cora.

The corridor was empty.

He grabbed the nearest midwife. 'Any idea where Cora, the new doctor, went?'

The midwife was carrying some equipment, obviously meant for one of the labour rooms. She looked momentarily confused, then smiled. 'Oh, the Scottish girl. Very pretty. She's away up to NICU with the new baby. I'm sure she said something about starting a new therapy.'

The papers in Jonas's hands started to crumple. He didn't look at the lifts. He ran straight for the stairs, taking them two at a time until he reached the fourth floor and the NICU.

By the time he was there, he could see Cora in one of the rooms, issuing instructions to the staff.

'What do you think you're doing?'

She looked up, completely unperturbed. All the other heads in the room turned towards him, and most of them *did* look perturbed.

'Outside. Now.'

'In a minute.'

'No, not in a minute. Now, Dr Campbell, or I'll order you out of my unit.'

Her cheeks turned pink and he could see her biting her tongue. She tugged at her scrub top to straighten it as she strode to the door. 'Carry on,' she said over her shoulder.

'*Don't* carry on,' said Jonas. 'Monitor the baby as you always would.'

He waited, letting Cora walk ahead of him. She thrust open both doors of the NICU and strode out into the corridor, turning on him in an instant.

'Don't you ever talk to me like that again.'

'Don't you ever attempt to put my staff in a vulnerable position again in my unit. I told you to wait. You moved, and attempted to start a procedure in *my* unit, without my permission.'

'We're running out of time. *She's* running out of time.' Her hands were on her hips, her words filled with passion.

'The research states the therapy should start in the first six hours after delivery. We are still well within that window.'

'Every minute matters.'

Jonas wasn't going to let this passionate woman beat him into submission. 'Dr Campbell, this is my unit. You don't go ahead without my consent. Have you even spoken to the parents—explained everything they need to know and gained their consent? Because I wasn't gone for long. Did you truly have time to have a conversation with them and explain what you wanted to do?'

He watched rage flicker across her face. 'Are you daring to suggest I haven't gained consent from the parents?'

'Can you show me it?'

'Of course, I can show you it! This isn't my first time at this.'

'Can you show me all the signed protocols and guidelines from every member of staff in the room with you in there? Can you show me your signed protocols and guidelines? I appreciate you've done this before, but not in this hospital. Not under the insurance of this hospital. And in order for you, and the hospital, to be covered, every *single* member of staff in that room involved in the therapy and the aftercare of that child needs to have read and signed the guidelines and protocols, *including you*.' He stepped right up to her. 'My job is to ensure the safety of both patients and staff. I will not allow you to bulldoze in here and put my staff at risk because you don't know how things work here.'

He saw her jaw tense. 'I gained consent a few days ago,' she said through clenched teeth.

'You spoke to the parents without clearing any of this with me?'

'I was giving myself a safety net. I always have this conversation with any woman who is in our antenatal unit if there is a chance they could deliver relatively early. It gives them a chance to ask any questions and take some time to think about it. I recognise that gaining consent after a difficult delivery, and with a very sick baby, can be fraught with difficulty. I only had to go back into Theatre and ask her if I could do what we'd previously discussed. And obviously she said yes.' Cora gave a giant sigh and ran her fingers through her messy hair, pulling it back again and redoing her ponytail. 'I didn't realise you needed staff to sign individual paperwork here.'

'You would have if you'd paid a bit more attention to how the unit works,' he said in a low voice.

The glance she gave him was an indication she was clearly weighing him up, trying to know when to push, and when to retreat.

'My staff and your patient are left unprotected unless all staff have read, understood and signed all the guidelines and procedures. That is what we do next.'

He didn't leave room for any argument, just moved past Cora and back into the unit. His instructions to his staff were clear. Two staff were to stay with the baby and monitor as normal, reporting any anomalies, while the rest spent the next half-hour reading all the new guidelines, asking Cora questions and then signing to say they knew what they were doing. Every additional staff member who was involved in looking after this baby while the new procedure was being trialled here would be required to do the same thing.

He knew she was agitated. She paced around the unit, planted a smile on her face to answer any staff questions, and wrung her fingers together while she waited for staff to read and sign what they should. When Jonas printed out a set of the papers and set them down in front of her, handing her a pen, she signed without even reading them. He raised his eyebrows.

'I sent the information to Elias. He won't have changed it—just completed it on your own templates.'

'Let's hope he did,' said Jonas with irony. 'Otherwise you have no idea what you just signed.'

He moved away to help a member of staff with another baby. The tension in the unit was palpable. Everyone had heard their spat. Everyone seemed determined not to get involved.

Once Jonas was satisfied everyone had read the protocols and guidelines, had signed, and it was recorded in their personnel files, he gave Cora a nod. 'Now everything is in place, you can get started.'

She almost flew across the unit in her haste to get started. Instructions flowed easily from her mouth. Jonas stood with his arms folded across his chest and watched the scene unfold.

She was direct. There was no ambiguity in any of her directions, and that made her a good teacher. 'Get the cooling blanket in place and monitor baby until the temperature reaches thirty-three degrees centigrade. Start the clock for a seventy-two-hour period. Continual monitoring of heart rate, breathing, blood pressure and temperature, with clinical observations of all extremities recorded every fifteen minutes. Any concerns at all, any readings that change, I'm right here. Talk to me. Use me. We want to do our best for this baby.'

Jonas watched as she put all instructions into the electronic records, and also set up visible charts around the crib. She'd just finished when both of their emergency pagers went off.

Jonas nodded to one of the other NICU doctors who'd signed all the protocols. 'Are you good here while we answer this?'

He nodded and they both ran down the corridor and back to the labour suite.

The sister met them as they burst through the stairwell entrance. 'You're not going to believe this. We have another.' She looked at Cora. 'You know, the sixteen-year-old girl you spoke to yesterday?'

Cora pulled back a little. 'The girl who presented with no antenatal care?'

The sister nodded. 'She's gone into early labour. Hard. The baby got in trouble with the cord around its neck. Assess for yourself, but I'm sure she'll meet the criteria.'

Jonas knew the sister of the unit well. 'Astrid, has there been a social-work referral?'

She nodded. 'The young mum is adamant she doesn't want to keep this baby. She's been hard to assess. She just turned up yesterday, with what turned out to be Braxton Hicks contractions. We kept her in when we realised her circumstances and that she'd had no ante-natal care. Emergency social worker saw her yesterday. Cora spoke to her yesterday, just as a precaution, in case she delivered early.'

Jonas put his hand on Cora's arm. 'This is a different set of circumstances. How was her state of mind? Did she understand what she was agreeing to?'

Cora nodded. 'She was a sad case yesterday. Very determined that she doesn't want to keep this baby, but close-lipped about everything else. I think she was dis-appointed she wasn't actually in labour yesterday. Told me she just wants to have this baby, sign the paperwork to give it up and leave.'

She took a deep breath and turned to Jonas. 'I know what you're asking me. Has someone pressured her into this? Is she actually a victim? Can she make rea-sonable and rational decisions?' She gave a nod of her head. 'She was very clear and articulate. Knew exactly what she wanted. When I asked her about the treatment she agreed immediately, but without any emotion. Just said, if it gives the baby a better chance of being adopted then fine.'

Jonas could hear a million thoughts crowding into his head about this case. 'Okay. She is the mum, and she's consented. We do want to give this baby the best possible start in life, no matter where it ends up. If she meets the criteria, then we'll take her up to NICU and start the therapy. But I want the duty social worker informed and I want someone to keep a special eye on mum.'

Jonas went to walk down the corridor, then stopped. He put his hand on his chest. 'Does she have issues with men?'

Astrid and Cora looked at each other, frowning. 'I'm not sure,' admitted Cora.

Astrid held up her hands. 'She's only met female staff so far. She hasn't told me she doesn't want to be treated by men.'

Jonas nodded. 'Okay, she knows both of you. Let's tread carefully here, because we don't know the background. Cora, you do the assessment of baby, Astrid, can you witness everything and record it, in case there are issues later?' He gave Cora a nod of his head. 'I'll wait here. If baby's suitable I'll help with the transfer back upstairs.'

He watched as they both made their way through to the delivery suite and picked up the phone to the unit. 'We may need a second team of staff for another baby. Can you start getting our other staff to read the guidelines and protocols? Call in extra if you need them. This could be a busy night.'

One minute she wanted to kill the man with her bare hands, the next he showed the maturity and professionalism of a manager who really understood a pregnant woman's journey.

She was struck by his thoughtfulness, even though she knew she shouldn't be. It only took her a few minutes to assess the newborn baby. She met all three criteria for treatment after her difficult delivery. Cora went to speak to the young mother, conscious that she couldn't let her own deep feelings affect her professional duty.

She'd been in the care system as a child and bounced from foster home to foster home. She'd finally been adopted by a couple who'd never had any children of their own and had a great life. When her adoptive mum had found herself unexpectedly pregnant, Cora had feared the couple wouldn't want her any more. But that hadn't happened at all. Instead, she'd managed to save her mother's life when she'd given birth unexpectedly and then suffered from a placental abruption. The emergency room operator had been cool and calm, giving the panicked fifteen-year-old Cora instructions every step of the way, and the whole event had set her career in process.

Cora couldn't remember her own mother, but had often wondered what set of circumstances had led to her being placed in the care of social services. She knew there could be a multitude of answers. She also knew what life in social care could mean for a child. After bouncing from place to place she'd got lucky with the Campbells, but she still had memories of feeling forgotten, left out and unloved in some of her foster homes. No one had ever been cruel or abusive towards her, but she'd lived her early days with the distinct impression that no one had really wanted her. And that stuck.

So, as she walked into the unit to speak to the young mum, she left all her feelings and memories at the door.

Five minutes later she blinked back tears and left the room. The young woman had been almost cold. Indifferent and uninterested in her new baby, she'd agreed again that her baby could have the therapy and was almost surprised she was being asked again. She was resolute in her decision, and also didn't want to go into her history or answer any other questions.

Cora respected the young woman's right to make a decision and knew she had to accept it.

As she came out of the delivery suite, Jonas was waiting near the crib, already monitoring the newborn little girl.

'She's really quite sick,' he said softly. 'Are we taking her for the treatment?'

Cora nodded as a tear slid down her cheek.

'You okay?' He touched her shoulder and she shook her head.

'Don't mind me, I'm getting old and emotional. Let's get this little one up to NICU where we can take good care of her.'

They readied the portable equipment to escort the little girl. 'What's her name?' asked Jonas.

Cora shook her head. 'She didn't want to give her daughter a name. Said whoever adopts her can choose the name.'

They both looked at each other. It was like a silent acknowledgement. They might have argued a short while ago, but things had to be put to one side right now. This baby was too important. There would be more than enough time to air their views about each other at a later date.

Jonas looked down and stroked the baby's hand. 'We'll pick you a name upstairs, lovely lady.'

Cora blinked back more tears. Today was just hitting her in all the wrong places.

By the time they got back upstairs, Astrid had solved their first problem. 'What a beautiful girl! You look like a Molly to me. What does everyone think of that name?'

There were a few nods, and moments later the temporary name was written on her chart. The next few hours flew past. Astrid had worked wonders and all staff currently in the unit had read and signed everything they needed to in order to be part of the team involved in the care of both babies. Molly's temperature was gradually lowered, and the clock was started.

Time ticked onwards and Cora watched both babies closely. Jonas had no interest in going home. This was a new procedure for his unit and he wanted to be there to support his staff. When the night shift filed in, none of them were surprised to see him near one of the babies. He often spent time in the unit if there were staff shortages, some really sick babies, or some parents who needed extra support.

Cora spent the first thirty minutes briefing all the new staff and getting them signed up. It was after midnight, when both babies were settled, that she finally sat down next to Jonas in one of the dimly lit rooms.

He pushed a box of doughnuts towards her. 'Perfect, I'm famished.' She sighed, then glanced around with her hand poised above the box.

He reached under the counter and pulled out a takeaway coffee.

'Where did you get that?'

He shrugged. 'There's a place nearby that does food

for nightshift workers. I gave one of our porters some money and asked if he could pick us up something.'

Cora looked around, clearly realising that most of the other staff were drinking from the same cups. 'You're really just an old softy, aren't you, Jonas Nilsson?'

He had an elbow on the desk and leaned his head in his hand. 'If you tell anyone that, I might have to stuff you in a cupboard somewhere,' he muttered in a low voice.

She gave a tired grin. 'It sounds like a half-hearted threat, but my brain is too tired to play verbal ping-pong.'

'And my brain is too tired to decipher what you just said to me.'

'Ping-pong. It's another name for table tennis?'

He shook his head and made a signal with his hands. 'You got me. My brain can't make the connection. No matter how much coffee and sugar I've had.'

She blinked. 'I think we've hit the night-shift slump. Let's get up and take a walk around. See if we can get some blood circulating again.'

He nodded and they slowly made their way around the unit, checking out monitoring stations and readings. Jonas nodded over his shoulder. 'Just as well those on the night shift haven't done a day shift too.'

Cora nodded thoughtfully. 'Your staff are good. I trust them.'

He smiled at her. 'So do I. Come on. There are a few on-call rooms just along here. You and I can grab a couple of hours' sleep. The staff will know where to find us if we're needed.'

She hesitated for a moment, looking unsure. 'Look,' he said as he pushed open the doors of NICU and took a few steps down the corridor. 'We're literally thirty steps away.' He pointed to the other door. 'And this one is forty steps away. It's better to lie down here than to have a parent see you sleeping in a chair in the office.'

She groaned. 'True.'

He ducked into the dimly lit kitchen in the corridor and grabbed two bottles of water from the staff fridge. 'Here, take one of these. There's a shower in the on-call room, and there should be fresh scrubs in there too.'

She leaned against the wall of the kitchen and closed her eyes. 'Are you trying to tell me something?'

He shrugged and leaned against the other wall. 'Some people like to shower before they sleep, some people like to shower after they sleep. I don't know your sleeping habits. Boy, you can be prickly sometimes.' The words came out in a jokey, sleepy droll.

She moved, coming shoulder to shoulder with him. 'Taught by the master,' she said ironically.

They stared at each for a few moments in the dim light. He could still see those green eyes staring at him. He wanted to know what she was thinking. What she was feeling right now.

The edges of her lips turned upwards. 'I can't work you out at all,' she whispered.

'Why would you want to?' came his throaty reply.

'Because you challenge me,' she said simply. 'And I think you might be the only friend I have in Sweden right now.' There was a wistfulness in her eyes that he'd only glimpsed before.

'Do you need a friend?' His hand moved automatically up to the side of her face, where he tucked a stray wispy strand of hair behind her ear. She instinctively took a step closer to him.

'Everybody needs a friend,' she murmured.

His own instincts took over, his mouth only inches

from hers. He could feel her warm breath on his skin and smell the light floral scent that danced around the edges of her aura. 'It's not nice feeling lonely all the time,' she said.

Her hand slid up to the side of his head, her fingers brushing through his short hair, pulling him forward so his lips were on hers.

Even though they were both tired, it was like a fire igniting some place beneath him. One of his hands wound around her waist, resting just above her bum, while the other moved to the back of her head.

Their kiss deepened. Not a mad, panicked kiss that he'd experienced at moments in his more youthful days, but something deeper, something more sincere.

None of this was normal for Jonas. He'd never dated a colleague before. He'd always just thought it wise not to. But Cora was different. From the moment he'd met her at the airport, she'd burrowed under his skin like some kind of persistent vice. Her confidence, demeanour and attitude both maddened and enthralled him. And the occasional flashes of vulnerability intrigued him. She'd already asked a few personal questions—ones he wasn't sure he would answer. One thing he knew for sure was that there was more to Cora Campbell than met the eye. Trouble was, did he want to push to find out more? She was only here for a matter of weeks. Could he really contemplate a fling with a visiting colleague?

Her hands moved and ran up the front of his scrub top, then she let out a little groan and rested her head against his, separating their lips.

He was surprised at how much that felt like a blow. So he stayed exactly where he was, feeling the rise and fall of her chest against his as they stood together.

As he watched, her lips turned upward again. 'I wondered,' she said with a hint of laughter in her tone.

'Wondered what?' he asked in amusement.

She leaned back. 'Just how good a kisser you would be.'

He was almost too scared to ask, but asked anyway.

She took a step back towards the corridor, her fingers curling around the edge of the doorway. She shivered before tossing a cheeky grin over her shoulder. 'A man of hidden talents. Definitely a ten,' she said as she moved out of his view and seconds later he heard the door of one of the on-call rooms close.

The temptation to follow her straight inside was strong. But she hadn't directly invited him. So he let out a long, slow breath, took a few moments to compose himself, then picked up his bottle of water and walked to the next on-call room, closing the door behind him and automatically flicking the tiny shower on.

What on earth had he just got himself into?

CHAPTER SEVEN

THEY DIDN'T DISCUSS the kiss.

For one whole, painstaking week, they didn't discuss that sweet, passionate, and extremely illuminating kiss—just danced around each other at work, exchanging small glances and smiles.

Jonas was a ten at kissing, of that there was no doubt. The ice Viking had ignited sparks that she'd kind of forgotten existed. Wow.

In fact, things at Stockholm City Hospital were turning out quite well. Both babies who'd had the hypothermia treatment seemed to have fared well. Of course, no one would know for a number of years if it had actually made a difference to their developmental outcomes. But Cora was positive as all the signs looked good.

A third baby had started treatment today and the staff, who had initially been a little nervous, were acting like experts now. They were a good team. Those who hadn't been present at either of the first sessions were all trained and on the rota for the third session to ensure everyone in the NICU got the experience and supervision they required.

Jonas had been around the last few days, helping with the supervision of staff. When he'd told her he was determined to make sure all staff had their questions answered, and would be confident and competent to practice, the man hadn't lied. He was diligent in his duty to his staff.

It was interesting to watch. She could tell that some staff loved his involvement, and a few thought it was a little interfering. But Jonas appeared to read his staff well, knowing who to back away from and who appreciated a glance over their shoulder.

So, if he could read all these staff well, why couldn't he read her?

She was beginning to replay the kiss over and over in her brain. The truth was, she wouldn't mind repeating it. But the even deeper truth was, she wouldn't mind getting to know Jonas a little better too. He intrigued her. It was almost as if he had a whole host of layers to break through before she finally got to the Jonas that lay beneath. Maybe things would have been better if they hadn't met in a workplace setting. He might be an entirely different person away from here.

All around the hospital, people were getting more and more in the festive mood. She was used to it. But Christmas sometimes made her feel as if the walls were closing in around her, especially as those particular dates loomed in the calendar. Even though they were still some weeks away, the twenty-third and the twenty-fourth of December were imprinted on her brain, a time when most people were entirely wrapped up in the chaos of panic buying and searching for that one last crucial element for dinner in the few days before Christmas.

What she badly needed right now was something to distract her from all this. Had she been at home, she'd have retreated to her flat, closed the door and the curtains and taken herself on some kind of sci-fi movie marathon. But being in the hotel was different. The Christmas decorations were beautiful. The maid had also put a small Christmas tree in her room and Cora felt like an old Scrooge when she tried to hide it every night by throwing her jacket or dressing gown over the top of it.

So, today when she was out walking through the older town, she was doing her best to scowl at all the beautifully decorated shop windows. Jonas and many of the other staff had encouraged her to explore Gamla Stan and they'd been entirely right.

The district felt like something from a children's story book. It was packed with cafés, museums, restaurants, tourist shops, galleries. Some of the building fronts were painted in vivid shades of red, yellow and green. Coupled with a dusting of snow and cobblestone streets, Cora half expected a witch on a broomstick to fly overhead, next to reindeer pulling a sleigh.

She lost several hours in the shops, buying some woodwork, jewellery, and then finding a sci-fi book shop with some very tempting board games. Wonderful smells continued to drift around her and it wasn't long before her stomach started to rumble.

She was peering in the window of one of the bakeries when she felt a tap on her shoulder. 'I'd recognise that green coat anywhere,' said the accented voice.

Her stomach leapt and she turned around to see Jonas holding a paper bag with a giant loaf inside. 'What are you doing here?' she asked.

He raised his eyebrows and lifted the loaf. 'I'm on a retrieval mission for the theatre team. I told them that when I came in at two p.m. today, I'd bring some bread for them.'

'You're working today?' He nodded. 'One of the

other managers needs a few hours off this afternoon. Her daughter is in a play at school.'

Those few words made Cora's heart swell. Jonas really was a good guy. 'What's the other bag?' she asked.

His face fell a little. 'It's Elias's favourite apricot pastries. I'll run them over to him later today.'

She nodded, then looked around and held up her hands, which were weighed down with bags. 'Okay, I've been shopping all morning and am looking for somewhere to go for a coffee and some cakes. Where do you recommend? They all look good around here.'

He nodded. 'Come along, I'll show you. Is it definitely cake you want, or something more substantial?'

'Oh, no, it's cake. Can you smell this place? I might just eat all the cakes. There's no way I can be here and resist eating cake.'

They walked along the street together, and when they were almost at the castle, Jonas nudged her, and pointed towards a cute-looking café. She spun around. 'Will you join me?' she asked. 'Or don't you have enough time?'

There was a large clock visible where they were standing and it was only eleven. But she had no idea what other plans he had for the day.

Jonas nodded solemnly and smiled. 'I think it's my duty to introduce you to all the cakes that Stockholm has to offer.'

He pushed open the door to the café and joined her at a table near the window. He glanced over at the glass-fronted cabinet. 'So, what's it to be? Scrumptious croissants, cinnamon buns, fruit and nut loaf, or blueberry and raspberry pie?'

'I swear I'm putting on ten pounds every time I inhale around here,' said Cora, watching as a waitress walked past with delicious-looking items on her tray.

'I want what they're having,' she said as the plates and mugs were slid onto the table.

'Well, that's easy, then.' Jonas said a few words to the smiling waitress as she passed by. She nodded and disappeared.

Cora gestured down at her bags. 'You didn't tell me how addictive this place is. Don't leave me unsupervised again. I'll likely buy everything and eat everything.'

She was smiling but Jonas's brow creased for a few moments. Didn't he know she was joking?

He looked down at the numerous bags she had sitting on the floor, the crease in his brow deepening as he stared.

Then he blinked and his pale blue eyes rested on her again.

'I'm sure that won't happen,' he said softly.

She unzipped her jacket, feeling instantly flustered. Cora had the distinct impression that she was missing something here.

The waitress appeared and put two delicious-smelling white hot chocolates on their table along with two portions of warm blueberry and raspberry pie complete with ice cream. 'Wow, ice cream in the middle of winter. I wouldn't have believed it if I hadn't seen it for myself.'

She wasn't quite sure what was on Jonas's mind, but she was determined to lift the mood. They'd kissed just over a week ago now, and neither of them had talked about it since.

As he took his first spoonful of pie, she decided to throw caution to the wind. 'So, tell me, do you kiss every visiting doctor that comes to Stockholm City Hospital?'

His eyes widened and he started to choke on his pie.

Several other customers turned to look and Cora had to jump up and give him a couple of claps on the back before he finally stopped. The waitress appeared with a glass of water and Cora sat back down in time to see Jonas wipe the tears that were streaming down his face.

'Are you okay?' asked the waitress.

He nodded. 'Fine. Sorry. It just went down the wrong way.'

She nodded, waiting a few moments before leaving.

Cora picked up her own spoon, now feeling badly instead of bold.

'Maybe a question for another time?'

Jonas shook his head and took a drink of the water. 'No. It's not. And no, I don't kiss every visiting doctor. You're the only one.'

She leaned her head on one hand. 'Ahh, so I'm special, then?' She wanted to joke, she wanted to flirt. She was still surrounded by all things Christmas and she wanted her mind to be someplace else.

He raised one eyebrow. 'Maybe.'

She grinned at him. 'You playing hard to get?'

His brow creased again and she waved her hand. 'Don't worry, it's an expression that probably doesn't translate well.'

He stirred his hot chocolate. It was clear he was thinking about something. 'Are you going to the Lucia procession?'

Now it was her turn to frown and shake her head. 'What's that?'

'It's next week. There are many processions of Lucia and they all take place in December. A young girl is asked to act as lady of light, or Lucia, as we call her. She wears a white costume and has candles on her head, and there is usually a singing procession following her.

There's always one in Stockholm and most of the hospital staff attend.' He paused for a second, then added, 'Or there's the night out beside the world's largest Christmas tree—you'll have seen it already at Gamla Stan. Or there's the living Christmas advent calendar. You might have seen it already. Every night, a window somewhere in Gamla Stan will open at six-fifteen p.m.—on Christmas Eve it opens at eleven-thirty a.m.—and one or more heads will pop out—an actor, a singer, a storyteller—and offer fifteen minutes of Christmas advent delight. If you look out for banners hung from windows that say *Här öppnar luckan*, you'll know where the surprise window will be that night.'

He was clearly waiting for a response, but, after flirting with him, Cora was finding it hard to say the word she wanted to: no.

She licked her lips and tried to find something appropriate to say. 'Is everything about Christmas? Isn't there anything that's just about Stockholm?'

She could sense his eyes on her for a few moments of consideration.

'Don't you like Christmas, Cora?' He asked the question in a gentle way that made her realise he already knew the answer. He was just giving her a chance to say what she wanted.

She bit her lip and met his gaze. 'I find it a bit tough. Family reasons. I want to be sociable with the rest of the staff—I do. But every single thing we do is about Christmas. I don't want to appear like a Scrooge because I don't love it quite as much as others.'

He reached over and squeezed her hand. 'You're right. Most of the trips this time of year are about Christmas. We can find something different to do. A visit to the Vasa Museum perhaps? Or we could do a boat trip—this city stretches across fourteen islands. You've only seen a few.'

She nodded gratefully as he kept talking.

'Maybe, though, if you don't have good memories of Christmas, it might be nice to create some new ones? And Stockholm is new to you—perhaps you could create some new memories here?'

Her skin prickled. He was being sincere, and it made her feel stripped back and bare. As if all her past experiences and fears were exposed. Her involuntary action was the same as always—to brush things off.

'Can I take that under advisement?'

Jonas looked puzzled again and she waved her hand. 'Just another turn of phrase. Ignore me.'

There was silence for a few moments as they both ate. The door to the café opened again, letting in a fierce gust of cold air, and another couple walked in hand in hand. Something twisted inside Cora.

She couldn't ever remember looking like that. So in love, so caught up in the moment that nothing else mattered. She tried not to stare as they stood at the counter together selecting cakes, then sloping off to one of the booths near the back of the café.

When she looked up she realised Jonas was watching them too. He shrugged. 'Oh, to be young.'

There was something melancholy about his throwaway words. And she was suddenly struck by the fact that for the last few minutes she'd been immersed in herself and not thinking about Jonas. She knew there was a story hidden deep down somewhere. It was in everything he said, everything he did, and the way he reacted to things. His need for process drove her crazy. But she'd seen how well he connected with patients. Part of her wondered if being in management was the right thing for Jonas. Management came with its own challenges—one of which was that it often took an excellent hands-on member of staff further away from the patients.

She glanced back at the younger couple. 'They're not so young,' she said, squinting a little to get a better look. 'Mid-twenties?'

Jonas nodded in agreement. 'Maybe.' There was still something wistful in his tone. She wanted to prod. She wanted to ask questions but wasn't quite sure how he might respond. Did kissing someone give her the right to dig deeper?

'You haven't mentioned family much—do you have family in Stockholm?'

He shook his head. 'My family stay in Sundsvall. It's about a four-hour drive. I moved to Stockholm to train to be a nurse and midwife and found that I liked it here. I've been here since I was eighteen.'

'Do you ever go back home?'

'Sometimes I visit my parents and my sister in holidays.'

'Are you going home for Christmas?'

He shook his head. 'I usually volunteer to work so other managers who have families can have the time off. I hope that when my time comes, someone will do the same for me.'

She was pretty sure her stomach was fluttering right now, and it wasn't the raspberry pie. 'You plan to settle down sometime?'

He leaned back in his chair. 'Some day. Doesn't everyone?' His eyes fixed on hers.

Cora hesitated. 'I sometimes wonder if I'm the settling-down type.'

His gaze was steady. 'Well, only you can decide that.

I guess it just depends what priorities you have in your life. And timing, of course.'

'You haven't met anyone you wanted to settle down with?' As she asked the question she noticed him shift uncomfortably and she cringed. Please don't let there be some dead wife in the background and she'd just monumentally put her foot in it.

His gaze was now fixed on the window to the street outside. Surely if there had been something, or someone, significant in his past, one of the other staff might have mentioned it? But then, the staff were loyal to Jonas. Would they really tell a temporary newcomer something private or personal about their boss? Probably not. Maybe she should tread a little more carefully.

'Not yet,' he said finally. She could almost see something turn on in his eyes—as if he'd never really given it much thought before, but now…now it was something he might consider. 'I guess I've just not been lucky.' He took a sip of his hot chocolate. 'Not met the right woman yet.'

She could swear there was something glittering in the air between them. So much unsaid. Her brain was screaming *How about me?* And, maybe she was crazy, but as he looked at her the corners of his mouth edged upwards, as if he were having the same thoughts as she was. When he spoke again, his voice was low. 'What about you? No Mr Right tucked away somewhere?'

She shook her head and laughed. 'Plenty of Mr Wrongs, Mr Never-Could-Be-Rights, and Mr Absolute Disasters, though. I tend to get too caught up in work to pay much attention to whoever I'm dating. I think I'm probably the worst girlfriend in the world.'

He held up his hot chocolate. 'I'll drink to that.'

She laughed and held up hers. 'What—are you the worst boyfriend too?'

'Oh, no, but I'm happy to drink to you being the worst girlfriend.'

'Cheeky!' She clunked her mug against his and ate some more of her pie. 'You said you're going to meet Elias. Do you think I might get to meet him in person at some point, before I leave?'

He wrinkled his nose. 'What—you have another, nearly three weeks? I'll see how he is today. Elias is a proud man. He wouldn't want to meet you unless he was at a stage where he could converse properly with you.'

'He's not there yet?'

'Maybe. He's improving all the time. I saw him again last week, and he was able to walk with a stick. He was still stumbling with some words, and his thought processes were a little delayed. Let me ask him when I visit later today. I'll let you know what he says.'

'Will you tell him about the babies?'

There was the briefest hesitation. 'Of course, I will. He'll want to know all about it.'

'And you'll tell him it's been a success?' she pushed.

'I'll tell him the procedures went well, and our staff training and monitoring systems are in place. I can't tell him it was a success as we don't know yet that it is a success. We won't know the outcomes for these babies for a few years.' This time it was him who was pushing.

'But the immediate outcomes were evident.'

He nodded slowly. 'Yes, but we have to view these things in context.'

Cora sat back with a sigh and shook her head. 'You don't want this to succeed, do you? You're so against change that no matter how well this works, you just won't let it continue.' Frustration was building inside her. She'd thought they'd made strides towards this being an implementable procedure at Stockholm City Hospital. A step forward for babies affected by hypoxic ischaemic encephalopathy. But every time she thought they'd made some headway, they seemed to jump backwards instead.

Jonas looked at her with an incredulous expression. 'Where on earth did you get that from? I'm just asking you to have a bit of context around the work so far and not to jump too far ahead. We've used the treatment on three babies, Cora. *Three.* Since when did that become a number that makes this treatment the one to use? You've been involved in research studies. You know that's not how this works. And we won't know the true outcomes for these babies for years.'

She leaned forward, pressing both her hands on the table. 'But this is *not* a research study. This is fact. The studies have been done. I'm here to teach, not to tiptoe around every person and constantly ask permission to breathe!'

Her heart was racing in her chest and her voice had become a bit louder, causing people to turn around and look at them, with a few raised eyebrows.

But Jonas wasn't ready to back down. He leaned back across the table to her. His voice was low, and hissing. 'But your research was done in the UK. A different population. A different demographic. A different healthcare and social care system. Things aren't automatically translatable. I shouldn't have to tell you that.'

Cora stood up sharply, her chair tilting back dangerously. 'You're impossible.'

Jonas leaned back in his chair. While she was boiling mad, he looked completely unperturbed. It was as if he was baiting her.

'And you're irrational.'

It was like someone jabbing a red-hot poker into her side. How dared he call her irrational? She was so mad she couldn't speak—not that he deserved a response.

She slid her arms into her jacket, bent down and snatched up her shopping bags, fumbling to fit them all in her hands before turning and storming out of the door.

The freezing-cold air did nothing to cool her temper. She stomped down the street without a backwards glance, determined to get as far away as possible from Mr Ice Viking.

She had a job to do. And he wouldn't get in her way. She wouldn't let him.

CHAPTER EIGHT

Two days later and she hadn't set eyes on him.

Cora was the ultimate professional. In the NICU she was all smiles. She'd written a few more protocols for the procedure and asked Alice for advice on how to put them through all the relevant committees.

Alice had waved her hand. 'Jonas will do all that for you,' she'd said casually.

'I like to see things through myself,' she'd insisted. 'Plus, I like to find out all the procedures anywhere that I'm working. Each hospital works differently, and it's good for me to get a handle on different operating procedures.'

If Alice had been suspicious, she hadn't said so, just scribbled down some names and numbers of people for Cora to get in touch with.

Forty minutes later when there had been a page from the antenatal ward that another of their patients had gone into early labour, she'd decided to go on down.

Her phone buzzed as she ran down the stairs. It was Chloe. They'd been ping-ponging messages to each other after Cora had raged about Jonas a few days ago.

Just thinking. Can't remember the last time you ranted about someone quite so much. If you ask me, there's more to this than a disagreement about work. Exactly how attractive is Jonas Nilsson?

Cora's mouth bounced open. Chloe was too smart for her own good.

Viking-like. But far too arrogant for me to care how attractive he is.

Dots appeared. Chloe was immediately typing a response.

You've kissed him, haven't you?

Cora actually stopped mid-step.

Why on earth would you say that??????????

She was shaking her head as Chloe typed back.

Knew it.

She let out a sigh and put her phone back in her pocket. Chloe could always read her like a book.

As she reached the labour suite, there was that eerie kind of calm. There was no sign of any staff, and the corridor was silent—never a good sign in a labour ward.

She made her way along the corridor, towards the emergency theatre at the end. Just as she reached the swing doors, a midwife burst through them, wearing a blood-stained plastic apron. She gave Cora a quick glance up and down before a flicker of recognition crossed her face and she pointed a gloved hand. 'NICU doctor?'

Cora nodded without speaking.

'Good, with me. Emergency.' The midwife gave a sharp nod of her head and pushed open the doors.

Cora could tell immediately that this was where the majority of the staff were. Someone was lying on the floor, and it took her a few moments to realise it was a fellow doctor, who was pregnant. She went immediately to assist, but a voice from the theatre table stopped her.

'No, leave her. We need you here.'

Cora's head flicked from one place to the other. Every instinct in her wanted to help her fellow colleague on the theatre floor, but there were three members of staff already around her. One of them caught her eye. 'She's diabetic. Had a hypoglycaemic attack. We can deal with this.'

Cora didn't recognise the obstetrician in the cap and mask at the theatre table, but there were twelve at Stockholm City Hospital and she hadn't met them all.

His voice was deep. 'I need a neonatologist. This baby will need resuscitated.' He was already cutting through the woman's abdomen.

Cora stepped to the sinks and gave her hands a quick wash. Turning around, she found a theatre nurse with a gown ready for her to step into, and another with a pair of waiting gloves, and a third placed a cap on her head.

She recognised one of the NICU nurses waiting next to the neonatal crib. She thrust her hands into the gloves, just as the obstetrician lifted out the silent baby.

As Cora took the baby, her motions became automatic. She'd unfortunately done this on many occasions. A voice she recognised was at her side and she looked up to see Jonas appear and tie a mask around her face. Some babies needed encouragement to breathe after delivery, but Cora knew nothing about the circumstances of this case, and this little one looked a little too flat for her liking.

She spoke clearly to the NICU nurse, who was just as well versed in this as she was, assessing airway, breathing and circulation. Jonas handed her a suction tube, as she tried to stimulate the baby to breathe.

Nothing. There was a noise behind them and she turned her head in time to see her colleague on the floor thrash out with her arms and legs. It was clear she was confused. Hypoglycaemic attacks frequently did that, and it could be a few minutes before things calmed down. In an ideal situation they would have taken her somewhere else, but for the next few minutes, the floor was probably the safest place for her.

Cora continued her assessment of the baby as Jonas systematically connected her to all the monitoring equipment. It was a little girl and her colour was extremely poor. Her pulse was weak but rapid and thready, and there was no respiratory effort at all, even with a bag and mask. After another few moments she nodded to Jonas. 'I'm going to intubate.'

She moved to the head of the crib and Jonas automatically put everything she needed into her hands. Airways could be tricky, particularly in small pre-term babies, but Cora slid the tube in with no problem and started the procedures to connect the little girl to the machinery.

Now it was Cora's turn to hold her breath, until the little girl's skin finally started to lose the dusky tone and pink up.

She spent the next few moments inserting a line. Premedication was usually given prior to intubation in the neonatal unit, but wasn't appropriate for intubations in the delivery suite. Cora wanted to ensure that now an airway was established she could do her utmost to ensure this little girl was given the medications that would assist her.

Cora finally lifted her head to look at the obstetrician while another nurse put an ID bracelet on the baby. 'I'm going to take this little one up to NICU.'

As another alarm sounded, this time for the mother, the obstetrician nodded. 'Thanks for your assistance. Jonas said you would step in.'

She exchanged glances for the briefest of seconds with Jonas, and then the two of them started to push the crib and ventilator out to the lift. Their doctor colleague was now in a sitting position on the floor and drinking some orange juice.

Once they were clear of the theatre, Cora pressed the button for the lift and looked at Jonas. 'What on earth happened in there?'

He frowned tightly. 'Everything. Eve passed out. One minute she was there and talking, the next she was on the floor. I had already paged you about the delivery and knew you were likely on your way down. Just as well, as at that point they lost the baby's heartbeat.'

Cora shuddered. Her eyes on her little patient. 'As soon as I walked into the labour suite I knew something was wrong.'

'Chaos?'

'The opposite. Not a single person and complete silence.'

Jonas closed his eyes for a second. 'Never a good sign.'

'Nope.' She touched the cheek of the little girl. 'Do we know a name?'

He nodded. 'Her mother told me before we got to Theatre that she intended to call her Rose.'

'You were already down there?'

He nodded again. 'Yes. There had been some issues on the antenatal ward, and the labour suite today.'

'What?' The question came out automatically, and as soon as she noticed the dark expression on his face, she wished she hadn't asked.

'Two staff were involved in a car accident this morning. One worked in each area. Both are serious, and are in general theatres, right now.'

'Oh, no.'

He inhaled deeply. 'I had to send some staff home, and I had to phone the families.'

She reached her hand over and touched his. 'That must have been hard.'

'That's the job. I've called extra staff in, and another manager.'

'And what about that doctor? I've never met her before.'

'The neonatologist? Eve has been off during her pregnancy. She's a Type One diabetic and had been having frequent hypos. She literally came back to work two hours ago.'

'Poor soul. She'll need to go off again. Will someone check her over?'

'I'll make sure of it.' He glanced at Cora. 'It's a shame. You would have liked working with her. She's a great doctor.'

As the lift doors pinged open, two of the NICU staff were waiting for them and grabbed one end of the crib and the portable ventilator.

They rolled smoothly into the NICU and spent the next half-hour getting baby Rose set up in the unit. Jonas disappeared while Cora spent some time with the frazzled dad who appeared upstairs, explaining exactly what was happening with his newly born daughter.

By the time Jonas reappeared with two ham bagels in his hand, Cora didn't even realise that four hours had passed since she'd first received the page.

As he sat down next to her in the office, and wordlessly handed her a bagel, Cora took a deep breath. 'Wow.'

He took a bite of his bagel and a few moments later gave an agreed, 'Wow.'

'Is Eve okay?'

He smiled. 'Angry, embarrassed, annoyed, and frustrated, but definitely okay.'

'That's what matters.'

He gave her a sideways glance. 'She wanted to meet you. Wanted to hear about your work.'

'Ah, that's nice.' She took a bite of her bagel. 'Maybe some other time. I'd be happy to go over the principles with her. Take it she's having a tough time with this pregnancy?'

He nodded. 'She's one of our most reliable doctors and she's been diabetic since childhood. But since she became pregnant, she's been plagued by unexpected hypoglycaemic attacks. It's a shame. She sat with me at lunch one day, ate everything, then stood up and literally passed out cold.'

'She wasn't showing any signs?'

'About two minutes before she passed out, she got a strange look in her eye—but she was still taking part in the conversation. She's been so well controlled for years that her blood sugar goes really low before she gets any warning signs.'

'Is there nothing they can do?'

Jonas actually looked furtive for a moment and paused.

'What have you done?'

He pulled a face. 'I phoned a company rep that I knew. There's a new thing that's been trialled. It's a patch that fits to the skin and sends a constant cellulose sugar reading to a phone. The phone can alarm for either high or low levels.'

'Did you get one?'

He glanced at his watch. 'Eve—much to her annoyance—is being monitored for a few hours in the antenatal ward. The rep will be here within the hour.'

Cora gave him an interested look. 'You have a good heart, Jonas Nilsson.'

He held out his hands. 'What? She'd do the same for me if I was in that position, and I know it. We're a team. We've got to help each other.'

She gave him a knowing smile. 'That's right. We're a team. We should help each other. I totally agree.'

The change in her tone of voice got his attention. He set the bagel down. 'Why do I feel like I've just been played?'

Cora shook her head and pointed at the half-eaten bagels. 'Tell me you got us something other than this?'

He sighed and reached into his pocket, pulling out two chocolate bars. Cora took hers, opened it right away and broke off a square of chocolate, putting it in her mouth without pausing for breath.

'You didn't finish your main,' he teased, pointing at the bagel.

She shrugged. 'I like to mix and match. I'll finish them both.' She narrowed her eyes and said warningly, 'Don't try and police my food. Quickest way to make me your enemy.'

'I thought I'd already done that,' he said casually, teasing her.

She ate another piece of chocolate. 'You definitely try my patience. This chocolate might be the only thing that saves you.'

He stopped for a minute, pushing his food away. 'Do we want to talk about what happened between us?'

'The kiss or the fight?'

'Touché. How about both?'

He had her there. Cora wasn't quite sure what to say. Talk about being put on the spot. 'Are you brave enough to go there?' She kind of preferred this casual flirting. Jonas had already learned more about her than most people she'd consider acquaintances. She wasn't entirely sure she wanted to reveal any more.

But on the other hand, finding out a bit more about her mysterious Viking wasn't entirely unappealing.

She licked her lips. 'Okay, then. I'll start with the kiss. I liked it. It was…interesting.'

He sat forward. 'Interesting?' He said the word as if she'd just insulted him.

She smiled at his reaction. 'Yes, it was.'

He frowned. 'Not enticing? Or amazing? I'd even settle for hot.'

Now, she was definitely laughing. 'Well, how would you describe it?'

He folded his arms. 'Unsure.' He was watching her with those pale blue eyes.

'And what does that mean?'

He gave her a half-smile. 'It means I think I need to try again, to be sure.'

'You do?' She couldn't help but smile as he leaned closer.

'I do.' His lips were inches from hers. As she inhaled, she could smell his aftershave. The soap powder on his uniform. The balm on his skin.

She put her hand on his chest. 'But we haven't got to the fight yet,' she said quietly.

'I thought we could just miss that bit,' he whispered.

'We could,' she agreed, highly tempted. But gave his chest a little push back. 'Or, we could get to the crux of the matter.'

He gave a resigned sigh and sat back on his chair, cracking open his own bar of chocolate. 'Which is?'

'Why you don't like my research or my work.'

He shook his head. 'Your research I don't mind. I've read it all. It's your methods I find…questionable.'

'Questionable?' Her voice rose an octave as he gave her a lazy smile, knowing he'd tempted another reaction out of her.

He waved a hand. 'I think we've established you're a great hands-on doctor. Fearless. Practical. Able to teach. Able to assist in an emergency.'

She gave an approving nod. 'Carry on. I like these thoughts.'

'I thought you might.'

She sighed and waited for him to continue.

'But you don't always see the bigger picture.' He put his hand on his chest. 'And you don't need to, because that's my job as the manager of this unit and all the staff to make sure that I cross every t and dot every i.'

'Is that a Swedish expression?'

He shook his head. 'No, I looked it up online last night to be able to explain what I meant to you.'

'You planned this conversation last night?' she said with disbelief.

'I planned we'd have it at some point.'

She broke off another piece of chocolate. 'What made you think I'd talk to you again?'

He reached his hand over and touched her skin. 'This.'

There was silence as the little buzz shot up her arm and tickled every sense in her body.

Her eyes were fixed on the spot he'd just touched. 'So, I haven't imagined it,' she said in a low voice.

'No,' he said huskily. 'You haven't imagined it.'

'So what does that mean...for us?'

'It means we have a little less than three weeks left to get to know each other a bit better.' He'd moved closer again, his voice low, his warm breath teasing the skin at her neck.

He smiled at her. 'So, what's it to be? The boat trip, or a visit to the Vasa Museum?'

Something warm stirred inside her heart. He'd remembered. He'd remembered that she didn't love Christmas so much, and wanted to try something different.

That mattered. A lot.

Her green eyes met his gaze. 'You decide,' she said quickly, before sliding her arms around his neck, and sealing the deal with a kiss.

CHAPTER NINE

IT SEEMED THAT he was losing his mind. And Jonas was sure that the gorgeous woman, currently on his arm, was the cause.

This should be harmless. This should be fun. Cora was only here for another few weeks. He already knew that she was due to fly back to London on Christmas Eve.

It had struck him as kind of a sad time of year to travel. But from the casual chats he'd had with Cora, he could tell she wasn't really thinking about it. Others might be fretting about late flights, and delays, and hurrying home to their family, but he already knew Cora didn't like Christmas much, even though he didn't know the finer details.

Today, they were huddled at the entrance to the Vasa Museum—in amongst a long line of tourists. Cora looked up at him with a smile. 'You bring me to all the best places,' she said, her breath turning to steam in the freezing air as she shivered.

He put his arm around her. 'It's warmer once we get inside. Think of this as your cultural experience.'

She laughed. 'It's a chocolate museum, isn't it?'

'You wish. But I know a nice chocolate shop we can visit later.'

'Promises, promises,' she muttered as the line slowly moved forward.

They made their way inside, and it took Cora a few moments to unzip her jacket and realise what was the main exhibit.

She let out a gasp. 'A ship? The Vasa Museum is a ship?'

He smiled and nodded. 'A bit of history. Pay attention. It's the world's only conserved seventeenth-century ship.'

The ship was mounted just above them, so everyone viewing could walk around and underneath and get a feel for the size and quality of the ancient ship.

Cora shook her head. 'How on earth did it get here?'

'It sank,' he said simply. 'A few minutes after being launched in 1628.'

She looked at him in confusion. 'But I still don't get it—this was at the bottom of the sea?'

He nodded. 'After over three hundred years on the sea bed, the *Vasa* was retrieved and preserved for the museum.'

'No way!' she said as she continued to walk underneath. 'No way was this under the sea for three hundred years.' She turned and wagged her finger at him. 'I've watched all those *Titanic* documentaries. Everything just disintegrates. This must be a replica. Isn't it?'

'I'll have you know we Swedes are a talented bunch. Ninety-eight per cent of this ship is original.'

She reached out to try and touch it, even though it was way above her head. 'But...that's impossible.'

He smiled again. He wasn't sure what she'd think of the museum and deliberately hadn't told her what it housed. But it was clear she was impressed. 'Did Vikings sail on it?'

Now, he laughed. 'We'd have to go back a whole lot longer for that. No, it was a warship, and the upper hull was much too heavy. That's why she sank. It's in such good condition because Stockholm has uniquely brackish waters, which basically fossilised the ship and kept her in great condition until her recovery.'

'I can't believe it survived,' said Cora in wonder. She slipped her hand into Jonas's as they continued around the structure.

'Well, a bit like the Titanic, the metal parts suffered. All the iron bolts disintegrated; only things like cannon balls and the anchor survived.' He gave a laugh. 'And the guns and cannons. They were looted years ago.'

Cora slid her jacket off. 'It's quite warm in here.'

'It's kept at a steady temperature to stop the ship deteriorating. If you came in here in the summer, you'd find it chilly and want a jumper.'

'Well, it's so cold outside it feels positively pleasant in here today,' said Cora. They'd walked around the boat twice now.

'Want to visit the restaurant upstairs? The food is quite good here.'

She nodded and passed by an exhibit of the timeline of the ship's preservation as they moved to the stairs. The restaurant was busy already, even though it wasn't quite midday, and they were seated at a table quickly.

'Okay, there's a rule,' said Jonas as the waiter took their drinks order.

'What's the rule?' asked Cora cautiously.

'They have a daily dish here—and it's always Swedish meatballs in a cream sauce with lingonberries. You have to try it.'

Cora smiled. 'I haven't tried any meatballs since I got here.' She picked up the fork at her place setting.

'But I have, of course, tried the meatballs at a very famous store in the UK.'

Jonas groaned and shook his head. 'No, they are an imitation. Now you're in Sweden, you'll try the real thing.'

Jonas ordered for them both as Cora sipped her white wine, and he his beer.

Her mood was good today. He hadn't seen those hidden shadows that occasionally flitted across her eyes. And it was clear she was enjoying herself. She asked questions at an alarming rate, and eventually he had to admit he didn't know all the answers, and bought her a guidebook for the museum.

They joked back and forward as their meal was brought to them and Jonas watched in pleasure as her eyes lit up at the first taste of the genuine Swedish meatballs. She gave a nervous smile. 'I hated to admit that I loved the ones back home, but these are really spectacular.' She leaned back in her chair with a contented glow. 'I swear, if I could come here every day to eat these, I might just move to Stockholm.'

Her words made him curious. 'You've always stayed in London—you wouldn't consider moving elsewhere?'

She shook her head. 'Well, obviously I'm from Scotland, and I trained at Edinburgh University and worked in the hospitals around there during my training. But, as soon as I qualified, because it's a more specialist field, there just seemed to be more opportunities in London. I had an offer last year of a job in Washington, and then the year before in Germany, but...' she paused as if she were contemplating whether to be honest or not '... I wanted to be in the same part of the world as my sister, Isla, when she was at university. And it's only just over an hour's flight from London. She has her aunt and uncle, of course, but we're close—guess that happens when you're there at the delivery—and I just wanted to be nearby in case she needed me.' She smiled sadly. 'But the truth is, she's all grown up now. She's the most independent girl on the planet. I wouldn't be surprised if she announced she was going to Australia to do her final year of university or something similar.'

Jonas shook his head. 'Wait a minute. Rewind. You were there when Isla was delivered?'

Heat flooded into her cheeks. But she'd said it out loud now. There was no point in lying about it. 'I delivered her. My mum went into labour early, fast, and very unexpectedly. We stayed quite far out in the country. My dad was miles away trading sheep, and it was just me and her.'

Jonas sat back a bit further in his seat. He wanted to know all about this. 'That must have been terrifying. How old were you?'

'Fifteen. Let's just say it was a baptism of fire. The emergency operator was great, calm as you like, and gave me really clear instructions. Isla was born within a few minutes. She was early and needed a bit of assistance with her breathing. The scariest thing was when my mum had a postpartum haemorrhage. I'll never forget seeing all that blood on the floor.'

'What did you do?'

'Exactly what the operator told me to do. They decided to send an air ambulance at that point.'

'How long did that take?'

She gave a distinctly uncomfortable smile. 'Nearly too long. Obviously, I had no oxytocin, and I spent a long time massaging my mum's uterus, trying to get it to contract and stop the bleeding. It was all I could do.'

'Wow, that's brave.'

She nodded slowly. 'In the end, both Isla and my mum were okay. Both stayed in hospital for a few weeks, and it lit a fire in my belly.'

He gave her a strange glance.

'Maybe it's another UK saying. It made me curious. Made me want to be a doctor. To help small babies like Isla and see if I could learn to do things to help them.' She licked her lips and took a sip of her wine. 'Honestly, it made me who I am today.'

He sat back and watched her for a while, loving the way the sunlight from the windows was catching the tones in her hair, and the glint of her green eyes. She was beautiful. Inside and out. Passionate about her work too. Yes, they might disagree about things, but Cora challenged him. She was the first woman who'd brought some light into his life in the last few years. She made him laugh. She made him furious. And he'd honestly never been so happy around someone.

But somehow he knew there was more—so much more to unravel about this intriguing woman. She still hadn't really told him why she didn't like Christmas, and if he asked now, it would feel like prying. She'd already told him a little of herself, but he was sure there were many more fascinating pieces to the puzzle that made up Cora Campbell. His stomach clenched a little. He'd been burned once before with Katrina. Was he going to let himself be burned again? Could all this blow up in his face?

He took a breath and made an instant decision. He would be patient. He knew Cora still had some secrets. But Jonas hadn't told her everything about himself either. He was rapidly losing his heart to this woman, and, at some point in his life, he had to take the chance. He had to take the chance to be happy.

'What?' she asked.

The word jolted him out of his reverie and he straightened in his chair. 'What?' he countered.

'You were looking at me funny.'

'I was not.'

Her expression was affectionate and her voice lowered. 'Yeah, you were.' Her hands circled the stem of her wine glass. 'So, I've told you what made me who I am. Now you need to reveal a bit of yourself to me.'

It was like being under an instant magnifying glass. He tried the casual wave of his hand. 'Nothing. What you see is what you get.'

She shook her head. 'No, it isn't. Why are you so pedantic at work? Why are you such a stickler for rules and regulations? I get that they're important. I know we have them for safety reasons. But, in my experience, on the odd occasion, it's okay to think outside the box.'

He visibly shuddered and she noticed straight away. 'See? You don't even like those words.' She paused for a few moments, clearly thinking. Her gaze drifted to the stem of the glass as she stroked her fingers up and down it. 'I've met a few people who act the same way that you do, and all of them had some kind of bad experience at some point in their career that made them a stickler for the rules.'

Her gaze lifted and met his. It was as if she'd just reached her hand into his brain and read everything he kept hidden there. He wanted to deny it. But, for the first time in a long time, someone was reading him like a book.

And it was Cora.

He took a long, slow breath, followed by a sip of his beer. 'Guilty as charged,' he finally said. If he was willing to take a chance with Cora, surely she would be willing to take a chance on him? He knew he was about to reveal the part of himself he didn't talk about much. There was always a deep-down fear that if he revealed this part of himself, a colleague might find him wanting. Might think he'd made the wrong decision and let his patient down. Would Cora?

She gave the slightest shake of her head. 'No. I need more than that.'

He sighed. 'It's just like you said. I had a bad experience. I learned from it. And I do my best to ensure that none of my colleagues end up in the position that I did.'

'And what position was that?'

He looked away from Cora. Her gaze was unnerving.

'I was newly trained as a midwife. Believe it or not, I used to be quite laid-back. I loved being a midwife. I loved working on birth plans and formed really good relationships with my expectant mums.'

'So, what happened?'

He was conscious that she kept gently pushing him to reveal more.

'I had a woman in the late stage of labour. She'd been really clear in her birth plan that she didn't want a Caesarean section unless there was no other choice. She'd had surgery as a child that had left her traumatised and was terrified of undergoing anything similar again. Her birth plan was meticulous. She had control issues, and having every part of her plan detailed in advance helped her feel more in control and helped alleviate her anxiety.'

Cora shook her head. 'Oh, no. I can guess what happened.'

He nodded. 'I made a mistake. I made a promise I eventually couldn't keep. I told her I'd do everything I could to make sure she didn't have a C-section.'

Cora winced. 'Ouch.'

Even now, he could feel a weight pressing down on his shoulders as he talked about the case. 'So, things went just like you'd expect. Baby's heart rate dipped dramatically, the baby was deteriorating and...'

'There was nothing else for it,' Cora finished for him. 'Your patient had to have an emergency C-section.'

He gave an enormous sigh. 'Exactly. And both mum and baby survived.'

'Both healthy?'

He nodded. 'Physically, yes. But mentally? Not so much. For mum, anyway. She complained about me— claimed I'd let her down. She suffered a really severe postnatal depression after the birth of a baby she'd very much wanted.'

'But that could have happened anyway,' said Cora.

'I know that. But I'm sure the whole delivery did affect her mental health.'

'So what happened about the complaint?'

He leaned back in his chair, his hands twisting the napkin on the table. 'I was exonerated. They said that my actions had saved the life of both mum and baby.'

'So why do you look so miserable about it?'

He leaned forward. 'Because I *did* let her down. I made her a promise that, in the end, I couldn't keep.'

Cora shook her head. 'So, you never had the "what if" conversation with her?'

He frowned. 'Of course, I did. That's how we had it documented that a C-section was only if there was no other choice.'

'And there was no other choice, was there?'

He ran his fingers through his hair. He hated talking about this. 'Of course, there wasn't. But the only thing that saved me in all this was the fact I had documented *everything*. And I'd followed every protocol to the letter. If I'd strayed in any way, they would have found against me.'

Cora held up her hands. 'You did what every good nurse, midwife or doctor does.'

He was still frowning at her. She was saying it as if it made perfect sense.

'Your practice was good, Jonas. You didn't do anything wrong. But that doesn't make you feel any less responsible. Or any less guilty. That's natural. I still remember every patient where there have been questions about care, or a complaint. It doesn't matter that they are few and far between, they stay here—' she pointed to her chest '—inside, grinding and grinding away. Making me ask the "what if" questions constantly. Making me go over every drug prescribed, every conversation I had. Wondering if I didn't read a situation correctly. That's normal. And neither of us would be good practitioners if we didn't reflect. If we didn't try and learn from situations that we wished had turned out differently.'

He gave a slight nod. 'But staff are sometimes slack. They don't understand how important it is to follow all protocols completely. Documentation and safe protocols can, at times, be the difference between a member of staff being charged with something, or not.'

'I know. I get it, I do.' She looked him in the eye. 'But don't you ever just want to park the bad experience, know that you've learned from it, and shake off the guilt? I can still see it sitting there, like a baby elephant in a cloud above your head.'

He let out a surprised laugh at that comment, then instantly became serious again. 'I'm the manager. It's my job to protect my staff.'

Cora agreed. 'It is. But it's also all staff members' professional responsibility to protect themselves. You can't be looking over every shoulder all the time. You can't work twenty-four hours a day.' She held up a cautious finger. 'And remember that we also learn from our mistakes—or our maybe mistakes. Reflecting on those can be even more important. And if you terrify staff with rules, they might be too scared to tell you about mistakes, or about near misses.'

Jonas leaned back, both hands flat on the table, thinking about what she'd just said.

'I can remember as a junior doctor drawing up morphine, double-checking the prescription and the dose with a nurse, then almost giving it to the wrong patient. Someone had swapped beds around while we'd been drawing up the medicine in the treatment room. When we went in to administer the dose, with the chart in our hands, the nurse went to read the name and date of birth from the patient's wristband. I have to admit to not really listening. And it took a few more seconds than normal to realise that something wasn't right.'

'But you didn't give it?'

'No, it didn't even get out of the tray. But for me, that was a near miss.'

He nodded silently and she held up her hand.

'Let me tell you about another. I was part of the arrest team. I got paged to a ward I was unfamiliar with. I reached the scene, and a senior nurse was standing next to a bed, looking stunned. I *assumed* that the nurse had already done the basic ABC checks before she pulled the arrest buzzer. You know…airway, breathing, circulation. So, as the most junior member of the team, I put my knee on the bed and leaned over to start compressions.'

'What happened?'

'I did one, and the elderly patient sat up and said, "Ouch!"'

Jonas put his hand over his mouth. 'She never.'

'Oh, she did. I got the fright of my life and I learned a valuable lesson. Never assume anything.'

'Who pulls an arrest buzzer without doing ABC?'

Cora raised her eyebrows. 'Who, indeed?'

Jonas was still contemplating what she'd said. Could his behaviour mean that staff were reluctant to report things to him? There was an electronic monitoring system in the hospital for any incidents or near misses. It was part of the induction training for any new staff. He'd always just assumed that staff would report the way they should. The thought that his dictate about rules and protocols might actually stop reporting issues was genuinely disturbing.

'Have you seen any incidents that should have been reported and weren't?'

She sighed sadly. 'And that is where the problem lies. Why did your mind go there first? Why didn't your mind say, *Hmm, maybe I should think about that*?'

'It went there too.'

'But that's not what you said.'

He sighed. Boy, she was tough. He put his elbows on the table and leaned forward. 'Okay, I don't want staff to be scared to tell me if something goes wrong.'

Cora nodded and smiled. 'Okay, now we're getting somewhere. I just think you have to strike a balance.'

'How do you feel about a balance?'

'What do you mean?'

'Most of the reasons we've fought is because I think you rush on into things. How about you stop and take a breath too. Try and strike a balance.'

She pulled a face at him for turning her words around on herself. She lifted her glass towards him. 'Maybe we should drink to that?'

The words were out of his mouth in a flash. 'I'd prefer to seal the deal with a kiss.'

She blinked and licked her lips. Once. And then twice.

And then she stood up and walked around the table towards him. He stood to greet her.

'Deal.' She smiled, as she stood on tiptoe to plant a kiss on his lips.

For a moment he thought it was going to be a fleeting kiss. But his body reacted immediately, bringing his hands to her waist and pulling her close. Cora's hands wound around his neck and their kiss deepened. They were in a public space so he couldn't do exactly what he wanted to do. But as he kissed her he breathed in her shampoo, her body lotion and her light perfume, a collision of floral scents that invaded his very pores.

She pulled her lips back, smiling, and murmured in a low voice, 'Sometimes, it's worth the wait.' Her warm breath caressed his skin. She rested her forehead against his cheek.

He laughed quietly. 'More than worth it,' he said as he stepped back with the sexiest smile on his face that she'd ever seen.

CHAPTER TEN

CORA STRETCHED OUT in her hotel bed and smiled. Last night they'd gone to see a movie in English and she'd eaten popcorn and drunk soda with her head on Jonas's shoulder.

The day before, flowers had been delivered to her hotel room. The beautiful pink and white blooms had started to open and the aroma was drifting across the air towards her.

Today, they were going to one of the Christmas markets. That would mean coffee and cake, and a chance to see all the items for sale. She jumped out of bed and quickly dressed in a warm green jumper she'd bought the other day that was threaded through with glitter. She pulled on her jeans and boots and wrapped a checked scarf around her neck. She was just sliding her arms into her green coat when there was a knock at her door.

'Ready to go shopping?' she asked Jonas, whose frame filled her doorway in a way that was far too inviting.

He leaned down and kissed her. 'New jumper?'

She nodded and pulled it out. 'Isn't it fabulous? I saw it in a shop window on the way home the other night and had to dash in and buy it. It's the perfect colour—even matches the coat you bought me.'

As she zipped her coat and grabbed her gloves, she ran a hand down the front of the jacket. 'You know, I've worn this every day since you bought me it.' She gave him a wink. 'It's brought me good luck.'

'Luck has nothing to do with it,' said Jonas as he pulled her forward for another kiss. 'I just have incredibly good taste.'

She kissed him in agreement and grabbed her bag. 'Should we go for breakfast first?'

'Oh, no!' He laughed. 'Wait until we get to the market. There will be food galore.'

It was only a short walk to the square where the Christmas market was held. There were a few across the city, but Jonas had suggested this was the best place to start.

There were around forty stalls, all red-painted wood, with a whole variety of items, and, true to his promise, the first thing Cora noticed was the delicious smell of food.

The place was already busy, both with tourists and locals. 'Where do we start?'

Jonas reached over and took her hand, threading their way through the crowd and stalls and finally stopping at one where the vendor was making pancakes. 'How about here?'

'Oh, wow.' They ordered coffee and pancakes, which were served on a wobbly paper plate. Cora tucked the coffee into her elbow and ate her pancakes as they drifted between all the other stalls.

'No way,' she whispered in horror to Jonas as she pointed at a sign. 'That can't be true.'

He grinned. 'Reindeer sausages? Oh, it's true. They're actually really popular.'

'You eat Rudolph?'

He didn't even blink. 'And Dasher, and Prancer, and Vixen, and whatever the rest of them are called.'

Cora shuddered and moved on. The next stall had Christmas cheese, crispbreads and handmade mustard. 'This is much more like it,' she said as she tried a few samples. The next had sugared almonds, honey, marzipan, *pepparkakor*—ginger snaps—saffron buns, home-made jams and marmalades and penny candy. Cora was highly tempted, but groaned. 'Those pancakes and that taste of cheese have ruined me. Take me away from all this food and show me things that can't do me any harm.'

He laughed and directed her to a range of other stalls all carrying different goods. Christmas music was playing as they wandered around the various stalls. She could even hear a few carols being sung. But Cora was completely distracted by the tall blond on her arm. Everything else seemed to dull around him.

Every now and then, people would come up and speak to him. More than one had a small child in their arms or trailing after them. It was clear from the faces of the mothers and fathers that these were children and parents who Jonas had met through work.

One woman threw her hands around his neck and kissed him on both cheeks, talking rapidly. Jonas took it all in his stride, happily meeting the twins she had in a double buggy and introducing Cora to the two little girls. She was impressed that he remembered the names of both the mother and the girls instantly and was completely at ease. When the woman finally left she turned to him. 'Another patient?'

He nodded. 'Long-standing patients. Twins were born very early. They are still under our monitoring programme.'

'The same one that the babies who've had therapeutic hypothermia will go on?'

He nodded. 'We nurse these patients for so long, I'm always interested in the long-term outcomes.' He wrapped an arm around her shoulder. 'No matter what you think of me, I get paged when any of our previous long-term patients come in for review, and I always do my best to go along and say hello, then talk to the paediatrician later.'

She gave him a curious glance. 'Is this official, or unofficial?'

He waggled his free hand in the air in front of them. 'Let's just say it's both personal and professional interest.'

'I knew you were a secret softy at heart,' she said as they moved over to the other range of stalls. They browsed easily. Cora bought some hand-knitted mittens that were the same colour as her jumper and parka, some white and red glassware, and a couple of Christmas-scented candles. She inhaled deeply as she chose them. 'I'll take these home,' she said. 'They'll remind me of being here.'

Something inside her stomach twisted painfully. Although she loved Stockholm, she'd found the time of year tough, as always. But now, the thought of going back to her empty flat in London didn't fill her with joy. Sure, it would be nice to sleep in her own bed again. But the bed at the hotel had been very comfortable. The staff at the hotel were lovely and hospitable, and she got that genuine vibe from the city too. By the time she flew home, it would be almost Christmas Day, and, unless she asked someone back home to help her out, she'd be arriving home to a relatively cold flat with no food. She'd already turned down the invite to go to her aunt and uncle's in the Highlands—mainly because the travel would be too complicated.

Jonas put a hand on her shoulder. 'You okay?' His gentle voice was like a warm hug around her heart.

'Of course.' She smiled. 'More shopping?'

There it was again. That odd expression on his face for the briefest of seconds. Then he gave her another smile and put his hand around her shoulder again. It was starting to become colder. Behind them the school choir started to sing more carols as they wandered past a market stall with traditional reusable Swedish advent calendars.

Cora was half tempted to stop and look. It had been a long time since she'd had an advent calendar, and these ones could be filled with tiny gifts.

'Want one?' Jonas asked.

She shook her head and watched as a woman walked past with a delicious-looking bag of chocolates.

'I'd like one of those, though.'

'Oh, I know exactly where that stall is. Let's go.'

He took her around to the back of the stalls, then across the road to a glass-fronted exclusive chocolatier. As soon as he pushed open the door and her senses were hit by the delicious scents, she couldn't help the wide smile that spread across her face.

'You said it was a market stall.'

'I might have been a stranger to the truth.'

'This place costs a fortune, doesn't it?' she whispered.

'Absolutely.' He nodded.

An aproned assistant appeared and happily guided Cora around the huge range of single chocolates on display. She couldn't help herself, and picked a whole range that were wrapped in a gold box with a flamboyant red bow. As they exited the store she turned to Jonas. 'I think I've just been very, very bad.'

'It's allowed,' he said.

She shook her head. 'No, what I mean is, I'm going to take them into the NICU. The staff might be distracted for the next day or so.'

'You bought them for the staff?'

'Of course, I did. Your staff are a great bunch. I love working with them.'

'Then why don't you stay?'

It was clear that the words had come from nowhere and seemed to shock Jonas just as much as they shocked Cora.

He seemed to take a breath and then added on a slightly more serious note, 'I suspect that Stockholm City will be advertising for a new clinical Head of Neo-natology in the next few months.'

'You don't think Elias will be back?'

He sighed, and she could see the pain on his face. 'Truthfully? I'd love him to come back. But I'm not sure that he'll want to. I'm sure his son and daughter will try and persuade him to retire. He might want to return a few days a week. But I think the running of the unit will all be too much for him.' He locked gazes with her again. 'So, at some point soon, I suspect we'll be looking for a new clinical lead.'

She was watching him carefully: he'd been partly shocked by his first direct invitation, but now she could see the idea start to settle on him.

'I'm not sure I would be the best person for the job,' she said, her automatic defensive mechanisms kicking into place. She wasn't entirely sure if he was suggest-ing the job, or maybe something else.

'Think you're not smart enough?' he joked quickly.

She rolled her eyes as they started to walk again. 'I definitely don't have a good enough handle on the language.'

'Try some immersive therapy,' he nudged. 'People always say it's the best way to learn. Move to a place, spend all day there, and try and speak the language constantly.' He gave a wicked grin. 'Or, there are some other immersive therapies we could consider.'

'Cheeky,' she nudged him right back, then stopped walking and looked around. 'It's a beautiful city, but I don't know enough about it yet. I know I've stayed at a great hotel. But I'd need to find out about renting or buying, where the good areas are, where the not so good are. The driving arrangements if I wanted to get a car. The living costs. Everything, really.'

'Sounds like you're trying to talk yourself out of the possibility.'

She gave a rueful shrug. 'I'm just not sure. I'd need to think about Isla. I know it's a short flight, but it's still a whole other country. Anyhow, we don't even know if a job will come up. There could be other amazing candidates. People that your hospital might go out to with offers, rather than advertise the job.'

He nodded his head slowly. She froze. The way he was looking at her was...unnerving.

'Is that what you're doing?' Every tiny hair on her body was standing on end.

The expression on his face told her everything she needed to know. 'They mentioned it to me yesterday. Gave me a few names that the board might consider. Asked what I thought of them.'

Something clicked in Cora's brain. She raised her eyebrows. 'But I wasn't one of them, was I?'

The pause was excruciating. 'No,' he admitted. 'But I think you should be.'

She leaned forward and grabbed the lapels of his jacket, heaving him towards her in the busy street. 'Jonas Nilsson, you didn't even consider me until right now, did you?'

He sighed as his arms folded around her. 'The truth is, I didn't consider *anyone* apart from doctors who are the heads of surrounding NICUs in Sweden.'

Cora held her arms above her head. 'But there's a whole world out there.'

He bowed his head and closed his eyes. 'I know that. But I think when any job comes up, you immediately look at all those you've worked with, and those close by. Heads of units that we speak to frequently because of transfers, or crib shortages, or imminent arrivals.'

She tilted her head to one side as she smiled up at him. Cora was feeling a little easier. For a few moments, she'd felt really on the spot. As if Jonas were asking about a whole lot more than a job. 'Think of all the wonderful people you might miss, thinking like that,' she teased.

He dipped his head, his slight bristles brushing the side of her cheek. 'And think of all the opportunities you might miss if you only look at the UK for job opportunities.'

'Touché.' She smiled and now he laughed out loud, knowing that she was teasing him about his word choice a few weeks ago.

She stared up into those pale blue eyes and her heart gave a little leap. What about staying here, living here, and working here? Jonas was the first guy she'd met in for ever who made her catch her breath, who made her skin tingle with one glance, and who challenged her, day and night. The sparks flew when they were in a room together. She liked it that he didn't always agree with her, and wasn't afraid to say so. Of course, he was wrong, but that didn't matter.

A tiny sprig unfurled deep inside her. The one that had been there since childhood. The one that told her she wasn't good enough, wasn't loved enough, to take up a post like this. She hated that it always appeared at times like this. Jonas hadn't thought of her first. He'd been working with her side by side—if he really thought she was good enough he should have thought of her first.

She pushed the feelings aside. He'd thought of her *now*. That was what was important. And he was enthused about it. Even though she didn't know if she wanted the job. The sprig inside was turning into something else—a beautiful rose.

'What are you thinking about?'

She smiled. 'A world of opportunities,' she admitted. She took a breath. 'I'm kind of cold. Want to come back to the hotel with me?'

He bent down again and whispered in her ear, 'I thought you'd never ask,' and slipped his hand into hers.

They walked along the street together, and she was conscious that her footsteps seemed to be quickening. She kept a firm hold of his hand when they reached the hotel entrance and she nodded to the doorman and receptionist as they crossed the lobby to the lift.

As soon as the doors slid closed, Jonas was kissing her again.

Now they weren't in public. He pressed her up against the mirrored wall of the lift and she wrapped her arms tightly around him as he kissed her until she was breathless.

When the lift slowed to a halt and pinged she stepped back and looked at him again. Her mouth was dry. But she knew exactly what she wanted the next step to be.

She licked her lips and held out her hand. 'Stay over.'

He hesitated, and for a second she felt a wave of panic. Was she overreaching? Misreading things between them?

But Jonas let out a soft laugh as the doors opened to her floor.

'Like I said earlier, I thought you'd never ask,' he said again, as this time he grabbed her round the waist, lifted her up and she wrapped her legs around him.

Cora couldn't help but laugh as she struggled to find her card for the door. 'Maybe a little unconventional?' she teased.

Jonas took it from her hand as she found it and swiped the door, carrying her inside and kicking it shut behind them.

Her heart swelled. A perfect day, and things could only get better.

CHAPTER ELEVEN

THEY'D QUICKLY FALLEN into routine. One night they would spend a night at Cora's hotel, then the next they would wake up together in Jonas's apartment.

He was surprised how quickly she seemed to fit into his life—in lots of weird ways. It felt entirely normal to see her snuggled up at the end of his pale grey sofa, or under the white blankets in his large bed. Within a few days her toothbrush remained in his bathroom, and he'd bought an extra one to leave in her hotel room.

'So, how're things going in love's young dream?'

The words jerked him from his thoughts. Alice was standing next to him in the NICU with a set of older notes in her hands. She was giving him 'that' look. The one that told him she could read every thought in his head and knew exactly everything he'd been up to in the last few weeks.

'I have no idea what you're talking about, Alice,' he said, doing his best to keep his face straight.

'Of course, you don't.' She smiled, patting his hand as she moved over to the computer screen.

'That's why you watch every step she takes, turn your head every time she laughs, and notice every time she talks to another member of staff.' She raised her eyebrows just an inch. 'And she, it seems, does entirely that same with you. The vibe between you both has changed.' She stepped a little closer and lowered her voice. 'And in case you think it's a secret...' she shook her head '...just so you know, we've been taking bets for a while.'

Jonas tried not to look stunned, but clearly failed when Alice started to quietly laugh. After another minute, he folded his arms. 'Who won?'

There was no chance for an answer as one of the alarms started to ping dangerously. As if by magic, all the staff in the unit moved smoothly. Resuscitating a tiny baby was always a delicate operation. One staff member automatically went to mum and put her arm around her, while moving her back, away from the crib, so others could do what they needed to.

Jonas and Alice joined the team, doing tiny heart compressions, bagging the tiny little boy and administering emergency medications, until finally the heart monitor started to blip reassuringly. A few moments later, the little boy's chest started to rise and fall rapidly as breathing was re-established, and his blood pressure started to come back up.

It was another hour before Jonas and Alice were back near the nurses' station. The phone rang and he answered it. 'Jonas, we've another baby on the way up. Meets all the criteria. Can you be ready? I'll be up in five.'

He put the phone down and gave Alice a nod. 'Another baby for the hypothermia treatment. Cora is on her way up.'

'Oh, is she?' said Alice wickedly, all the while moving off to prepare one of the side rooms.

Jonas shook his head as he moved after her. 'Is this

what it's come to? Is this what I'm going to have to put up with at work every day?'

Alice grabbed a drip stand to pull into the room and threw him an interested look as she attached the machine to the stand. 'You have no idea how much pleasure it gives me. How much pleasure it gives us all.' Her hand reached over to his arm as he was preparing the crib. 'Jonas, you seem so happy around her. Mad at times. Then delighted at others. Honestly, if you let this one get away, I'll make your life a misery afterwards.'

The words stopped him cold. He looked at the older woman, who might have made a million mistakes in her life, but he'd never know it. Her gaze was honest, sincere and playful all at once. It yanked at every heart-string he'd ever had.

'You wouldn't have to, Alice. I'd be there already.' The honesty of the words was like a bucket of ice-cold water emptying over his head.

He was frozen. Thinking about how much Cora actually meant to him.

Alice was routinely going about her business. 'Have you told her?'

His eyes darted to Alice. She was so cool and casual about things—as if this were an everyday conversation that they were having.

But it wasn't. And they both knew it.

He loved the way she could be so matter-of-fact about things. It was one of her greatest traits, and why the entire hospital staff looked up to the experienced sister of the NICU. She was unflappable, to the point, entirely professional, and all with a little gleam in her eye.

The slightly scary thing was, he knew she would make his life a misery if he didn't up his game and speak to Cora.

So he was entirely honest with her. 'Of course, I haven't told her. She's due to go back—' He stopped as something came into his head. He'd been about to say 'back home', but realised that he got the general impression from Cora that, right now, nowhere really felt like home to her. 'She's due to go back to London in two weeks.'

'Sounds like you're running out of time, Jonas.'

He shook his head as he plugged in some of the other pieces of equipment. 'Yeah, don't rub it in, Alice.'

She bumped him with her hip on the way past. 'Don't say I didn't warn you.'

The NICU doors flew open and Jonas pushed everything out of his head. It didn't help that Cora's face was the first one he saw, and he instantly drank in everything about her. It was amazing how quickly she'd got under his skin, and he didn't mind one bit.

But as he worked methodically, helping the team get set up for the treatment, his mind kept going back to Cora. He'd already unexpectedly asked her if she'd considered staying, and it was abundantly clear it had never crossed her mind.

To be honest, until that point, it hadn't crossed his either. But as soon as it had landed there, it had just made perfect sense, and it had made his heart lurch in a way that had surprised him.

But inside his head, there were a few tiny doubts. His judgement had been wrong before. His ex had proved that. And every time he saw Cora loaded down with shopping bags, it just rang alarm bells in his head. She'd done and said absolutely nothing to make him think she could be anything like Kristina. But then again, Kristina had done nothing to raise alarm bells either. Maybe his whole judgement was just questionable?

And if he couldn't get past that, how could he have any other kind of conversation with Cora? He shook his head as he put some recordings on a chart. He'd told Cora the most significant event in his life. And she'd talked it through with him with empathy, understanding and reassurance. She hadn't doubted his practice for a single second. And that meant something to him. But could he actually say those three little words to her? Last time around it had spelled disaster for him. Could he be brave enough to try again?

As the team set to work, lowering the new baby's temperature, he moved out of the room to let them continue their work. The start-up procedures were the most labour intensive and, once they were over, the unit settled down to a steady hum of activity. There, in the waste basket near him, were the remnants of a box of chocolates with a familiar logo. The first box Cora had brought in had disappeared in one day. She'd bought a second, and this was clearly the remnants of the third. It struck a chord with him about how she felt about the staff here. They'd wanted to learn from her, and it was clear she relished the opportunity. How would he really feel if Cora was a permanent fixture around here?

Jonas grabbed his jacket and took a walk. He was already long over the hours he should have worked and wanted to clear his head.

Snow crunched under his feet as he walked towards the city centre. Lights glowed everywhere. Before he knew it, he was outside her hotel—the one he'd taken her to on that first day. Cora was still back in the unit. He knew that. He took a few moments to walk around the square. Another Christmas tree had appeared, decorated with pink lights. There seemed to be trees all over the city this year. He hadn't got around to putting his own up back at his apartment. He was usually a bit more festive. But he knew there were still more layers to Cora Campbell. She'd told him she didn't like Christmas much, and it had seemed wrong to push it on her by decorating his apartment. She'd remarked that she frequently just closed the curtains in her room at the hotel to block it out.

As Jonas watched other tourists and some local families walk past, his heart was sad. Christmas wasn't for everyone and he could accept that. But what he really wanted to do was to make some new memories for Cora. Give her something else to think about. He'd already suggested it, but he still wasn't sure if she wanted to take him up on that.

As much as he wanted to do something, he knew deep inside he had to let that be Cora's decision to make. He had no idea what her experience of Christmas had been, or if she was ready to try something new.

Something flooded over him like a wash of warm water in the icy cold. Even though he'd compared Cora and Kristina in his head, he knew in his heart that Cora was nothing like Kristina. They weren't even in the same ballpark. And even though he'd said those three words to Kristina in the past, the way he felt about Cora couldn't even compare. It was so much more. So much better. So much fuller. Any feelings he'd had for Kristina were a pale comparison to what he felt about Cora.

This was love, pure, unadulterated love.

As he walked past a nearby shop, something in the window caught his eye. Before he had time to think much longer, he ducked inside, coming out five minutes later with the gift tucked in his pocket. Would she like it?

He wasn't sure. He could only wait to find out. Because he knew what he needed to say to her. He just had to find a way to let those words out again. His heart knew exactly how he felt about Cora. But could he actually tell her?

Cora looked around the unit. The little boy, Sam, was steady now. She'd been seriously concerned about him earlier, and she could only hope that the treatment would help him. Now, she needed to find Jonas. Something had happened today, and she wanted to tell him, and get a sense of what he thought.

'Anyone know where Jonas has gone?' she asked one of the nearby staff nurses.

The girl turned to a colleague and held up her hand for a high five. He slapped it and they both laughed. 'What?' asked Cora.

The nurse shook her head. 'We've just been waiting for confirmation—but it doesn't really matter, we already knew.'

Cora smiled. 'So, does anyone know where Jonas has gone?'

She nodded. 'He headed out earlier. I think he said something about a walk. He'd been here for around twelve hours; he probably needed some head space.'

Cora wrinkled her nose. When she'd woken this morning, Jonas had been gone with a scribbled cute note next to her bed. She'd just imagined he'd had some things to do. She hadn't realised he'd come into work early.

She made a few final checks, then grabbed her jacket, zipping it up and pulling out her phone to text Jonas. He answered straight away, and as she pushed open the doors of the unit, something came into her head. She looked over her shoulder. 'Okay, then, who just won the bet?'

'Alice,' they both answered in unison.

'Of course.' She nodded. 'I should have known.'

She couldn't stop smiling as she left the hospital and headed to meet Jonas. It was dark, but the streets seemed even busier than normal.

Jonas appeared through the crowd and slung an arm around her shoulder. 'Do you remember that boat tour I promised you?'

She nodded. 'But it's dark, I won't see anything.'

'This is a special tour. Perfect for night time. We cross under twelve different bridges and see most of the city.' He bent down and whispered in her ear. 'There's even Swedish *fika* on board.'

'Coffee and cinnamon buns? You got me.'

They boarded the boat at Strömkajen. Cora stood at the railing on the boat and watched as the white craft pulled out into the black water. All around them, across the city, white lights were sparkling, outlining buildings, and giving the whole city a glow. Soft music played in the background as a guide gave them a little information about the history of the city, and the bridges they passed underneath. They even passed through the lock that connected the Baltic Sea to Lake Mälaren.

As it got colder, they ducked inside and grabbed some coffee and a cinnamon bun. 'Want to sit down?' Jonas asked.

She shook her head. 'Actually, I'm really enjoying this. Can we take these outside?'

He nodded and they went back to the railing. Cora watched the wonder of the passing sights. The inner city, the Old Town, Södermalm and Lilla glided past. Her heart was warm. The twinkling festive lights only added to the experience. She put her head on Jonas's shoulder. Between the steam from their breaths, and the steam from their coffee cups, it made the cold night air seem even more special.

She was starting to love this city, and the people in it. For the first time in for ever, the thought of Christmas didn't fill her with sadness and dread. Jonas had suggested—without asking tricky questions—that it might be time to make some new memories. And somehow, being in an entirely new place, with a wonderful man and a great bunch of staff, was making it a whole lot easier. Maybe it was timing too. But it was almost as if the dark cloud that seemed to descend around her shoulders at this time of year had forgotten where she was.

Snuggling up with Jonas, and looking out at this new place, was perfect.

'Hey.' His lips brushed her ear. 'What's up?'

She turned towards him and slid her hands around his waist. 'Nothing's up,' she said with a smile on her face. 'I'm just happy.'

'Happy?' He pulled her closer. 'Now, that sounds good.'

She nodded. 'One of the directors of the hospital came and found me today.'

He didn't look particularly surprised. 'They did?'

She gave his chest a gentle slap. 'They told me that— as well as another suite of candidates—they were considering me for the position of Head of Neonatology.' Her voice was shaking a little.

'And what did you say?'

She stood on her tiptoes and kissed one of his cheeks. 'I listened carefully...' she kissed the other cheek '... and said thank you very much...' she dropped a soft kiss on his lips '...and that I'd wait to hear from them.'

She slid her arms around his neck. 'Do you think someone put in a good word for me?'

He gave her a small smile. 'They might have.'

'But is there any chance that person might be a bit biased?'

He laughed. 'It doesn't matter if I'm biased. The board listens to lots of people. They'll have spoken to your colleagues back at the Royal Kensington, they'll have asked many of the other professionals you've worked with over the last few weeks. They want someone they know will fit well with the unit. Someone who can help us maintain our standards and reputation.'

She let her fingers run through his hair. 'You think someone like me—a woman who makes your blood boil at times—can do that?'

He slid one hand under her thick jacket. 'Sometimes blood boiling means a totally different thing,' he said with a soft laugh.

She pressed closer as she looked over his shoulder. 'This place has been surprising. I've never really considered a proper move before. Even when I was offered a job in Washington a few years ago, I never truly, really considered it properly.'

'And now you will?'

She nodded and pressed her lips together. 'If they ask me.'

'Will you talk to your sister first?'

She blinked back some tears and nodded. 'Absolutely. But I have a feeling that Isla will tell me to chase my dreams.'

'And what are your dreams?'

The question circled around her brain. She immediately wanted to say that she didn't know. But, deep down, parts of her did know. Jonas drove her crazy and

she loved that. She'd never wanted to be around someone so much. Waking up next to him every morning
had quickly given her the vibe that she was entirely in
the right place.

But could she trust him with her heart?

She wanted to. She really, really did.

CHAPTER TWELVE

'HEY, HOW ARE you doing?' Jonas leaned forward and put his hands on Elias's shoulders, kissing him on either cheek as he opened the door.

Elias looked distinctly shaky. He had a stick in one hand and had limped slowly to the door. 'How's my unit?'

'Interesting,' said Jonas as he followed Elias inside and closed the door behind him. His heart fell as he saw a few boxes piled up in one corner. It told him everything he needed to know. But for Elias's sake, he pretended he hadn't seen them as they walked slowly through to Elias's large kitchen and sat down at the table. Jonas noticed that the coffee was already made.

He sat a bag on the table and started emptying it. 'Favourite marmalade, bread, biscuits, and those peppermint creams that you hide in your top desk drawer.'

Elias smiled, and Jonas breathed another sigh of relief. Both sides of his face were moving in perfect symmetry.

His hand shook a little as he determinedly poured the coffee. Another sign. These hands that had inserted thousands of central lines over the years into tiny veins would not be doing that again.

He kept all emotion from his face. He knew that

Elias's heart must be breaking. Work had been such a huge part of his life after his wife had died. And now that had been taken from him too.

'What do you mean by interesting?' asked Elias. 'How's the new doctor working out?' There. He had a glint in his eye. The main part of Elias was completely intact.

Jonas couldn't help the smile spreading across his face. 'She's good. Feisty. Challenging. But definitely an excellent doctor.'

'Asked her out yet?'

Jonas choked on his coffee. 'What?'

'A bright, intelligent, good-looking woman? What's wrong with you? From the first second I spoke to her, I thought you would be an excellent match.'

Jonas was incredulous. 'You invited a doctor to our hospital because you thought she would be a good match for me?'

Elias shook his head. 'Of course not. I invited her purely because of her research—which is outstanding, and I hope you've got everything set up for us to continue when she leaves. The match part came later. That video conferencing is a fine thing. Her manner. The passion for her job. That accent. She isn't married, is she? Because I thought she would be perfect for you. I'm just annoyed I haven't got to play matchmaker and take full credit for it.'

He dipped one of the biscuits that Jonas had brought in his coffee.

'You're an old rogue.'

Elias's eyes shimmered with pride. 'I knew it. You do like her.'

He sat back in his chair and gave a self-satisfied sigh. Then, his expression changed. This time his face was full of sadness. 'I tendered my resignation last week. But you know that, don't you?'

Jonas nodded his head. 'I suspected. The board of directors approached me about possible candidates for Head of Neonatology.'

Elias looked interested. 'Who did you recommend?'

'Franz Kinnerman from Lindesberg, Ruth Keppell from Lund, Astra Peniker from Kalmar...' He paused for a second. 'And Cora Campbell from the Kensington.'

Elias tapped his fingers on the table and nodded. 'I also recommended two out of the three. But I asked them to pay particular attention to the performance of our visiting consultant.'

He smiled at Jonas. 'I take it my matchmaking is going well?'

Jonas took a breath. He wasn't quite sure how to answer.

'Come now, Jonas. Tell me you've put that whole episode with Kristina behind you. It's time to make new horizons for yourself. Take a chance on love again.'

Jonas shook his head. Elias was one of the only people he'd confided in about what had happened with Kristina. He reached over and grabbed a biscuit. 'I don't remember asking for love advice.'

Elias tapped his hand on Jonas's arm. 'But I won't be around much longer to give it to you.' His expression changed again. 'My son has persuaded me to sell up and move down next to him and his wife.' Elias looked around his home with the wide windows showing the land around about him. 'Forty years I've lived here. But all good things...' He met Jonas's gaze again. 'It's for the best. But who will be here to keep an eye on you and give you advice about life? I feel as if I should leave you in a safe, but sparky pair of hands. And I think they are distinctly Scottish.'

Jonas burst out laughing. 'Wait until I tell Cora you called her sparky.'

'You should have brought her with you today. I would have liked to have seen you two together. See if there really are sparks flying.'

Jonas was serious now. 'She asked. She wanted to come and meet you. I told her I had to wait until I'd seen how you are.'

'Well, bring her back when she wants to know more about running the unit. I'll give her all the tips she'll need. Or...' there was a wicked gleam in his eyes '...you could always just invite me to the wedding.'

'Elias!'

'What?' He held up his hands, his face the picture of innocence. 'Can't let a good one slip away. And Christmas is always such a lovely time of year for a proposal. It's when I proposed to Ann, you know. Under the giant Christmas tree at Skeppsbron.'

Jonas took a sip of his coffee. 'Christmas isn't her favourite time of year. I don't exactly know why. I didn't want to push. I just suggested that since she was in a new place, it might be nice to make some new memories.'

'With a new person?' Elias gave a nod. 'Wise man. But you should ask. Always ask the difficult questions, Jonas. Then she'll know you care. That you want the good, and the bad.' He gave a soft smile. 'But you know that, don't you? You only have a few days left—don't leave it too late.'

Jonas nodded slowly. 'Let's just say, I have a plan.'

He glanced at his watch. 'I'll have to run. I'm the duty manager at the hospital this afternoon.' He stood up and reached over and gave Elias a giant hug. 'Next time I come, I promise I'll bring Cora with me.'

'Be sure you do.'

Jonas pulled on his jacket and left, pausing outside for a moment to take a deep breath. So much of what Elias had said to him rang true.

But what was most important was that he was right. Time was running out.

And it was time to look to the future.

CHAPTER THIRTEEN

SOMEONE HAD PRESSED fast forward on her life. Last time she'd looked at the calendar there had still been nearly two weeks left in her time here.

But it felt as if she'd blinked—and that time had gone.

Every night had seemed shorter than the one before. Waking up next to Jonas had become excruciating because she'd realised that soon it wouldn't be happening any more.

She'd spoken to Isla the other day, who'd told her she was spending Christmas with their aunt and uncle and wouldn't be coming down to London.

Cora had made a half-hearted scramble to look at when her flight got into London, and any possible chance of reaching the Highlands safely, even though she'd known it was completely futile. Alternative flights to Inverness airport were full. It seemed that most of the Highlands wanted to get home on Christmas Eve.

But what she couldn't get out of her head was the dark cloud that continually settled around her shoulders at this time of year. It had arrived again—even though she'd hoped it wouldn't.

Being in Stockholm had been the perfect distraction at first. But maybe it was time to accept that, no matter what else was going on in her life, she would never get over these feelings associated with Christmas.

And this, doubled with the fact that she hadn't quite managed to figure out exactly how she felt about Jonas—or how he felt about her—was making her lose sleep at night. She should be over the moon with the time she was spending with him. But now it just felt like a double countdown looming over her head. The countdown to bad memories. And the countdown to leaving Jonas behind.

She hadn't heard anything about the job, which likely meant they had another preferred candidate. It would seem ridiculous to let her go back to London, and then offer the job to her. And even that was completely crazy. She hadn't come to Stockholm even thinking about the possibility of a job change. It hadn't been on her radar at all. But, after falling in love with Stockholm, and the staff at City hospital, and falling in love with Jonas, she had such mixed feelings about going back home.

Cora froze. She was tying her shoelaces and her hands just stuck in mid-air. She *loved* Jonas. She loved him. The thought had entered her brain so easily, and the realisation struck her like a blow to the chest.

She sat back up and let out some slow breaths. It was early evening, Jonas would be here in a while, but she'd planned to go for some fresh air. She grabbed her jacket, and looked out at the square, and blinked back a few tears.

Did she really want to go out there? In amongst the glistening white lights and people excited about Christmas?

She pulled her hat over her head and grabbed her gloves. As soon as she reached the foyer of the hotel, the receptionist shouted her over. All the staff knew her by name now. There was a large tray of cookies on the reception desk and Cora could smell them instantly.

'Help yourself, Cora. They've just come up from the kitchen. They're still warm.'

Cora smiled. 'They smell delicious. Thank you.'

'We'll really miss you when you head back to England. Will you come and visit again?'

It was like a little light going on in her head. She'd been so encompassed by the thoughts of going home, and everything that was ending for her, that she hadn't even thought of her holiday time. Wow. Her head must be really muddled.

'I'd love to come back again, and if I do, I promise I'll stay here.' Her footsteps felt a little lighter as she walked out to the square and started to meander her way around in the dimming evening light.

The shop window displays were all familiar to her now, and she couldn't pretend that she didn't have favourites. The traditional carved pale wooden trees behind a white chequered window were lovely. Another shop had a whole array of small glass ornaments with splashes of colour. The effects were mesmerising. She'd already bought a little sculpture with splashes of green, and a mini square with a pink drop in the middle. Now a wall hanging with a flash of red across the middle was catching her eye. It was the size of a large dinner plate—did she have enough space in her luggage? Who cared? She could buy another suitcase if needed.

She continued along the street, stopping to buy a soft grey jumper for Isla, and a decorative studded bangle.

The air was icy and there were several stalls set up in the middle of the square. She wandered over and decided to be brave and try another cup of warm *glögg*.

She sat down on a bench, ignoring the cold as she watched the world go by.

She wasn't even seeing the Christmas decorations now. She was just seeing the people. The families and couples, all walking along laughing and joking. Tears blinked in her eyes as she saw a man and a woman with a teenager and a baby in a buggy. It gave her instant flashbacks to what her family must have looked like to others.

And before she knew it, she was in floods of tears.

'Cora!' The joyful shout came from the other side of the square. Jonas looked really happy. He practically sprinted across the square to join her, and she quickly wiped her tears away.

'I wanted to talk to you,' he said, slightly breathless, a wide grin across the face that she loved.

'What is it?'

There was a weird kind of pause. He sat down on the bench next to her and looked as if he was trying to decide where to start. He bent down and kissed her. Cora responded instantly, because Jonas's touch to her was as natural as breathing air.

When they separated, his arm was still around her shoulders. 'Have you made a decision?'

Her stomach squeezed. 'About what?'

'About where we're going for dinner tonight?'

Every muscle in her body sagged. For some strange reason she'd hoped it would be an entirely different question. Have you made a decision about wanting to stay here? Have you made a decision about when you're coming back? Have you made a decision about what happens next for us?

But maybe she was just imagining the connection between them both. After all, she'd only just realised herself that she loved this man. They hadn't talked about love. They hadn't talked about anything to do with when her time with the Kensington Project was up. And that suddenly struck her as odd.

If Jonas felt the same way she did, surely he would have started a conversation with her by now?

For reasons she couldn't entirely explain, tears started rolling down her cheeks again. It was as if every emotion had just burst to the surface and was overwhelming her.

Maybe he thought she wasn't good enough for him. Maybe he didn't want her the way she hoped he did. Maybe, yet again, she would be the child left alone at Christmas. The feelings were overwhelming, coming out of nowhere. There was no rhyme or reason to them. She knew she could try and be rational and think herself out of them. But she couldn't stop the heave in her chest, or the overwhelming feelings of not being good enough. They were swamping her, making it almost difficult to breathe.

'Cora?' There was instant concern on Jonas's face.

She stood up and shook her head, trying to breathe and stammer the words out. 'I...don't feel up to dinner tonight. I can't do this. I think it's best if I just go back to the hotel.'

He looked at her as if those words had stung, and she knew instantly it was the delivery. She hadn't added the word 'alone' to her dialogue, but her tone had made certain the implication was there.

He reached for her hand. 'No. Don't go. I wanted tonight to be special. I wanted to talk to you. What's wrong?'

The words just erupted from her belly. 'Nothing. Everything. I don't know.' She held out her shaking arms, letting the paper cup of *glögg* fall at her feet. She looked around her at the people, families, and all the signs of Christmas in every part of the square. Even though she knew they were outside, it was as if the walls were pressing in all around her. She couldn't breathe. She couldn't be here. She couldn't do this.

She turned and ran, ignoring the fact her clumpy boots slowed her pace. If her head had been straight, she would have gone back to the hotel. But nothing was making sense to her right now. Every corner she turned seemed to take her to another festooned street. Christmas lights and decorations had never bothered her quite as much as they did now.

Flashes appeared in her head. Holding her mum's cold hand. One minute she'd been there, full of life and laughing, and the next minute she'd been gone. Nothing could save her. Then the flash of her father's withered face on the pillow, his pallor sicklier than any shade of white or grey. The laboured breaths and wheeze. And the memories of hating every second of seeing the bright, vibrant man that she loved in pain. The cancer had come quickly after her mum had died, and Cora always thought he'd had no strength to fight because his heart was already broken. It was agonising, but that was what was left in her memory. And over the years it had grown bigger, instead of fading. It had pushed all the best memories out of place. And with it was the overwhelming sensation that Cora had failed both of her parents.

The final breath had been a relief to them both, and, for that as well, the guilt was overwhelming.

Cora had reached the harbour now, panting, and, catching hold of the barrier in front of her, she clung on, knowing there was nowhere left to run.

She didn't even hear his footsteps, but knew instantly the arm around her was his. For a few moments he didn't speak, just stood with his chest against her back, his arms around her, and his own rapid breaths matching her own.

'I hate seeing you like this. Tell me what's wrong, Cora. I want to help.'

She couldn't find the words; exhaustion was sweeping over her.

He turned her around to face him. 'I wanted this night to be good between us. I wanted to talk about what comes next.' There were deep furrows across his brow, and he was clutching her array of shopping bags in his hand.

'What comes next is, I get on a plane and go home. Isn't it a bit late to have the "what about us?" talk?' It came out much more bitterly than she wanted it to. But her heart was aching. Every moment felt like another realisation. If he'd wanted to talk about them, shouldn't it have been mentioned long before now?

He hesitated, and it made her heart plummet inside her chest. 'I was waiting,' he said cautiously.

'Waiting for what?'

She saw him swallow awkwardly. 'I thought they were going to offer you the job today.'

Those feelings that she was trying hard to push away swamped her again. They hadn't wanted her. She wasn't good enough to be offered the job.

His pale eyes looked fraught with worry, and she wasn't quite sure how to read it. 'Well, they didn't. But, so what? Why would that make a difference to any talk about us?'

She stepped away from him. 'What? Can there only be an "us" if I'm right here? On your doorstep, where it's convenient? Is that why you waited to have this discussion? And now I've told you that they haven't offered me the job, I can see how awkward you feel. I take it that rules out any discussion for us at all?' She put her hand on her chest. 'How am I supposed to feel? Has this all just been a convenience for you? Because it hasn't been for me. And now I'm finding out just how important I am in your life. I won't be working here. I'll be back in London. I've been here for a while now, Jonas. We could have had the "what about us?" conversation at any point.'

The words were coming out so quickly, she almost couldn't breathe. 'And today? Tonight?' She let out a hollow laugh. 'It couldn't be more fitting. This is my worst time of year. You nearly had me fooled for that too—that I should try and create new Christmas memories. But how can I do that? No matter where I am in this world, I'm always going to feel like this—alone.' She closed her eyes, hating herself for spilling everything out to him. Her voice shook. 'You've no idea how much I hate this date. This is the date that my mum died from an aortic aneurysm after going into hospital with back pain. A year and a day later, my dad died from cancer on Christmas Eve. And things don't get better with time—no matter what well-meaning people say. They just amplify and haunt me. How can I create new memories when the bad ones take me over—no matter how hard I try?'

Her shoulders started to shake. Jonas had his arms around her instantly, propping her up, taking her weight as her legs started to crumple. 'Let me help you, Cora. Let me help you. We can get through this together. You should have told me. I had no idea how hard this was for you.' His eyes glanced towards the bags he gripped in his hands—her bags. And there it was again. That weird look.

And his earlier words didn't soothe her, they just injected her with a force of solid determination. He still hadn't said the words that mattered most. And now, she realised, she didn't want him to. She didn't want him to react to this situation by saying something he didn't actually feel. He'd never given her a true indication that he wanted a long-term relationship with her. Her heart twisted in her chest. She loved this man, but it was clear he didn't have the same strong feelings that she did. It was easier to end things here and now and walk away with a bit of her dignity intact. But something inside her flared as she saw his eyes still fixed on the bags.

'Why do you do that?' she snapped.

'What?' He looked confused.

'You.' She thrust her hand towards him. 'Every time you see one of my shopping bags you get a weird look on your face. I know you don't like shopping, Jonas, but you really need to get over yourself. People all around the world shop!' She'd thrown her arms upwards now and the expression on Jonas's face changed, filling with hurt and regret.

He took a deep breath. 'I'm sorry,' he said slowly. 'The bags just reminded me of a past experience. Every time I see them, it just takes me back.'

Her eyes narrowed. 'What past experience?'

He shook his head. 'An ex, with spending habits that left me in a world of debt. Every time I saw you clutching shopping bags, it brought back memories.'

Her brow wrinkled. 'That's ridiculous. Why on earth would I leave you in debt with my shopping? I have more than enough money of my own.'

Her brain was spinning. Was this the mysterious

ex she'd heard a few of his colleagues hint at? One had even mentioned they'd thought Jonas might have planned on asking her to marry him.

Every part of her body bristled. He'd never mentioned his ex to her before. He'd never confided in Cora, and that made her realise that he'd never taken their relationship that seriously.

As the thoughts churned in her brain he nodded and closed his eyes. 'And when you say it like that, I seem like a complete fool. But I couldn't stop the memories, and it became more about my bad judgement than anything else.'

She stepped back as a cold wave of realisation swept over her. Nothing about this had been as it seemed. Maybe the connection between them had all been in her head?

She straightened and looked at him. 'I'm going home, Jonas. I'm going home tomorrow. I'm sorry that they didn't offer me that job, but, in a way, I'm not. Because now I know. Now I know this would never have worked between us. And it's better this way. It has to be.'

She turned quickly, walking swiftly back towards the centre.

He was alongside her in an instant. 'Cora, stop, let me talk to you. Don't walk away. I don't want things to be like this between us.'

She stopped walking for a second and looked him in the eye. 'This is exactly how things are between us, Jonas, which is exactly why I should leave. Now, stop.' She held up one hand. 'Leave me alone. I can't be anywhere near you right now.' She took a deep breath. 'I'm going to keep walking, and you—' she pointed at his chest '—are going to leave me alone.'

And she started walking as quickly as she could—

even though her vision was blinded with tears and her heart ached.

All she could do was keep walking. Right on back to London. She'd wanted to trust him with her heart, but it was clear that she couldn't.

CHAPTER FOURTEEN

HE WAS AN IDIOT. He was an absolute prize idiot. The words had been on the tip of his tongue last night—even before he'd noticed she was crying—and he half wished he'd blurted out the *I love you* as soon as he'd seen her.

Instead, he'd been distracted by the pile of shopping bags around her feet. And in that moment of distraction, which had made him think about bad memories, he'd lost his momentum and opportunity.

The way Cora had looked at him last night had been like a knife to the heart. Had he totally misread everything? She'd seemed almost cold. He couldn't help but wonder if she'd always meant to break up with him—had never considered anything serious between them. If that were true, his *I love you* would have been sadly misplaced and awkward for them both.

Although he'd wanted to run after her last night, her story about why she was so sad at Christmas had floored him. He'd known it was something significant. But the look in her eyes when she'd told him about losing both her mum and dad so close to Christmas, one year after the next, would have broken the heart of the coldest ice man. And when she'd told him to let her walk away, even though every cell in his body had protested, he'd known he had to listen. And his head had filled with crazy doubts. Maybe Cora had only ever wanted a temporary fling. Even with the potential job offer, she might just have been placating him. Letting him think she would consider it, when she really just wanted to head back to London and get on with her life.

He still couldn't believe that she *hadn't* been offered it. And it almost felt as if she'd blamed him for that too last night. Or maybe his head was just too full of conflicting emotions to actually think straight.

So, he'd let her walk away. If she didn't love him, then this was for the best.

But it had been an achingly long night. He hadn't been able to sleep for a minute. He'd played things over and over in his head. What if he'd done something different? What if he'd chased after her when she'd walked away, and admitted that he loved her?

He'd been in work since six a.m.—after toying with the idea to walk to the hotel and deciding not to. He would wait for her here. It was her last day in Sweden. He wanted her to come into work, say goodbye to the friends she'd made, and then he would ask if he could have some of her time.

He wanted to wear his heart on his sleeve and tell her that he absolutely loved and adored her. That last night, he'd had a special gift for her in his pocket. He wanted to tell her that was what his plans had been. A nice restaurant. Some good food. Some wine. And a chance to tell the woman he loved that he wanted to spend the rest of his life with her.

He only prayed she would still let him.

The clock ticked past in slow motion. He paced near the unit. He paced near the labour suite. He paced near the paediatric ward. But Cora was nowhere. He asked and asked, but no one had seen her.

He wandered the management corridors, wondering if she'd been called to some kind of meeting. He still couldn't believe she hadn't been offered the job. But it had never even entered Jonas's head that Cora would consider that part of a reason to be together. He'd already decided last night that if Cora wanted to return to London, he'd ask if he could join her.

But he had to find her first.

A colleague had asked him to verify some documents for him, and Jonas scribbled his signature and passport details, before ramming his passport in his back pocket and pacing the corridors again.

Alice came and found him in the corridor. Her face was sad. 'She's not here.'

'I know she's not here. I've been looking everywhere.'

Alice sighed and put her hand on Jonas's arm. 'Did you message her?'

'Of course, I did.' It came out much more snappily than intended.

Alice pressed her lips together and gave an understanding slow nod. 'Well, she texted me.'

His head shot up. 'What? What did she say? Where is she?'

Alice's voice was soft. 'At the airport. Her flight leaves in the next two hours.'

'What?' Panic gripped straight across his chest like a vice.

He looked around madly.

'You'll need to be quick,' she whispered.

Jonas didn't hesitate. He grabbed his car keys, his jacket and started to run.

His car was in the car park at the hospital. It was the middle of the day, so traffic wasn't too heavy in Stock-

par据

holm, and he did his best to stick to the speed limit on the way to Arlanda airport.

By the time he reached the airport, the slow entry to the car park and the excruciating line of people trying to file into a parking space made him want to explode. He dived out of the car, and raced to the airport entrance doors, his eyes immediately scanning the boards for her flight. Some part of him felt a wave of panic when he couldn't initially find a flight to London. Then he realised. LHR—Heathrow. The abbreviation had thrown him.

He ran towards the security entrance, scanning all people sitting in chairs, around the washrooms and in the stores along the way. There was no sign of Cora.

As he reached the security entrance, one of the guards eyed him suspiciously. 'Ticket?' he asked.

Of course. He didn't get past here without a ticket. 'Can I put a call out for someone?'

It was as if the man could read his mind. He raised an eyebrow. 'Will they come if we call them?'

His stomach clenched. He darted back through the crowds of people slowly milling about the airport as if they had all the time in the world, straight to one of the ticket desks. He slammed his credit card on the counter. 'I need a ticket.'

'Where to?' asked the girl behind the desk, pulling back a little.

'Anywhere,' was his instant response.

Her brow furrowed and she gave him a suspicious glance. Just what he needed—her to call security, and him to get ejected from the airport.

'The love of my life is in the departure lounge. I need to get in there—and to do that I need a ticket.'

'The love of your life?' The girl gave him a hard stare.

Jonas nodded then screwed up his face. 'I just haven't told her that yet.'

The girl's eyebrows raised. 'Are you asking her to stay, or do you want to go with her?'

'What?'

'You said you need a ticket. Wouldn't it be wise to buy a ticket to the same place, instead of just any ticket?' She didn't wait for him to respond—just continued with her hard stare as she folded her arms. 'After all—you can't just expect her to come back home with you. If you love her, you have to be prepared to go where she is.'

Even though he didn't have time for this, and his heart was currently racing, he leaned forward and smiled at the girl. 'You're that kind of quirky character in the movie, aren't you? The one that almost stops the guy reaching his girl?'

She nodded. 'What can I say?' She made a sign with her fingers, 'Hashtag, team girl. Have you any idea how many stories like this I hear from hapless guys who just haven't got their act together?'

'Okay, I'm a shameful, pathetic human being. Now let me buy a ticket to London Heathrow and send me on my way.'

She gave him an approving nod, took his credit card and passport and her fingers flew across the keyboard. A minute later she handed him a printed boarding card, and a receipt. She sighed and said, 'Okay then, go be a hero and don't screw this up.'

'Thank you.' The words had barely left his mouth when he started running back through the hall towards the security check area.

He thrust his boarding card towards security.

The queue seemed to deliberately crawl forward. Pat-

downs took for ever. Jonas was watching the clock on
the wall behind the check-in desk; it seemed to be on
fast forward. He could also see a board filled with flight
information. The boarding gate number was up for Cora's flight, along with the flashing words *Go to Gate*.

He was a few seconds away from pleading with the
people ahead to let him skip the queue when another
checkpoint was opened and a guard waved him over.
He'd never moved so fast. He stuck his belongings in
the tray to be security scanned, held his hands out to
be patted down, collected his tray, pushed his shoes
on his feet and rammed everything else in his pockets,
and then he started running all over again in the direction of the gate.

A few people shot him an amused glance as he
sprinted past. The message on the flight screen had
now changed. *Now Boarding*. There were already a few
people in the line.

He ran straight to the front, ignoring the glares and
craning his neck to see the few people who'd already
walked into the tunnel to board the plane. He didn't
recognise any jackets. He took long strides and looked
at every face in the waiting line. Nope. None of them
were Cora.

He turned back and ran to the front again. 'Can you
check a name for me to see if they've gone through to
the plane?'

The attendant, who was scanning someone's ticket,
didn't even look up. 'Go to the back of the line, please,
sir.'

He wanted to argue. But that wouldn't do any good.
He'd only get thrown out, and right now he needed to
be in this airport, in the departure lounge.

His brain kept whirring. Maybe he should go back and check the shops? She might still be shopping.

He darted back and scanned the nearest tourist souvenir shop, the duty free, a perfume shop and a bakery and coffee shop. No Cora. No sign anywhere.

There was a buzz.

'Last call for Flight G654 to London Heathrow. Would the last remaining passengers make their way to the boarding gate now?'

When he ran back along the corridor, he was suddenly very conscious that there was absolutely no one waiting to board. There was only one attendant, glancing at her watch and looking slightly annoyed.

His brain freaked for a moment. What if Cora had changed her mind and gone back to Stockholm? Could he really take that chance? He might end up on a flight for no reason.

But he couldn't take the chance. Not for a second. Not when Cora was at stake. Worst-case scenario, he would end up on a flight for no reason and have to take one back.

He handed his boarding card over and walked down the longest flight bridge in the world. He hadn't even looked at his seat number.

The air attendant smiled and gestured to him to walk down the entire length of the plane. He could hear the door being closed behind him, but all he could do was scan the faces in the seats. As he got nearer and nearer to the back of the plane, his heart sank. He couldn't see her dark hair anywhere.

He got to the last row, and someone lifted their head.

A head with dark hair. Cora. She had been rummaging in her bag that was shoved under her seat. Jonas couldn't believe it. He glanced at his ticket. Then slid into the seat next to her.

She sat up straight away. And he realised she must have recognised his aftershave.

Her face was shocked. 'What are you doing here?'

She looked around as if it were some kind of bad joke. But no, the doors to the plane were closed, and the plane had started to taxi to the runway.

'I came to find you.'

Her face grew tight. 'But why?'

'Because I didn't get a chance to say the things to you that I should have.'

She blinked and waited a few seconds. 'And what should you have said?'

'That I love you, I'm crazy about you and I want to be where you are. And I don't care if that's London, Stockholm or anywhere else.'

She drew in a shaky breath and shook her head a little. 'I'm on my way back to London, Jonas. Why tell me now?'

'Because I'm an idiot. Because I was scared. Because I let myself get tied up in past experiences, because the truth is, for me, you were just too good to be true.'

'You got on a plane to tell me this?' There was an edge to her voice, and the last thing he wanted to do was upset her. He had a purpose for being here and had to get to the point.

'I waited all morning for you at the hospital. I was stupid enough to think you might show up at work today. I wanted to come to the hotel this morning, but thought that was just too creepy.'

The corners of her lips edged up for a second.

But they went back again as she slowed her breathing. 'I've been here for seven weeks, we got closer and closer, and you never told me that you loved me, you never really talked about the future—just danced around the subject.'

He reached over and put his hand over hers as the plane lifted off from the runway. 'You're right. And I'm sorry. But don't leave like this. I don't want you to leave like this. If you go, I go. I can't imagine not waking up next to you in the morning. This morning was the worst ever. To turn over and find a big empty space was the worst feeling in the world. I kept telling myself that I'd see you at the hospital. I'd talk to you. I'd persuade you to give me a chance to explain. Tell you all the things I should have told you last night before you walked away. Then Alice told me about your text.'

'She was texting me literally every hour, on the hour.'

'She never told me that.'

Cora raised an eyebrow. 'She's a very persuasive, persistent woman.'

She shook her head again. 'But your whole life is in Stockholm, Jonas. What on earth will you do in London?'

He kept his face grave. 'My whole life will be wherever you are, Cora. If you'll let me.' He slipped his hand into his pocket. 'I didn't get it. Your whole Christmas feeling. When you told me last night, you broke my heart, because I just wanted to be there for you.'

She closed her eyes and spoke quietly. 'And I pushed you away. Because that's what I've learned to do. I don't talk about it with anyone. Most of my colleagues back home already know—so no one brings it up. I just volunteer for the Christmas shifts, and no one asks why.' She lowered her head. 'I got so used to not telling anyone, that I just couldn't cope last night. I was overwhelmed.' She kept her head down, but squeezed his hand. 'You told me to try and make new Christmas memories, and I did. I started to. I started to make them with you. Then I felt guilty. That I didn't deserve to make them, and I was betraying my mum and dad by even considering moving on.' She looked up in surprise when Jonas wiped away a tear that slid down her cheek.

'We don't ever have to do Christmas, Cora. If you don't want to, then that's fine with me. We can take holidays and go off to some remote cabin for a few days and just be ourselves, just chill. Take some time away from everything.'

She shook her head and breathed deeply. 'No, Jonas. I'm going to do what I should have done years ago. I'm going to go to a counsellor and talk my way through this. Maybe I'll never feel better, but I have to try.' She gave a soft smile. 'Maybe I should try to make new memories.'

He stroked her cheek with his finger. 'And I want to be by your side. Whatever your decision, it will be fine with me. What I have with you is too special that I can't even contemplate a life where we're not together. I've never loved someone the way I love you. Not even close.'

By now the plane had climbed high into the sky. Cora glanced out of the window. 'You're actually coming to London? You know today is Christmas Eve?' There was still a wave of sadness in her eyes.

'And this is a day you shouldn't be on your own. I'm happy to fade into the background and give you space, or, equally, just give you lots of hugs.'

Cora didn't cry. She just laid her head on his shoulder. He whispered into her hair. 'I'm hoping a really kind-hearted woman will let me bunk up with her tonight, and maybe for a whole lot longer.'

'You really don't want to go back to Stockholm?'

'I can be a midwife anywhere,' he answered promptly, and he truly meant it.

'And I can be a doctor anywhere too,' she said simply.

'Then the world is our oyster.'

She nodded as the air attendant approached with drinks for them both. As she set them down, Jonas reached for the item he'd taken from his pocket. 'My timing isn't great. But I had something for you.' He smiled. 'I bought it a few weeks ago, but wanted to give it to you the day before you left—without realising what I was doing.'

She took a sip of her wine and wrinkled her nose. 'What is it?'

'It's a message.' His voice was steady. 'Things are a bit different in Sweden. You might think we do things in reverse.' He swallowed and flipped open the small velvet box. 'In the older days in Sweden, this was an engagement ring.'

Cora leaned forward, her eyes wide at the simple gold band, with a thicker one next to it.

'We both wear them,' he said steadily.

She hadn't said anything yet, and his nerves were making him fill the gap. 'I promise I'll buy you a diamond later—but we usually save them for the actual wedding.'

Her eyes were wide as she turned to face him. 'What exactly are you asking me?'

Jonas didn't hesitate for a second. 'I'm asking you to marry me, Cora, and pick where we live together. I love you. I was a fool not to tell you sooner, but I promise I'll spend the rest of my life telling you every day.'

Her finger brushed the gold rings in the box. She smiled. 'Aren't I supposed to buy you a ring?'

'I decided to save us some time.'

She kept staring at him in wonder. 'When did you buy these?'

He groaned. 'Will you just answer the darn question?' He'd drunk some of the wine given to them by the air attendant, but if she didn't give him an answer soon, he couldn't swear it would stay down. No one ever spoke about how nerve-racking it was for a guy to ask the woman he loved the biggest question in the world and wait for an answer.

She slid one hand up the side of his face and through his hair, pulling him towards her. Just as their lips were about to touch she gave him his answer. 'Yes,' she whispered.

And they kissed, forgetting about the world outside and concentrating only on each other.

EPILOGUE

'READY?' CORA GRINNED at Jonas as he tugged at the kilt she'd made him wear.

'Is this supposed to be comfortable?' he asked, straightening up.

'Absolutely not.' She kept smiling. 'You're supposed to spend the whole night in terror that you'll turn too quickly and the whole world will see what they're not supposed to.'

He shook his head. 'I'm not sure about all this "true Scotsman" tale. Did you make it up? Because I can tell you right now that any Norseman with this on would wear boxers.'

She walked up and put her hands on the lapels of his Highland jacket. 'But tonight, husband, you are an honorary Scotsman.' She winked. 'And you did lose the bet.'

He sighed and grabbed his wallet, stuffing it into his sporran. 'I never thought you'd hold me to it.'

'You're quite handsome as a Scotsman. Maybe we should try this more often.'

Jonas let out a disgruntled noise as he grabbed her hand. 'Let's go before this Christmas party starts without you.'

Cora took a final glance in the mirror at her floor-length red satin gown, grabbed her purse and made her way down the hotel corridor with her new husband.

They'd married quietly, only a few days before, with her sister as bridesmaid, and Jonas's friend as best man. Their reception would be held back in Sweden after Christmas. All their friends and colleagues back at Stockholm City should have received their invites in the mail today.

They'd arrived in London nearly a year before and as soon as they'd landed Cora had received the call from Stockholm City asking her to be Head of Neonatal Intensive Care.

She'd accepted immediately, then spent the few days after celebrating with Jonas, before packing up her things, renting out her flat and moving to Stockholm permanently.

Tonight was a double celebration. Their wedding, and the Royal Kensington Christmas party to celebrate the achievements of all the staff who'd been part of the Kensington project over the last fifty years. Organising had been a logistical nightmare, but Cora had taken on the challenge with pride after Chris Taylor had asked her to. Her first calls had been to her fellow three Kensington Project recipients that year. It seemed that the project had had a big impact on all of their lives. Tonight, she would get to see some of them for the first time in nearly a year.

The large ballroom in the hotel was decorated with green boughs and red bows.

Pictures of all those chosen to be part of the Kensington Project over the years lined the walls. Chloe, Scott, and Stella all stared back at her with pride on their faces. Cora glanced quickly at the four people who'd had the honour this year, wondering if their lives would change as much as her and her colleagues' lives had.

A waiter was standing in the entranceway with a silver tray of glasses filled with champagne. Cora had only taken a few steps when Chloe ran over and threw her arms around her. Chloe's green dress was gorgeous and her curly hair was piled up on her head.

'What took you? Aren't you staying here, same as us?'

Cora nodded and gestured to Jonas. 'My husband needed a hand with his kilt. It seems he's not used to wearing a skirt.' She kept hugging Chloe tightly. 'You look fabulous. Are we still on for tomorrow so I get to see this gorgeous baby?'

Chloe grinned, her eyes sparkling at the mention of the baby she'd had back in July. 'Can't wait. We'll meet you at St James's Park.'

A deep laugh sounded behind them as Chloe's husband stepped out from behind her to put a kiss on Cora's cheek. Sam, the general surgeon from Kingston Memorial who'd captured Chloe's heart, automatically started teasing Jonas. 'Don't bend over too quickly.' He laughed good-naturedly.

'Hey, don't start this party without me.' Stella, their colleague from Orthopaedics, glowed in a silver fringed dress as she wrapped an arm around both of them. With her dark bob, she looked as if she'd stepped straight out of a nineteen-twenties movie.

'You look fantastic,' said Cora, kissing her cheek. 'I wasn't sure if you'd want to make the journey from Toronto.' Like herself, Stella had decided to relocate after meeting Aiden and his small son when she'd travelled to Toronto as part of the Kensington Project.

She reached out to shake Aiden's hand.

'Where's Scott?' asked Chloe.

'Right behind me,' said Stella as she nodded over her shoulder.

They watched as Scott, their handsome American cardiology colleague, danced his way across the floor to them, his arm around his wife, Fliss. He clinked glasses with them all as soon as he arrived.

The girls all wrapped arms around each other and started to laugh and joke, ordering a bottle of champagne from a passing waiter and sitting down at a table to exchange stories.

As the music started a little while later, all four men appeared on cue to take their partners onto the dance floor.

Cora slid into her new husband's arms and wrapped her arms around his neck as the slow Christmas song started.

'Happy?' he asked.

'Delighted,' she whispered. 'And this year, I get to have my first Christmas Day in Stockholm. I can't wait to make a whole host of new memories to keep for ever.'

Cora had been seeing a counsellor back in Stockholm and was slowly unpicking her feelings of guilt and grief. Jonas was with her every step of the way, and she'd never been happier.

'So, what are our plans for tomorrow?' he asked. They only had another few days in London before flying home again.

'We're meeting a gorgeous baby, and then...' she gave him a special smile '... I have a few ideas about what we could get up to.'

He looked at her with amused suspicion. 'And what might that be?'

She spun around under his arm before pressing up against him. 'What do you think of this dress?'

Jonas's eyes ran appreciatively down the figure-hugging floor-length red dress. 'I adore it. Is this a trick?'

'Could be. My plans include doing my best to ensure I don't fit into this dress next year. But I might need some help with that.'

He spun her around the dance floor. 'Oh, I think I can help with that. I think we should practise.' He dipped her low, then pulled her back up. 'Let's do our best to expand this family.'

And Cora stood on her tiptoes and planted a kiss on her husband's lips. 'That, darling, is music to my ears.'

And they danced their way around the floor again.

* * * * *

IN HIS SIGHTS

DANICA WINTERS

To Mac.

Thanks for always believing in me.

Chapter One

It was impossible to change a person. However, it was possible to change a person's opinion—given the right motivation. And, as it so happened, death was one hell of a motivator.

Jarrod Martin looked at the man strapped to the chair in the center of the interrogation room, deep in the guts of Camp Four within the confines of Camp Delta, also known as Guantanamo Bay or Gitmo. The air was hot, reminding him of his days in Iraq, but heavy with the dank humidity and the scent of sweat and fear.

As soon as he was done here he could make his way back out into the world...a world that didn't outwardly appear to be at war. And yet, no matter where he was in the world or under what regime, there was always some unspoken or unacknowledged war—even at his new home in Montana, and it was one of the many reasons he was in no rush to head there.

For the good of the people and for himself, he was here—the man sent in to rectify security threats and take down terrorists.

"Cut him loose," he ordered, looking to the two agents he had been given as guards.

"Sir, this man is a known criminal," the agent nearest him said. He looked to be about twenty-five, and Jarrod swore he could even see a smear of milk on his upper lip.

He held back a chuckle. "What's your name?"

"Agent Arthur," the man said.

"Well, Agent Arthur, I didn't ask for your opinion." The last thing he wanted, or needed, was someone questioning how he did his job. He'd been involved in interrogations long enough to know what did and didn't work—and he didn't need some know-it-all rookie his boss had stuck him with rocking the boat.

"My apologies, sir," the man said, walking over to their suspect and unlocking his restraints. "I just thought—"

Jarrod shot him a look that said *shut up* in every language. "His feet, as well," Jarrod said, motioning in the direction of the shackles.

The rookie zipped his lip and set to work. Jarrod took one more look over his suspect's file, for effect rather than the need to know. He'd seen more than his fair share of these kinds of guys—the corporate jerks who thought they were above the law…right until they found themselves sitting in his interrogation chair.

Daniel Jeffery, the young CEO of Heinrich and Kohl gun manufacturing, sat back in his chair and looked around the room. He looked like a wolf that had just been set loose from a snare. Jarrod held back a mirth-filled smile. Given enough time, he would turn this wolf into a pup who would beg to do his bidding.

"How are you doing, Daniel? Do you need anything? Water? Sandwich?" he asked, trying to ingratiate himself with the man.

Daniel brushed off the legs of his dress pants, attempting to rid himself of the detritus of captivity. "I could use a latte and a fresh set of clothes," he said. "I don't know why you think it was okay to bring me here. I've done nothing wrong."

Sure, he could argue all he wanted. But if he was innocent, the CIA would have never called STEALTH, Jarrod's independent military contractor team and the CIA's harbinger of dirty work. He and his team were like the Ghostbusters of bad guys—the government always called them in when they'd run out of legal ways to handle those who needed to be dealt with.

In fact, it had been a running joke among his brothers and sisters to the point that he had programmed his phone to notify him with the *Ghostbusters* theme song whenever they messaged him. And back at home, after a few rounds of whiskey, their nights always devolved into poor renditions of eighties hit songs.

The thought of his family made his core clench. He needed to be with them, especially after the death of their sister Trish, but he couldn't bring himself to face them...not yet. For now it was so much easier to stare down corrupt businessmen, killers and thieves. They were people he could understand.

Jarrod motioned to the other guard. "Would you

please run and get Mr. Jeffery a coffee?" He turned to his detainee. "You take cream and sugar?"

The man shook his head.

"Great," Jarrod said, glancing back to the guard. "And grab him a pair of Gitmo's finest. I'm feeling like a tan jumpsuit would be a good fit. It's not quite as nice as the suit Mr. Jeffery has there, but it will get the job done."

The agent gave him a tight nod and left the room as the detainee started to argue. Agent Arthur stepped closer to the man but stopped when Jarrod shot him a look.

Jarrod could remember the days when he had been a young, dumb newbie, just waiting to jump in and take control in every situation. Thankfully, he'd had his father to show him the ropes in STEALTH—and the man, though he had his fair share of faults, had been as patient as a saint. In moments like these, he reminded himself of his father's words: *The only thing you can do well without thinking is falling in love. The rest of the time you got to shut your mouth and pay attention.*

"Now, Mr. Jeffery, do you know why you are here today?" he asked, taking a chair from the corner and moving it directly in front of his detainee.

"All I know is that I was visiting our company's office in Washington, DC, when you and a bunch of fed clowns thought it was okay to come in and take me down like I was some kind of goddamned mob boss." Daniel pointed at Jarrod, his actions aggressive and angry. He would need to calm the man down.

"I'm sorry you feel like it was an invasion of your

professional life," Jarrod said, trying to empathize. "I know you're the boss and under a lot of public scrutiny." He held Daniel's eye. "It's my goal to get you back home as quickly as I can. I'm your advocate. And perhaps we can even make this all work in your favor."

The man sat in silence for a moment. "I appreciate that." He stared daggers at Agent Arthur, who stood in the corner.

"Absolutely," Jarrod said, even though he was struggling to keep his personal judgment of the man at bay. "So, according to what I've been told about your case, they believe you may have been selling state secrets to foreign governments—North Korea, to be exact. Is there any merit to their claims?" he said, careful to distance himself from the authorities.

Daniel gave him a look of complete disbelief. He opened his mouth and shut it a few times before finally speaking. "I... I don't know about any of that. And I sure as hell didn't sell anything to North Korea." Strangely, his gaze kept slipping to Agent Arthur as though he feared the man.

"If that is the truth, then I think everything should go well here today." Jarrod sat down in the chair across from Daniel. He put his knee between the man's knees, just close enough to be inside of his personal space, but not so close as to make him clam up.

"So, you believe me?" Daniel asked.

He didn't believe the guy any further than he could throw him, but he wasn't there to be judge and jury— he was only there to find out exactly what this detainee knew. "Unless you give me a reason to mistrust you, I think we can be friends. I believe in the American system of justice—innocent until proven guilty."

In reality, almost everyone who worked in law enforcement felt exactly the opposite. Everyone was guilty of something. Maybe not for the crime they were investigating, but there wasn't a single soul out there who wasn't guilty of some wrongdoing—and it was his job to find out exactly what.

The man let out a long exhale. "But what about him?" He paused, pointing in the direction of Arthur with his chin. "I wish I knew what you are doing here." There was an odd strangled sound to Daniel's tone.

"Don't worry about him," Jarrod said, waving him off.

"How do you work with all these meatheads and not lose your mind?"

Jarrod chuckled. "I know you met us on a crap day, but some of them aren't so bad. I'm sure you've got employees at Heinrich and Kohl who are about the same way—duller than a butter knife."

The man laughed, loosening up. "You know it. There are days where I swear some of my employees ate paint chips as kids."

Good, he was establishing camaraderie.

"Any of those employees at H&K got it out for you?"

The man shrugged, staring down at the floor. "If you're a giraffe, there's always going to be hyenas nipping at your ankles."

"You think any of these hyenas could be behind this leak?"

Agent Arthur shuffled his feet like he was growing

bored with the interrogation. No doubt, he wanted to handle it differently, but Jarrod didn't care. What he really wanted to do was send the rookie out, but the CIA had made it clear that he needed a guard with him at all times. They should've known by now that he could take care of himself, and yet that kind of hubris made him more like the rookie Arthur than he cared to admit.

Daniel looked over at the offending agent and then back to him, weighing them both in a glance. "There's always someone gunning for me. I'm sure that whatever it is you think I did, it was done by someone else. I have no interest in implicating myself in some political nonsense. I already have more than enough to keep me busy."

"You're not hurting for money or resources?" Jarrod asked.

"No, I make a really good salary. Our stocks are running high, and the long-term forecast looks great."

Though the man was nearly the picture of innocence, Jarrod didn't buy everything Daniel was saying. The CIA wouldn't have brought him here if Daniel didn't have some strong motivation to sell secrets about his weaponry and government contracts.

"Let's go back to this idea of your hyenas," Jarrod said. "Is there anyone you suspect might have set you up?"

Daniel looked torn, like there was something he wanted to say. He looked at Agent Arthur and then back to Jarrod. "For starters…" He stood up.

Agent Arthur took a step toward him, the action unnecessarily aggressive. "You need to sit down," Agent Arthur ordered.

Daniel ignored the man, instead reaching in his pocket.

"Get your hands out of your pockets, now!" Agent Arthur roared.

"Agent, take a step back," Jarrod said, trying to regain control. They didn't need this getting out of hand when they were just starting to get somewhere.

Daniel pulled what looked like a pen from his pocket. As he moved, a picture fell down, drifting to the floor. The team must have frisked the man, and he had gone through a metal detector.

"Where did you get—" Jarrod started.

"Put down the weapon!" Agent Arthur yelled, pulling his gun and pointing it straight at the man's center mass.

If Jarrod hadn't been shocked, it would have made him laugh to have the agent call a pen a weapon.

Daniel clicked the pen, and as he did, a shot rang out. The percussive blast roared through the room, momentarily deafening him. Instinctively, Jarrod's hand went to his gun.

Daniel crumpled to his knees and dropped the pen. His hands moved to his chest. Blood seeped from a tiny hole directly over his heart. He looked at Arthur, then down at his hands. Blood collected at the creases of his fingers and dripped downward. "Arthur, you two-faced bastard."

"What in the hell did you do, Agent? It was a goddamned pen!" He rushed to Daniel's side just as he slumped to the ground.

"He was drawing a weapon. I thought he was a threat," Agent Arthur said, waving his hand at the offending man like his choice to shoot was obvious. "My actions were completely justified."

Applying pressure, Jarrod tried to stop the bleeding even though he knew his efforts were in vain. The blood soaked through the man's clothing and spread over the ground, wetting Jarrod's knees. So much blood.

He looked to the pen. There was something off about it, and as he picked it up, he noticed that it had a tiny pill-like plastic piece filled with powder instead of a nib. He could only guess what was inside, but he wouldn't have been surprised if it had been cyanide.

Beside the pen was a picture of a young woman. She had long brown hair and a playful, confident smile. He flipped the photo over with the tip of his fingernail, careful not to disturb the evidence. On the back it read: "She will be next."

This time, death had won, but if he acted fast, and found the woman in the picture, perhaps he could stop another person from falling victim to life's fickle master.

Chapter Two

She hated this, being stuck in yet another stupid meeting. Sometimes she could have sworn her job was to do nothing more than listen to the mindless ramblings of the H&K board and their endless stream of guests.

Mindy Kohl looked down at her watch, trying to subtly check the time without making the members of the Swedish parliament, the Riksdag, think she was being rude. She had to follow the rules of etiquette or risk offending the leaders who would determine the fate of her company's expansion, but it didn't make her any less squirmy.

She hated this job. Pandering was best left to those who enjoyed the thrill of the hunt and the glory that came from winning. It was really no wonder her half brother had loved it, right up until he had become CEO of Heinrich and Kohl. Even in his new role, he'd still hovered, constantly reminding her that she was to do her best, as they had much to lose.

Then again, not everything was terrible about her new position: it afforded her a great deal of travel and leisure—though this time she got to stay home in the heart of NYC. She was relieved that after this brutally long and drawn-out meeting, she could go home.

There was a man standing to her left beside the table. His name badge said Jarrod Martin. She didn't recognize the man, but he appeared to be in his early thirties and comprised entirely of muscle. He'd come in with the entourage that accompanied the parliament members, and was likely acting as a guard. But, instead of bringing her comfort, every time she looked at him, she felt an unwelcome warmth cascade through her.

If only it were a year ago, when her life had been focused on nothing more than giving in to the whims of her heart, she would have easily made the man her lover. She caught herself glancing down, hoping to see if his back was as scrumptious as his front. She wasn't disappointed.

Her contact, and lead ambassador for the Riksdag, Hans Anders, cleared his throat as he took the floor. He was sitting three down from her at the conference table. His fingers were tented in front of him as he spoke, a look of distaste forming when he addressed Mindy directly. He clearly thought a woman in gun manufacturing was some kind of farce. She'd always thought that the Swedish were more progressive when it came to empowering women, but clearly there were some men in every culture who thought it best for a woman to stay in the kitchen.

Needless to say, she hated the bastard.

"Furthermore," Hans continued, "it is not in our best interest to allow a machining plant in our countryside. While we welcome international businesses with open arms, by bringing in a gun manufacturer, it could be misconstrued as our implied consent and role in the international gunrunning trade."

"Sir, while I appreciate your thoughts and hear what you are saying, I humbly disagree," she said, forcing herself to remain seated even though all she wanted to do was stand, face him down and put an end to this argument. "My company is in no way an advocate for international violence. We pride ourselves on our stellar record within the global market. While we cannot control where or how our guns are used, the same can be said about many other incredibly lucrative businesses—such as pharmaceuticals. Would you deny a person access to a lifesaving medication because you are afraid of the medication being misused?"

Hans opened his mouth, no doubt wishing to rebut, but she didn't give him the chance to speak. She had the floor, and no matter what some man thought, she was going to keep it.

"What you are talking about is a what-if, while you—and the entire Riksdag—should be focused on the bottom line of our proposal. This year alone, our plants in the United States have brought in $7.2 billion in taxable income. We believe, should you allow us to open our plant, we will either match or exceed this figure every year for your country."

Hans looked as though he had swallowed a sour grape. Money always took precedence. Really, this endeavor would be a win-win for both parties. All she had to do was prove it.

"Why don't we take a little break, and we can come

back and discuss this further after lunch." Hans stood up and shuffled through the papers of her proposal.

Though Hans wasn't the head of the parliament, he sure acted like it. Without his approval, this would go nowhere. She'd spend the next six months apologizing to her brother and the board, and trying to find a suitable replacement for the warehouse and manufacturing building they had purchased in Sweden.

"That sounds wonderful," she said. "And please note, my family's company always strives to create a healthy environment for employees. It would be an honor to have our company located in a place that has an empowered and ambitious workforce."

Smiles appeared on the faces of the men and women around the table.

Maybe she wasn't so bad at pandering after all.

The guard to her left, Jarrod, stepped closer to her. "If you'd like, I'd love to escort you to lunch. I hear there's a great deli just around the corner."

Her mouth watered, but she wasn't sure if it was because of the man who'd asked her or the prospect of salty, fatty meats. Either way, she was happy to oblige. "Of course, though I thought you were with the parliament members." She motioned to the group around them.

He smiled. "I doubt anyone will miss me. As it is, I was brought here just to be a visible presence in the meeting room."

"Oh yeah? Did they think that I was the kind of woman who would jump on the table and threaten them if I didn't get what I wanted?" She stood up and made a show of her petite, but heavyset frame. "I'm hardly equipped—or likely—to throw my weight around."

"I've always found that one shouldn't underestimate the power of an angry woman." He laughed.

"If you don't feed me soon, you'll get to see exactly how hangry I can get," she teased.

"Well, I'm only going with you if you promise not to take me down," he said with a laugh.

A wave of torrid thoughts washed through her mind. She couldn't help the heat that rose in her body and colored her cheeks.

She tried to cap all of her dirty thoughts, but it was a losing battle. She hadn't had sex in six months. A girl only had so much willpower.

Maybe she could just take him during their lunch break. They had an hour, and with the way she was feeling, that would leave them plenty of time to cuddle afterward.

Oh goodness, what was wrong with her?

Maybe going with him to lunch wasn't such a great idea after all. If things were going to devolve into some midday rendezvous, she was probably better off staying in her office.

Whenever her body took the lead, it never seemed to end well.

When she had been younger, to say she had been a bit of a party girl was an understatement. Until her father's death, she had been spending her time—and her father's money—shopping, traveling, hanging out with her friends...and having her heart broken by men.

Throughout the years, people had told her she was

spoiled. However, she had never really seen it that way. Though she had been economically gifted, it came at a price. Her mother had died when she was young and her father's success had taken its toll. During his rare appearances at home, he had spent all of his time in his office yelling at hapless underlings or business associates. He rarely had actual free time, but when he did he liked to spend those days on the golf course. Mindy didn't blame him for his parental failings. However, she was extremely tired of having to justify how she had become such a headstrong and wild woman—she couldn't have been anything else, thanks to her free-range childhood.

She allowed the members of the Swedish parliament to exit in front of her in a gesture of goodwill. Jarrod stayed by her side. His arm brushed against hers, making the hairs on her skin stand at attention. It was as though there were a charge between them, something resembling static electricity, but she tried not to pay it any mind. Maybe it was nothing more than her thousand-dollar shoes scuffing against the carpet. It struck her as funny that even now, after all of her dalliances with men, it was still possible to mistake attraction for actual electricity.

That was what it was—her attraction to him was science. They were like two magnets drawn to each other by nature's cosmic forces—nothing more. But dang, those forces felt good.

She waited for a few moments, until they were alone in the room, and then she turned to Jarrod. "Look, if you have a job to do, we can always meet after work."

It came out sounding far more lurid than she had actually wanted it to. Rather, she had hoped it would be an invitation for a real, grown-up date...one that wouldn't resemble anything like the Netflix-and-chill dates of her past.

He gave her a melting smile. She got the impression that a real smile was something he didn't experience often. "I appreciate the offer, but I'm here for your protection." There was something in the way that he spoke, like each beat was measured and well thought out, which made her wonder if there was something he wasn't telling her.

"I don't believe I'll need a bodyguard with a bunch of old Swedes."

Jarrod's smile widened, but a veil of mystery moved over his eyes. "I don't believe that was quite it." He helped her with her jacket, slipping it over her shoulders, and then he handed over her purse and phone.

It wasn't particularly cold outside, but fall in New York was a mercurial thing. One minute it could be sunny and seventy, and the next snow would be floating from the sky with a nor'easter on its heels.

They rode down in the elevator, sandwiched between strangers and so close that she could feel his breath against the back of her neck. Their bodies touched as she was pressed farther into the elevator with each descending floor. Heat radiated from him, and she tried to stop herself from moving any closer. They were already treading on dangerous ground.

It seemed to take forever to get to the lobby, and she counted her breaths in an attempt to think about anything besides the painfully handsome man behind her. If she closed her eyes, she could make out the shapely contoured goatee and the slight curve of his lips. Oh, those lips. She could kiss those lips.

She shifted her weight from one foot to the other, and once again brushed him—making a fire course up from where their bodies had touched, burning into her cheeks.

When the elevator doors opened, she nearly sprinted out—it was her only chance of escaping. Yet, as soon as she reached the glass doors at the front of the building, she turned around and waited for him.

She could control herself. If nothing else, this was a test. If she could refrain from jumping his bones, she had made significant strides in her personal development. If not, well... She'd have a little more work to do when it came to her boundaries.

"You okay?" he asked, finally catching up to her.

She nodded. "Absolutely, though I have to admit I have a hard time in such enclosed spaces."

He gave her an odd look, like he was deciding whether or not he should believe her. "From the meeting, it seems as though Hans has something against you. What did you do to the poor guy?"

She was thankful he was changing the subject. "Actually, Hans has always had a thing against my family. My father purchased a building and started developing it for H&K's expansion some five years ago. Hans has been blocking our move into their country ever since. We've finally reached a place in our growth where we're going to have to do something or start looking at other countries. Unfortunately, our father invested a large sum of money into the development of this plan and if we walk away now, we'd lose all of the time and money that has gone into it."

Jarrod gave a thoughtful nod. "Did your father ever let you in on why Hans didn't want you there?"

She shook her head as they walked out into the New York air. She both loved and hated the way the city smelled of people—sweat and body odor—cars and industry. In many ways, she didn't miss this city when she spent time at H&K's DC offices.

Though she hadn't talked to him in a couple of days, Daniel was probably chomping at the bit to learn how this meeting had gone. They had a lot riding on this deal and it was her first run of this kind. Just the thought of letting him down made her stomach ache.

Ahead of them in the mash of people was Hans. His bald head looked like something on a bobblehead doll, bouncing as the man walked among his guards and the other members of the parliament.

Her heels clicked on the concrete and they stopped at the crosswalk. "From what I know about Hans," she said, motioning in the direction of the devil in question, "he had a distaste for my father. I think it had something to do with a former business deal gone bad. Something in the nineties. My father never went into great detail, but it's abundantly clear that Hans is the kind of man who can carry a decades-long familial grudge."

"I know all about those," he said.

"Where are you from?" she asked.

He looked at her for a moment, like he was deciding if he wanted to answer. Or maybe it was more about how much he wanted to reveal to her—she couldn't be sure.

"My family is from here, the Bronx, actually. However, we just moved to Montana. I'm here finishing up some last-minute things before heading west."

"Montana?" She'd heard wonderful things about the state and its picturesque scenery and wildlife. "Aren't you afraid of the bears?"

"Once again, I find angry women far more terrifying."

"That sounds like it comes from some dark and horrific place. I'm going to need to hear that story," she said, giving him a teasing smile.

"I wish I were kidding, but I have a faint bite mark from one of the women I had to guard. It's just above my knee," he said, lifting his leg like she could see the mark beneath his dress pants. "I swear it gets sore to the touch before any major storms."

"That is the most ridiculous thing I have ever heard. And I would hate to ask what the woman was doing that had her at knee height." As she spoke, he seemed to gain a bit of color.

The crowd shuffled and they were pushed nearer to Hans, who was standing precariously close to the passing New York traffic.

"Sir," Mindy said, tapping Hans on the arm, "you may want to take a step back. Cabs pull right up to this curb."

Hans gave her a look like she had murdered his first

grandchild. "Are you kidding me?" he asked, his voice flecked with his Swedish accent. "First you think you can tell me what I should do with my power inside the parliament, and now you even wish to dictate how I cross the street? You Americans think you know everything."

As the last words fell from his lips, there was the screech of tires and a man's yelling. The sound was strangled, some foreign tongue that Mindy didn't recognize. But even not knowing exactly what the man was saying she could tell by the look on Hans's face that it wasn't good. As the car grew closer, something pitched out of the window. From where she stood, it looked like an envelope. As it hit the ground a plume of white powder erupted into the air. Jarrod grabbed her and threw her to the ground, covering her with his body.

She couldn't breathe, but she wasn't sure whether it was because of his weight or how he had pinned her. As she struggled, her throat burned and her eyes began to water. She tried to push Jarrod off out of some instinctual need to survive. After what seemed like an excruciating amount of time, he rolled off her. As she took a breath, her lungs burned.

He looked as she felt. Tears were streaming down his face and there were dabs of saliva at the corners of his mouth and goatee. She glanced around, a few paces away from them, where Hans was lying on the ground. He was coughing, his body in a fetal position. When he rolled over, she could see that his eyes were swollen shut and blisters had erupted on the skin of his eyelids. There was blood dripping from his face and mouth.

Hans moved as though he was looking at her, even though he couldn't possibly have been able to see her. And then she heard the scream, her scream. Hans reached out in her direction, but she didn't move. She couldn't.

Though she knew she should act and help the man, she feared moving any closer to him. Hans rolled on the ground, his body convulsing.

Whatever the man in the car had thrown at them, it must have been some sort of poison.

Reaching into her purse, she grabbed a wet wipe. It would probably do nothing to help, but she couldn't simply watch Jarrod deteriorate like Hans.

Jarrod took the wipe from her and cleaned his face. "Thank you." He looked dazed, but he got to his feet, tugging her up with him. "We have to get out of here. Now. You're not safe."

From what she could see around her, no one was safe.

She grabbed her phone, dialed 911 and threw the device to the ground in hopes that it would be traced— she could get another phone, they were a dime a dozen.

Jarrod took her hand and pulled her away from the area. She wanted to stay to help, but Jarrod was right. The safest place for them right now was as far away as they could possibly get from the effects of the powder while they waited for EMTs to arrive. For once, she didn't just have herself to think about… Now, she also had Jarrod.

Chapter Three

It had been a long and painful night stuck in the confines of Mount Sinai Beth Israel Hospital. The place was constantly in motion, just like the rest of New York City. It reminded him entirely too much of Camp Delta. Every time he tried to close his eyes after the nerve agent attack, he found himself thinking of all the lives that had been extinguished around him just within the last month. First Trish, then Daniel, and now Hans—everywhere he went, it seemed as though he left corpses in his wake.

Throughout the night, he had made his way down the hall and to Mindy's room to check and make sure she was doing better. For the most part, she had seemed only mildly phased by the chemical attack, but the EMTs had been adamant about bringing them in for all kinds of testing. Luckily, aside from some irritation in his lungs, he had been given the all clear—a far cry from what had happened to Hans, who had died almost instantly on scene. They had taken his body to the morgue, where he was being kept in isolation until they could determine the chemical that had been used in the attack.

He ran his hand down his face and sat up from his hospital bed. Somewhere down the hall he could make out the shrill beeps of an IV pump that had run dry, the monotonous trill of an EKG machine, and the thump and whoosh of a ventilator. The whole place stank of the terror of the long-ill and bedside commodes.

He couldn't stand being in this place another minute. It was worse than being a prisoner of war. At least there, he would have felt he had better odds of making it out alive.

He went to the closet and opened up the melamine door. His clothes were MIA, but there was a small white plastic bag with Beth Israel printed on the side. It contained his wallet and small personal belongings.

He should have expected as much. Of course, they would have disposed of anything that could have been contaminated. He was just fortunate that the hospital staff had stopped using full-blown bodysuits—ones that looked like something straight out of a nuclear war zone—every time they had come in to check on his status.

Thankfully, they hadn't been forced to remain in isolation for long once it was established that the nerve agent used had already dealkylated and run through its half-life. Leaving nothing to chance, he'd already made sure to have the hospital staff send a sample off to his people within the CIA.

A draft worked its way through the back of his gown. It was going to be a breezy walk.

Unlike him, Mindy had seemed to welcome the reprieve from her daily life. She had barely woken once since they had been brought here, possibly an effect of the sedative they had received. His dose had worn off rather quickly, but it had left behind lethargy.

All night he had been thinking about who could have pulled this off and why. He'd come up with many options—ranging from the Swedish government itself all the way to his enemies within the Gray Wolves, a crime syndicate responsible for his sister Trish's death in Turkey.

The Gray Wolves hadn't been exactly quiet about their distaste for Jarrod and his family—and their leader, Bayural, had left them with a warning that he would soon be coming for the entire Martin family. Jarrod had no doubt that the man would come through on his word.

Still, the attack wasn't typical of something the Gray Wolves would have put together. They were far more crass and deliberate. They certainly weren't the type who would hit and run; rather they would face him down as they drew their weapons. Bayural wanted him and his family to know exactly who was pulling the trigger and why.

So, in essence, he had been left with no real answers—only more questions.

He tied the back of his gown as tightly as he could and made his way down the hall one more time to Mindy's room. Nurses rushed from one room to the next.

At the nurses station stood a man who appeared to be visiting the floor. Jarrod guessed he was in his midthirties, with a high and tight haircut and a stiff back. As Jarrod approached, he made sure to walk closer to the wall, masked by the comings and goings of the staff and visitors, and outside of the man's direct line of sight. Something about him felt off, but he couldn't attribute that feeing to anything obvious about the man's appearance.

Jarrod passed behind him just as the man said something to the nurse at the counter.

Had the people responsible for the nerve agent attack found them? They had to have known they would end up at a hospital.

To be safe, he and Mindy had to get out of there, but at the same time, he didn't want to alarm her. She'd had enough happen in the last twenty-four hours. If she caught a whiff of their being under further attack she might bolt—and likely end up dead.

He tapped on the closed door of her room, and the TV inside the room clicked off. "Come on in," she said.

His body clenched at the sound of her voice. He had known she would be fine, but there was still a tremendous amount of relief in hearing her sound so healthy.

He looked toward the nurses station one more time, but the suspicious man had turned and was now walking down the hall in the direction of Jarrod's room. He opened her door and slipped inside. He was probably making something out of nothing.

"Hey." He walked over to the window, carefully holding the back of his gown shut.

"Hey." She gave him a look that made him wonder if she was as much at a loss for words as he was.

What could they say about what had happened out there on the street? The nerve agent attack wasn't something a person was forced to endure very often.

For a moment, he considered making a joke about the weather, but he remained silent.

"Feeling okay?" Mindy asked.

He nodded. "You?"

She nodded. "Were you a man of this few words yesterday, too? Or is this something new?"

He cracked a smile. "I have no idea what you're talking about. I'm super chatty."

"Wow, if that's true then you must think I never shut up."

He laughed. "I know for a fact you are quiet sometimes. Last night, for example, you only snored a little bit."

She covered her face with her hands but peeked between her fingers, the action uncomfortably endearing. "You did not come in here when I was sleeping, did you?" she asked, sounding slightly embarrassed that he would have seen her in such a vulnerable state.

"Not in a weird way," he said, trying to make her feel better. "I just wanted to make sure you were doing okay."

She motioned down her body. "As you can see, I made it through unscathed. And I am so ready to get out of here."

"Have you looked in your closet?"

She shook her head. "Why?"

"Well, you and I are going to have matching gowns on the way out. That is, if you want to go AMA with me." He hitched his thumb toward the open door, beckoning her. He tried not to sound hurried or alarmed, but his thoughts kept moving back to the man at the nurses station. If one of them had been the intended target of the nerve agent attack it would be no time at all before the perpetrators found them and finished them off.

"I should've known you were a rebel." She got up from the bed and walked over to the closet. When she opened the door, there was only a plastic bag filled with her wallet and personal items.

"Crap." She took the bag out and put it on the bed as she rifled through it.

"What?" he asked.

"My phone. It's missing."

"You threw it on the ground, remember?" He could still hear the sound of the glass of the phone crunching as it hit the concrete. He was impressed she had thought to sacrifice her phone for the greater good.

"Dammit... Okay, first stop, I need a new phone." She looked up at him, appearing somewhat frantic at the prospect of being cut off from the outside world.

"If you need to get ahold of someone, like your boyfriend or whatever, you can use my phone." He lifted the bag he was carrying for her to see. "It's in my briefcase." He reached inside his bag and pulled out his cell phone.

He had twenty-seven text messages. Most of them were from his sister Zoey, who had pulled data about the attack and immediately pieced together what had happened. The farther he read down into her texts, the more frantic they had become, with the last unanswered text reading, I'm on my way to NYC if I don't hear back from you. Plane leaves in three hours.

That had been two hours ago.

He tapped out a quick message to let her know that he was okay, but no doubt she would still be beside herself with concern. It was one of the things he loved about his brothers and sisters—or rather, sister...now that Trish was gone.

God, he was never going to get used to that.

He was nowhere near ready to go to Montana and face his family and the ranch without his sister. Though logically he knew it wasn't his fault, he still felt responsible. He was the one who had picked the job. He was the one who had put their family right in the middle of the Gray Wolves crosshairs. If he had just jumped on another ticket and taken another contract instead of this one, they could have been a thousand miles away and unknown to the men who now wanted them dead.

"Everything okay?" Mindy asked, looking at his phone as she walked over to the sink and washed her hands. "Your wife freaking out?"

He couldn't hold back the laugh that escaped him. "No wife. No kids. No home base."

"Ah," she said, drying her hands. "I see. You are the rootless man."

"Is that this generation's way of asking if I'm a playboy?" he asked.

She giggled, the sound melting away even more of his resolve to stay emotionally detached from the beautiful woman standing in front of him with nothing on but a hospital gown. "You aren't that much older than me, are you?"

He wasn't stupid enough or young enough to fall into the trap of asking her exact age, but he guessed she was about twenty-eight. "I'm sure we are within a few years of each other. But I turned in my cool card years ago."

"Clearly," she said, grabbing a clean hospital gown that was folded and sitting beside the sink.

"What are you doing?" he asked.

"You may not care about flashing the outside world, but I need a little more coverage." She indicated her backside.

He laughed. "You and your rear end have nothing to worry about. You have me for coverage."

"Are you saying you want to…cover my rear?" she asked, giving him a disbelieving and yet alluring smile.

He would have been lying if he said no, so he grabbed her bag. "I admit nothing."

"Okay, I see how it is." She took the second gown and slipped it over the first, this time putting the back in the front. "There, now you won't be so tempted…"

Two little hospital gowns and the bedhead she was rocking wouldn't stop the way he was feeling about her. His only option was to get the answers he needed and then get the hell out of Dodge. If he stayed with her too long, he'd have to face his most challenging enemy—his feelings—and as the leader of his family and STEALTH he didn't have time or the freedom for such a mind-set.

He peered out the door of her room and waited for a nurse to turn the corner. "Let's go."

She followed behind as he tried to seem as nonchalant as possible while making their way to the back stairwell.

He held the door open for her, and she started downward. Her footfalls echoed in the concrete stairwell, sounding like spring raindrops clearing away the dusty remnants of his wintery soul.

He took one more glance behind them, but the man from the nurses station was nowhere to be seen.

Yes. He was making something out of nothing. Perhaps the attack had been intended for Hans and they had merely been bystanders.

Regardless, they were lucky to be alive, and it was his mission to keep it that way for as long as it took to get the information he needed about Mindy and her family's role in the stolen government secrets.

At least, that was what he needed to tell himself in order to remain at arm's length from this woman. If he let this get personal, he was going to find himself in trouble. And trouble was one thing already rampant in his life.

"I get that we are leaving AMA and all, but why are you acting like we're being chased?" she asked, stopping at the entrance to the second floor.

He wanted her to keep moving, so he made his way past her hoping it would urge her along.

"You don't think whoever was behind this attack was coming after me, do you?" she pressed.

Her…him… Hans… He couldn't be sure.

Maybe whoever had pitched the nerve agent was trying to take all three down in one fell swoop.

"Is there a reason you think that may be the case?" he asked, giving nothing away.

She looked away from him, but not before he saw the flicker of concern and fear move across her face.

She held secrets, but he was certain he could get her to loosen her grip and hand them over to him. All he needed was a little more time, a bit more pressure and an increment of fear. Maybe now was the time to talk of murder.

Chapter Four

The Lyft driver hadn't spoken to them, which was just fine by Mindy. She hated the formality and awkwardness that came with forced small talk with a single-serving stranger. It wasn't that she wasn't nice or didn't want to be kind to others; it was just that with everything in her own life, giving any more emotionally—even ten minutes to a stranger—threatened what little control she had left. She was so tired.

As they arrived at her Upper West Side brownstone, Jarrod got out and walked around to her side, opening the car door for her. The gesture was as welcome as it was unexpected. It was a rare New York man who still had manners, or perhaps it was just that the prep-school kind of men she dated had let manners fall by the wayside. Maybe this man could finally bring a bit more civility and old-world charm into her life.

"Thanks," she said, holding her hospital gowns in place like they were a Givenchy cocktail dress instead of the blue checkered fabric that had been worn by countless others.

She couldn't wait to take a shower. Yet, if she left

him alone in her apartment, she would be the one devoid of manners. Assuming that he was coming in. He probably had better places to be, including reporting back to his Swedish bosses.

"You are welcome, ma'am."

Oh no, he didn't… Old-world charm be damned.

"Ma'am? Really?" she asked, raising a brow. "What am I, eighty?"

He laughed, the sound rich and baritone, as strong and virile as the man it belonged to. "I'm sorry, I guess my upbringing is showing. I didn't mean anything by it."

She didn't believe that for a second. Maybe he hadn't meant to call her old, but he had meant to imply that she had the upper hand in whatever social hierarchy lay between them. On one hand, the feminist in her loved the idea of holding the power, but on the other, if they were to become anything more than friends… Well, he didn't seem like the kind of man who would be willing to have the woman in the driver's seat. But he had yet prove he was the man she assumed he was.

She fished in the hospital's plastic bag until she found her keys. "You're fine."

None of what she thought or felt about the man really even mattered. This was nothing, just a man being chivalrous after a near-death experience. She couldn't project some kind of hero fantasy on him. He barely even seemed interested in her.

"I appreciate you taking time out of your schedule to see me home," she said, unsure whether or not she should ask him in or let him go.

The thought of being alone made her hands shake, and she struggled to put the key into the lock.

"Here, let me help you with that," he said, taking the keys and unlocking the door.

Damn.

She hated being this weak in front of a man like him. Her confidence was her armor, and up until the moment she'd met Jarrod, it had been seemingly impenetrable. Now here she was, so far away from her safe emotional space.

Yep, he had to go.

Still, she hated the thought of being alone.

If she had been the target of the attack, for all she knew, there could be someone waiting just behind these doors. The thought made chills tumble down her spine.

She had to be confident. She had to be strong. She had to let him leave and walk through the door alone. It was the only way she could fall back into her normal life.

"Do you mind if I use your restroom?" he asked.

Ugh. There went her mantra and any measure of self-control she had left. She could hardly let him stand out here on her stoop, but letting him in now wouldn't be just good manners—she would be letting him into her life.

"Go for it," she said, slipping off her Hermès flats, the only piece of clothing the hospital hadn't cut her out of. She pitched them into the garbage pail inside the coat closet.

He watched her with curiosity as she closed the

closet door. "You know, your shoes are probably fine to keep. Whatever they used on us, it's worn off by now."

"It's all right," she said with a shrug.

"They looked expensive."

They had been, but it didn't matter. If she kept them she would think of the attack every time she put them on. She would already have to pass by the street corner every time she went to her office. She didn't need any more triggers—at least none beyond the man who stood in front of her.

"It's okay, I have another pair just like them." That wasn't entirely true, but she wasn't ready to completely open up to him. "If you'd like, you are welcome to use the shower upstairs. We can call out and get you some new clothes, as well." She looked him up and down, trying to estimate what size he wore, but a flirtatious expression forced her eyes away.

"If you wouldn't mind, that would be great. You'd save me from going back to my hotel room in a hospital gown. Did you see the way the Lyft driver looked at me when he came to pick us up?" He chuckled.

"We really did look like two escapees, didn't we?" She waved down at her gown. "This is one look that I'm happy to see go. In fact, I may take a shower in my en suite when you take yours."

He raised a brow. "How big is this place?" He stepped into the living room, and his gaze moved to the original Picasso that hung over the mantel.

She'd always loved that piece, a bit of surrealism in a traditional world. In a way it reminded her of herself, a woman working in a man's world. Sure, it wasn't unheard-of to have a woman hold a seat on a board, but a woman at the seat of a gun manufacturer's board was unusual.

She shrugged. "Big enough?" She gave him a half grin in an attempt to downplay her elaborate dwelling.

"Is that a real Picasso?" he asked, pointing at the colorful painting.

She nodded. "He was a friend of the family's in the 1930s. He made it specifically for my great-grandfather, but he never particularly liked it so it sat in storage for years until I took over the place."

Jarrod walked across the room, staring at the painting. "Beautiful." He looked back at her. "Why don't you have security staff?"

The thought of hiring security had crossed her mind many times, but she rarely spent enough time here to concern herself. She'd have to start looking into changing things. "I'm new to living completely in the public eye and drawing all the scrutiny that comes with it. My father was the former CEO for Heinrich & Kohl. That is, until he passed away last year."

"I'm sorry to hear about your father's death. From what I've heard, he was a good man."

She was surprised that, working for the Swedes, he had heard even a single good word about her father. "So, you know about my family?"

"A little bit, but not much. Just what I could glean from the meetings I've attended."

She wasn't sure if he was trying to be vague or if he really didn't know much about her. Either way, it was strangely endearing. "What do you do for the Riksdag?"

"I don't work for them," he said, all of his attention back on the painting.

"Okay, so who do you work for?" She walked over to her white couch and sat down, arranging her gown to cover her knees.

He turned to her, and his gaze dropped to her hands. She covered her naked ring finger with her other hand, his simple action making her feel almost naked...and vulnerable.

"I work where I'm needed and when I'm called upon."

"That sounds dangerous." And sexy as hell. "If you tell me, would you have to kill me?" she teased, but from the tense look on his face the joke had fallen flat.

He was silent for a moment too long. "Let's just say I'm a man who understands the value in keeping a personal life sacrosanct."

Maybe they had more in common than she had initially thought.

"You're naive if you think that you're safe," he continued.

She felt her hackles rise. "I don't know who you think you are—"

"I didn't mean any offense," he said, raising his hand and motioning her to stop. "I was just saying that I don't think I should leave you here alone. At least not until the NYPD and the FBI get their hands on whoever was behind the attack."

"I'll hire people," she said, trying to gain control over her anger. Whether or not he had meant it, it had still hurt. She didn't need anyone telling her that she was stupid.

"I'm sorry again," he said, sitting down beside her on the couch. "I really didn't mean it like that. Please forgive me." He looked her straight in the eyes and took her hands in his.

Sweat rose on her skin as she stared into his bottomless blue eyes. She wasn't sure she had ever seen eyes that exact shade before. They reminded her of the color of the deepest ocean, and it seemed that they held just as many mysteries.

But she couldn't forget who she was or change for any man, no matter how handsome. "I don't appreciate being put down. Ever. I know it was unintentional, but don't think that you can talk to me that way."

He looked contrite, bowing his head. "I know. I made a mistake. I just... Well, I don't want to see you get hurt."

What bothered her the most was that he was right in his castigation of her. It had been naive of her to think that she was safe on her own here. She had chosen this place, without a doorman, living a life halfway between obscene wealth and a recent college grad. Her brother had warned her that this day would come, the day when things would change and she would have to start really taking her life and safety into consideration. With a business like theirs, it was only a matter of time until they were on the receiving end of the guns they made. They worked in a volatile business, one full of secrets, underhanded deals and political warfare.

Until now, she had thought they had done a pretty good job of staying out of it.

When it came to dealing with corruption, it was best to walk away—no amount of money was worth dying for.

"I appreciate your apology." She paused, studying his thick, wavy hair. "It's too bad you're working for someone else, or else I'd think about bringing you on as my chief security advisor."

He jerked, looking up at her.

As his gaze pierced through her, she wished she hadn't spoken so fast although she had meant what she said. He would be a valuable asset to her life, especially when it came to her well-being and safety. She wasn't sure that he would be as sound an addition when it came to her heart. Though she was almost certain she could trust him, she wasn't sure she could trust herself.

"I—" he said.

"The shower is upstairs, third door on your left," she said, intentionally interrupting him, fearing what he was about to say.

"Oh, okay," he said, some of the tension leaching from his voice.

"Towels are in the linen closet in the restroom." She motioned toward the stairs, afraid that if she spent one more moment alone with him she would say something else that would bring him even deeper into her life.

He nodded and silently made his way out of the living room and up the stairs. His footfalls echoed on the marble steps, their sad sound cascading down upon her.

As the sound quieted, she exhaled long and hard. She needed to get a grip on herself.

She sat down on her couch, picked up her landline telephone and dialed her brother. Daniel's phone went straight to voice mail. "Hey, Danny, I hope everything is going well in DC. Things up here… Well, give me a call when you can." There was a crack in her voice as she spoke. No doubt Daniel would pick right up on it and be worried. "I'm fine, everything is fine, but I hope Anya's okay. Just call."

Ugh.

That wasn't how she had anticipated that going. Once he got her message, she would have to talk him down off a cliff. He'd always been the worrying type. She hung up the phone, half expecting to get a call from him, but nothing came.

She waited for a moment before ascending the stairs to the third floor and to her bedroom. It was just as it had been yesterday, understated but tasteful. She could still pick up the scent of her Mademoiselle perfume as she entered the bathroom.

It was as if nothing had happened.

A towel hung on the hook next to a clean washcloth and bathrobe. The cleaning lady must have come, and all had been replaced and freshened. In fact, the only thing out of place in the entire house was her.

She pulled off her hospital gowns and tossed them in the bin as she turned on the shower and waited for it to warm. Steam began to rise around her as she stood examining herself in the mirror. For all intents and purposes, she seemed the same. Same eyes, same nose, same cheeks, but nothing felt the same. In one moment everything had changed.

She wasn't entirely sure if it was because of the attack or because of the strange feelings she was experiencing with Jarrod.

It was though she were drawn to him by some invisible force. The words that came out of her mouth even worked to pull him closer. At the same time, all she wanted to do was push him away.

She wrapped a towel around her body and made her way out to her closet. Surveying the racks of clothes, she wasn't sure whether she should go with business attire, or leggings and sweatshirt. Whatever she wore, it would send a message to him, but what she wanted to do was put on comfortable clothes and binge-watch Netflix all day.

She grabbed a pair of jeans and a T-shirt. A happy medium, for them both.

As she reached into her drawer of undergarments, a draft brushed against her bare shoulders. She started to turn, but a hand wrapped around her neck.

She dropped her clothes. "What in the—"

"Shut up, dammit." A man's hot breath wafted against her skin.

She tried to turn around, but as she struggled, the man's hand tightened. Reaching to her left, she grabbed her Manolo stiletto.

"You can thank your boyfriend for this." His accent was thick, guttural.

"Who are you?"

The tip of a knife pressed into her side. And his hand loosened slightly.

She stole the moment. Raising the shoe, she slammed it down as hard as she could into the man's thigh. She rolled out of his grasp, grabbing her other shoe as he dropped to his knee in pain. He yelled, something in a foreign language she couldn't understand but was sure was a string of expletives.

The man struggled to stand up, limping on his good leg, slashing at her with the knife. She pressed back into her closet as blood poured down the man's leg. She had hit him perfectly in the inner thigh.

"Don't come any closer," she yelled. "Jarrod is coming. He's here. He'll kill you. Jarrod!"

The man lunged at her with the knife. She watched his eyes darken and his shoulders move toward her. His breath froze as the knife in his hand moved immeasurably slowly and the world stopped around them. She held the shoe high and bore it down. The heel pierced the soft, pudgy flesh of the man's neck.

Blood pulsed from the hole she'd left as she drew the shoe back and slammed it down again.

The man fell as the red fountain sprayed from him, coating the clothes to her right. In a few beats, it slowed. The pool of crimson blood grew around him, staining the faux fur area rug that adorned the closet floor.

She stared at the shoe that was protruding from the man's neck. The swooping swan-style jewels on the shoe were covered in tiny drops of blood.

Dang.

She'd always loved those shoes, even though they were too narrow and had done nothing but sit in her closet since the day she'd bought them.

At least she had finally gotten her money's worth.

No matter what—or who—was to come, she couldn't be taken by surprise again.

Chapter Five

"Oh," Jarrod said, standing at the doorway of the closet. He held the towel tight around his waist as he stared at the scene in front of him. "Yeah. Okay," he said, stunned by what was unfolding.

"I… I…" Mindy stammered, pointing at the dead man on the floor.

"It's okay," he said, sidestepping around the man's body and moving to her. Like him, she was wearing nothing more than a white bath sheet. "Don't worry about this," he said, looking down at the knife that still rested in the fat man's hand. "Are you okay? He didn't cut you anywhere, did he?"

She seemed surprised, as though she hadn't even thought to check her body for any harm. She glanced down at her body, inspecting it. "I… I think I'm fine. Just… I don't know."

"You're in shock. This is normal. You have been through a lot in the last forty-eight hours." He took her gently by the arm and helped her navigate around the body and out of the closet. "Let's just get you into the shower and then we'll get out of here."

There was blood on her hands and splattered over her white towel. In an effort to keep her from being even more traumatized, he moved her through the bathroom and kept her from seeing herself in the mirror. He let go of her and turned his back. "Hand me the towel. Then get in. I'll get you some clothes. Anything you prefer?"

His question was met with silence. After a moment, there was the click as she opened the shower door, and then she gently handed him the towel.

He walked out of the bathroom, loudly closing the door behind him so she could be more comfortable. He made his way back to her closet and the body.

The dead guy was in his midthirties, obese and starting to bald. His features were familiar, but he wasn't sure from exactly where.

There was no way anyone from the Gray Wolves could have known where he would be, or with whom, unless they had been following him. It didn't seem possible. This man had to be here for her.

Which brought him back to the reality that, regardless of any feelings he held for the woman, he couldn't do anything about them. He had to find out the truth and that was that.

He sent a quick email, with picture, to his people at the CIA and followed it up with an email to Zoey. Between his teams, it would only be a matter of time before he had an ID on this guy. Meanwhile, he had to get her out of this apartment and out of New York.

Only one safe place came to mind—Montana.

The Widow Maker Ranch, his family's new acquisition, was the safest place he could think of. There, they would be surrounded by family and out of the limelight.

However, if Mindy was more involved in the underbelly of the gun world than he assumed, it might well be like inviting the fox into the henhouse.

There were plenty of people on the lookout for him and his family. There had to be a bounty on their heads.

He couldn't bring trouble back to his family.

But where else could he take her? She was a somewhat well-known figure in the world, had been in her fair share of magazines as an up-and-coming heiress to the H&K fortune. He had even once seen her on the pages of *People* at a benefit at the Met. Anonymity would be hard to come by.

She was a major liability no matter where they went or what he chose to do with her.

His phone buzzed with an email from his handler at the CIA acknowledging what had gone down. Thankfully, they would take care of the body and get rid of any evidence once he and Mindy left.

At the far corner of her closet, there was a rack of men's suits and incidentals. He glanced down at his towel. He had planned on calling out for fresh clothes, but they didn't need anyone else coming or going from this house.

He grabbed a pair of the suit pants and a white button-up shirt. He'd have to go commando. Even if he found some skivvies around there, putting on another man's underwear was a step too far. The pants were a size too large and the shirt was a bit snug in the shoulders, but both would work well enough to get them out of this place and onto a flight—anywhere away from here.

He grabbed her a pair of jeans and a comfortable-looking shirt. The top had little blue flowers, bright and cheery but still tasteful—just like the woman it belonged to. Hopefully, he wasn't way off the mark and she'd like what he'd picked out. He glanced down to the clothes she had dropped on the floor. They were similar. Good. But what if they would remind her of what happened?

He grabbed a floral print dress as a second option for her. It was pretty, and he was sure that she would look beautiful in whatever outfit she chose. And for the first time in his life, he chastised himself for not knowing more about women's fashion.

He set the clothes on her bed. The entire room was huge, and the bed at its heart reminded him of a sled skating on a gray wooden tundra. At the foot of her bed was a faux fur throw blanket, much like the one that lay under the corpse in her closet.

His fingers brushed against the blanket as he laid out her clothing. It was so soft, comforting...perfect for making love.

No. He couldn't go there.

He dropped his clothes onto the bed beside hers and started getting dressed. As he did up the last button, his mind wandered to who had worn these clothes before him. Their mere presence meant that she had allowed some guy to have his personal items here, and yet she hadn't mentioned any significant other. Neither had her file. According to what his handler had given him, her last major relationship had been five years ago to an investment banker who now worked on Wall Street. The guy had grown up with a silver spoon and went to NYU on a full ride, no doubt thanks to his family's donations to the dean of admissions' retirement fund.

On the other hand, it was possible that these clothes belonged to a new man, someone that the agency didn't know about. They certainly weren't infallible.

He shook his head. This woman and her world were a million miles apart from where he had come from and where he was going. She was an American princess and he only got close to her world by being a hired gun for the American government.

However, if push came to shove, his life seemed better; at least he was free to do whatever he wanted without falling under scrutiny from John Q. Public. Whatever she did, she probably had to answer to her board of directors, the tabloids, Twitter, Instagram, Facebook and, until recently, her brother.

He needed to tell her. Or, at the very least, she needed to find out.

She walked from the bathroom, toweling her hair dry. He hadn't thought a woman with wet hair was sexy before, but with her standing there, dabbing at her water-darkened locks, she looked like something out of a vintage magazine ad. With red lipstick, she could have been a spitting image.

When she saw him, she stopped in her tracks. "Oh." She stared, no doubt because of the clothes he was wearing. "I… I'm glad you found those. I had totally forgotten I even had them."

"I was hoping you or your boyfriend wouldn't mind." He silently prayed that she would put his non-sensical fears that she was seeing someone else to rest.

"Don't worry, there's no boyfriend."

"Do you have a lover…anyone that may come knocking at the wrong time?" He felt stupid for saying the word *lover*. Even to his own ears it sounded archaic and laced with Victorian-style prudence.

Her brow arched and she looked at him like she had heard something in his tone she didn't appreciate. A droplet of water slipped down from her forehead, dotting the edge of her hairline and sliding its way along her neck until it stopped at the perfect V-shaped hollow at the base of her throat.

Hell, he wanted to kiss that droplet away. He could imagine it now, moving closer to her. Pulling her into his arms. Licking away the drop from her skin. It probably tasted sweet thanks to her shower, maybe even smelled of some exotic flower. His body stirred to life at the thought.

He turned away, wishing that he'd had boxers on after all.

"No. No one like that," she said, walking behind him and moving to her sleigh-like bed. "Don't turn around, I'm going to get dressed."

There was the sound of her towel dropping to the floor behind him. Desire dictated that he turn, but respect stopped him from listening to his baser instincts…no matter how badly he wanted to scoop her into his arms and throw her onto the fur on the bed and make love.

He caught a glimpse of her, from her shoulders up, in the glass of a framed photo. If he moved just a bit he was sure that he could have a full view of her, but he forced himself not to. He didn't need any more reminders of how sexy she was and how badly he wanted her.

"I called a friend at the DOJ. If you want, I think we have somewhere we can go. Somewhere you will be safe," he said, forcing himself back to the task at hand.

"What about *him*?" she asked, motioning in the direction of the body.

"Don't worry. I told them what happened. For now, you aren't in any trouble, but they may want to question you. In the meantime, they just want you to get somewhere safe."

"And they put you in charge of that? Ever since I met you, people have been dropping like flies around me. I think I might be safer just getting away from you."

He snorted. He couldn't tell her the truth of who he was or why he was here—he'd be directly out on his ass if he did—but that didn't mean he couldn't hint. "Don't start looking over here to find the cause of what has been happening. I'm just a simple civil servant. Who would want to come after me?" he lied.

"When that man came at me, he said that I could 'thank my boyfriend' or something," she said, her voice muffled as he assumed she pulled her shirt on over her face. "I think he was talking about you."

"It's not likely. No one in the world would think we were in a relationship."

"Oh," she said, and there was a twinge of hurt in her voice. "I guess you're right, but who else could he have been talking about?" She walked close to him on her way to the bureau, where she grabbed a pair of light socks. She slipped them on—but before her feet disappeared, he made out the white tips of a fresh pedicure. This lady must have lived one hell of a life.

He shrugged. "Who knows what this guy was thinking. Until we get a positive ID on him, it's going to be hard to know anything. He didn't give you any other clues, did he?"

"Did you pat him down or whatever?"

"Yeah, there was nothing. Would've been nice if the bastard had carried a wallet, huh?" He chuckled.

"With whatever it is that you do, do you deal with this kind of thing a lot? I mean dead guys and stuff?"

He'd seen more death than he would ever care to admit. He'd spent more than one afternoon standing on-site at mass graves in the Fertile Crescent. The most recent had been in Syria after a chemical weapons attack by the local government. He could still recall the stench of the bodies, the clouded, shrunken eyes of the dead and the hum of flies…oh, the flies. They alone could have been the stuff of nightmares.

"Are you okay?" she asked, touching his arm with her shower-warmed fingers.

"Yeah, fine. I guess I'm more tired than I thought I was. Hell of a week, this one." He located a suitcase in her closet and brought it out to her. "Pack what you are going to need."

"How long do you think we're going to be away?

Wait… You're going to stay with me, aren't you, Chief Security Advisor?"

He smiled, and part of the protective coating on his heart chipped away. "You got it. At least, if that's what you want."

Her fingers moved down the hair of his arms, leaving a burning trail behind. "There is nothing that I would want more, though…" She paused.

"What?" he asked, touching his arm where her fingers had just been.

"I need to get in touch with my brother before I go anywhere." She opened her bag, completely unaware of the turmoil within him. "I tried to call him earlier, but it went to voice mail."

Now he wasn't so sure that he wanted to tell her about her brother's death after all. All of his normal interrogation techniques and practices were quickly plummeting out the window. He had to stop breaking the rules when it came to this woman. Though their circumstances were about as unconventional as they were uncomfortable, he had to try to get them back on track.

However, he had a feeling that she was already scared enough as it was, even without knowing that her brother had been gunned down by an agent.

He couldn't believe he had gotten himself so compromised with this woman, and so quickly. This wasn't his way. Normally, he was in, out and done. One day, one interrogation, one paycheck, and then shipped off to the next location. It was the way he liked it. Wham, bam, thank you, ma'am.

As it was, they had already spent more than their

fair share of time together. He'd hate to think the effect she'd have on him in a week if he did decide to take her to Montana.

"Why don't you try to call him again?" he asked, feeling sheepish in feigning such deplorable ignorance.

She couldn't find out what he knew or his role in this. She would hate him forever if she did.

She walked over to the head of her bed, picked up the phone and dialed.

"I'm going to go make some phone calls of my own. I'll come get you when I'm done," he said, walking out of her bedroom.

She nodded, but she was distant, no doubt worrying about her inability to get in touch with her brother.

He called his sister Zoey, but she didn't answer and his mind instantly moved to what Mindy must have been feeling. His gut ached. There was no way, absolutely no way he could be the one to break the news to her. Maybe she didn't need to know right now.

But if he didn't tell her, she might not agree to seek safety. They'd be back to square one.

And if she found out, she would be an even bigger wreck. He would have to console her. And as much as he desired to bring her into his arms, he had to stick to his guns and try to keep her in the professional zone.

He texted Zoey a message and instructions. Hopefully, she would come through. If not, they would probably be staying in New York—the heart of the target. If they did, he wasn't sure he could save her from being taken down if their enemy's aim was true.

Chapter Six

She stared at the receiver. Daniel's voice mail. Again.

Something was definitely wrong. She hung up and dialed his house. His live-in nanny, Esmerelda, picked up. "Hey, Mindy, how's it going?"

"I'm okay," she lied, throwing things in her suitcase in a feeble attempt to pack. "Hey, you haven't talked to Daniel today, have you?"

"Actually, he hasn't been home for a few days. As far as I knew, he was supposed to be home last night." There was the sound of a washing machine in the background, reminding Mindy of all that Daniel's life entailed—a life that was a far cry from her own.

The flicker of panic she had been feeling grew into a full-blown flame. "And you haven't heard from him?"

"Nope, I tried calling him this morning. Anya wanted to talk to him, but it went straight to voice mail."

Mindy glanced in the direction of her closet. What if he had been jumped, as well?

"I'll be there in a few. Please pack Anya a bag." She hung up the phone without waiting for Esmerelda to answer. She could apologize for her gruffness later; for now they had to get the hell out of there.

She walked downstairs with her suitcase and made her way into the living room, where Jarrod was waiting. His foot was tapping as he typed something on his phone. He was frowning as he worked.

Though he was incredibly handsome, he almost edged on a hot mess. Strangely enough, it was endearing, the way his hair matted against the side of his head and how his shirt was tucked in the back. She would've hated it if he had been perfect while she was so characteristically out of sync with her normal life.

"Jarrod?" she asked, her voice soft and unassuming. If she was going to have him help her with Anya, she needed to present this to him as gently as possible. If Jarrod was like most guys she'd known, having a child in tow would be the last thing he'd want.

He looked up from his phone. "Perfect." He hurried over to her, grabbing her suitcase and wheeling toward the door. "Let's go."

Making their way outside, they waved down a taxi. As Jarrod put her suitcase in the trunk, she gave the driver directions to her brother's house in New York. Jarrod sat down next to her in the back seat. Though there was enough room between them to fit another person, she suddenly felt entirely too close to him.

As they drove through the borough, Jarrod seemed glued to his phone.

"Is everything okay?" Mindy asked.

He clicked off his phone and looked over at her. "Yeah, it'll be fine. Just making sure we have airline tickets and everything is in order when we arrive at LaGuardia."

"Actually, we're going to need a third ticket." She gave him a guilty grin. "I want to take my niece with us, wherever it is we're going. I still haven't been able to reach Daniel, and I'm afraid something might've happened to him."

Jarrod's eyes widened slightly. "Your brother has a daughter?"

"If your friends at the DOJ don't let us take her, I don't think I can go. I need to make sure she stays safe. And if my family is under attack, it's vital she be protected."

"I see." He nodded as he chewed on the inside of his cheek. "How old is she?"

"She's five." Mindy paused, unsure of exactly how much she should tell him about her niece.

"Okay, I'll make sure she has a ticket with us."

Surprisingly, he didn't sound as upset as she had assumed he would be. Maybe he really wasn't interested in her as anything more than a job. In a way the realization came as a relief, even as disappointment also swirled through her.

"There's something else," she continued. "Anya has special needs."

"Allergies?"

"Actually, she has Down syndrome. We have to get her. I need to make sure she is safe."

He looked at her for a moment. "That's fine, but we're going to have to move some things around."

"I think it would be for the best."

"Do you think she's going to be worried about her father?" Jarrod asked.

"Well, I'm sure she's going to notice that her father is missing. He doesn't spend a lot of time with her, but he's really been trying ever since he…"

"He what?" Jarrod asked.

"Anya's mother wasn't from the United States." Mindy tensed. "At the time of Anya's birth, she was living in Russia. When Daniel heard he had a daughter, he tried to convince the woman to bring her to the United States, as the care and resources are better. Instead, the woman tried to extort money from him…to the tune of $1 million."

"Did he give it to her?"

She nodded. "He wouldn't refuse her money to take care of their daughter. However, it soon came to light that instead of using the money for their child, she put Anya up for adoption."

There was a long silence between them and the air was filled with the wailing of ambulances and the constant street noise of the city. She wished he would say something to give her an idea of what he was thinking.

"Does your family have this kind of drama?" She tried to laugh, but the sound came out strangled.

He snickered. "Every family brings their own kind of drama, but there is no family out there that doesn't have issues."

She would take that as a yes.

The taxi came to a stop in front of her brother's building. Jarrod seemed a bit surprised, but helped her out of the cab and grabbed her bag as she made her way toward the building.

The doorman welcomed her with a warm greeting, but she didn't hear exactly what he said so she just smiled. Jarrod followed behind her as they made their way over to the bank of elevators. She didn't have to say anything to the man waiting inside. He pushed the button for her brother's floor.

Again Jarrod seemed surprised, this time probably at the level of service, which once again made her wonder exactly how and where he had grown up. He'd said something about the Bronx, though he hadn't gone into a lot of detail. Maybe that was a good thing.

"Anya is a sweetheart. You are going to really like her," she said. "Do you know where we are going to go?"

Jarrod glanced at the bellhop and his features darkened, almost as though he was afraid the man was listening into their conversation—which, undoubtedly, he was.

"I'm so excited about a little vacation," she said, trying to cover her mistake. "I'm thinking Rio will be nice this time of year."

He looked bemused at her feeble attempt.

Thankfully, it didn't take long to get to the tenth floor. Esmerelda was waiting at the door when she knocked. "Hey," she said, opening the door. "Who's your friend?" She gave Jarrod an admiring glance.

"I'm just her driver, ma'am," Jarrod said. "But it is wonderful to meet you." He sounded prim and proper, matching the almost-fitting suit he was wearing.

Mindy tried to disguise her surprise.

"Well, it's nice to meet you, driver." Esmerelda gave him a nod.

"Is Anya ready to go?" Mindy asked.

"She should be. I put her in charge of picking a few stuffed animals she would like to take along." Esmerelda turned and walked toward Anya's bedroom. "How long are you planning on keeping her?"

"I don't know, maybe a week. I'll try and get ahold of Daniel again, but if you talk to him first...just let him know she's with me." She was careful not to reveal any unnecessary details.

Anya was sitting on the floor in her room. She was coloring, her wide strokes spreading off the edges of the paper and into the area rug, but, thanks to the brand, they weren't leaving marks behind.

"Anya, sweetheart," Mindy said, moving beside the girl and sitting down next to her. "How are you doing, honey?"

Her brunette head popped up and she gave Mindy a look of pure, unfiltered love. "Anta!" she cried, using the name she had recently assigned her. Anya smiled, her round face filled with joy as she jumped up and looped her arms around Mindy's neck. "Presents?"

Mindy laughed. Of course, that would be the one word the five-year-old would say perfectly.

"Not today, sweetheart."

Anya let go and went back to her coloring. Sometimes Mindy had to force herself to remember not to feel guilty or hurt. Anya was always going to be a girl who wouldn't mask her true feelings. And right now, that honesty was to be respected.

"Anya?" she said, trying to draw her attention, but Anya was concentrating on a horse on the paper. "Anya, I was hoping that you would want to go with me on an adventure. Are you all ready to go?" she asked, careful to make it something they both wanted. The last thing she needed was for the girl to have a meltdown. Time was not on their side.

Anya stood up and, without saying a word, ran to her bed. She grabbed a stuffed unicorn, complete with big sparkly eyes. "Let's go." She walked to Mindy and threw her hands up in the air, wanting to be picked up.

Hopefully, Daniel was fine. But in case they were right and Daniel was...*compromised*...this was the only option she had. And yet, it felt strange to put her trust in Jarrod, a man she had only just met. However, he was a man who had already risked his life for her. He had known what to do with the dead man in her closet.

Her brother would probably have something cynical to say when he found out about her relationship with Jarrod. He would certainly question the man's motives.

As much as she realized she ought to, she hated to let her mind slip to those thoughts. There were already enough questions roaring through her. Right now, she needed answers.

As she lifted the little one and hugged her to her chest, there was no question in her mind—when it came to this child, the only answer was to do anything to keep her niece safe, even if it meant placing her trust in a man she barely knew.

Chapter Seven

He had planned on the two of them simply boarding a plane and hightailing it out of there, masked by the anonymity of airport crowds. That was no longer an option. As soon as they walked out of Daniel's apartment pushing Anya in the stroller, all eyes were on them. It was like no one had ever seen a kid with special needs before and it irritated the hell out of him. He couldn't imagine what it must have been like for Mindy, having to deal with the sideways glances and hateful comments that she probably received when she was with Anya.

As they waited for their Uber, he glanced down the road, looking for anyone or anything that seemed out of the ordinary. Most were consumed by their phones, chatting away as they passed through their day glued to the screen. As much as he hated it, he was no different from anyone else in that regard. His job required he be accessible.

Anya babbled away in her stroller, laughing sporadically at her private jokes. He had so many questions for Mindy about the little girl, but he didn't want to be anything like those people who treated Anya as some kind of curiosity instead of just a child. Whatever he needed to know, she would inevitably tell him or he would learn himself.

"Hi, baby girl, are you hungry?" He put his fingers to his mouth in a feeble attempt to sign.

Anya kicked her feet, sending one of her sandals into the gutter.

"Hey now," he said, running after the shoe. "You're going to need those if you're going on an adventure with us." He pointed up at the sky. "We're going to go on a plane. Have you ever been on a plane?"

The girl stared at him with her beautiful, round blue eyes and then glanced to Mindy, as though she were looking to her aunt for answers.

"You can talk to him, sweetie. Mr. Jarrod is a very nice man," she said, sending him a sweet smile.

"Mister? Wowzah, Anya, can you believe it? I'm a mister!" he said in mock surprise. "I gotta say, I've been called lots of things but never Mr. Jarrod. It has a pretty nice ring to it." He smiled at the little girl as he gently pushed a stray bit of hair out of her mouth where it had been trapped in a bit of syrup that must have been from this morning's breakfast.

"You nice?" Anya frowned.

"Most of the time. Yep, I'm pretty nice," he said, but as he spoke his thoughts moved to all of his days spent in war zones and pulling the trigger when the jobs had called for it.

He couldn't help but find it just a bit strange that to many, he was the man of their nightmares, and yet here he was getting an opportunity to play the hero. He could get used to this.

"Do you have puppy?" Anya asked, still very serious.

He smiled. "Um, nope. But someday, maybe. Do you like puppies?"

She gave him a vigorous nod. "I wanna puppy."

He glanced around, keeping an eye on their surroundings. There was a man standing at the corner who kept looking over at them. As Jarrod watched him, the man turned back to the phone in his hand.

Jarrod's phone pinged. It looked as though, thanks to the addition of his new ward, Zoey had gotten them a private plane. Not only would he get to hang out with a beautiful woman and her cute niece, it also looked like they would be flying in style. Things were starting to look up.

His phone pinged again. The driver had canceled.

Strike the looking-up thing. He ordered another car, but they were ten minutes out. Hopefully, they wouldn't get close to arriving and cancel as the last driver had.

"I no go." Anya reached down and started to fumble with the buckle that was holding her small frame. "No, no, no." She repeated over and over.

"Anya, you can't get out of the stroller, sweetheart." Mindy squatted down on the other side. "You need to stay in there while we wait." She reached under the stroller and took out a bag of fruit snacks from her purse.

"I don't go," Anya said, smacking the crackers out

of Mindy's hand and sending them flying across the concrete sidewalk.

A dark-haired woman in a long coat looked down at Anya and sneered. She slowed as she stepped over the mess on the sidewalk. "You know, they have genetic testing," she said, like they had committed some kind of crime by choosing to have Anya.

The comment pierced his heart in a way he had never experienced. "Who do you think you are, lady?"

"I'm someone who would never saddle a kid with a life like that."

The woman had no right to speak as she had—what did she know?

"Love doesn't count chromosomes. So why don't you just keep walking, you piece of trash," Mindy said, standing up and lunging toward the woman like she was about to pummel her.

The woman hurried away, likely returning to the bowels of hell where she had ascended from.

He was taken aback by Mindy's sudden shift into mama-bear mode. When she turned back to face him, her cheeks were red and there were tears dotting the corners of her eyes. She dabbed them away with the backs of her hands.

She came back to Anya, who was still fumbling with her belt. "Anya, baby," she cooed.

Anya looked up with a frown on her face. He wasn't sure if the girl understood what the woman had said, but he hoped that for her own sake she hadn't. Anya was already going to have a hard enough time without having to face the judgmental and negative attitudes of others who had no business talking.

"I no go," she said, seemingly oblivious to the melee that had occurred.

"Where don't you want to go?" he asked, trying to give Mindy a moment to collect her rage and blink back her tears, though she had every right to be angry.

Anya threw her hands down to her sides and huffed, looking up at the sky like the mere question was exasperating. "No. Planes. No."

"Are you afraid of flying?" he asked.

She wiggled back and forth in her seat as though she could get out that way. "I go kinder."

He gave Mindy a confused look.

She sighed. "Honey, we can't go to Kindermusik today."

"I wanna bell. Bell!" Anya screamed at the top of her lungs.

In case they weren't already being gawked at, now they had everyone's attention.

"Anya, we don't get to play music today. No." Mindy shook her head, unflappable against the five-year-old's will.

"Anta, I wanna play," Anya repeated, giving her a pleading look.

He would have found it impossible to say no to that face, but Mindy just shook her head.

Anya started to cry, loud and long wails.

"You know, we have a private plane. I'm sure that we can wait an hour or two before we have to take off," he said, watching in agony as Anya's temper tantrum spiraled out of control.

Mindy tried to comfort her. She whispered softly in the girl's ear, but instead of calming her, it seemed to have the opposite effect.

Mindy glanced up at him. "You really don't mind?"

"Absolutely not." He glanced down at his phone. An hour one way or the other wouldn't pose a problem. Time wasn't their enemy; rather, it was the unknown. Maybe while they were taking a break he could check into things, talk to his sister and his contacts, and see if he could get a little further in their investigation.

On the other hand, he wasn't sure giving in to the girl's temper tantrum was the right strategy. If they gave in now she would use the same strategy to wear them down anytime she didn't get her way. But, for right now it seemed like going to the music thing was the only option that would calm her down.

"Is it within walking distance?" he asked.

"Yeah, it's only a couple of blocks. If we hurry, we can still make it on time." She checked her watch. "Anya doesn't do well with spontaneity." She gave him a pinched look.

He canceled the Uber. "It's okay, I know plenty of people who take change even worse than her." On occasion, that someone was him.

A class where children played kazoos and snare drums sounded like an instant headache, but he wasn't about to let Anya down. She was already going to go through so much change in her life, thanks to the death of her father....

His chest ached as he realized how big a role he had inadvertently played in altering this girl's life forever. He owed her a debt far greater than he could ever repay. Sitting through a developmental class seemed inconsequential in comparison.

As they walked to the class, passersby continued to stare at their impromptu family.

"Is this normal?" he asked, motioning in the direction of an older woman who was craning her neck in order to look into their stroller.

"I know what you mean," Mindy said, glancing around them at the people who were suddenly no longer staring. "I'm still getting used to it, too. Anya has only been living with Daniel for about six months, and I only get to see her a few days a week." She paused for a moment. "I hope I didn't embarrass you back there… you know, with the woman and all. I should have had better control over my emotions. But, seriously, that woman deserved a smack to the jaw."

"I don't disagree with you in the slightest. Actually, I thought it was sexy as hell." He gave her a wide, alluring smile.

She cocked her head, looking at him like she wasn't sure whether or not he was teasing.

He raised his hand in testament to his truth. "No, really."

She laughed and, reaching over, she took his hand and lowered it. "Only you." Instead of letting go, she slipped her fingers between his and let their interlaced hands move between them. "It takes a special kind of man to watch his *friend* nearly take a woman down, and then like her more for it."

"First, she was abhorrent; and second, I'm nothing if not special...in everything I do," he said, chuckling.

"Oh, you are a cocky one, aren't you?" She giggled, the sound high and full of perfect happiness, and a little more of his hard shell chipped away.

Walking hand in hand with her at his side while they pushed the stroller, it struck him how much they appeared to be a family. The thought thrilled him just as much as it terrified him. In a way, it reminded him of everyone waiting for him back in Montana.

He could still remember the day his parents had brought the twins, Trish and Chad, home. They had been such little things that in his six-year-old mind he had thought they were dolls...that was, until Trish had started crying. A lump rose in his throat.

His phone pinged. Zoey. Of course, she would text him the moment he had even a tiny thought about his other sister.

Zoey was checking their status. Letting go of Mindy's hand, he texted her back, telling her about what had come up. As it was, it would be a quick flight into Missoula compared to commercial flights, which would not have landed until close to midnight.

He slipped his phone back in his pocket.

"Everything okay?" Mindy motioned to his phone. "Your girlfriend looking for you?"

He lost his footing, tripping himself, then quickly correcting with a nervous laugh. "Uh, ha. No. It was my sister."

"Sure."

"What, are you jealous or something?"

"Ha." She maneuvered the stroller over the curb as they crossed the street. "Are you always this full of yourself, or are you being this way just for my benefit?"

He wasn't sure of the right answer. "If you play your cards right, everything I do could be for your benefit."

She stopped and stared at him, a shocked grin on her face. "Wow. Just...wow." She gave an amused sigh.

He was just as surprised as she was that he had said it. He didn't have room in his life for a full-blown family. Right now he didn't even have a lifestyle that would work for a pet.

"You know you don't mean that," she said, starting to walk again.

Though she was right to call him out, he wasn't sure she wasn't wrong. He had a habit of saying exactly what he meant, in fact to the point that sometimes people called him callous for his lack of filter between his brain and his mouth. Then, he'd always thought it best to let people know where they stood with him— at least when it came to his private life.

Again, he reminded himself that this woman and this child were work.

Yes, she was right. He hadn't meant it. He *couldn't* mean it, no matter how badly a part of him yearned to have a typical America life.

He was grateful as they rounded the corner and saw a brightly colored sign for Kindermusik. He walked ahead and opened the door for them.

"You ready for this fun?" Mindy asked with a wink.

Thanks to their arrival into his life, as far as he was concerned, the fun had already started.

Chapter Eight

Though Mindy had taken Anya to her music class twice before, she didn't remember it being quite so loud. A little boy was sitting over in the corner, waiting with his mother for class to start, slapping two pieces of wood together and screaming at the top of his lungs. Not far from him was a girl with tears streaming down her face, her whining approaching the decibels that only dogs and bats could hear.

A group of toddlers ran around her legs, brushing against them as she unstrapped a wiggling Anya from her stroller. As soon as her feet touched the ground, Anya toddled after the kids in vain hopes of catching up.

"Hey," she called after them, but none of the children paid her any mind. "Anya here. Hey!" she yelled, but as she hurried she tripped and fell to her knees. She crawled for a few feet then, giving up, sat and watched the kids make another lap around the waiting room.

The boy in the corner stopped screaming just long enough to look at her, then picked up his wailing again.

"Oh. Wow. No." Jarrod backed up until he was pressed against the wall. Terror marked his features.

"Yes, this is happening. Remember, you agreed that we should be here," she said, raising one eyebrow.

"Yeah, I clearly lost my freaking mind." He motioned toward a child who was actively doing something in their diaper. "I am not emotionally prepared for this. No."

The distinct aroma of a full diaper wafted over. She tried to ignore it, but she could have sworn that it was growing more pungent by the second. Just as she was about to concede that, like Jarrod, this was the last place she wanted to be, the door to the back opened. A woman in her midfifties with bottle-red hair and a yellow broom skirt stepped out. Her neck was adorned with a variety of macaroni necklaces that were likely made by the throngs of children who passed through her doors every day.

"Children, children," she said in a quiet, singsong voice. "One, two, three, eyes on me."

The kids quieted down and stopped running.

The woman clapped, the sound as gentle and reminiscent of Mr. Rogers as her voice. "Well done, my little butterflies."

Mindy could feel Jarrod rolling his eyes next to her. She couldn't blame him. For a man like him, who was clearly more comfortable kicking ass and taking names, standing through this musical, artistic love-fest probably felt just about as comfortable as a colonoscopy.

She giggled.

The front door to the shop jingled and a man wearing a red shirt walked in. The little girl in his arms was crying and her face was contorted with rage as she attempted to wiggle free from his grasp. From the look of things the girl was in the throes of a nuclear meltdown.

The instructor glanced over at them, and as the little girl saw the woman, she quieted down.

"My name is Lily Lilac Peppercorn," the baby-whispering instructor said.

Oh, that name had to be so fake.

"I'm your instructor today with my little helper..." She pulled her other hand out from behind her back and a sock puppet with blue hair came into view. Together the woman and the puppet made all the colors of the rainbow. Just when Mindy thought things couldn't get worse.

"This is Jacques. Jacques, can you say hi?" The woman wiggled her thumb and the puppet jerked violently.

A few of the kids cheered at the unexpected assistant, but one or two moved into their nanny's legs. At least, she assumed the women at their sides were their nannies. She glanced around. Jarrod was one of only two men. The rest of the caregivers were women, and most had the look of paid help. A couple were even complete with candy striper–like uniforms. It made sense. Few of the people in her social circles who had kids were ever seen with them. They had staff to take care of their children's daily needs and requirements.

Ms. Peppercorn kept talking in her singsong voice as Mindy walked over to Anya and scooped her up into her arms. Though she was five, she was markedly smaller than the rest of those in her age group. Anya clapped her hands on each side of Mindy's face, joyfully playing a beat to the tune of the woman's voice.

Maybe it wouldn't be so bad after all.

"Why don't you all follow me in so we can get started," the woman said, giving the kids little waves as they flooded through the doors with their caregivers.

Mindy walked forward but stopped as she noticed that Jarrod wasn't behind her. She turned back. "Oh, come on now, there's no chance that I'm going to leave you out here while I go in." She took his hand and pulled him forward.

"I…but…" he protested.

"Emotionally ready or not, here we go," she said, smiling at him as Anya continued to play drums on her cheeks.

There was no way she could do this alone. As they walked into the room, the man in a red shirt elbowed his way through the crowd, almost as though he was trying to get closer to the only other man in the group.

Her mind turned to Daniel. He was normally the one to bring Anya down here, when he wasn't traveling for work. It was the one thing they normally did together, but since they had picked up the girl, Anya had yet to mention her father.

Part of Anya's personality was that she often wasn't as emotionally present as other children her age. It was just another of the facets of Anya's being that had proved to be more of a struggle than either she or Daniel had been prepared for.

When Mindy had learned about Anya's diagnosis, she had thought that it wouldn't be that hard to adapt their lives to meet her needs. If anything, she was bringing *extra* to their lives. Yes, she would need extra time, extra attention, extra love, but in return she would give them all the extras that they needed in their lives, as well. And though it had been harder than she had first anticipated, all the extras were worth it.

And yet, wasn't that what all relationships were based upon—the little extras? She gave Anya a squeeze as she thought about how much she loved her.

She looked to Jarrod and thought about the things he had done for her just in the short time since they had met. As she watched him, he reached up and scratched at his scruffy goatee. He played with it, almost as though he were using the hair on his face to comfort himself in the same way a child would turn to a beloved teddy bear.

She didn't have time for a relationship. In many ways, having her niece in her life was significantly easier and far less dangerous for her heart than having a man. Though they both had the power to break her heart, Jarrod seemed far more likely to do so.

She glanced down at their hands and then up to his face. There were the start of fine lines around his eyes—he had the face of a man who had seen what life could bring. He was clearly a good man, but that didn't mean he saw the world the way she did, or that he could promise he would keep her heart safe if she chose to give it to him for safekeeping.

But she was jumping ahead again. He had made no

promises. He had barely hinted at anything beyond friendship. In fact, she barely knew this man. Still, even though they had just met, it didn't change the pull she felt every time she thought of him. She had to fight her feelings and pull them back before she was too far gone. Vulnerability wasn't a luxury she could afford. Not now. Not ever.

The lady leading the class handed out tambourines. Jarrod's face was pinched as he looked at the instrument. If she hadn't known better, she would have thought that someone had just handed him an active warhead—though, perhaps he would have looked slightly more at ease.

She sat Anya down and took her tambourine. "It's going to be okay, Jarrod. It's only an hour." She could have sworn he looked even more tormented at the mention of time.

"All right, everyone, let's sing while we count with our tambourines," the instructor said.

Surprisingly, Jarrod found the beat and pretty soon he was even helping Anya shake her tambourine in unison with the other children. After about ten minutes, and three songs and something Ms. Peppercorn called a happy heart yoga pose, Mindy saw the start of a smile on his face. Sure, he could act all tough and manly, but no man could resist the joy of seeing children completely enjoying themselves. She would have gone so far as to say he even looked comfortable.

And dang it if it didn't make her like him even more. By the end of the class, he was singing with Anya at the top of his lungs, and thankfully the tambourines had been put away. They'd gone through kazoos, drumsticks, whistles and harmonicas, and her head was throbbing. It didn't escape her that after all her teasing, she was the one paying the price for the cacophony. Karma was rearing its ugly head.

The man in the red shirt had moved closer during each song. And, out of the corner of her eye, she could see him watching Anya. In an attempt to shield her from the man's gaze, Mindy pulled Anya in closer to her legs and farther out of the man's field of vision.

As the class came to an end, the man kept looking over at them. The child beside him was peering up at him, and though they had seemed to enjoy themselves, the child looked almost frightened at the prospect of leaving with him. It struck her as odd, but she questioned herself for judging anyone with their child. She wasn't really a parent. She didn't know enough about kids to really understand exactly what dynamic was happening, so to jump to any conclusions was out of the question.

She nudged Jarrod. "Look at that guy," she said, motioning with her chin toward the man and the child.

As he glanced over at them, the little girl at the man's side rushed away from him and over to the instructor. The man frowned and looked over at them. He noticed them staring, and instead of going after the little girl and bringing her back, he moved toward the door. As he turned, Mindy made out the telltale bulge at the man's hip. He was carrying a gun.

The guy looked back at them, giving her a menacing grin and mouthed the words *you're dead*.

As they approached the man, one of the moms stepped in her way, saying something she barely heard about organic produce. She tried to push past her to go after the man, but the woman seemed hell-bent on telling her something about the health benefits of going vegan.

The man's hand dropped to his gun, like any minute he would start shooting.

The woman said something about asparagus.

Mindy bit her tongue, but all she wanted to do was tell the woman that no one cared, especially when there was a killer in their midst.

The man smirked and sidestepped out the door, their eyes locked until the moment he disappeared outside.

What in the hell was going on?

The little girl wrapped her arms around the instructor's legs as the rest of the children and their guardians streamed out of the room.

Jarrod moved after the man, but Mindy stopped him. "Wait…"

He looked as though he was about to argue but stopped and took a breath. "We need to get our hands on that man. Find out who he's with."

He was right, but as much as she wanted the information, they had to get out of there. "For all we know, we are going to get jumped the second we walk out of here. We need to go somewhere we can be safe."

He chewed on the inside of his cheek. "If he's waiting outside, he's stupid."

"Anya," she said, leaning down, "are you ready to go?"

Anya stood up and wrapped her arms around her legs, just like she must have seen the other little girl do to the instructor.

"Do you know this little girl?" the instructor asked as she made her way over to them.

Mindy shook her head.

"She said she didn't know that man." The woman picked up the little girl and pulled her into her arms. The girl buried her blond head into the woman's neck, and her back shuddered as she sobbed. "He took her from the park. I bet it was the one two blocks down."

"Her mother…" Mindy said, looking to Jarrod as she thought of how the poor mother must be feeling right now, realizing that her daughter was gone. "If he's willing to kidnap a child without fear of reprisal, who knows what else he is capable of. He has to be found."

"Call the police," Jarrod said. "I'll see if I can get my hands on him before it's too late."

The instructor hurried to the phone and dialed as he rushed out with Mindy and Anya behind him, leaving their stroller.

"Stay here," he said as they reached the sidewalk in front of the building. People brushed by, moving between them in their rush to get wherever they were going.

She shook her head. "You can't leave us."

"I'll be right back," he urged. "Really, my going alone is the only chance we have to catch this guy. Go back inside."

Though she wanted to keep her protector with her,

she had to let him go. They had to find out what was really going on…and who their enemies were.

"Go." She waved him on. "But be safe."

SOMETHING ABOUT THE way she looked at him, like she was torn between needing him and pushing him away, pulled at his heart. Her green eyes reflected the world around them, the masses of people and the confusion, but at their center was a call to him. If she asked for just about anything, he wasn't sure he could refuse her.

He was just lucky she wasn't asking for his heart.

Forcing himself to turn away, he rushed in the direction the man had gone.

The odds weren't in his favor, but he had to try. He wasn't the kind of man who could watch an innocent child be victimized and then do nothing about it. This man was a lowlife who seemed to believe it was acceptable to use a child as a weapon of war, and as far as he could tell, a war was exactly where they had found themselves.

And war was far better than being home. In war, he could cut down his enemy and watch as their blood peppered the ground. There was some amount of justice, unlike with Trish's death. Bayural prided himself at being untouchable. Which meant as soon as Jarrod went home to Montana, he would be forced to come face-to-face with his failure—and he wasn't a man who could fail.

About a block down he spotted the kidnapper. He thought about calling out, yelling for someone to grab the man, but most people weren't like him. Most didn't want to get their hands dirty. Most people put self-preservation above a call to arms given by an absolute stranger. Maybe people were smarter than him in that regard, but he knew how to grab life by the horns and ride it for all it had.

He didn't wait for the walk sign; instead, he ran, weaving through the slow-moving bumper-to-bumper traffic. The driver of a black Tundra honked as he dodged out in front of it. He smacked the hood as the vehicle sped up, forcing him to jump and slide over their hood. As his feet touched the ground, he flipped the driver the bird. The driver returned the motion with both hands.

Okay, so maybe Jarrod wasn't so different from other people. Just like the rest of the world, he wasn't above biting back. And, if he got his hands on the bastard who had kidnapped the girl, he would tear that sucker up.

The man in the red shirt turned and glanced in his direction at the sound of one last honk. Even from almost a block away, Jarrod could see the look of recognition on the man's face, but it quickly turned to a look of desperation.

Jarrod ran toward him, pushing his way through the crowd. It was at times like this that he wished he was back with his team. A quick call on the handset and this guy would have already been taken down to his knees. As it was, here he was playing a game of cat and mouse.

He lost sight of the man as he rushed in the direction he had last seen him. By the time he made it to the spot he'd seen the guy, he was gone.

Luckily, a woman in a frumpy brown wool peacoat pointed to the left. "He went that way. Into the deli."

He wasn't sure if he should listen to the woman. In a place like NYC it was sometimes hard to tell which side of the law a person cheered for. But her tip-off was all he had until the police showed up. That was if they showed up.

The girl hadn't been hurt, only abducted and a bit shaken up. In some circles, something like that barely warranted their becoming involved. There were murders waiting to be solved and kids that were actively missing. For them, this girl's story actually ended pretty well. But he didn't hold himself to the same standard. As jaded as he was by war and the travesties that came with it, he couldn't be just a passive observer.

He rushed into the deli. The place smelled like smoked meat and expensive cheese, and it was so packed with people that there was standing room only and even that was in high demand. The man must have known NYC to have picked such a popular deli, a deli where he could quickly disappear in the crowd and slip out of Jarrod's grasp. That was, assuming the guy was even in the place.

From where Jarrod stood, he could almost see the front counter through the rustling field of heads and shoulders. He wasn't a small man, but standing there in such close quarters with everyone else made him feel utterly insignificant.

This was hopeless. He should have just stayed out

of this and ignored his need to be a hero. Perhaps his ego had run away with him in thinking he could make a difference. Here, without his family and team, he was only a single man standing against evil.

Or maybe he didn't have to be quite as alone. He pulled out his phone. He maneuvered between people until he spotted the guy in the red shirt near the back door, leading to the kitchen. He was scanning the crowd, no doubt searching for Jarrod.

Before the man had a chance to spot him, he snapped a picture. The kidnapper pressed open the swinging door and slipped into the back.

Beside Jarrod stood a man who had to be at least six foot seven and pushing three hundred pounds. Jarrod tried to go around him, but he moved to block Jarrod's path.

"Out of the way. Police business," Jarrod said, but as he moved to take a step the big man didn't budge.

Instead, he glowered down on him, anger and impatience in his eyes. "Sure," he said with a smirk. "Look, man, you can get in line like everyone else." He jerked his thumb in the direction of a nearly nonexistent line that was more a mash-up of bodies.

The man behind him nodded in agreement, and though he wasn't as big, he looked like he was itching for a fight.

"I'm not here for a damned sandwich. I'm here to do my job. Now get out of my way," he urged.

"Flash the badge or you get your ass to the back of the line, man," the tall guy said, and this time his voice took on a harder edge and his body stiffened as though he was preparing to throw a punch.

Though Jarrod was tough, looking at the guy's biceps made him question his prowess. The dude's arms were as thick as his thighs. One well-placed punch and he would be eating through a straw for at least a month.

Fighting this guy would be about as worthless as continuing the chase.

He had the kidnapper's picture. With Jarrod's team, that was just about as good as a death warrant.

Chapter Nine

She wasn't a doormat, no way. But right now, standing with Anya and staring down the sidewalk in the direction that Jarrod had disappeared, she felt weak.

It wasn't that she needed him, she reminded herself. No. What she *needed* was to know they were safe. And as much as she had thought she could protect herself, this week had proved otherwise.

And perhaps that was what made her feel weakest of all—she had been unable to save herself.

For her entire life, she had convinced herself that she could handle anything and that she was braver than most, and yet when the nerve agent had been thrown at them, she had merely stood there. Jarrod had saved her life.

And now, here he was seeking justice for a child he didn't even know, and soon he would be whisking them away to some unknown place where they would be out of the killer's sights.

If she could have willed his return, she would have. Anya fussed. "Hungry, Anta. Hungry."

"Okay, sweetie. We will get food soon."

"No. No. Now." She whined, the sound a screechy wail.

Mindy reached into her purse, fishing around for some kind of snack. At the bottom of her tote was a semi-crushed bag of Goldfish crackers Daniel had given her the last time she had watched Anya.

Anya, having seen the oily bag, opened and closed her starfish-like hands as her whine turned into desperate grunts.

"Don't eat all of them in one sitting," she said, handing Anya the bag. "When Jarrod gets back we will go get some food. Okay?"

Anya ignored her, instead she yanked the ziplock bag open, tearing the sides in her rush to get to the few whole Goldfish crackers that remained.

When Jarrod appeared in the distance she could have sworn the clouds broke and a sunbeam illuminated his presence.

He didn't look at her as he walked toward them, surrounded by strangers.

It always struck her how, in this city of millions, a person could still be all alone. In many ways, the way he looked, completely oblivious to the world around him, was how she often found herself feeling.

Sure, she had shirttail friends, and friends spread around the globe, but more often than not, she spent her time dealing with emails, invoices, patents and lawyers. And even when she did get the chance to hang with her friends, it was like they had all reached the same place in their careers…the point of no return.

Looking at Jarrod's muscular, sinewy arms and perfect V-shaped body, she couldn't help wondering if she had reached the same place with him, as well. There was no question about her level of attraction to him. It had been months, if not years, since she had felt this kind of burning inside of her when she looked at a man. And perhaps the best part was how much he appreciated that she was a smart, capable and professional woman.

Which reminded her... She tried to straighten her body and appear not to be in full-blown panic mode. He couldn't know all that she was feeling. If he did, he'd realize how unstable she felt.

As he approached she looked for signs that he'd been in a fight, but he appeared unscathed. A wave of relief washed through her, making her realize that it wasn't just her and Anya's safety she had been concerned with.

"Did he get arrested? Do we need to go to the station and give a statement or anything?" she asked in a single breath.

"What?" He looked at her like he was trying to decipher what exactly she had just blurted out.

"Did you get him?" She tried again, this time more measured.

His face contorted with anger and disappointment. "He got away, but I got a picture of him."

What would a picture do? It seemed utterly worthless. She thought of the old adage "a picture is worth a thousand words." Right now she could think of at least that many to tell him how disappointed she was that he let the kidnapper slip through his fingers.

Maybe he wasn't who she needed in a bodyguard after all.

"What happened?" She tried to not sound as if she was interrogating him, even though that was exactly what she was doing—or maybe, it was more of an interview for the job he was already doing for her.

"Whoever this guy is, he knows the city. He definitely used it to his advantage." Jarrod directed his attention down at Anya. "But don't worry, my team will track him down. My sister has already sent my brothers after him. By the end of the day I'm sure we'll know everything from this guy's cell phone number to the size of his shoes."

Though Jarrod seemed self-assured, she didn't want to point out that they were still trying to figure out exactly who had attacked them. If his siblings were as talented as he was making them out to be, it didn't seem right that they were still at a loss. Or maybe she was just being cynical.

"How's my girl Anya doing?" Jarrod asked, squatting down beside the girl, who was still digging into the bag.

Anya didn't bother to look up at him. Instead, she shoved a handful of crackers into her mouth.

"Are you hungry, sweetheart?" Jarrod asked.

Anya finally looked up at him and nodded. "Happy Meal?"

"No way," Mindy said.

As they made their way down the city block, it almost felt surreal. Only moments before, they had been chasing down a kidnapper. Now they were going on with their day as though nothing had happened. She couldn't make sense of her life. It seemed to ebb and flow between danger and safety in a way that made her almost question her sanity. She couldn't keep going on like this.

"Happy. Meal," Anya insisted.

Jarrod passed her a pleading look. He might not want to argue with the little one, but that didn't mean they could give in to Anya's whims. Things had a way of spiraling with her. If they didn't stand their ground now, Anya would learn that they were a soft touch. And the next time, when they really meant no, Anya would push even harder.

On the other hand, soon Anya would be back with Daniel and her nanny and Mindy wouldn't have to deal with the repercussions. It might be a little passive-aggressive, but with the disappearing act Daniel was pulling, he kind of deserved it.

"I'm sorry, sweetheart," Mindy said. "But we'll get you something that will make your tummy happy."

Anya threw her arms over her chest in an angry huff.

For Anya, the reaction was mild. Finally Mindy was getting this caregiver thing down. The last time she had told Anya no, and actually stuck with it, the little one had gone into a full ten-on-the-Richter-scale tantrum, and Daniel had been forced to step in to handle things.

Hopefully, everything with Daniel was okay. It wasn't entirely unlike him to up and disappear for no reason, although since Anya arrived, he had been much more grounded. The last time he had done this was when he found out about Anya being put up for adoption. He had raced off to Russia without telling anyone and had returned with the girl under his wing.

Maybe he had another child out there, or he was rescuing someone she knew nothing about. For now, she would have to give him the benefit of the doubt and assume that his reckless behavior was nothing more than one of his flights of fancy. And yet there was a twinge of something inside of her that said there was more to this, that he was in danger.

She pushed the thought aside. Daniel was fine. She was making something out of nothing.

An Uber pulled up next to them, and the driver rolled down his window. "Are you Jarrod?"

Jarrod nodded. "Thanks for finding us."

The driver stopped just long enough for them to scurry into their seats before taking off to the airport. Anya sat in Mindy's lap, which was not ideal. If they needed to do any driving in their next location, she would need to find a car seat.

After making the Uber driver stop at a corner fruit stand and buying a bag of fruit for Anya, they made their way to the airport. They drove onto the tarmac where their private jet waited. As they got out, she made sure to hand the driver a hundred-dollar bill for adding the stop. The guy looked surprised at the money, but it disappeared into his pocket without protest.

She would have given almost anything to have an existence like their driver's. Sure, his life probably had its ups and downs, but instead of worrying about life and death, he had to worry about which bridge to avoid and where traffic was the lightest.

More than anything she wished she could just *be*.

The pilot welcomed them with a handshake and a smile before helping them board. He and Jarrod spoke to each other, but instead of speaking in English, it sounded something like French.

If only she had taken it in school. As it was, she felt like an outsider standing in the middle of their conversation.

The plane was larger than it looked, with two rows of leather airline seating in the front and couches in the back. In the farthest reaches of the plane there was a door, and even from where she stood she could see a bed adorned with a fresh-cut bouquet of sunflowers. Their giant droopy heads were perched on the pillow, sunny and warm in their welcome.

A flight attendant walked out of the back bedroom and nodded at Mindy and Anya. "Welcome, ma'am. If there is anything I can help you with, please do not hesitate to ask. Would you like a glass of champagne to get your flight started? Perhaps orange juice for Ms. Anya?"

"That would be wonderful, thank you," Mindy said. "Would you like one as well, Jarrod?"

He nodded, but his attention turned to Anya, who was pulling at his suit pants.

The attendant walked toward them and took the bag of fruit from her. "Would you like me to chop these up for you?"

She felt silly for having made them stop to get something for Anya. Of course there would be food on the private jet. Yet, from the way that Jarrod had talked about their flight, it had sounded more like a puddle jumper than something Hans Anders would have used to fly around the world.

It wasn't that she wasn't used to traveling in lavish style; it was just that Jarrod, with his rugged looks and penchant for danger, seemed like the opposite of posh. He seemed like the kind of guy who would be more comfortable holding one of her guns deep in the jungle somewhere, waiting and watching for the moment he could take someone out. At the same time, though, it was hotter than hell to see a badass like him surrounded by luxury. It was like she was getting the best of both worlds.

The flight attendant made her way to a small kitchenette near one of the couches in the back of the plane and started putting together their drinks, complete with gold-trimmed stemware.

"Go. Go," Anya said as she plopped down in the front seat.

"Do you want me to sit with you?" Mindy called to Anya.

Anya shook her head and pulled her stuffed unicorn from her backpack and buckled him in the seat next to her.

Mindy followed Jarrod down the narrow aisle, stopping when she came to Anya. She quickly buckled her seat belt. "You have to stay in your seat when we are flying. Unless you need to go potty. Okay?"

Anya didn't pay her any mind, instead pulling at her confining belt.

Mindy readjusted her purse as she stood up. Nestled inside was a diaper for the girl. Maybe she should have checked to see if she needed to be changed before they had gotten here. As it was, she only had a single diaper and it would hardly be enough for even a day, let alone however long it was going to be that they would be away. "Do you need to go potty now?"

Anya shook her head. "We go?" she said, her words somewhere between a question and a statement as she pointed out the window and toward the airplane's wings. "Dada?" she added.

Jarrod twitched, the action so minuscule that if Mindy hadn't been standing right behind him, she might have missed it.

"I...uh... We are hoping to meet up with your daddy soon." She tripped on the fear the words created within her. What if her feeling had been right and there really was something going on with her brother? What if he was hurt, or worse?

She looked over at Anya as she took the seat next to Jarrod. Anya was pulling at her wayward curls, wrapping her hair around her finger and letting go like her hair was just another of her toys. Anya looked over at her and smiled, the action so unexpected and pure that she felt her heart skip a beat. This was love.

And true of love, terror rested on its heels.

What if Daniel remained missing? Mindy wasn't sure she was ready or right for the job of being Anya's mom or guardian or caregiver. Sure, she knew how to help her, to guide her through the day, but being a mom was totally outside of her comfort zone. It was such a foreign concept that she couldn't even really imagine it.

Her thoughts moved to her own mother. It was strange, but she couldn't really remember exactly what she looked like, though she could still remember the scent of her mom's skin and her Shalimar perfume. She had always loved floral pantsuits and high heels, and no matter what was happening, she was always dressed to impress.

Her mother had completely bought into the myth that was "the perfect life." Go to school, work on herself, exercise, uphold societal beauty standards, marry, have children, get the dog and the white picket fence and then die. Well, all except she had raced to the finish line and had died when Mindy was merely eight years old.

She had been the one to find her mother in the bathtub, pills scattered around the marble floor. Even now, sometimes when she closed her eyes for the night, she could still see her mother's lifeless expression and her slack jaw…as if she had spoken her name one last time as she had slipped from this world and into the next.

Mindy couldn't imagine what her mother must have been going through to make such a choice, but she didn't hate her for it. If anything, she felt only a deep sadness and guilt. If only she had acted better, behaved better, listened better or paid more attention to her mother's instructions, perhaps her mother wouldn't have made the same choice. Now she understood those feelings were those of a child who thought that everything was her fault. But even with that acknowledgment and understanding, at her core she still felt guilty.

If she had been *more* for her mother, there was no way her mother could have left her.

She and Daniel had never really talked about her mother. Daniel's mother, her father's first wife, had attended the funeral, but instead of mourning she had mostly doted on her son. It had made Mindy dislike the woman in the moment, but over the coming years they had made progress with their relationship. Right up until she had shacked up with her pool boy, a man half her age, and turned away from Daniel.

There was nothing wrong with a woman choosing a younger man, but it was wrong that the woman had forgotten the son she had previously used as a crutch when he no longer served her purposes.

Which brought Mindy back to the impossibility of being a mother. She was totally not ready; nor did it feel like she ever would be. Her life was a thing of beauty as it was. Everything, until recently, had been centered on logic. One decision led to another, which led to another. Each time she simply had to ask herself if the outcome fit their business model and marketing plans. If not, she made a different choice. Mothering was nothing but a series of ambiguities. And ambiguities were not something she was prepared to handle.

Not only that, but just looking at her and Daniel's mothers, maybe it was best if she didn't go down that road… If her life was anything like theirs, she could only see it ending in disaster.

The attendant brought them each a glass of champagne and Anya's orange juice, along with a peanut-butter-and-jelly sandwich—Anya's favorite. After Anya ate and went potty, Mindy had another glass of champagne and fell into the comfortable flight's lull.

Jarrod was doing something on his phone, and after about an hour Anya fell asleep, her head propped up against the window as if she were hoping that she could spend her dreams in the clouds. Mindy nudged Jarrod and smiled as she pointed across the aisle toward the girl.

"Ah, what a sweetheart. I bet we wore her out," he said.

"Why don't we move back to the couches, that way we don't disturb her?" she whispered, unbuckling her seat belt.

Jarrod nodded and followed her. She couldn't help staring at the door that led to the bedroom. It was silly and completely asinine, but all she could imagine was slipping her hand in his and leading him back there.

She would have pushed him down onto the bed, then let him watch as she slowly stripped down in front of him. He would have loved her pink lace panties and matching bra.

But that was all it could be, a fantasy.

She sat down beside him on a couch, and even though the jets drowned out some of the sound, she could hear his every breath. The sound was mesmerizing, and once again she found herself thinking of more carnal things.

She wasn't some love-struck teenager, but for some reason, whenever she was around him it seemed like she was reverting to her old ways—make love first and ask questions later. But that couldn't be who she was anymore. She was a professional woman, and as a professional she had to consider more than just her feelings when making a decision, especially when it came to her heart.

His hand rested between them, and she kept glancing down as she wondered how it would feel to take his hand. Now, in this place and nearly alone, she would revel in his touch and the rough calluses that adorned his skin. He had the hands of a man, with one tough patch just below his naked ring finger and another between his pointer and thumb. Actually, it was the callus of a man who handled firearms—often. Far more than a simple security guard would.

She thought about pressing him for more answers about who he really was, but no matter how many questions she asked, he wasn't the kind of man who would willingly supply her with information. Her only hope to really know him would come with patience and time, neither of which she had in spades.

His phone sounded and he pulled it from his breast pocket. *Hotstuff*—that was the caller.

Unless it was a pizza place, there was only one other explanation—his girlfriend was on the line.

He shot Mindy a look and stood up as he answered the phone. "What's up?" he asked, his tone in direct opposition to the name that had flashed on the screen.

Was it possible that the woman on the other end of the line was his ex? Still, if she was calling it had to mean there were still feelings lingering between them.

A niggle of jealousy crept through her, or maybe it was anger that he could have lied to her. Either way, she wished she had stayed in her seat and closer to the comfort of Anya. She shouldn't have let herself imagine anything with him.

Questions first.

"Are you kidding me?" he said, walking over to the bar and pouring himself a scotch. He took a long swig, emptying the tumbler and refilling it.

The last time she had seen a man drink and talk in that manner was when Daniel had gotten the first phone call about Anya. While the situation with his daughter had ended well, it had been a long journey in getting her to the States and under their care.

Oh goodness, what would she do if Jarrod was learning he was a father?

There may have been an increase in cabin pressure, but she was certain that her heart had just dropped into the soles of her feet.

She thought of Daniel and the moment he'd found out he'd become Anya's primary guardian. He had looked so excited, but he'd also looked just as terrified as Jarrod did now. It wasn't that she would have minded dating a single father… That was fine. But what if this new responsibility—or whatever it was that he was learning—took precedence over a relationship?

Jarrod flopped down across from her on the other side of the plane and dropped his forehead into his hands as he grumbled words into his phone. She wasn't completely sure, but it sounded as though he said something like "I can't believe it." From his tone, they weren't the words of a man who was relieved. Rather, they were the words of a man who had been broken.

Chapter Ten

There were fools, and then there were complete idiots—and he was definitely in the latter group. Why hadn't he seen it before?

Jarrod stared down at the industrial carpet of the plane's floor as he tried to make sense of what Zoey was telling him.

"Chad is going to be okay. The bullet just grazed him." Zoey's voice was soft, completely unlike her usual no-nonsense tone. It only made him feel worse. He'd messed up so completely. He should've taken the kidnapper down when he had had his chance, and instead he let the man go. He should have killed him, right there in the middle of the deli, consequences be damned.

"You can't beat yourself up over this," Zoey continued, almost like she could read his mind. "You didn't know they belonged to the Turkish crew. How could you have? They just as easily could have belonged to the people trying to gun down your new girlfriend."

He jerked, gazing over at Mindy. She was hardly his girlfriend. Zoey was just trying to get a rise out of him.

"Either way, I should've taken him out." He shifted, feeling the cool steel of the gun strapped to his ankle.

Mindy looked at him, questions in her eyes. There was a softness there, and it tore at his soul. Normally, he didn't mind keeping a secret—especially when it came to securing his family's safety and anonymity. However, Mindy was different from most. There was something about her that made him want to draw nearer to her. He wanted to whisper secrets into the wisps of her hair and take solace in her arms.

Maybe that was what made him the biggest idiot of all—any person who believed they could trust a stranger was setting himself up for disappointment.

"Are you going to tell her the truth before you get here?" Zoey asked.

"What do you think I should do?" he asked.

"The fact that you're asking tells me you are already compromised enough when it comes to this woman."

That was exactly what he was—compromised. "That didn't answer my question," he said.

"I've a feeling that you are going to do whatever you want, regardless of what I tell you. So, whatever you decide to tell this woman, just make sure you stay safe." Zoey sighed. "Love you, bro, see you soon." Without waiting for him to answer, Zoey hung up.

Did Zoey know something about Mindy that she wasn't telling him? Was Mindy more than she was pretending to be?

All he really knew about her was that she needed him. Maybe that was what he was attracted to. Perhaps he was reveling in his ability to be the white knight although, in reality, he was exactly the opposite. He was a spy in her life, regardless of how much he wanted to be something else.

"Everything okay?" Mindy asked, standing up and walking over to him.

He opened his legs and took her hands and pulled her closer until she was standing between his knees. He looked up at her, taking in the luscious curves of her lips and the gold flecks at the center of her green eyes. He could get lost in her eyes. In fact, that was exactly what he wanted to do. He didn't want to have to question anything anymore. He just wanted her.

"Everything will be fine," he lied. He doubted everything would be okay, especially if Mindy learned that the man at the music class and the man she had killed in her closet had been sent by his enemies and not hers.

He could only imagine what she would say when she learned they were being attacked on all fronts. Rather than being a safe haven, he was only bringing more danger into her life. In fact, if it hadn't been for his enemies and their attack on his life, Mindy and Anya may well have stayed in the city. They could've just gone on living their life... and eventually heard the news about Daniel.

The thought of her brother's death made his entire body clench.

Every bad thing in Mindy and Anya's life was because of him.

If they ever found out the truth, they would hate him. And he wouldn't blame them.

He was struck by the irony in his situation. On one hand, he wanted to tell her who had been stalking them in the city so she could stop thinking someone was after her. And then on the other hand, he was keeping far worse secrets, though he would have liked to think that the secrets he kept were saving her from heartbreak.

But was he really saving her? Was it within his right to keep the truth from her? Or was all of this a feeble attempt to save himself from having to face the consequences from his own series of mistakes?

"You are lying to me. I know when something is wrong." Mindy squeezed his hands and gave him a sweet smile. "I hope you know you can tell me anything."

He jerked. She couldn't have known what he was thinking—he had a better poker face than that—and yet it was like she could read him. He both hated and loved that about her. Few people in this world seemed to have the ability of really being able to know him just by looking into his eyes, and the fact she seemed able to do so terrified him.

He opened his mouth to speak, then closed it again, unsure of exactly what he should say. He hadn't been this big a mess in a long time. He liked it when his life was cut-and-dried, logical, linear. And yet, here he was, befuddled by the beautiful woman standing between his legs.

"I know there's something going on here that you aren't telling me, and I know it's about a woman." She shifted her weight from one foot to the other, nervous.

"I get that relationships can't always be categorized as boyfriend and girlfriend or whatever, but if you're dating somebody, that's okay. I'm cool with it."

Oh, hell. Here he had thought she had seen right through him, but what she was really worried about was whether or not he was emotionally available. He wasn't sure if he was relieved or even more concerned.

"I... No... The woman on the phone, that was my sister. She just had some new information about what happened back there and the picture I took."

Mindy relaxed visibly and let out a long sigh. Her hand loosened in his, but she didn't let go. "Oh," she giggled, sounding slightly embarrassed. "Sorry. I didn't mean to pry. I guess I just have been hurt by so many guys I always assume the worst."

"Are you telling me you're a train wreck when it comes to relationships?" He laughed, glad to take some of the pressure off him and all of his thoughts.

"Hey, *if*—and I'm not admitting that I am—but, *if* I am, it's because of the men I've been in relationships with." She paused. "There's been more than one ex who had calls like the one you just had. I would be stupid to fall into the same trap. I like to think I've learned a thing or two."

"Wouldn't we all like to think we've learned our lessons? That we will never be hurt again?" he said, but as he spoke he stared out the windows into the steadily darkening sky.

"So, I guess I'm not the only one who's a bit of a train wreck." She reached up and ran her fingers through his hair.

The simple action made his breath catch in his throat. He'd forgotten how good it felt to have someone's fingers twist in his hair. His pulse quickened as she cupped his face with her other hand. "Jarrod, I want you to know that I'm grateful—for everything. You've done so much for me and Anya. And, I promise, no matter what happens, just as you have saved us from getting hurt, I will do my best to keep from hurting you."

Just when he had thought he couldn't feel any more at odds with himself, she had to go and say something so tremendously sweet, and soul crushing. It wouldn't have hurt so much if for just a split second he had thought she hadn't meant it, but from the depth in her gaze and the soft lilt of her words, he knew she meant every syllable.

A flood of thoughts of morality and desire moved through him, and in its wake were dreams of what could be.

He stood up and wrapped her in his arms. This woman, this beautiful person, could be his future. She could be his everything.

He pressed his lips against hers. They were as sweet and all-encompassing as the woman they belonged to. And, as he ran his tongue over their curves, he noted that she still tasted of champagne, and it didn't escape him that its flavor was the epitome of the woman it belonged to. She was refined but complex, full of secrets but then whispering of unarguable truths, and beneath it all there was a sweetness that spoke to years spent perfecting itself. Like the flavor on her lips, she was true perfection.

And damn, he wanted her.

All of her.

If she was a bottle of champagne, he would taste her every drop.

Hell, champagne or not, he would savor every bit of her and their time together.

She took a breath, breaking their kiss without moving her lips away from his. "Jarrod... What about Anya?"

"She's down for the count."

She sighed.

He expected her to tell him that this was wrong, ill-fated, even out of line perhaps, but instead she looked up at him, her eyes vibrant. "Take me to the back," she whispered. Her breath brushed his lips. "I want to feel you, all of you."

He was instantly hard, in fact, painfully so. He ached to take her here, now, on the floor, on the counter. It didn't matter. He couldn't wait.

He lifted her up, and she wrapped her legs around his waist as he carried her to the back bedroom of the plane. She shifted her hips, rounding herself against him and making him impossibly harder. He would have to slow her down, no matter how badly he wanted to rip off her clothes and show her exactly how she made him feel.

Thankfully, the flight attendant had disappeared long ago, but he still checked over his shoulder one more time as he stepped into the bedroom and closed the door behind them. For the next hour, or as long as Anya was napping, Mindy was all his.

She ran her fingers through his hair, wrapping it around her fingers and giving it a pull as she took his lips with hers, the action commanding, even aggressive, and one hell of a turn-on.

He moaned into her mouth, and she rocked against him.

Laying her down on the bed, he moved down between her legs. Rubbing his hand over her, he moved his other hand down her leg and pulled off her shoes. He hadn't noticed until now how red they were, almost like a candy apple…the same color her lips had been when he'd first seen her at the meeting. He dropped the shoes to the floor with a thump and moved to take off her pants.

Covering her was a thin layer of pink lace and nothing more. As badly as he wanted to rip them open and take her, he forced himself to slow down, to take pleasure in unwrapping the gift that she was.

"You are so beautiful," he said, leaning back and taking in the sight of her half-naked body.

"You haven't seen all of me," she said with a self-deprecating chuckle. "Just wait until you see how my jelly rolls." She put her hands on her stomach.

Sure, she wasn't a size two, but that didn't matter to him. If anything, he was glad she wasn't. He wanted a woman who was true to herself, true to the needs of her body, and true in her choice of giving her heart and body to him. He wanted her for her and not some stereotype of perfection that was thrust upon them by the world.

In his eyes, regardless of what she thought, she was perfect.

He undid her buttons, revealing a bra exactly the same color as her panties. She had to have planned that, which meant one of two things, either she was the kind of woman who needed to control her life to such an extent that she always wore matching underwear, or she had hoped that things would advance to where they were right now.

"My, Ms. Kohl," he said with a shocked laugh, "were you planning on taking advantage of me?"

She giggled. "You wish."

"Then what is this?" He ran his fingers over the edge of her bra, grazing her nipple with his fingertip ever so lightly.

She moved into his touch. "So, you think just because a woman wears sexy underwear she must be planning on bedding a man? Sir, you are the one who has problems. Can't a woman just want to feel sexy?"

He laughed. Damn, this woman was a challenge, and he loved every second he spent with her that much more for it. "My apologies. I guess I just hoped—"

"That I wanted you?" she said, finishing his sentence.

"A man can wish."

"Do you really need to wish?" She sat up on her elbow and kissed him as her hand slid down and took hold of him. "I've wanted you since the first moment I laid eyes on you at that meeting."

If he was to be honest with himself, he had wanted her even before that, a longing that started when he became acquainted with her file. Hell, maybe seeing her face was the real reason he had made sure he infiltrated her meeting with the Riksdag all in the name of the CIA.

There were just a handful of moments in his life when he felt there was something that was meant to be, almost fated. Meeting her and finding himself between her thighs was one of them. Though he didn't know how this thing would go, there was no question in his mind that this place—and with her—was exactly where he was supposed to find himself.

He silently thanked the Fates.

His prayer was met with the sound of a twisting door handle and the bang of a locked door that was trying to be forced open.

"Anta," Anya said, her voice muffled only slightly by the thin plastic door. "Anta, I hungry."

Mindy sighed, letting go of him and rolling out from underneath before slipping her pants back on. "One minute, sweetheart. I'm on my way." She gave his shoulder an apologetic squeeze.

Jarrod flopped down on the bed as a surge of adrenaline coursed through him thanks to the guilt and fear of being caught.

He was sure the Fates were laughing at his pain. Hopefully, he and Mindy would get the chance to have the last laugh.

Chapter Eleven

It was nearly midnight when the plane touched down on the tarmac. The asphalt was bumpy and little more than a farmer's field with a strip of asphalt, even though it was the private airfield. After they came to a stop, Anya unclipped her belt and ran toward the cockpit and the pilot. "We here?" she called, her voice so high and full of excitement that Jarrod couldn't help smiling.

"Yep, baby girl, we are here." Jarrod stood up and took her by the hand as she toddled from one foot to the other before tumbling to the floor. He helped her up and held out his hand to Mindy.

She looked tired. Her eyes were dark and her hair was falling loose from the clip she had put it up with. She tried to force it to submit as they made their way down the stairs.

There was a black sedan waiting for them and it took them straight to the ranch. As they got out of the car, Zoey stepped outside the main house and waved.

"How was your flight?" she asked.

Mindy flashed Jarrod a guilty smile. "It was good, but it got a little rough about midflight."

He checked his laugh. Zoey would already be looking for something in their relationship to pick apart, and he didn't want to even hint about what had happened—or rather, *hadn't* happened—back on the flight.

He didn't need Zoey questioning his judgment. He was the head of both the family and the STEALTH team, even if Zoey constantly took it upon herself to put him to the test. Though she was his junior, she always seemed to be at odds with him, like somehow it was his fault that she was the youngest.

In a way, Mindy was a bit like Zoey. They were both incredibly strong willed and among the most determined women he had ever met. Hopefully, they would get along.

And hopefully his secret role in Mindy's life wouldn't yet come to light and put their budding relationship in jeopardy.

Zoey opened the back door to the car. "Hiya, little one," she said, giving Anya a high five as Jarrod got her out of her car seat. She introduced herself to Mindy with a handshake. So far, so good.

Anya wiggled in his arms as Zoey stretched her arms to take the girl. Anya, the girl to whom few were considered strangers, pushed him and motioned for him to let her down. She made her way over to Zoey and wrapped herself around her legs in the smallest bear hug he'd ever seen.

Zoey laughed as she hugged the girl. She motioned them inside. "We have everything ready for you guys. We don't have much in the way of furnishings in the house, but what we do have is yours. So make yourselves comfortable," she said, giving Mindy a little nod.

Maybe his sister had grown up a bit since he had last seen her. Or maybe she was feeling the weight of Trish's loss. Trish had always been the glue that had held the family together and the one to call Jarrod and Zoey to the table when they were at each other's throats.

However, he would do anything for Zoey and she the same for him. And, if anything, her constant pressure had only forced him to work that much harder and for that, they had all benefited.

Mindy took Anya by the hand, pulling her from Zoey's legs and lifting her into her arms. "This little one got a nap, but it is well past her bedtime. Is there anywhere specifically that you would like for her to sleep?" Mindy smiled.

Zoey pointed up the stairs. "Up there, third door down the hall. I made up a bed for both of you. There's an attached bathroom with everything you need to wash up."

Wow, his sister really had thought of everything.

With a thank-you, Mindy and Anya made their way upstairs. As soon as they turned the corner to the hall and were out of view, Zoey turned on him. "How much does she know? Did you tell her about STEALTH?"

"I haven't told her about us—or anything else. I was hoping that we could get this all sorted with the Riksdag first. I don't want to overwhelm her with everything all at one time."

"That's a cop-out and you know it. You aren't giving

this woman enough credit. She is going to figure out what's going on, and then where will you be?" Zoey shook her head. "She has an MBA from Brown—graduating first in her class. She is the type who is going to question the world around her."

"You're right, but what we do shouldn't be on her radar...unless she learns the truth about the kidnapper."

"I'm taking it that you didn't mention his identity to her on the flight?"

He gave her an exasperated look. "Why are you drilling me before I'm even in the house? Can't this wait until morning?"

"You are seriously going to come at me just because I want a little information? I'm helping you, remember?" Zoey rebuked.

He sighed. "Sorry, I'm just tired. It's been a hellish couple of days."

"Apology accepted." Zoey started upstairs, Jarrod close on her heels. "And for now, I'll let Chad and Trevor know where we stand."

"How is Chad doing?" Jarrod asked.

Zoey waved him off. "He's fine. You know Chad—he's tougher than nails and the wound wasn't too bad."

"Sounds like he got lucky," Jarrod said, giving a relieved sigh.

He considered telling Mindy the truth about who he and his family were—it wasn't too late to share some of the truths about STEALTH and his role in her life. But he feared opening up. She was smart. She was going to ask questions, and those questions would only lead to catastrophe.

For now, all he could do was avert disaster and keep anyone else from getting shot. If his family came under fire again, he doubted they would be lucky enough to stay alive.

MINDY ROLLED OVER in the bed and glanced at the clock. It was early but sunlight was starting to creep in. Her body, still on New York time, screamed for her to rise and get to the business of her day. Without a doubt, she had probably missed at least a few hundred emails, most of them urgent, thanks to the loss of her phone.

No wonder she hadn't missed the dang thing.

Getting up, she was careful to not rustle too much. Anya was still asleep on the bed beside her. It had been a long, fitful night for them both. Sleeping next to a child was a bit like sharing a bed with a fish out of water. Anya, though she had been completely asleep, flipped and flung her body around in her ever-pressing need to get comfortable.

As Mindy slipped from the room, her lower back pinged where Anya's wayward foot had found her a few hours earlier. Coffee. Ibuprofen. Phone. And back to work. Just because she had been out of the loop for the last few days didn't mean that the world had stopped. And with Daniel being MIA, she could only imagine the state of things at H&K. There had to be someone available to run the ship.

She made her way down the hall, walking by an open bedroom door. Inside, Jarrod was asleep. He was sprawled out on the bed, taking up nearly the entire thing, and he reminded her of her fight for space with the little fish. He was definitely a man who spent most of his nights alone in his bed. The thought made her smile.

For a second, she considered going into his room, getting into bed with him and finishing what they had started last night, but instead she simply closed his door. What had happened last night on the plane, while fun, had been a bad idea. With sharing bodies came sharing hearts, and hers was already a hot mess.

She needed to get her life back in order and under control before she would be ready to open herself up to what a physical relationship would entail. Even before the last few days, starting a relationship would have been questionable at best. Now, thoughts of starting a relationship were completely asinine.

Her focus had to be on removing herself and Anya from the crosshairs, and then she needed to resolve the obstacles preventing her plants from opening up in Sweden. Until that happened every day was a money-losing day for the company. When Daniel found out, he was going to be furious that she hadn't done her best to watch the bottom line.

Though, thinking about it, he'd be one hell of a hypocrite if he dared to call her out when he'd failed to tell her where he had gone and why. Actually, when he came back, she was going to make it a point to give him a piece of her mind.

Making her way to the kitchen, she found Zoey sitting at the table, tapping away on her computer. "Oh," she said, "good morning. Is it okay if I get some coffee going?" she asked, pointing at the empty coffeepot on the nearly barren kitchen counter.

"Hey," Zoey said, looking up from the screen. Her eyes were red and tired looking, making Mindy wonder if she had even bothered to go to bed the night before. "Go for it. Or if you want, I can do it." Zoey moved to stand up, but Mindy stopped her with a wave of the hand.

"You stay there. I'll grab you up a cup, too." She walked over and started to fill the carafe. "Did you get any sleep last night?"

Zoey shook her head and clicked off her computer before Mindy had a chance to take a good look at whatever was on the screen. The way she moved made her wonder if Zoey was hiding something.

Jarrod hadn't talked about his family very much and, until now, she hadn't really thought to ask much about them. She tried to quell the anxiety and distrust that moved through her as she made the coffee. Zoey was helping with the investigation—nothing more.

Zoey slipped her computer into the case by her feet. She started to stand up, but then stopped herself and reached back into her case. "Hey, I have something for you." She pulled out a phone and handed it to Mindy. "Jarrod said something about you losing yours, so I updated my old one and set it up for you. It's not much, but it will get you through until you're back in the city."

"Wow. I…uh, thank you," Mindy said, taking the phone from Jarrod's sister and clicking it on. It was almost identical to her old one. As she scrolled through it, she was struck by how much Zoey seemed to know about her, though—admittedly—the phone thing might have just been a coincidence. "I appreciate you doing this... I thought I was going to have to hunt down a new one out here in the middle of nowhere."

Zoey laughed, the sound loud and reverberating through the seventies-style kitchen and over the percolating sounds of the coffee maker that was likely from the same era. "I figured as much. You'd almost have better luck finding gold than finding a good smartphone out here." She grabbed two cups from the cupboard and poured them each a mug of the only half-brewed coffee. "You should have seen me when we first got out here. I thought I had found the actual middle of Nowhere, America."

Mindy laughed. "It's a far cry from the city. I'm not gonna lie, I don't think I've ever heard crickets that loud before. Even with the windows closed in our bedroom it sounded like they were in the room with us."

"Knowing this place, they may well have been." Zoey gave her an apologetic smile, as if their home was a poor comparison to what she'd been used to in the city.

"That's not what I meant at all... I guess I'm just not a country girl. I like the amenities that come with city life—constant sirens and all." She took a sip of her coffee, strong and bitter.

"I bet you are thinking about espresso at this very minute. I know I am." Zoey laughed.

She feigned ignorance as she buried her face in her mug and suffered through the next drink of the boiling hot road tar. "I guess making coffee should be put on my list of skills that need a little more work." She reached over for Zoey's cup, but the woman pulled it away.

"No, I don't mind a hearty cup of coffee. In fact, when we've been working overseas there are times when I would give my left leg for even this."

"What is it that you do?" she asked.

Zoey's face tightened. "Well, I've been in the investments game for a long time. Once in a while I travel around and look into whatever our next investment will be, as well as checking my current ones."

Though Zoey's answer made sense, something about it rang false, and she was once again reminded to check her cynicism.

"What kind of things do you invest in?" She knew she should drop the subject, but at the same time she just had to stir the pot and get to the bottom of why she was feeling suspicious.

"This and that," Zoey said, giving a vague wave.

"Jarrod said that you are a genius when it comes to tech. Have you been following everything with Elon Musk?" she asked, trying to make conversation and go a little bit deeper with the woman.

Zoey nodded. "He's an interesting man, but I tend to steer clear of his promises. Though, years or so ago, I went to one of his dinners in Hollywood when he was looking for investors in his latest project. That turned out to be PayPal. So as many successes as I have had, I've had just as many failures and missed opportunities."

"Can you imagine how much those stocks would be worth now?" Mindy asked.

"Millions. That was, if we had played it right. But investing is a gamble. What works for one may not work for another. I mean just look at the Bitcoin boom some time ago. Our company made a substantial profit, but others we know lost nearly everything they had and had to start over. Most of the time, we've been lucky."

"Is that why you all moved here—you got lucky?" Mindy sat down at the table as Zoey stood up, walked over to the counter and poured a bit of sugar into her coffee.

"Yeah, that and a few other reasons." Zoey's face was again pinched, but Mindy wasn't sure if it was from the coffee or from something else. "Did Jarrod tell you about Trish?"

She shook her head.

"Oh," Zoey said, staring into her cup. She took a long breath. "Trish is our sister. She died. A few months ago. It's been hard on the family."

"I… I'm so sorry." Mindy tried to not feel hurt that he had kept a secret so big from her. And on the heels of that was a twang of pity. Here she had been so consumed with her life's upheavals that she hadn't paused for a moment to consider he had things going on in his private life, as well.

Zoey shrugged, but she could tell from the look in Zoey's eyes that it pained to even mention her sister's name. They must have been close.

The door to the kitchen opened and Jarrod walked in. There was a sleepiness to him and his eyes looked heavy. "Hey," he said, walking over to the pot of coffee and pouring himself a cup. "I thought I heard someone talking down here." He glanced over at her and gave her a tired, sexy grin that reminded her entirely too much of their time together on the plane. Her cheeks warmed.

"You hungry? I think there are some frozen waffles or something." Zoey motioned for him to help himself.

"What, no breakfast feast this morning?" he teased.

Zoey gave him a look. "You know how to cook. Feel free to make yourself at home."

"Oh, come on now, sis, you know you want to make me breakfast."

Mindy stood up. "I can make myself useful and start breakfast if you like. It's the least I can do for your generosity in having me here."

Jarrod's smile disappeared, and there was a strange look on his face as he turned to his sister. Zoey cocked her head, quickly glancing between them like she was trying to understand why Mindy would offer to be so nice.

"Seriously, it would be my pleasure. I don't want to impose, and if this is a way I can make your lives easier—"

"No," Zoey said, standing up and walking between her and the stove. "My brother is just kidding around—he knows I hate to cook. Besides, he's lucky that he isn't eating expired MREs while holed up in a cave somewhere. He should consider himself lucky." She glared at him, but there was a faint smile playing across her lips. She walked to the freezer, pulled out a box of Eggos and threw them at him. "Here. Now, stop your whining."

Nearly dropping his cup, he caught the box as it hit him in the ribs.

"While you're at it, why don't you whip up a couple extra for me and Ms. Kohl. We have business to discuss." Zoey grabbed her phone and clicked it on.

"Did you find something?" Jarrod asked.

"Actually, we may have," she said with an excited grin. "The sourcing came back on the chemical samples you sent me from the attack."

A black hole formed in the center of Mindy's chest. She was desperate to hear who may have been behind the attack on Hans, but at the same time, she wasn't entirely sure she was ready. As soon as they located the source and found out who was responsible everything was going to change. It was possible that Jarrod would even leave her here. He had no reason to stay with her and Anya now that she was tucked into the safe harbor of his family's ranch. He was definitely the kind of man who was more comfortable traipsing around the world on a moment's notice than sticking to one place.

Not to mention what it would do for her professionally and personally if her company or her brother had something to do with the attack. Their futures might well be in jeopardy. Not only would their business with Sweden be deemed out of the question, she could easily find herself on the fast track to prison.

But Daniel couldn't have had anything to do with the attack. He would never have ordered such a thing. He wasn't the type. And he certainly wouldn't have done something so rash and put her in danger. That is, unless he was tired of having her at the company. What if he wanted it for himself? As of now, they were profit sharing. Sure, they were both making a decent amount of money, but with her out of the picture he would be making millions more. And he had Anya to support now… Maybe he felt he needed that extra income.

She tried to calm herself and put those kinds of thoughts out of her mind. Her brother didn't hate her. Sure, they weren't the closest of siblings, but for half brother and sister they were certainly a lot closer than most. But then again, Daniel was all business. He was always about the bottom line and how to put more money into his pocket.

Jarrod walked over to her like he could somehow sense her turmoil. "You okay?" he asked, leading her out of the kitchen and away from his sister. "Why don't you just sit down out here on the couch? Let me talk to Zoey for a while, unless you want to come along?" He sat a plate of waffles down on the table in front of her.

"No," she said, shaking her head. "I'm fine. Just…" She didn't know exactly what to say to convey her true feelings of terror and uncertainty. "I need to take a break, maybe get some work done."

"Okay, babe. But know that I get what you're feeling. You've been through a lot in the last couple of days. But everything is going to be okay. You have me." He walked her over to the couch and flicked on the television to some stupid early-morning talk show and handed her the remote. "If you want, just take a break. Veg out for a bit."

As he smiled, relief moved through her. Yes, for the first time in years, she finally felt as though there was someone she could trust.

Chapter Twelve

Jarrod could kick himself for the charade he was being forced to play with Mindy. He made his way to the kitchen, looking back one more time to make sure that she was settled on the couch.

She trusted him.

Hell, from the look she had just given him, her feelings had developed past the almost one-night stand. He might have imagined it, but he could almost have sworn that he saw genuine emotion in her eyes.

For her sake, he was going to have to nip that in the bud. Nearly sleeping with her on the plane had been one heck of a mistake—one he couldn't repeat, no matter how much he wanted to take her in his arms and bed her.

He grabbed his mug and stood in front of the sink, taking a long drink as he remembered how sweet Mindy's lips had tasted. If only he had been able to taste all of her.

"How long have you loved each other?" Zoey asked. "Is this a new development or would you say that you loved her from the first time you laid eyes on her?"

"Zoe, you can be a real pain in the ass sometimes. Did anyone ever tell you that?" he asked, turning to face his sister.

"You. And all the time." Zoey picked up the waffles and returned them to the freezer. "So, really, is this thing you have going with Mindy going to cause a problem with your work? If it is, then maybe it's best if you let me get the truth out of her and you can nose around her company. You know our handlers at the CIA aren't going to patiently wait around for answers, especially once they find out that you are screwing the biggest lead in their case."

"Knock it off, Zoey. You don't know what you're talking about. We haven't *screwed*. We won't *screw*. And if we did *screw* it would be none of your business." He spit the words like they tasted as pithy and dismissive as they sounded.

"Actually, it is my business, Jarrod. It's *all* of our business. If you don't fly straight with the CIA, it's going to affect us all. They are working overtime, just like I am, to get us out of the Gray Wolves' sights. You can't risk pissing them off. If Bayural finds us, we are as good as dead. We have to show the director that we are up to whatever task they give us. And that *you* can keep your pants on."

His sister had a point about their connections within the CIA, but that didn't mean that she had any right to treat him like this. He was the head of this family, not her, no matter how badly she wanted to take the helm. He wasn't stupid and he surely didn't need her treating him like an idiot. At the same time, there was no use picking a fight with her nearly the second he came home. She was just making a show of her role in the family, nothing more. In a few weeks, they would be back into the swing of things and working together in a way that suited them both.

"You just worry about you." He dumped the rest of his coffee in the sink, letting the bitter contents swirl down the drain. He had enough of a burning in his gut. The last thing he needed to do was throw a little battery acid on top of it. "About the nerve agent attack, what did you find out?"

She walked over to the kitchen door and peeked out, checking on Mindy and making sure that she was still watching television. "It looks as though they used a nerve agent called VX. It was the same one that killed the North Korean leader's brother. But this time the attackers chose to turn it into a powder form—and that was likely the only reason you both survived. Had they made it into an aerosol, there is nearly a one-hundred-percent chance that you and Mindy would have never walked away."

"Then I guess it's good that I'm lucky," he said, trying to make light of the attack.

"Yeah, right. That, or the people who threw it weren't looking to kill en masse, rather just a few targets."

"If that was the case, why didn't they just shoot them? Or take care of Hans in his hotel room?"

"My best guess is that they may well have been trying to send your girl, and maybe you, a message. It's more than possible," she said, coming closer so that she could whisper to him, "that this could be somehow connected to our enemies in Turkey. Maybe it was a quick hit by an offshoot gang from the city. Maybe it was just a screwed-up attack. Maybe they meant to go after you and thought they were close enough. Maybe it was supposed to send a message to our family."

"I thought you said you had answers. If I wanted to have everything even further up in the air, I could have taken this all to Chad and Trevor."

"Hey, jerk." Zoey punched him in the arm with a little laugh. Finally they were making some sort of progress with one another, even if it came off as ribbing. "There is more. As far as the sourcing, like I said, we got a manufacturing point. In fact, based on the strontium levels contained within the source compounds, it appears this batch was made in North Korea."

Turkey and North Korea had well-known ties within the black market, and there had been whispers that there was a secret armistice between the two opposing governments that made them common enemies of the United States, whispers that he knew to be true. Which meant he very well may have been the target in the nerve agent attack and that perhaps this had nothing to do with Mindy and Daniel as he had previously assumed.

It only made him feel more like scum.

MINDY CLICKED ON her phone and entered the passwords required to sync her account. As of this morning, she had close to seven hundred emails that had piled up since she had been gone. While most of them could wait, there were plenty that needed her approval or insight. She moved down the list, approving everything from compliance statements to work orders that had defaulted thanks to her brother's absence.

Maybe she had made a mistake in coming to Montana. Maybe she and Anya would have been better off holing up in one of her factories on the West Coast, taking in the warm fall weather on the southern California coastline.

Then again, there was no way she would have refused Jarrod's offer to bring them here. He could have asked her to go to the moon and she would have followed him.

She would have to work on that...at some point.

There was a press release about Hans's death. From the Riksdag's letter, it appeared that there would be a private service for the man, and a public memorial would take place next week. If the situation was different, and her safety wasn't in question, she would have flown to Sweden in order to pay respects to the man and his family. It was the least she could have done, though they weren't exactly what she called allies.

The man, though he had impeded her company's progress, hadn't deserved to die—and certainly not as he had.

She emailed her personal assistant, telling him to send flowers.

Near the bottom of her monstrous inbox, she nearly missed it, but there was an email from Daniel. It didn't have a subject line.

Thank goodness, you're all right, she thought. *At least I can put some of my fears to rest.*

She clicked it open.

A video started to play.

It was all over the place and she could hear voices yelling in English, but the sound was garbled as though someone had a hand over the phone's mic.

Her brother's face flashed on the screen. His dark eyes were filled with terror. He was wearing his business suit. The phone fell, scanning over carpet, carpet that matched that found in their offices in Washington, DC. The screen went black.

Daniel yelled. "What in the hell are you doing? Why are you arresting me?"

"Put your hands behind your back!" a man ordered.

"Where's your warrant?" Daniel called.

The camera jerked, and a man's black wing tip shoes came into the screen. The view shifted again like someone had kicked his phone out of his hand. As the phone skidded over the floor, the video blurry, a face came into view. Standing over the phone, his face stoic and emotionless, was Jarrod.

Chapter Thirteen

She was numb. Though she should be angry, hurt or confused, she felt nothing. Or maybe it was just that she felt everything all at once. Maybe it was shock.

Yes, shock.

Or maybe she was dreaming. There's no way that could have been Jarrod standing over her brother during his arrest. Jarrod wouldn't—no, *couldn't*—have kept a secret like this from her for so long.

Maybe he had a twin brother. He'd said something about his brothers. But as she thought it, she knew she was lying to herself.

Though the mere thought sickened her, she replayed the video. This time, as she watched, tears streamed down her face, dripping onto her chest as if they could somehow mend her shattered heart. If only it was that easy.

She paused the video and zoomed in on Jarrod's face. There was no mistaking him. There were the blue eyes that only last night had been fixed to her face, his hands that had traced the curves of her body, and the lips that had promised her solace from the storm of her life.

Jarrod had lied to her.

He had betrayed her.

And the entire time he had told her that he was there to protect her, to keep her safe.

She had wanted to give herself to him, this man… this *liar*.

The door to the kitchen opened, and he and his sister walked out. She wanted to scream, to purge all of her anger. Instead, she stared at him and said nothing.

What could she say? There were no words that would fix what he had done or repair her broken trust.

He took one look at her and stopped. Zoey was saying something and seemed unaware that anything was wrong with her brother and the way he was looking at Mindy.

"What happened?" he asked, the words barely above a whisper.

She wanted to take her phone and shove it in his face and make him watch the despicable video. But it would do nothing except give him more time to come up with some excuse.

She would not allow it.

"Where's Daniel?" she asked, sounding far calmer than she felt.

"I don't—" he started.

"Don't you *dare* lie to me." Her words were laced with rage.

He looked over at Zoey as if she could supply him with the answers.

"Answer me, Jarrod."

He glanced back at her, and there was a look of despair in his eyes. She didn't care how he felt. He *should* be sorry. Hell, he should've been *far* more than sorry. He should've lain at her feet, begging for mercy, and instead he had the audacity to try to continue lying to her. She could never forgive him for what he had done to her, for what he was doing to her now.

What a fool she had been.

Then again, perhaps she was foolish only for trusting him. People were forced to trust one another sometimes. Her only mistake was trusting the wrong one.

"I'm so sorry, Mindy." Jarrod moved toward her, but as he advanced, she stood up and backed away.

"Stay where you are. I want you nowhere near me," she said, bitterness dripping through her words.

"I didn't have a choice…" Jarrod said.

Zoey looked between them and left the room without a word. Her exodus made Mindy wonder if she knew about Jarrod's betrayal. The sting from his actions worsened.

"Who told you?" Jarrod leaned against the couch as though it was the only thing keeping him from falling.

The simple action only angered her further. How dare he be so upset. This was his fault. This was all his doing, yet he seemed almost as shattered and hurt by the revelation as she was.

"Daniel sent me a video while he was being arrested. It was taken during his arrest. You were in the background." She paused. "Don't bother lying to me any longer. I now know exactly who you are—you're my enemy."

Jarrod sat heavily on the arm of the couch. "Mindy, please don't think that. I promise I never wanted you to get hurt. I only wanted to help you. I wanted to clear your name." He paused. "I never wanted Daniel to die."

Holy crap.

What was he talking about? She sat on the fireplace hearth, folding her knees to her chest.

Daniel is dead.

She dropped her head to her knees as she realized that she had forgotten how to breathe.

Daniel was her lifeline. He was her everything. He was the only family she had left.

Except Anya.

And what about Anya?

Who would care for her now, now that he was *dead*? The word rattled through her like a cascade of marbles falling through a steel grate.

Breathe in.

The oxygen tore at her air-stricken lungs, making them burn, but the pain was nothing compared to the agony of this new revelation.

Jarrod had a role not only in her brother's arrest but also in his death. It was too much to bear.

How could Jarrod even dare to look her in the eyes this entire time?

Once again, she found herself filled with questions, and she had no idea where to begin in order to get the answers she needed.

Moreover, she wasn't sure that she could handle

more bad news. One more heartbreak and she would likely meet her own death, as well.

There was a tickle upon her cheek, and she realized that she was crying. She bit her cheek, hoping to stanch her tears. Jarrod had no right to see her at her weakest. He didn't deserve to share in any of her emotions. He deserved to go straight to hell.

She wiped the tears from her face. The most important question she could think of slipped from her lips. "Why?"

"I didn't want him to die because—"

"No," she said, trying to read the truth or a lie in his face. "Why did you kill him?"

"My God, no..." Jarrod stammered. "I didn't... I didn't kill your brother."

He couldn't expect her to believe him. Not after what she'd just seen. "Don't lie to me, Jarrod. At least treat me with some amount of respect after everything you've done."

He shrank in the seat. "Mindy, I think you have this all wrong. I didn't kill your brother. I don't wish you any ill will. And I know you probably don't think you can trust me right now, but I swear to you that I'm on your side."

She didn't know exactly what he meant when he said he was on her side, and right now she didn't even want to ask. No doubt, he would simply feed her some other rehearsed line.

"I know nothing about you. You and your supposed family, you all may be putting me on." She checked the tears that once again threatened to fall. "I want... No,

I *have* to get out of here." She stood up and walked to the window, turning her back on him to hide another wave of tears.

She couldn't be weak, not now, not when she was so vulnerable.

"Mindy, no." Jarrod moved closer, stopping beside her. "You don't have to leave. At least let me explain myself about what is going on. Then, if you like, you can go. I will even drive you to the airport and get you a private jet home. I swear." There was a softness to his voice that made her want to fall into his arms even though he was her enemy. She just needed someone she could trust implicitly. Someone who would hold her right now and tell her that everything was going to be okay.

But she couldn't fall into the trap that was Jarrod Martin.

"If you didn't kill my brother, then who did?"

"Your brother's death was an unfortunate accident." Jarrod sighed. "We were questioning him and my colleague misread the situation. He thought your brother was holding a weapon and he was forced to act."

"Forced to act?" she repeated, chuckling at the macabre absurdity of his words. "First, who are you really? Is everything you've told me before now been a lie? Is your name even Jarrod?"

"My name really is Jarrod. And all the feelings that I've had for you are real. I meant everything I said to you."

"You just omitted some key details." She turned to

face him, new rage filling her. "You can't possibly believe you're worthy of my trust."

She could see her words strike a nerve.

"I... I know," he said, sounding as broken as she felt. "I hate myself for what I have been forced to keep from you. When I took this job, I thought I could keep my feelings for you at bay. But you're unlike anyone I've ever had to work with before."

She couldn't listen to his words. If she did, they had the power to break her heart. "*Work with?* Doing what?"

He hesitated for a moment, as though trying to decide whether to tell her the truth. She glared at him and his reticence seemed to wither away.

"My family and I are also business owners, but our business is slightly different from yours. We own and manage a company called STEALTH. We're independent military contractors, and—"

"You are *mercenaries*?" What did mercenaries have to do with her brother?

What had Daniel been doing?

"We're not mercenaries, we're contractors—an entirely different thing."

"Do you kill people in the name of the United States government?" she asked, trying to make sense of what he was telling her.

"On occasion, but that is rarely our mission."

"Okay, you are only mercenaries *on occasion*. Please tell me how that isn't being a mercenary?"

"That isn't all that we do. Like with your brother."

"And yet he ended up dead, strange." Her anger flared.

"In your brother's case, I was there working as a hired contractor, which included interrogating him for the CIA. My background makes me what some would call an interrogation specialist."

"The CIA?" She paused, at a loss. "Why would the CIA want to interrogate Daniel?"

"They had reason to believe he was selling state secrets to foreign governments."

"You thought my brother was a *spy*?" She choked on the word.

He didn't say anything.

A sickening realization welled within her. "Do you think I'm a spy, as well? Is that why you brought me here?" She swallowed back the lump that formed in her throat. "Did you set the whole thing up with Hans? Did you manipulate me into thinking that you were my friend?"

"I am your friend. I am your ally. And no, I didn't have anything to do with Hans's death." He paused. "I have my people within the agencies looking into the attack. The biggest break we have had so far was what Zoey just told me about linking the nerve gas to North Korea."

She was so confused. He still hadn't told her whether she was under investigation by the CIA. And somehow they had ties to North Korea? What had happened to her almost-boring life?

"What does all of this have to do with me and my family?" She stopped for a moment. "Was Daniel selling secrets to North Korea?" The implications nearly brought her to her knees.

Daniel wouldn't do this kind of thing. He'd only been the head of the company for a year now. He couldn't have gotten himself in this much trouble so quickly—or could he? What had Daniel been doing behind her back?

The thought of her brother and Jarrod betraying her... She really had no one.

If only she could reach out to Daniel and ask him what he had done. And why.

How could he have gone against the family when he had a child who depended on him?

She reminded herself to breathe. This was it. She was going to have a full-blown panic attack.

There was a deep pain in her chest, and she could swear that her arms were numb.

Her vision tunneled and blurred.

Then her world went black.

Chapter Fourteen

"So, you finally had to tell her?" Zoey said with a pitying look on her face as she rushed into the room, no doubt flushed out of hiding by the sound of Mindy hitting the ground.

He knelt beside Mindy and pushed her hair back from her face. There was a thin sheen of sweat on her forehead and her pulse was rapid, but he was sure she was going to be okay. Or at least that she would wake up.

"And I'm guessing, based on the state of your girlfriend, that it didn't go quite as well as you were hoping?" Zoey continued.

Mindy started to blink, but she didn't seem to be focusing on anything in particular as she struggled to regain her bearings.

"Be quiet, Zoey," he said, lifting Mindy into his arms with an *oomph*. "I don't need your judgment right now."

Mindy rolled into him, her head against his neck. "You're going to be all right. I've got you," he cooed.

Mindy answered with a weak nod.

"I heard you telling her about STEALTH. Do you really think that was your place?" Zoey continued on her rampage.

He stared daggers at his sister. "You told me to tell her whatever I thought was necessary. It was god-damned necessary that she knew that I'm on her side... that I didn't want her or her brother to get hurt."

"And yet here we are." Zoey motioned toward Mindy. "Don't you think you should leave the poor woman alone? Let someone else handle this investigation?"

Damn Zoey for putting him on the spot. And damn her for being right. Damn it all.

"Do you want to take this over? Were you in the room with Daniel?" He seethed. "I know you think you have all the answers. I know you think you're smarter than me, but until you know everything, and until you feel what I'm feeling, just be quiet and get out of my way." He pushed past her as he made his way down the hall and to the stairwell. He carried Mindy up the stairs, nearly running away from his sister.

As he made it to the upstairs hall, Anya came walking out of her room. She was rubbing her eyes. Before she had the chance to see him and the state her aunt was in, he ducked into the nearest bedroom—his own.

He closed the door quietly behind them with his foot. Hopefully, Mindy wouldn't be furious to find herself in his room. She was already having a hard enough time trying to work through everything. It was really no wonder that she had fainted.

There was the sound of Anya humming in the hallway. She sounded sleepy and she grew louder as she came near his door. She stopped and walked into the bathroom that was nearest them. From the sound of her singing, he could tell she hadn't bothered to close the bathroom door as she went to her business.

Mindy was growing heavy in his arms. His biceps burned as he held her, unsure of whether to take her to her own bed or simply put her down in his bed and hope for the best. So far, hoping for the best had been biting him in the ass.

His shoulders ached.

He gently laid her on his bed. It would be easier to explain to her than to Anya. He could almost imagine Anya and her questions now. No doubt there would be questions about their friendship.

He pulled a blanket over Mindy and tucked it gently under her arms before making his way out and into the hallway. Anya was just walking out of the bathroom.

"Good morning, sweetheart," he said, trying to sound like his world and his hopes for the future weren't crashing down around him. "Did you sleep well?"

"Uh-huh," Anya said, looking up at him with her big sleepy eyes.

There was the sound of footsteps ascending the staircase, and Zoey made her way onto the landing. Taking one look at them, she smiled. "Hiya, big girl, are you hungry?" She stuck out her hand. "How about I take you downstairs and rustle us up something to eat while Jarrod gets ready for the day."

"I want Anta," Anya said, looking around.

"She's taking a nap, sweetheart," Zoey said, moving closer and taking the little girl's hand. "Let's let her sleep a bit more before we wake her up. After your big, long flight last night, I bet she's tired. Do you want to tell me about your plane ride? Did you have fun?" She pulled the little girl up into her arms as she started to make their way toward the stairs. She looked back at Jarrod and mouthed the words *I'm sorry.*

The only thing his sister had to be sorry about was that she hadn't stopped them from getting into this predicament. Yet, even if she had spoken out against him taking this job, he was sure he wouldn't have listened. When it came to his feelings and how he acted upon them, he would never be more than a fool.

He walked into the bathroom, grabbed a washcloth and wet it. Mindy was still on the bed and her eyes were closed. Part of him wondered if she had woken while he had been in the hall and was now faking being unconscious just so she didn't have to face him.

He wouldn't have blamed her.

If only she understood he was simply doing his job, and he had only brought her here to keep her safe. He had really been acting out of what he had believed were his best intentions—though, looking back, part of the reason he had wanted to keep her safe and out of harm's reach was because he was falling for her.

And look where those damn feelings had landed them.

He sat beside her on the bed and ran the cool cloth over her brow. She stirred a bit at the chill, but her eyes remained closed.

She wasn't faking it, but she clearly wasn't in a damned hurry to come back to him.

There was the buzz of her phone from her pocket.

It buzzed again.

He had been behind Zoey giving her the phone and getting her access to work, but he was surprised that people were already trying to get ahold of her. He looked down at his watch. Then again, they were on Eastern Time. Though it was early morning in Montana, it was late morning there. And she probably hadn't told anyone where she had gone. At least, he hoped she hadn't.

His family's secret popped into his mind. If Mindy had notified someone that she was here, and revealed who she was with, it would put his entire family at risk of being found by the Gray Wolves. If the organization heard even a whisper of where they might be, they would descend upon them.

It was all his fault.

If only he could go back in time and turn down this job. If only he could have faced Trish's loss and the family's grief instead of running and hiding himself behind the emotional walls of his work, it would have saved them all a great deal of heartache.

Then again, he would have never met Mindy.

Even if things weren't turning out as he had hoped, at least they'd had one wonderful night together. Though they hadn't completely given themselves to one another, it was still one of those nights that he would hold on to forever. Sometimes the preamble to making love was even more exhilarating than the act itself. If they had gone all the way, and if it was impossibly better than the moments they had shared, he would probably have died from ecstasy.

Her phone buzzed again, sounding even more insistent.

Reaching down, and careful not to invade her privacy, he pulled the phone from the pocket of her sweater.

There, on the screen, was the name Arthur.

His first thoughts were of the rookie that had taken Daniel down. He laughed at his reaction. Agent Arthur wasn't actively pursuing this lead. And, if he was, Jarrod's handlers at the CIA would have told him.

And he doubted that Agent Arthur was the kind who would go behind his superior's backs, at least not this early in his career. Something like that, disobeying orders, would get him sent straight back to the civilian world.

Still, he couldn't shake his illogical fear.

What if Mindy had been playing him instead of the other way around? What if she had known about Daniel's death the entire time and had just been using him so that she could come here and infiltrate his family for the Gray Wolves? What if she was here to kill him and his family?

What if he had set a Wolf loose in their home?

He stood up from the bed as he stuffed Mindy's new phone into his pocket.

Mindy moaned from the bed and her eyes fluttered open.

He wasn't sure what to do. There she was, lying in

front of him, her pink lips parted as though she was waiting for his kiss.

For the first time, he realized that this confusion, this complete loss of bearings, must be exactly what she was feeling, as well. That is, if she wasn't a spy for the Gray Wolves.

She moaned again, and this time it carried the soft hoarseness of one who had just made love. The sound pierced the feeble shell he had been trying to build around himself.

There was no way she could have faked this. She had been taken to her knees by his revelation.

He couldn't project his guilt onto her. No. He was the one who had made mistakes.

He knew he was trying to rationalize, but he couldn't have told her who he was before or his role in her brother's death. No. He had done what he had to do. Being covert was as much a part of his job as meetings with dignitaries and the like was a part of hers.

His anger surprised him. He tried to stanch it, but the more he thought of his justifications, the angrier he became. It wasn't just anger with her, but rather the entire situation.

Mindy opened her eyes. He knelt down. "Why don't you stay here and rest. I'll come up and check on you in a little bit. In the meantime, I'm going to go and make sure that Anya has breakfast."

Mindy moved to argue, but as she sat up, she was taken with what he assumed was another feeling of faintness.

"Just rest. When you feel better, we can talk," he said, trying to keep his tone neutral.

She nodded and laid her head back on his pillow.

As he closed the door behind him, he couldn't help feeling thankful that for once a woman in his life hadn't argued with him.

He sat down at the top of the stairs, not ready to face his sister. Taking out Mindy's phone, he opened it up using a password he had noticed her using. Luckily, he got it right on his first try.

On the home screen were the icons for her email as well as the notification that she had missed a call. He needed to be careful not to leave any tracks of his snooping. If she found out, there was absolutely no way he would ever get back into her good graces. As it was, there was only a slight chance of reconciliation between them.

Opening up the phone icon, he scrolled through her call log.

Picking through the numbers, he tried to see if he recognized any, but none stood out. He turned to his own phone and looked up Agent Arthur's cell. Out of curiosity and a desperate hope he was wrong, he did a search for the number. Nothing came up.

He felt a bit of relief in finding out that his fears about her double-crossing him were completely unfounded, but there was still something nagging him that he couldn't quite put his finger on.

Mindy hadn't seemed like the type who would play him, at least not intentionally.

On the heels of that thought was the realization that he was being a hypocrite.

Even if she was working against him, how could he begrudge her—what if she was only doing her job?

No. She wasn't working against him.

He just needed to make things right between them, and make her understand his actions. Then, perhaps, they could go back to where they once were, lying in each other's arms and whispering late into the night. She could be his and he could be hers. They could belong to one another forever.

And maybe that was nothing more than a pipe dream, and he had screwed up the only future he had ever truly hoped for.

He clicked on her photo album in the cloud, hoping to see a picture of her smiling, anything that could help ease the pain that was filling his heart.

There were dozens of pictures of her and Anya playing in Central Park, one of them on the boardwalk on the Jersey Shore, and another where she was laughing and Anya's face was filled with mischief. In every photo, she and Anya looked sublimely happy. It was almost as if the two of them were only truly happy when they were together.

Which made him wonder… If things did go his way, and they reconciled, would there be any room for him in their little club of two?

From the top of the stairs, he could make out the sweet trills of Anya's voice drifting up to him from the kitchen. The sound was broken by the ting of a metal spoon on a cereal bowl and the echoes of his sister's laugh.

He could see how easy it was to love a girl like

Anya. She was the epitome of innocent sweetness. There were no questions about the little girl's thoughts or feelings—she just put them out there without fear of consequence or reprimand.

If adults were the same, life would be easier in so many ways.

He closed his eyes and tried to envision a future with Anya and Mindy. He could almost see them now, sitting downstairs with his family eating breakfast. When they were together, really together, it would become his mission to make a full spread—ham, eggs, potatoes, toast, waffles, pancakes, sausage, bacon and even beans for his brothers Chad and Trevor, who could eat everything in sight. Trevor had always loved when they'd spent time in England and had the chance to gorge themselves on the full fry-ups.

He smiled at the thought of them all together.

Again, the ache for Trish returned.

He couldn't help but wonder if the grief that came with her loss would ever go away.

Anya laughed, the sound bright and cheerful.

What would happen to her when she learned of her father's death? Would she feel the same way he did about Trish? Would his absence from her life be a constant sting, or was Anya still young enough that his loss wouldn't be as hard to deal with as it would have been if the girl was older?

The ache in his chest intensified.

If only he had stopped Agent Arthur from hurting the man. If only he could have seen what was to come.

If only, if only… He had to stop. He had to take control of the situation. It was his only choice. He couldn't stand by and hope time would dull the pain and anguish caused by his mistakes. He had to move forward and do everything in his power to make things right.

Renewed, he stood up and started to walk down the stairs.

Mindy's phone rang in his hand once more.

Again the caller was "Arthur," and the familiar twinge of angst filled him. He ignored the call and sent it to voice mail.

He started to close the photo app, planning to cover his tracks, but as he did, the photo album he'd been looking at flipped to another. There, standing at what looked like a company luncheon, complete with a spread of firearm prototypes of all sizes and colors, was Mindy. Standing behind her, and to her left, was none other than Agent Arthur.

So much for hope, and so much for "if only." Now he was left with one choice alone: to kill or be killed.

Chapter Fifteen

The door to Jarrod's room slammed open, hitting the wall behind it so hard that the door handle stuck in the drywall. "Are you kidding me?" Jarrod said, his voice somewhere between a terrifying yell and a sobering accusation.

Mindy tried to sit up in bed, but as she moved, her head throbbed. "What? What is it?" As she looked up at him, rage and hurt in his eyes, she was brought back to what had happened between them.

"You've been lying to me," he said, pain flecking his voice.

She swung her legs over the edge of the bed, trying to force her body to submit to her will and simply regain her equilibrium. "I don't know why in the hell you're pissed off at me, when I'm the one who has every right to be angry here."

"I admit that I screwed up." He took a long breath as though he was trying to control his temper. "I kept the truth of who I was from you, but I did so for both of our benefits. But how dare you judge me when you're keeping your own secrets from me."

She was at a loss. "What are you talking about, Jarrod?"

He thrust her phone at her. "Why didn't you tell me that you've been working with Agent Arthur?"

She had no idea what he was talking about. "Agent Arthur?"

He clicked on the screen, using a password that she hadn't given him yet he seemed to somehow know. She thought about asking why he thought it was okay to steal her password and invade her privacy, but they were well past that point. Now, as far as she could tell, they were both at a place of all or nothing.

If she hadn't fainted, she had no doubt that he would have had her ass on a plane at that very moment.

"Who is this?" he asked, pulling up a picture of the company's last summit meeting.

There was a large group of people in the photo. When the photo had been taken they were in the middle of reviewing next year's weapon prototypes. They were going to unveil a new line of long-range military-grade rifles.

Her engineers had put a great deal of time and effort in the design. In fact, it was the line they had intended on manufacturing in Sweden.

The thought made her stomach clench as she thought of Hans and the Riksdag. And Daniel.

"Who?" she asked, looking at the many faces of people standing around her in the photo.

He pointed at a tall and muscular man standing behind her in the picture.

"That guy?" she said with a chuckle. "Oh, you are

being ridiculous if you are worried about him. That's one of my assistants, Arthur McDuffy."

Jarrod made a strange wheezing sound as he dropped her phone onto the bed beside her. "Did Daniel know him?"

"They might have seen each other, but rarely. Why?"

Jarrod shook his head, saying nothing as he stared down at his toes.

"Now, was there a reason you thought it was okay to go through my things?" She shut off the screen on her phone and slid it under her leg. "If you want, I can go find my purse and let you look into that, as well. Or, you could just ask me about whatever it is that you think I'm guilty of."

He stared vacantly at the place where she had tucked the phone beneath her leg.

"I bet this is just your way of taking the pressure off you. Something you learned in the CIA? You know, the old bait and switch thing? Make me look guilty of some nonsense thing in order to make me think that you aren't the worst kind of man on earth?" As she spoke, anger roiled through her, washing away any remnants of the feebleness she had been feeling. "Well, guess what? You are the one who is in the wrong here. I've done nothing."

She stared at him waiting for a response. He didn't move.

"You asked me to listen to your side of the story, to hear why you did what you did. I get that you didn't think you had a choice, but you know what, Jarrod? I don't forgive you. You lied to me. You played Anya and me for fools. And no matter what comes, or what risks are waiting for us, I want to go back home."

He jerked. "You can't."

"Why? You want me to stay here?" she rebuked, knowing that she was calling him deeper into the fight. She gave a dry, angry chuckle. "You've done nothing but manipulate me. Enough is enough, Jarrod."

"I know you aren't going to listen to me, but I wish you would." He paused. "I didn't bring you here to manipulate you. I just wanted to help."

"You keep telling yourself that," she said, crossing her arms over her chest and protecting what little there was left of her heart.

"You have every right to be angry," he said. When she didn't respond, he continued. "How long have you known McDuffy?" He finally looked her in the eye.

She shrugged. "You aren't about to change the subject on me."

"Just answer me." He wasn't angry, just insistent, which made her come to a screeching halt.

What was he getting at by going after Arthur? And what did it matter?

"I don't know." She thought for a moment. "I guess he's been working for me for about the last six months."

Jarrod turned away from her and slowly paced around the room. "How did he get hired?" Before she could answer, he continued, "Did you run any sort of background check on the man?"

"That kind of thing is my HR team's job, but I'm sure they were done." She paused. "Do you think he had something to do with the nerve agent attack, or something to do with Daniel?"

He snorted like he knew something that she didn't. Her anger rose to the surface once again.

"Look, Jarrod, if we are going to get along...and if you want me to forgive you for lying to me, then you and I are going to have to get something straight. You have to tell me the truth. We have to be honest with one another. Or else, what is the point? I won't be able to trust you and you won't be able to trust me."

As it was, even if he was honest with her, she wasn't sure if she could ever really trust him again. He had broken her heart into a million pieces. Her trust was completely shattered.

"Let's just say that I know Arthur."

She could have sworn he said something under his breath that she couldn't quite hear.

She sighed. He still wasn't telling her anything. She should have seen him for the interrogation specialist he was. "Arthur formerly worked for my father. He was one of several of his assistants. How do you know him, Jarrod?"

She could have sworn Jarrod's face paled.

"Did he have access to any private information?" he asked.

"Not my files." She nibbled at the corner of her cheek. "At least I don't think so."

"And what about your father's?" he pressed.

She shrugged. "I don't know. It was rare that my father even let my brother and me into his office, let alone have any kind of dealings with the day-to-day running of the company."

"And yet you and your brother were left with the company after your father's death?"

He sounded so judgmental. What was he trying to insinuate?

"Look, I've done the very best I could, given the circumstances of my father's death. I have worked hard to understand and run the company the way he would have wanted." She stood up, readying herself for another battle with the man with whom she had previously shared her bed.

"I'm sorry," he said, taking her hands in his.

She wanted to pull away, but she yearned to feel his touch once again. When he had been with her on the plane, his touch had reawakened a part of her that she had given up hope on.

If he truly didn't have anything to do with her brother's death, and had been merely a bystander as he claimed, then perhaps there was room in her heart for forgiveness.

She may have caught him in a lie, but he didn't have to tell her about his investigation. In divulging the truth to her, he had opened himself up to far-reaching consequences. If the CIA found out that he had acted against their best interest, his job—and maybe even his life—would be in jeopardy.

Not for the first time, she was reminded that he had put his life on the line for her.

But it didn't negate the fact that he'd kept the truth of her brother's death from her.

Still, she didn't pull away from his touch.

"Now, are you going to answer me, Jarrod Martin, or do I need to sit you down on this bed and interrogate you as you have interrogated me?"

His lips formed a smile, like he found what she was saying to be some kind of turn-on instead of the castigation it was intended to be. She considered correcting him, but oh, that smile. She loved that smile.

"Ask away." He let go of her hands and sat down upon the bed.

"How did my brother die?"

"Do you really want to know?" he asked, giving her a look of pity.

"I just need to know if he suffered." The lump returned in her throat.

"No, don't worry, it was quick," Jarrod said, taking hold of her fingers and giving them a reassuring and apologetic squeeze. "During my questioning, the rookie agent, Agent Arthur was there."

"My Arthur?" she asked, some of the faintness she had been feeling threatening to return.

"The one and only." Jarrod nodded. "Your brother moved for something in his pocket and pulled out a pen. Agent Arthur mistook it for a weapon and shot him in the chest. At least that was how it seemed at the time. Now I have to assume he intended to kill him all along."

"What happened to Arthur?" she asked, moving to sit back down on the bed beside Jarrod.

"I'm sure his actions are being investigated by the CIA. Though spooks have a different set of standards, shooting someone in the middle of interrogation isn't something they are going to ignore."

"And you think Arthur was out to murder my brother?" Her words came out as a whisper, like they were some kind of secret that she could barely utter.

"Until I saw that photo, the thought hadn't crossed my mind. But now I'm sure that was his intention." Jarrod reached up and pushed a loose hair behind her ear. "Are you feeling any better?"

She had been until now. Just when she thought her world couldn't be more in turmoil, there was another twist.

"Do you think it was Arthur who was selling our company's secrets to North Korea?"

Jarrod nodded. "Everything seems to be pointing that way. My best guess is that he was compromised by North Korean agents when he worked for your dad. They probably paid him well for his services."

She leaned into him, letting him wrap his arm around her. "Did you try and save my brother?"

He sighed. "There wasn't time. I should have seen Arthur going for his gun, but I missed it. I'm so sorry, babe."

She felt herself soften as he called her by the pet name. Though she was deeply saddened by the loss of Daniel and the lies that were unfolding around them, she didn't have it in her to completely turn Jarrod out. She was angry and hurt, but without him at her side she was left with no one. As it was, she was already more alone than she had ever been. She needed him. And gauging from his rapid heartbeat as she drew closer, she could tell that he needed her, too.

Right now, they were each other's rocks, and the world around them was their hard place.

Chapter Sixteen

Jarrod was at a loss. Although he had finally gotten a break in the case, he was unsure of what to do. If Agent Arthur truly was a double agent for the North Korean government and the CIA, he would be a very dangerous suspect to pursue.

And if he did go after Arthur, he couldn't leave Mindy and Anya in his sister's care. Not when she was here alone. They would be vulnerable to attack. If the Gray Wolves found them, there would be nothing to stop them without him here. Sure, they were tough women…and his sister was one heck of a shot, but he wasn't willing to take the risk.

He also couldn't take Mindy and Anya with him.

What would happen if the North Koreans found out that their agent and source had been revealed? He couldn't know for sure if they would simply let Arthur fall under the hatchet or if they would stop at nothing to prevent him from being taken out. No doubt, if they thought that he and Mindy were the only ones who bore witness to the truth, they would come after them in order to protect their investment.

Jarrod couldn't be certain that Arthur truly belonged to the North Koreans. He would have gone through rigorous background checks and training to become a CIA agent, not to mention his work as an undercover agent within Mindy's company. So, either Jarrod was missing something, or Arthur and his people had someone working for them within the agency.

Of the two, he had a feeling it was the latter.

Double agents, though difficult to identify and pin down, weren't hard to come by. They were much like police officers in the sense that in order to be a good police officer one must also have the mind-set of a great criminal. Only an uncorrupted moral compass set the two apart.

"What are we going to do, Jarrod?" Mindy asked, and as she spoke her body vibrated against his, filling him with a strange sensation of never wanting to be apart from her again.

Giving in to that desire, to keep her at his side always, would only put her in more danger than he already had. And yet, here he was, the one she depended on for answers, and he only had more questions.

"I could go to my people at the CIA, but I'm worried that they may have a leak." He took his phone out from his pocket and sent a text off to Zoey. The sooner she could get to work, the better. They were already behind the eight ball when it came to this investigation. And now, with his concerns about a leak in the agency, STEALTH was the only group he could trust.

Zoey's code name popped up on the screen as she pressed for more information. As quickly as he could, he told her exactly what they knew. She was their greatest weapon when it came to finding out secrets.

"I'll strip him of all of his access. I have some great people on my staff, especially in IT." She smiled up at him. "Your sister isn't the only one with a corner on the hacker market."

He didn't doubt that for a second, but if her people were as good as she thought they were, how in the hell did they miss Arthur stealing secrets in the first place? Still, they could be put to work in the meantime.

"Why don't you call your people. Have them start going through Arthur's computer. See if they can dig up anything that would indicate that he is, in fact, the man behind this."

"Okay," she said, but she didn't move from his arms, almost as if she was as reluctant to pull away from him as he was to let her go.

"I'll have Zoey work on our side. She can dig around. See what she comes up with." As he spoke, he wasn't really thinking about anything other than how she smelled of fresh sheets and shampoo.

He didn't recall her taking a shower since they had gotten to the house, but at some point, she must have. He took a deep breath, pulling the scent of her soap deep into his lungs.

"You smell good," he said as lust stirred in his body.

Though he was well aware that this wasn't the time, he couldn't help himself. He wanted her. More, he wanted to sweep her up into his arms and carry her away from all the stress filling their lives. He wanted to be her hero. He wanted to be her lover...until the end of time.

Leaning closer as she looked up at him, their eyes met. From the way she gazed at him, he could see that she felt the same confusion, the same needs and the same wants.

He grazed his lips over hers, soft and questioning, making sure that he wasn't misreading her.

She moved into him, reaching up and taking hold of his hair with her hand, pulling his lips hard against hers.

Damn, it felt good.

He leaned back slightly as he thought of everything he had just told her. "I'm sorry, Mindy. About your brother and all the deception."

Her lips moved into a smile as they brushed against his. "Shut up, Jarrod Martin. Just shut up and make love to me."

There was no misreading that.

She must have needed a respite from the confusion as much as he did. And though he questioned whether or not this was a good idea, his body and its desires held precedence over the logical part of his mind—sometimes a man needed to follow his heart.

She pressed him down onto the bed and straddled him. He took hold of her hips as she moved her body over his, reminding him exactly what part of his body was in charge at the moment.

"Mmm," she moaned, rocking back against him.

She was wearing his old Nirvana T-shirt and as she moved, he could make out the subtle curves of her breasts and the hardening of her nipples. Oh, how he wanted to take those little nubs and run them over his lips before popping them in his mouth. He could almost hear her now, moaning his name as he flicked her nipples with his tongue until she was nearly in pain with ecstasy.

She leaned down and he ran his hands up her sides, pulling her lips into his and driving his hips against her so she could feel exactly what it was that she did to him.

Damn, he wanted her.

He kissed her lips and then positioned her head so he could trail his lips down her neck. As he kissed her, her lips found his neck as well and he could feel the subtle graze of her teeth against his skin as though she threatened to devour him. The sensation made him groan with both desire and warning.

"No teeth," he groaned.

"Just like you, Jarrod Martin," she said into the crease of his neck, letting her hot breath brush against his skin where she had just played rough. "I do what I want."

He laughed, and as his body moved, she shifted on him, reminding him exactly who was in control.

He could only love her more for it.

"I hope you realize that I have wanted this, and you, from the first moment I laid eyes on you," he said, pressing himself against the thin fabric of her panties.

"Is that right?" She shifted off him and he reached after her, but she playfully moved out of his reach. "What is it that you want exactly, sir?"

He wasn't sure what game she was playing with

him right now, but he liked it. "Well, ma'am, I want to watch you take off your shirt."

"Oh, yeah, is that right?" She reached down and toyed with the edge of the shirt. "How badly?"

"So badly, that if you don't, I may just have to rip it off you. And that's one of my favorite shirts." He smiled.

"You would be willing to destroy your favorite shirt just to get to me?" she teased.

"That's the least of the things that I would do to make love to you."

"Oh, is that where you think this is leading?" She lifted the edge of the shirt higher, over her belly button, exposing a pair of fresh black lace underwear. They weren't the same kind as before; rather, they hugged her hips like a pair of hands. Exactly where his fingers ached to be.

"I believe it was you who told me to make love to you, ma'am." He grumbled, reaching for her again, but instead of giving in, she moved farther from him on the bed.

"If you are lucky, I just may let you. But you are going to have to play your cards right, *sir.*"

He threw himself back into the pillow, groaning as he ran his hands over his face and tried to regain control over the flood of desire he was feeling.

She brushed her fingertips against his legs and up his thighs. She found the elastic band of his pajama pants and, running her fingers under it, pressed the fabric down his legs and over his feet. He heard the fabric hit the floor beside the bed.

"Do you like it when I play with you?" she asked.

He uncovered his face and looked up at her. "I would like it better if you would take off your shirt before I have to do it for you."

She laughed, the sound high and unmarred by the world outside of his bedroom. Humming a little song like something from a risqué movie, she lifted the edges of her shirt until he could see the bottoms of her breasts. Rubbing her hands over her nipples, she gave him an impish smile. "Is this off enough for you?"

He reached for her, and this time she didn't pull away. "Hardly," he said, his voice gravelly and harsh with want.

He kissed the little space between her breasts. The skin was soft. She arched like she was begging for more than his kiss. Running his lips over her skin, he found the curve of her breast as he moved his other hand under her shirt and thumbed her nipple gently as he moved his face back and ran the scruff of his goatee against the little trail of wetness his kiss had left behind.

Her body stiffened at the sensation of soft and scratchy.

"Yes," she whispered.

Not daring to play nice, he took hold of her hips and moved her back on top of him. He pressed himself against her, only a slip of fabric between them.

It didn't escape him that all he had to do to enter her was press the cloth to the side. But no, he had to take this stolen moment for all it was worth. If this was the only time they made love, he wanted to make it the best she'd ever had.

Pushing up her shirt, she took hold of it, and lifted it over her head, exposing her body to the cool mid-morning air.

Her nipples were the color of cherry drops. Leaning in, he sucked one into his mouth. It tasted almost as sweet as it looked.

Damn, he was one lucky man.

She shifted against him, but he didn't play along. Instead, he moved his hand down her belly and moved her panties to the side. Ever so gently, he thumbed her as he had thumbed her nipple. Her body was taken with a gentle but sharp spasm as he found and worked her.

"Mmm," she said, her head leaning back as he stroked her. "Yes, Jarrod, yes." Her words were like satin, smooth and silky, giving away the pleasure she must have been feeling beneath his touch.

"I'm yours, my lady. This day, this time, is for your pleasure." He slipped his fingers inside of her as his thumb continue to circle.

She moaned, and the sound made her shudder against his fingers. If he had his way, it wouldn't take long to satisfy her...the first time. And once she found release, he would enter her and hopefully make her find the edge once again.

Gently, and without stopping, he flipped her over so that she lay open for him. For a brief moment, he paused and stripped her panties from her so that he could have complete access to her naked body.

He sat there, gazing at her. He loved the subtle

curves of her waist and that place where they met the luscious roundness of her hips. She really was a thing of beauty.

Moving between her legs, his mouth found where his thumb had been. She tasted even sweeter than her nipples had. In fact, he could think of nothing more delicious. It was as if they were made for one another— each the other's nectar and ambrosia.

She moved beneath him, taking his head in her hands and moving him exactly where and to the speed she liked.

"Yes, Jarrod, yes..." she moaned quietly.

Just when he thought he couldn't find anything hotter, she had to go and moan his name like that.

Her breath caught, and he could feel her body shift and sway under his mouth.

She stiffened as her body pulsed with his touch as she found the place he had been leading her.

He kissed away her wetness and she pulled him up to her lips. There was something kinky and hotter than hell in the way she kissed him, and it made him love her more. It was a special woman who wanted to share in everything.

Releasing him from their kiss, he moved down her body and rested his head on her heart. For a moment, he lay there, listening to her heart and the rhythm that told him how he had made her feel. He had done it, brought her to this place of joy and relaxation.

"You can hardly think we're done," she said, her voice swathed in the remnants of euphoria. "One cannot have true pleasure without the other."

He grew impossibly harder at the promise laced in her words.

"That's where we disagree," he teased. "Nothing pleases me more than watching you turn to putty under my touch."

She giggled and he looked up from her chest. "Is that what I am to you?"

He laughed. "And what am I to you?"

She opened her mouth to speak, but he could see a storm cloud roll into her eyes, and she closed her mouth as though she were second-guessing herself.

"Nothing?" he teased, hoping that she would open up to him.

"If I'm putty," she said, her impish smile returning, "then you are the form that I shape myself upon." She sat up, moving atop him. She dipped him slowly into her.

If he had his way, this is how he would be taken from this world...spending the day in bed with the woman he loved and buried deep within her.

No matter what happened in their future, he would be forever thankful that, for now, they were one.

Chapter Seventeen

By the time she was dressed and ready to go downstairs it was approaching evening. The smell of hot food had drifted up from the kitchen and she realized she was starving.

As they made their way into the dining room, Zoey gave them a knowing and highly entertained grin. Anya was sitting in a booster seat beside her and there was a swath of half-colored pages that had been ripped from a coloring book spread around the table.

"You guys have a nice day?" Zoey's smile widened. "I hope you got everything sorted."

Jarrod cleared his throat as a rush of embarrassment burned through Mindy. She hadn't thought about the rest of the household. Really, how could she have when she had been gifted hours in the comfort of Jarrod's embrace?

That man certainly knew his way around her body. If she had another chance, perhaps he could show her again all the ways he could make her feel with just his thumb.

Anya turned toward her. "Anta!" she cried, throwing her hands up in the air and dropping her crayon on the dining room floor.

"Hi, little one, did you have fun with Ms. Zoey today?" she asked, moving over to the girl and giving her a quick hug.

"Uh-huh," Anya said, reaching for Mindy's hand with her pudgy fingers.

They were sticky with what Mindy could only assume was peanut butter and jelly, Anya's favorite afternoon snack.

"Thank you, Zoey, for watching her for me." Mindy let go of Anya's hand and, wiping her hand off on her jeans, sat down across the table from her.

"No problem," Zoey said with a nod. "While you guys were *working* I found some things I thought you all might find interesting."

Mindy tried to ignore the feeling of embarrassment that filled her. Just because Zoey assumed she knew what they were up to upstairs, it didn't mean that there was anything to be ashamed of. She and Jarrod were both adults and they both… Well, they both had to know that there wasn't any possibility of a future. No matter how badly she wanted there to be one.

Though she had forgiven him and they had made love, there remained a gap between them. Perhaps it was the fact that he had lied to her, or maybe it was something else, but there was something that was making her hold back from falling completely and utterly in love.

"Anta, we see Dada?" Anya said, reaching for another crayon.

And there it was, the wedge that was driving her and Jarrod apart.

There was nothing she could do to bring them together when a child stood in the world between them. Now that she knew Daniel was dead, she had to focus on Anya. She was the only person the little girl had left. First, Anya had been discarded by her mother, and now, with the death of her father, she was completely alone. If something happened to Mindy, she would have no one.

The world had already taken enough from Anya. Mindy couldn't let her be hurt more.

But she also couldn't keep the truth from the little one about her father's death. She had the right to know that her father was gone. Yet, Mindy couldn't bring herself to utter the words that would undoubtedly break Anya's sweet heart.

"I don't think you are going to see him today," Zoey said, seeing Mindy struggle for words.

"Okay," Anya said.

Relief passed through her. Though she should have been honest with Anya, the truth could wait. There were so many things happening right now, not to mention the fact that Daniel's body hadn't been released to his family. As far as the government was concerned, she had yet to find out about her brother's death.

Sometimes, a reprieve could be found in the shadows of truth.

"You color for a bit, okay?" Zoey said, but Anya barely acknowledged her; instead, she leaned down and started chaotically coloring the picture of a cat. Zoey stood and motioned them to follow her outside.

As they walked out, they noticed a car waiting in the driveway. "Who's that?" Jarrod asked, pointing toward the blue sedan.

"This is your driver," Zoey said, walking them to the car. "He is going to take you to your private jet." She stopped, clearly not planning to elaborate.

"No," Mindy said. "I can't leave Anya."

Zoey sent her an acknowledging smile. "Don't worry about Anya. She and I are going to go over to Dunrovin Ranch. We have family there, including kids that she can play with. We will hole up there until you find Arthur and *neutralize* the situation."

Was she saying that she thought the only solution for Arthur and the spying was to kill him?

Jarrod stopped before they reached the car. "What did you find out about him?"

Zoey glanced over at her brother. "I dug into H&K's records and found—"

"Wait," Mindy said, cutting her off. "How did you gain access to our records?"

Zoey gave a dry laugh. "Did you really think I gave you that phone without a way to keep track of what you did with it?"

So, she had been hacked by the Martins, as well. Mindy sighed. Maybe one day she would no longer be surprised by the family that seemed willing to do anything to get to the answers they needed.

Their family was one that she would have liked to have called her own. Instead, she'd had a globe-trotting brother and a father who had kept them out from underfoot to such an extent that she was only just learning how dangerous his world had been.

"If you could gain access so easily how do we know it was Arthur who stole the data?" Mindy asked.

"Do a lot of people have access to your phone or your personal computer?" Zoey asked, a frown darkening her face.

"No, but—"

"And what about your brother's network? Did anyone have access?" Zoey pressed.

Mindy shook her head. "Daniel didn't have an assistant who had access. Anything that came through his secretary went through separate channels. With Arthur, on the other hand, I thought he could only access certain emails."

"From everything you and my brother have told me, and from what I've been able to piece together, Arthur is our man," Zoey said. "He is definitely up to something at H&K. Now, whether or not that is obtaining and selling military secrets is up for debate, but I have a feeling that we are going to get to the bottom of this soon enough."

Mindy wasn't sure that she had the same level of faith as Zoey, but she also didn't have the same access to data as Jarrod's sister.

Once again, she was thrust into a position where she was being forced to trust this family.

It hadn't even been twenty-four hours since the truth had been supplied to her, and yet there wasn't time to waste rehashing any wrongs. She had granted her forgiveness, but was she ready to trust them?

"Okay," Mindy said, taking a deep breath to alleviate the stress and anxiety that filled her. It did little to help. "But if something happens to me, I want Anya to stay with your family. She doesn't have anyone else. Fake adoption papers, fake whatever you have to, but I don't want her going back to Russia, or falling prey to a broken foster care system. Do I have your word?" Mindy took one more look in through the living room window at the little girl coloring at the dining room table.

"Don't worry. No matter what, I have your daughter under my care. If anyone dares lay a finger on her, I will kill them." Zoey reached up and took hold of Mindy's shoulder. "I will take care of her as if she was my own."

Zoey's words ripped at her. If she'd had the chance, she might have said the same thing to her brother before his death. Instead, he had likely died not knowing what the Fates held in store for the ones he loved.

Once again, she found herself not wishing to follow in her brother's footsteps.

Zoey hadn't whispered a single word to him about her plan. No doubt, she had thought it best if he and Mindy didn't know what was in store for them, but it pissed him off. Once again he was reminded of what it must have felt like for Mindy to be kept in the dark.

He and his brothers and sisters, before Trish's death, had prided themselves on not falling into the trap cre-

182

ated by keeping secrets. They had all vowed that they would not keep things from one another. Yet, here they were, and here he was once again having to confront his sister's desire to lead the family.

Maybe he shouldn't fight her on it anymore.

Then again, there could only be one leader. More than that would lead to chaos.

Maybe the best thing Jarrod could do was to let Zoey take the controls. She could prove herself, or else she could learn exactly how hard it was to keep order within the family, especially with so much happening right now.

This could be her moment to sink or swim.

If she succeeded, then he could step back and finally enjoy living without the constant pressure of leading the family. He could relax and maybe even follow his heart with Mindy.

For once, he wouldn't have to fight with her. If nothing else, that was a win.

"Before we go anywhere, Zoey," he said, "where are you sending us?"

"With how much we've been through lately, and the liability that comes with running tech, I'm only going to tell you this once, and in person." Zoey glanced toward the car that was waiting for them. "I tracked down Arthur. He's holed up in a hotel room in Stockholm."

"What is he doing there?" Mindy asked.

"From what we know about him," Zoey said, "he's probably getting off US soil in case the CIA chooses to crack down on him for his role in your brother's death."

"But why Sweden?" Jarrod asked.

Zoey shrugged. "Your guess is as good as mine."

He couldn't help but wonder if Arthur was deeper into this than even he had imagined. What if he had something to do with the hit on Hans Anders, as well?

Maybe he had intended for Mindy and Jarrod to get caught up and killed in the melee.

On some level it made sense. It seemed more than possible that after killing Daniel, Arthur had decided to go after Jarrod, as well. At Camp Delta, the day Daniel had died, there hadn't been cameras rolling. Which meant that Jarrod was the only witness to Daniel's murder.

That, in and of itself, was more than enough motive for Arthur to want him dead.

He couldn't wait to get on the plane, fly across the Atlantic and lay a beatdown on the man.

He took Mindy's hand and led her toward the sedan that was waiting. "We will be back here as soon as we can," he said to Zoey as she walked the last few feet to the car with him. "While I'm gone, you are running things. She and I will be off devices as much as we can to keep anyone from tracking us."

"Just call me when you can. You are going to have a stop in New York before heading over the Atlantic, but from what the pilot has said, it sounds like you'll be there by tomorrow morning, their time."

"Do you have any clue how to find Arthur when we get there?" Mindy asked, opening the car door and putting one leg inside.

"According to the app OpenTable, he made a reservation for tomorrow night at the Wine Cellar at the

Grand Hôtel," Zoey said, helping her into the car. "You both have bags packed and waiting for you on the plane. If you need anything, use cash. Stay off the radar as much as possible." She closed the door on Mindy's side of the car.

"Thank you," Jarrod said, realizing how much work his sister must have done. "Seriously, I appreciate it."

"No matter what happens, you will always be my big brother, Jarrod." She threw her arms around him and gave him a hug.

From the way she held on to him, he could sense that she was frightened. With all their ups and downs, he hadn't really realized how much Zoey loved him.

"I love you, sis. Take care of things while we're gone." He gave her a quick kiss on the cheek.

"You got it." Zoey let go of him and watched as he got into the car. "And hey, bro, make sure you and Mindy come back safe. I want to watch you two get married."

Chapter Eighteen

The flight felt short, but it could have been because he and Mindy had spent most of it locked in the back bedroom making love until they had both fallen fast asleep.

The pilot had made a stop to refuel at a private airstrip near NYC, but he and the staff aboard the plane had done little to interfere with their private time.

Jarrod couldn't have thanked them enough, and when the pilot announced their descent into Stockholm, a profound sadness filled him.

He glanced over at Mindy. Her green eyes were heavy with sleep. She gave him a drowsy and satisfied smile. "Good morning," she said, "are you ready for this?"

All he was ready for was to live his entire life with her in his arms. Screw the world and all the madness within it.

He knew that was impossible. They had to go back to their lives. And that meant he had to make sure Arthur was no longer a danger to Mindy—and that meant that he had to clear her name of any possible wrongdoing.

His family's plan was to come together at the Widow

Maker Ranch and live out their days in seclusion and peace. At least until the Gray Wolves were under control and they were no longer in fear for their lives. As such, once everything was handled with Arthur and Mindy was once again safe, she could come back to the ranch. If she was willing. He knew she had an entire business to run on her own, thanks to Daniel's death.

Their time together might be coming to a close. Sure, they could try the long-distance thing, but such relationships were often destined to fail. Life always got in the way. First, they would go out of their way to meet up together—missing meetings and throwing caution to the wind. But over time, when the bloom left the rose, business would once again come first and life would take over. They would slowly move apart until neither could really recall exactly why they had ever gotten together in the first place.

It was better to realize now that whatever they had would be best left behind. It would be easier on both of them, instead of deluding themselves into thinking that they could make it work—no matter how much he loved her.

She blinked, her impossibly long eyelashes brushing against her cheeks. He wished he could tell her how he felt, that he loved her, that he wanted to be hers forever, and that he would do anything for her.

However, if he gave in now and told her how he was really feeling, it wouldn't just be him that he was hurting…and he had promised that he would do anything to stop her from being hurt further. He had to keep his word.

The plane jerked as the wheels touched down on the tarmac.

Mindy set about getting her clothes together and putting them on as he watched. If things went well, they might very well be bringing Arthur back with them on their next plane ride. This could be their last time alone.

Reaching over, he helped her button her pants. And before she could turn away, he took her one more time into his arms and gave her a kiss that felt entirely too much like goodbye. She looked up at him as he let her go. There were questions in her eyes, and behind those questions was a darkness as she, too, must have realized what he had been thinking.

She knew as well as he did that what they had together was over.

The ride to their hotel was quiet and filled with melancholy. They passed by beautiful waterside and antiquated architecture, which would have normally given him joy. This time all he could think about was the sadness that filled him.

Maybe he could move to New York and stay with her and Anya. But then, she hadn't spoken of a future together. And just like him, she was probably guarding herself from becoming too emotionally attached. That, or she held no feelings for him at all.

It pained him to realize the truth of their arrangement.

He normally wasn't the kind of man who fell for a woman, so maybe this was his karma. In a way, he couldn't deny that he deserved what he was getting from her.

Though she had seemed to forgive him for his transgressions, she had never really told him so in as many words.

Maybe she had spent the night with him to ensure that he would be hurt as badly as she was. Or perhaps she had taken him in an attempt to make herself feel better and to forget about the pain in her real life. Maybe she had known it was over before it began.

As their car came to a stop in front of the hotel, he looked across the water to the royal palace. It was no coincidence that Arthur was here. He had to have been somehow involved with the Riksdag, or possibly Hans Anders's murder.

Come hell or high water, Jarrod would get to the bottom of this.

Not for the first time, he wished he could call his people at the CIA. He wished there was somebody he could trust to be on his side and tell him more about Arthur.

If Arthur really was a double agent, then it seemed likely he may have also been behind the suspicion of Daniel and Mindy. Perhaps Arthur had even been spreading rumors that she was somehow involved with Hans's murder, and in an effort to expunge himself from any possible guilt, he was here trying to sell his innocence to this Swedish Parliament.

Bottom line, Arthur was a bastard.

In broken Swedish, he thanked his driver and helped Mindy out of the car. The driver motioned that he would be taking the bags into the hotel for them. Jarrod handed him a healthy tip in kronor.

The man took the money with a wide smile and stuffed it into his pocket before escorting them to the lobby door where a bellman waited. The driver said something to the man and, though the well-dressed bellman was already at attention, he stood a bit straighter.

"If you wouldn't mind," Jarrod said, "could you please make sure our bags arrive safely in our rooms?" He handed the bellman the same tip he had given the driver.

The bellman nodded, and the money disappeared as though in the hands of a well-practiced magician.

They weren't at a HoJo in the States, that was for sure.

As they made their way into the foyer, they were met with brilliant marble floors, fresh-cut flowers and crystal chandeliers that cascaded down from the ceilings. The place was quiet, though a few guests were making their way to and from the elevators and up and down the grand staircase. The hotel smelled of something clean but dripping of class, something reminiscent of white tea and sage. The palatial foyer opened up into a group of rooms and the luxury hotel's front desk, where a woman in a suit waited with a smile.

He would have to ensure that he had the right attire for such a place. The thought made him miss the ranch, and it reminded him of just another thing that was so different from NYC and Mindy's life. With her lace panties and high-end clothes—well, all except his Nirvana shirt—she was totally out of place at a Montana ranch.

He slipped his hand into hers, pretending just for a moment that they were something more than what they could be.

She gave his hand a squeeze as she smiled over at him, and, though they were both terribly underdressed, he found himself right at home. He had her.

When they checked into their rooms, they were booked as Mr. and Mrs. Martino. He couldn't help but notice the faint rosiness rise in her cheeks at the moniker that his sister had assigned them.

Maybe it wasn't so crazy to hope that she had feelings for him that went beyond a one-night stand.

Taking their respective keys, they made their way up to the suite Zoey had reserved for them. The main room was enormous, and it looked out upon the waterway and the palace. He hated to think how much this would be costing the company. If he had been alone, he would have not put himself up in such a magnificent room. But he was glad his sister had chosen this for them. If nothing else, he and Mindy could spend their last night together in the lap of luxury. Perhaps she would think that he wasn't that different from her after all.

The door clicked shut behind them and as it did, he could hear the air rush from Mindy. "Wow," she whispered.

"Zoey did well." He chuckled. "I think she'll manage to take care of everything while I'm gone."

"Is that her role in your family, to make sure everything runs smoothly?" Mindy asked, walking across the large room and stopping in front of the window. "I would have assumed you were the head of the family."

Did she just implicitly know where his sore spots were, or had he let something slip during their time together?

"I'm oldest, but as you can see I'm hardly the one in control."

"Actually, I know a little bit about that, as well." She moved the leather chair that sat beside the window and motioned for him to come sit beside her.

"Oh, really? But you work under your brother. I thought—"

"He was my boss? Yes, he definitely was. He ran the company. But in our personal lives, he was always a bit of a mess. I mean, look at Anya, for example." She turned to him as he sat down beside her. "I've always had to step up when it comes to him. It was the main reason that I never really wanted to be a part of my father's company."

Every time he thought he knew this woman, she surprised him, and that enigmatic quality was just one of the many reasons that losing her would tear his guts out.

If there was even a chance that he could make a future with her, he would seize it with both hands. And no matter what happened, he would fight.

Chapter Nineteen

They arrived early to the dining room and, after giving the hostess what Mindy knew to be at least a thousand dollars in kronor, they made their way to a private table. From where they sat, they had a perfect view of the wine cellar and yet were out of sight from anyone who sat below.

Thankfully, when she had unpacked the bag Zoey must have curated, she had found a red Chanel dress, complete with matching heels and a clutch. She couldn't have picked a more dazzling or sexy dress herself. As she sat down, the hem of the dress threatened to expose more of her backside than she desired. In an attempt at modesty, she perched forward on her seat until the hostess had retired from their room.

Jarrod, having noticing her predicament, made his way around the table and helped her stand. She adjusted her dress slightly and found her proper seat. "Thank you, my kind sir," she said with a forced formal air.

"You know what happens when you start calling me sir," he teased, giving her a mischievous grin. "This may be a private dining room, but I doubt that's what they have in mind." He touched her bare shoulder and his warm fingers made her cool skin prickle to life. "But, hey, if you're game, you know I am."

She laughed, the sound bouncing around the walls of the small stone room, making it sound more like the morose cascade of raindrops.

As though he, too, heard the faint sadness in the sound, he stopped smiling and sat down. "But really," he said, looking around the centerpiece, "you look beautiful."

She ran her hands down the satin of her dress, straightening some invisible wrinkle. "Thank you. Your sister has good taste."

"I like you in that dress almost as much as I'd like you out of it," he said, giving her the same look he had when he'd first kissed her lips.

If she could have caught that look in a memory and saved it in her soul, she would have. But, as it was…

"Jarrod, are you going to be okay?" she asked. She wanted to reach across the table and take his hand, which wouldn't be smart, knowing what she needed to say.

"What do you mean? Because I'm imagining you out of that dress?" He grinned, but she could see in his eyes that he knew exactly where this conversation was going. "You may give me a heart attack, but I think I'll recover."

She couldn't help the little smile that played on her lips. "No, you know what I mean."

He sighed, unfolding the linen napkin that was in the shape of a swan and placing it in his lap. Though she was certain that it was some nervous tic and a way for him to evade the topic, she followed suit.

"Jarrod, when we get home…"

"I know. I know," he said, resignation in his tone. "I've not been able to think of anything else since we landed. I've worked this through a million different ways."

"But you know how this has to end, just as much as I do—don't you?" she asked.

He nodded. "But do we really have to talk about it?"

He was right. There was no sense hashing over their destiny. Some battles were lost before a person could ever even step foot on the battlefield.

Still, what she truly wanted was for him to tell her that she was wrong. That they could make this work. That if they both just believed in love enough, they could triumph over whatever obstacles stood in their way. She wanted him to tell her that love—their love—was all it would take for both of them to find true happiness and peace.

Even though their lives had been in upheaval since they had met, she couldn't deny that what they had was special. Jarrod knew it, as well. That was what was making this just that much harder.

She had been waiting all of her life to meet a man like him, a man who could make her laugh at the lowest points in her life, a man who could make her forgive even the greatest missteps with the simple curve of his smile. She hadn't truly believed in soul mates… that was, until she had met him. Now she couldn't imagine her life or her future without him. He had become as much a part of her as her soul. If the world was to strip him away from her, she would be left with an empty shell.

She needed him to be whole.

But she couldn't argue with what had to be. There was no sense in pursuing something that was fated to die.

She'd had her fair share of relationships in the past. Long-distance didn't work. Relocating would be difficult for either of them, and unless he felt as strongly about her as she did him, it would be pointless. He couldn't. If he did, how could he be sitting there ever so calmly and staring at her with those big blue eyes?

She had to let him go. For the sake of her own heart, there was no other choice. If she didn't keep the last little bits of her guard up, she would end up as battered as the stone walls that surrounded them. No matter how hard she tried to grasp at the sounds of laughter, everything would turn into the sandy rasp of a mournful wail.

Their sommelier came up and, in heavily accented English, gave them the list of wines that the cellar was serving that night. The bottles ranged in price from moderate to so expensive that they hadn't bothered to put the prices on the list—including a Bordeaux from 1794.

She ordered the chardonnay and he followed suit. As the waiter disappeared, Jarrod turned back to her. From the look on his face he wanted to say something, no doubt wanting to continue their conversation from before. She couldn't bring herself to give it any more energy.

"What are we going to do with Arthur?" As she changed the subject, Jarrod's features drooped.

"On the slim chance that he actually shows up... To be honest, I haven't got a clue." He peered over the ledge of the private balcony and to the cellar below. "I have to admit, I haven't been giving this enough headspace. I think my mind has been on other, more pressing, matters."

As was hers. If she had her way, Arthur wouldn't show. At least not now. Instead, they could spend one more night together.

"This place totally reminds me of one of those episodes on *The Bachelor* where the man takes the woman on a one-on-one," she said, motioning around the romantic cellar and the racks of wine that adorned its walls. "Think about it. We could do the whole thing...a band, fireworks at the end of the night..." *And a one-way ticket to the fantasy suite.*

"Don't tell me you're into reality television," he said with a soft laugh.

"Hey now," she teased, "we are all allowed one vice. Mine just happens to be that I love to watch modern-day romances, no matter how screwed up the premise. I mean what woman would patiently wait for a man to take her on a date while he's busy bedding other women?"

He laughed.

"But," she continued, "if you ignore all that non-sense, it really is a cute love story." She took a sip of the water that was sitting on the table as they waited for their wine. "Can you imagine telling your children that you spent your dates in foreign countries, at private concerts by big-name talent, and falling in love?"

"Except for the big-name talent and fireworks bit, I think that you and I would be able to tell our children exactly that," he said.

She felt the air rush from her lungs as the sommelier brought out the chardonnay that they had requested and poured them each a taste.

Had Jarrod really just insinuated that he was falling in love with her, that *they* could have children together? Her chest tightened with giddiness.

She sniffed the wine as the sommelier waited for the approval on their wine selection, but given the attention she was paying to the wine, she could have been sniffing turpentine.

"Will this selection work for you?" the sommelier asked, holding the bottle at arm's length in front of her so she could see the label.

She nodded, afraid that if she actually tried to speak her words would come out as a high-pitched, excited squeak.

The waiter appeared from around the corner and entered their room as the sommelier left the bottle and made his way from the table. "Sir, madam, it is my pleasure to serve you this evening." As the man gave them the preamble of specials and what kind of cuts of meat they were serving in the restaurant that evening, she inched her toes out of her shoe and moved it under the table to find Jarrod's foot. She ran her stockinged toes under the edge of his suit pants and up his leg.

He gave her a look of lusty surprise just as the waiter stopped talking. The waiter stood waiting for him to speak, but Jarrod appeared panicked, as though he had been paying as little attention to the man as she had.

"Um, yes, thank you." Jarrod waved away the menu the man offered. "Instead of picking, would you please have the chef prepare whatever dish he recommends for us this evening?"

Apparently, Jarrod liked to live dangerously even when it came to gastronomies. She wouldn't be surprised if the dinner came out and was comprised of sweetbreads and other mystery meats. But what did it matter? As it was, she wasn't feeling hungry for anything other than the look he kept giving her as she ran her foot farther up his leg.

Even though the waiter couldn't possibly have seen what was happening under the table, he promptly took his leave. She couldn't have been more grateful.

There were the sounds of men's voices as someone entered the main cellar area below. Peeking over the edge, the bald head of a man came into view. As the man turned, she could make out his round, pudgy features. She recognized him as one of the members of the Swedish parliament from the meeting that they had held in the city. Though she couldn't remember the man's name, she recalled that he was one of Hans's subordinates and the next in line to the man's seat.

Walking behind the man, she recognized her former

assistant, Arthur McDuffy—if that was his real name. "Look," she whispered.

The sight of him made bile rise up in her throat, and she forced herself to sit back, hiding herself from the men below. From the smattering of voices, they were part of a larger group.

Chairs scraped on the stone floor as the men sat down. She could hear Arthur making small talk with the men around him. They spoke of the weather, their flights and the state of their families. It drove her mad.

She moved to stand, to charge downstairs and face the man head-on. What did it matter? They didn't have a plan. Instead, Jarrod reached out and took her by the hand, stopping her. He shook his head.

She considered shoving his hand aside, but she stopped. She couldn't think about just herself—she had to think about Jarrod and his safety, as well. And that was to say nothing of Anya, who waited at home for them. She promised herself that she wouldn't leave the girl alone. That meant that she would have to handle this situation with caution.

No matter how badly she wanted to go in with guns blazing.

It felt like justice—to kill the man who had killed her brother.

If she was lucky, she would still get the chance. However, if she attacked right now she was more likely to go to prison than she was to get her revenge.

She had to play this smart. Jarrod motioned for her to come near him so he could whisper in her ear.

"When Arthur attacked your brother and killed him,

your brother was reaching for this." Jarrod reached into his pocket and extracted a pen and a photo of her.

She swayed on her impossibly high heels. Jarrod took her by the waist and made her sit on his knee. He wrapped his arm around her. "You're going to be okay," he whispered.

"But why? Why did he have this?" She paused. "And where did you get it?"

"Zoey can get her hands on almost anything. Seriously." He chuckled. She had no doubt that Zoey was capable of anything. The woman was a powerhouse.

"Do you recognize the pen?" he asked as she took her picture from Jarrod's hand. There was a splatter of blood on the bottom, just over her heart. She tried to not think of it as a sign, but rather as her brother's attempt to remind her of exactly what she had to lose.

She glanced over at the pen still in Jarrod's hand. It was silver and rather unremarkable. She shook her head. "I don't think so. Why?"

He let go of her and twisted the pen open. Instead of a regular nib at the end, the pen had a white capsule at its tip. He closed the pen's nib, like he somehow feared its contents.

"What is it? The powder, I mean?" she asked, motioning toward the pen, fearful of touching it.

"At the time, I didn't know. I assumed it was some sort of cyanide capsule."

She stared at her reflection in the pen's mirrored surface. "Do you think he was trying to kill himself? To die instead of allow you to interrogate him?"

"I don't know if he was intending on using it on

himself or on Arthur, but before he had the chance, Arthur shot him."

She covered her mouth with her hands as she tried to work through everything Jarrod was telling her. "Why didn't you tell me all this before?"

He put the pen back into his pocket. "I didn't think it mattered. Until now I thought it was just one of those details that didn't play into the larger picture. That was until I found out about Arthur."

"And now?" she asked between the spaces in her fingers.

"Well, with the attack on Hans," he said, motioning toward the men who were still talking loudly below, "I'm wondering if the powder inside this pen might be linked to the nerve agent attack."

"Do you think Arthur planted it on my brother? That he intended on poisoning him? Then us?"

"I thought about that," Jarrod said, nodding. "In some ways it makes sense. Maybe Arthur had hoped to kill him with it. Or maybe Daniel had it before he stepped into the interrogation room. And I can't help wondering if your picture is somehow tied in, as well."

He turned the photo over, revealing the threatening note.

It appeared that her brother had died trying to protect her.

She started to stand, but he stopped her. "I didn't tell you this so you would fly off the rails. Right now, I need you to stay on point with me. Don't let your emotions get us into trouble."

She reminded herself of the Swedish prison that waited for her if something went wrong downstairs. "Okay," she said, trying to quell her rage. "What is it that you think we should do?"

"We need to get Arthur alone."

"I've got it." She stood up, this time resolved to keep herself from flying off into a murderous rage... at least for now.

If they did this right, they could take Arthur down. She would have to be patient. In fact, they could probably kill him and be out of the country before anyone was any the wiser.

Their waiter returned carrying a tray of bacon-wrapped figs covered in warm honey. He set them down on the table between them. "Compliments of the chef. And he wishes you the most wonderful of evenings. He is looking forward to enrapturing your senses with tonight's delicacies."

Mindy forced a polite smile. "Please extend him our gratitude."

As the waiter turned, Jarrod called to him. "Excuse me?"

"Yes, sir," the waiter said, turning back to face them.

"Would you please tell the man, the one in the dark suit in the lower room, that she—" he motioned to Mindy "—wishes to meet him in the hall?"

The waiter glanced over at her and gave her a presuming smile. "Absolutely."

"Along with her invitation, would you please include a glass of one of your finest wines?"

"Sir, our wines are sold by the bottle."

"Then, by all means, please present him with the bottle."

The waiter gave a well-practiced bow. "And may I ask who is sending the bottle, sir?"

She moved closer to the waiter. "Just tell him it is from his secret admirer."

Admirer or adversary, what was the difference? Right now, all that mattered was taking him down.

The waiter nodded and excused himself from their room.

"You do realize that is likely a hundred-thousand-dollar bottle of wine you just ordered," she said.

"If it gets him out of that room and away from the other members of the Swedish parliament then I will have to consider it a smart business expense." He smiled. "That's what tax write-offs are for—isn't it?"

"I doubt it will be the first homicide that ended in a tax write-off." She laughed. "I really do need to start taking notes from your playbook." She ran her hands down the front of his suit jacket, and ever so carefully she pulled the pen from his pocket.

He didn't notice as she wrapped it in her hand and held it out of sight.

"I'm at your mercy," he said, with a slight tip of his head.

She didn't question it. For as much as he was at her mercy, she found herself happily following the requests of the man. In a world full of lies and betrayal, they had found each other.

He stood up and took her by the hand. "I'll step into the kitchen while you wait for him in the hall. He may panic when he sees you." He paused to look her straight in the eye. "If you feel in danger in any way I want you to get the hell out of there. You run. Don't try to face him down, and don't do anything stupid, just get him to stay there. If he is the man we think he is, he may come in hot at you."

Though she heard what he was saying and she wanted to heed his warnings, she wasn't sure she would actually be able to do as he asked. "I'll try. You just stay close."

He looked nervous, but maybe that was how she looked, too.

She walked out of their dining area and followed Jarrod to the kitchen door, where he stepped inside. Through the window she could see the kitchen staff had stopped and were staring at Jarrod. With the placement of a bill in the head chef's hand and what she assumed was a thank-you for the figs or possibly a quick explanation of what he was doing in their private sanctum, the staff returned to their normal business hurrying around the kitchen.

That man knew how to grease a palm.

In their high-stakes world, she would do well to learn from him. Maybe one day she would be just as smooth, but for now she had only started.

As she made her way back toward the main cellar, she tried to stay in view of the small circular window that looked out at the hall and to the dining room. Jarrod would have to be careful to remain unseen.

Their waiter made his way out of the main dining room. "He is on his way, madam. Is there anything else you might need from me for now?"

She shook her head. "Thank you."

The waiter returned to the kitchen and disappeared through the door to where Jarrod was waiting.

She stood in the hall for what felt like an hour but was likely only a matter of seconds. Time lost all meaning as she stood there, thinking about Daniel, about the attacks, about Anya and the world she would have to go home to, and all the damage Arthur had done in her life.

Finally Arthur made his way out of the dining room. He was carrying a glass of red wine and as he looked up and saw her, she could have sworn she saw a little ripple in the liquid, as though his hands were starting to shake.

He would have been stupid not to be afraid.

"Ms. Kohl, I didn't know you were going to be here in Stockholm. I thought you were still in the States."

"Ah, no," she said, the mirth dripping from her voice. "Surprise trip. I had to come in and check on the H&K assets. Always doing business…isn't that right, Arthur?"

He moved closer to her but was careful to stay just outside her reach, almost as if he feared she might lash out at him. "When did you arrive in Sweden?" He swallowed hard, making his Adam's apple jump like a bullfrog.

"We just arrived this morning." She gripped the pen in the palm of her hand, swirling it with her fingers and making sure the nib was exposed. If the contents of the pen were cyanide, Arthur would be down and dead within a matter of seconds...probably less than the time it had taken for her brother to die from Arthur's bullet.

"We?" he asked, looking around them.

"I came with a friend, someone who has been looking out for my best interests ever since that horrific event in the city."

Arthur couldn't meet her eye. "Yes, I'm sorry I didn't get to come see you in the hospital. I had—"

"You can hold your excuses and your lies, Agent Arthur. I know exactly who you are and what you've done to my family and my business." She lowered the pen in her fingers, but before she killed him, she had to get her closure. "You've been exposed."

"Is that why you've come here? Because you think I did something to you?" He looked confused, but his gaze darted around the empty hallway. "What have I been exposed as?" he asked, sounding glib.

She couldn't believe that he was trying to act innocent. Ignorance wasn't a defense.

"I found out about your role in Daniel's death."

His mouth dropped open. "I don't know what you are talking about," he said, but now some of the glibness had disappeared from his voice.

He turned his back to the kitchen and she saw Jarrod glance out at them. She gave him an almost imperceptible nod, and at the signal he silently opened the door to the kitchen and moved in behind the man. From under his jacket, he reached behind him and pulled out a handgun. Her time with Arthur was quickly running out.

"I know you killed him. Don't deny that you pulled the trigger. You knew your lies were catching up with you. Danny must have found out about your role in selling our family's secrets to our enemies. I bet that when he figured it out, you had him arrested. I know about your role in the CIA...and that you're working both governments. In fact, I bet you're making a hell of a lot of money." All the weight lifted from her chest, but her hatred for the man remained.

"Mindy, you have me all wrong," he pleaded, putting his free hand up in surrender, like somehow the simple action could save him from her rage.

"I allowed you into my life. You took my secrets... my family's secrets...and you sold them to the highest bidders. Then you murdered my brother in cold blood...and then you tried to kill me with the nerve agent. That was the real reason you suddenly left my side for an 'urgent business trip.' Were you going to North Korea so you could pick up your money?" She gripped the pen in her hand so hard that she could feel the metal clip on its side cutting into her palm.

"If you think that's true, then it's time you get a new source." Arthur leaned around her as if checking to make sure none of the members of parliament were in sight.

"What I can't figure out is why you are here. What business could you have with the Riksdag?"

She tried not to look as Jarrod took another step

closer. He raised his gun, aiming it straight for the back of Arthur's head as he waited for her signal.

But she wasn't ready. No. Nor would she be. This was one killer that she had to take down herself. She had to avenge her brother's death.

"I know you think you know everything about me. But trust me when I tell you that you have this all wrong. I'm not the man you think I am."

"Don't you dare ask me to trust you," she seethed.

"You're right, that was the wrong choice of words. But at least hear me out."

As badly as she wanted to jab the pen into his jugular and end him, she found herself wanting to hear. A strange gnawing in her gut told her something wasn't quite right.

"I do work for the CIA. I did kill your brother." He gave her a pleading look and the wine in his glass sloshed against the sides. "I'm sorry. I didn't want to kill your brother. It wasn't my intention."

"But it was the only way you could keep the truth of your corruption from coming to light…"

"No," Arthur argued. "I wasn't the one selling your family's secrets to North Korea. It was Daniel. And you weren't ever supposed to be here."

"Liar." She took a half step toward him.

"No, I have proof. He wasn't acting alone," Arthur said. "Don't do anything stupid. I'm here to—"

He was interrupted by the rattle of rifles and body armor as eight men charged down the hallway and turned into view at the corner by the kitchen. Jarrod turned to them, a look of surprise on his face as he lowered his weapon.

She was shocked. How had she and Jarrod gotten this so wrong? Arthur moved around her and she stepped closer to Jarrod.

"What in the hell is going on?" she whispered, watching as Arthur's team moved in file down the hallway, clearing the doorways as they moved toward the cellar's main dining area.

Arthur turned to Jarrod and nodded. "I should have known that you would get yourself wrapped up in this."

"What are you talking about, Arthur?" Jarrod snarled. "What's going on?"

He turned to face them both. "Mindy, we discovered that your father had been selling secrets for the last five years. When he tried to remove himself from the arrangement with North Korea, they poisoned him. Much like they had planned on poisoning you."

She felt the fight dissolve from her. "You were trying to protect me? If that's true, why did you kill Daniel?"

"Daniel was an unfortunate loss. We hadn't intended on killing him, but the Koreans were breathing down his neck. We think he went for the pen knowing I would be forced to act and pull the trigger."

"You didn't have to kill him."

"If I hadn't, the Koreans would have… And they probably would have killed you, too."

"And what about the nerve agent attack? I suppose you are going to say that was the Koreans' doing, as well?" Jarrod asked.

"The attack is actually what brought us here." Arthur nodded toward his team. "Your father's and brother's roles in supplying weapons to North Korea had come to light within the Riksdag. That was one of the reasons Hans was going to do everything in his power to shut your company down—and never allow you access to Sweden. Your brother had an agreement with North Korea, and thanks to this the North Koreans stepped in. They needed you to continue your work without any hindrances. They bought several of the members of the parliament and they were the ones who helped arrange the hit. Your brother and his cronies had one hell of a business going—they were making money from every angle." Arthur paused as he gave a stiff, ruthless laugh. "If you think about it, North Korea is part of the reason your family's company is so profitable."

She felt a wave of sickness overtake her as she realized her entire life had been bought and paid for with blood money.

"Now, I'm here working with the Säkerhetspolisen, or SAPO, and luring out those that the North Koreans had paid to help with the hit," Arthur said, putting his finger to his lips as he handed her his glass of wine. "Stay back. I don't want either of you to get hurt."

Chapter Twenty

There was screwing up and then there was royally screwing things up, and this time he had definitely hit an all-time low. Jarrod holstered his gun as he pulled Mindy close to him. If there was going to be a firefight between the joint task force and the rogue members of the Swedish parliament, he needed to get Mindy out of there.

But as he nudged her to move back toward the kitchen and away from the fight, she refused to budge.

"Jarrod, is Arthur telling the truth? Were my brother and father really doing all that?" she asked, sounding broken.

He stared down the hallway at the joint task force. From what he could see, it looked as though the man at the front of the formation was definitely CIA, as was the man behind him. The next two appeared to be in a different kind of tactical gear, and their weaponry was definitely from UN. Behind them were members of the SAPO.

"From the looks of it, our investigation was only

the tip of a much bigger iceberg." He looked at Arthur. "He was right."

"But I thought you said that the CIA sent you to investigate me? How did you not know about the rest of the operation?"

The blood drained from his face. The CIA had used him as their pawn and he had been too stupid to see their game for what it really was. And now he had to admit that he once again wasn't the man she thought he was.

"I think they sent me to keep an eye on you. If they'd really been suspicious, you would have had CIA agents assigned to you. They must have wanted me to keep you out of danger during their raid on your family."

"But...why?"

He sighed. "Like I told you, I'm a government contractor. STEALTH works for groups all over the world just like the CIA. And, as contractors, sometimes our job isn't to know everything that is going on with a case. That's why they call us in, to handle the odds and ends bits that could land them in hot water if they ever fell under investigation. As a contractor, we are held to different standards—especially when working internationally. We don't have to play by the rules of the Geneva Conventions."

"You make it sound like you are badasses."

"And yet, here I stand in front of you looking like a chump." He hung his head playfully before giving her his most melting smile.

"But what about the man in the city? The man in Anya's music class? Was he a part of this, too?"

And the next hatchet fell. *Crap.* He had almost forgotten about the man and the life that was waiting for him when he got back home. "Mindy, you aren't the only one with enemies. I think that man... Actually, I know that man was a member of a group called the Gray Wolves—a group that is actively targeting my family."

"What?" She leaned back against the wall behind them.

From down the hall, Arthur called out to his men and they rushed the dining room, guns aimed at the men inside. There were the sounds of bodies being dropped down to the floor and handcuffs being clicked.

Thankfully, and almost surprisingly, there wasn't the sound of a single round being fired.

Maybe the CIA didn't want to pick up the tab for a rack of hundred-thousand-dollar bottles of wine.

Arthur's mission appeared to be a complete success. Especially compared to STEALTH's handling of the mess.

Though perhaps he was looking at their situation from the wrong angle. Instead of thinking of it as being played by the CIA, he had gotten a once-in-a-lifetime opportunity to spend time with a woman who might be his soul mate.

"Who are the Gray Wolves?" she asked.

"When we were in Turkey on a mission for the CIA, we had a run-in with the Gray Wolves, a Turkish crime syndicate. My sister Trish was killed," he said, emotion clogging his throat. "Well, we managed to take out a lot of their men…and cost the leader and his organization millions of dollars. As a result, they put out a hit on us."

She nodded. "So the man in my apartment and the one from the music class—Gray Wolves? How can you be sure Zoey and Anya are safe?"

"The Gray Wolves don't know about the Montana ranch. We're very careful to keep it that way." He gave her a feeble and apologetic smile. "I'm so sorry, Mindy. I'm sorry that I have made your life such a disaster."

"You *did* do that." She took a long drink from the wineglass Arthur had handed her. She laughed as she caught Jarrod gawking at her. "Did you seriously think that I would let this good a wine go to waste? You really don't know me."

He laughed, thankful that she seemed to finally find some peace with the situation. If nothing else, perhaps they could be friends when they got back to the States.

She leaned in closer to him and he could smell the rich hues of strawberry and oak from the wine on her breath. "Another thing you may not know about me… I have a thing for men who are real."

"You mean you like *chumps*?" he asked, looking deep into her green eyes.

"Not chumps," she said with a little giggle. "But I've dated enough men who think they are the world's greatest catch…men with more money than they even know what to do with…men who have no real drive in life. I love a man who can take his lumps and admit when he is wrong."

"You mean you could love a man who would take

you on a worldwide adventure, only to learn that he had screwed up from the very beginning?"

She leaned even closer to him, her lips on the cusp of his ear. "But wasn't it one hell of an adventure?"

He couldn't deny that fact. Looking back at his career, he'd never missed the mark on a case so badly before. However, this was probably the best case he had ever worked on.

She drew his earlobe into her mouth, giving it a light nibble as she kissed him. "And as far as loving you," she said, letting go of his earlobe. "If you give me half a chance, I could love you until the end of time."

A wide smile took over his face and he wrapped his arms around her, careful not to spill her glass of wine. "Why, Ms. Kohl, I think you're declaring your love for me."

"I know you warned against me calling you sir, and now I see why. If you call me miss one more time I'm going to have to take you upstairs and show you exactly how unladylike I can be."

"Would you rather I call you Mrs.?"

Mindy smiled as she drew back slightly and looked up at him. "Will you marry me?"

"I don't have a ring, and unlike *The Bachelor* I can't give you the final rose. Well, I would, if I had one..." He stammered. Dammit, this was going all wrong. "What I mean is, yeah, I'd love to marry the hell out of you."

She laughed, the sound mixing with the footsteps of the task forces and their detainees as they marched down the hall beside them.

As they walked by, Arthur gave them a wink. "I'll see you guys back in the States. If you need anything, or have any questions, you know where to find me."

Jarrod flipped the guy the bird as he laughed.

All he cared about now was Mindy. "Ms. Kohl, it appears as though we finally may have a bit of time alone."

"And for the moment, it appears no one is trying to murder us."

He laughed. "Are you going to be bored if no one throws nerve agents at us?"

She shook her head, a playful smile on her lips. "Is this what it's going to be like, married to you?"

He couldn't believe this was really happening, that in just a matter of moments his entire life had changed for the better. Even so, he couldn't completely give in to the happiness.

"Are you sure that I'm what you want in your life? I mean, what about Anya?"

She gave him a kiss on the cheek. "I know that you and your family are among the safest places that we could possibly be. But I'm going to need her approval. Oh, and she has to have a spot in our wedding."

"But aren't you going back to NYC? You have the company to worry about…and now that you're down an assistant…"

"I have a feeling that we're going to start moving in a new direction. But I'm not going to worry about any of that right now. Just like the rest of our lives— you and I are going to have to just figure this thing out as we go." She ran her hand down his cheek as their gazes met. "Now, sir, take me upstairs and show me what adventure means to you."

Epilogue

Anya ran out of the front door of the Widow Maker Ranch's main house as they drove up and parked in the driveway. Zoey was close at her heels.

"Anta!" Anya called, throwing her little round hands up into the air as she waited for Mindy to come sweep her into her arms.

"Hi, sweetheart," Mindy called, waving at her niece as she and Jarrod stepped out of the car. "How did it go?" she asked Zoey as she made her way over to Anya and pulled her into her embrace.

The little one smelled of Cheerios and fresh air, and it reminded her of exactly what she wanted for the girl.

"Everything went great. And from the sounds of it, far better than your trip." Zoey gave Jarrod a hug.

Jarrod let go of his sister and sent Mindy a sly grin.

She was glad that they had waited to tell Zoey and the rest of the world their good news. It had been a fun weekend spent in the safety of the hotel room in Sweden, telling each other everything about themselves and their pasts, down to which kind of toothpaste was their favorite.

"Actually, it wasn't too bad." Mindy smiled as she sat Anya on the porch and knelt down in front of her. "Before we go inside—Anya, I have a little surprise for you." She reached in her purse and pulled out a Barbie dressed in a bridal gown.

"Oh, she pretty." Anya took the doll and pulled it to her chest, smoothing the doll's hair like it was her own personal baby.

"Look, Anya." She motioned for her to more closely examine the doll's hand. "She has a ring on."

Anya nodded as she stared down at the doll's hand. "Anta?" she asked, confusion on her face.

"Look." Mindy stretched out her hand so both Zoey and Anya could see the diamond ring that Jarrod had bought her. "Jarrod gave me this."

Zoey squealed beside them, and she jumped from foot to foot and wrapped her arms around her brother's neck. "Yeah, you guys! I knew it!"

"Always the family planner." Jarrod laughed, giving her a quick peck on the cheek.

"But first," Jarrod said, turning back to the little one. "I have to ask… Do you think it would be okay if your auntie marries me?"

Anya toddled over to him. She wrapped her arms around his legs, the Barbie still in her hand, and looked up at him, giving him a wide smile and an enthusiastic nod.

He lifted her into his arms.

"Okay," Anya said, snuggling into his chest. She reached out for Mindy. "You're Anta." Then she pointed to herself. "I'm Anya."

"Yes, baby girl. I'm Anta and you're Anya."

"Uh-huh," Anya said, smoothing her doll's hair. "Anta and Anya. I just like you." She gave her a sweet smile. "I love you, Anta."

Mindy moved to them and wrapped Anya and Jarrod in her arms as tears filled her eyes. "I love you, too, little one."

Anya rested her cheek against hers. "And Jarrod?"

"Yes, baby girl, I love Jarrod, too." She smiled as Jarrod wrapped his arm around her and pulled her tighter into their new family's embrace.

"I love you, too, my girls," Jarrod said, looking over at his sister.

For once in her life, Mindy was at peace. At least for now. The future, though she knew it would bring its own set of troubles and upheavals, looked bright. She would spend it with the people she truly loved, and she had no doubt that their lives would be nothing less than wonderful.

* * * * *

HOTTER ON ICE

REBECCA HUNTER

To Mr Hunter, who has entertained so many of my crazy ideas over the years, including the one about staying in a hotel made of ice and snow in northern Sweden. I love this journey we're on together! xo

CHAPTER ONE

WHY THE HELL is he taking so long?

Alya Petrova had peeled herself out of bed at six thirty in the morning to be on time for this meeting. Now she found herself sitting at the Blackmore Inc. conference-room table alone, fifteen minutes after the hour, staring out blankly at Sydney Harbour, waiting for Henning Fischer to show up.

In the world of virtual communication, Henning was the most reliable person she knew. Apparently, those skills didn't translate into real-world punctuality.

Being nervous as hell wasn't helping. What would it feel like to meet the surveillance expert she'd talked with over the phone for the last three years? She knew almost nothing about Henning himself. His name had floated around in conversation for as long as she'd worked with the elite security service Blackmore Inc., and she had gathered scraps of information from her former bodyguard, Max Jensen. Surveillance specialist. Ex–Australian Federal Police officer. Who never, ever appeared in person.

So, of course, she'd turned to the internet, which was surprisingly stingy on Henning Fischer–related information. A couple track and field championships from years ago. An occasional statement by him in connection with police work. And only one clear photo, an official-looking portrait from his cadet days. Physically, he was striking, his dark brown eyes intense. Though the photo showed only to his shoulders, it was clear he was built. She had stared at that photo more than once, trying to connect it with the man whose voice rumbled through her phone. She couldn't make it fit.

This was the person who had watched over her through her front hall security camera, giving her a boost of support on her weakest days, those vulnerable times she'd worked so hard to move past. She hadn't wanted to lean on someone else—a man, no less—for comfort, but Henning had been a safe bet.

Now that distance between them was about to disappear. Soon he would walk through the door, a flesh-and-blood man, not just an idea. Okay, *maybe* she had developed a tiny bit of a crush on him. It had been a completely harmless escape when she thought she'd never meet him, a safe place to put all sorts of fantasies.

But her modeling shoot on the Great Barrier Reef had changed everything. When her former bodyguard devoted all his off hours on the island to her sister, Natasha, the two had fallen in love. Alya had definitely seen that one coming. Shortly after, Max

stepped down from working one-on-one with all clients, including her. That one she hadn't seen coming, though, in the end, it was for the best. Alya had
taken this change as an overdue nudge to reassess
her security situation. A lot had changed in the three
years since she had moved an ocean away from her
stalker ex, and she didn't really need a bodyguard
in most cases anymore. Surveillance of Nick, her
ex, was enough.

This week was the exception: a fashion shoot on
the other side of the world was a long way to travel
without security. But with Max no longer working
in that role, a new plan had been hatched: Henning
would take Max's place.

The longer she waited in this quiet conference
room, the more the anticipation buzzed through her.
She had imagined many versions of him, but what
would it feel like to be close to the real Henning all
day long? Standing next to him, almost touching, his
deep voice in her ear...

Alya stood up and started for the door, looking
for a distraction. Maybe the receptionist would point
her to the coffee machine?

She crossed the room, slowing as a familiar voice
came through the closed door. Henning's. After
three years of phone calls, she'd know it anywhere.
Alya froze, her hand just shy of the door handle.
Did she continue her search for coffee or return to
her seat?

Then the door opened, and she was buried in his

chest. His hands closed around her arms, steadying her. His warm, musky scent… Relief hit her first, and then—*oh, God*—something powerful. Urgent. His breaths were sharp and erratic in her ear. He towered over her, his presence everywhere. *Oh my*, her harmless crush was sooo not harmless anymore.

"You okay?" His voice was a familiar rumble, and the sound of it in person turned the fluttering inside into molten lava.

Alya nodded against him, too stunned to speak. Her fingers, her arms, her breasts, her stomach—everything tingled with awareness. Was her body calling to him or answering his call? It felt like both. After things went so terribly wrong with Nick, she had had a growing suspicion that she was just too wary to feel this…captivated by a man. Wrong, so very wrong. Her reaction to Henning was bone-deep and intoxicating.

There was no good explanation for what she did next. Alya lifted her hands and touched him, pressed her palms against his stomach. Checking if he was real. Yes, he was definitely a solid, warm, very real man. Henning sucked in a harsh breath, and his muscles twitched, turning rock-hard under her touch. His hands tensed around her arms, and a low growl came from deep inside him.

Alya froze. Shit. She was feeling up Henning Fischer, uninvited. In the Blackmore Inc. conference room. What the hell was wrong with her? She stepped back.

"Sorry. That was totally out of li—" She met his gaze.

The first thing she saw was his eyes. Dark brown and even more serious than his picture had let on. Intense enough to steal her breath, and for a moment his gaze flared even hotter, darker. A rush of awareness ran through her, aching, burning.

Then she saw the scars.

Jagged, unnaturally smooth, down the left side of his face. Skin that had been stitched and patched together. Her eyes widened. The old, grainy photo online had shown him as good-looking in a clean-cut, impersonal sort of way. But he was so, so far from clean-cut now. Alya followed the longest scar that tugged at his left eye, distorting one side of his face, then disappearing into the collar of his shirt.

His big body, the scent of him, the rawness in his voice, his dark eyes, the scars—all of these pieces came together into one thought as she stood in the doorway gaping at him: this man knew trauma. He understood it. Her heart jumped and pulsed in her chest, expanding. She understood it, too.

Shit—how long had she been staring at his scars?

Too long. When her gaze flickered back up to his, all the burning intensity she'd seen seconds before had vanished. His face was shuttered closed, giving nothing away, and his expression was cool, impersonal. The only hint of emotion he showed was the rapid ticking of his pulse at the base of his neck.

Slick introduction, girl.

Time to start over, preferably in the way regular people introduced themselves.

"Sorry again. I'm Alya, in person," she said. "And doing a crap job at making a good first impression."

Henning blinked down at her, his gaze softening a little. "Henning Fischer, very much in person. As you clearly noticed."

"Clearly," she said dryly, trying to preserve the last of her dignity in this exchange. Was he teasing her about feeling him up or about staring at his scars? Probably both.

The tiniest hint of a smile tugged at the uninjured corner of his mouth. Heat was rising into her cheeks, as he studied her in the quiet room. She studied him right back.

"Max should be right in," he finally said, gesturing to the conference table. "You know how this works."

Yes, she did. She had sat across from Max at this table many times, going over her security details. But never once had she been so fully aware of each breath, each movement, the way she was right now with Henning.

Alya took a seat and flipped open the folder in front of her, skimming through the papers in it. Henning sat down facing her, silent, alert, an overwhelming physical presence. He radiated a protectiveness that wrapped around her, settling inside her. It was the same feeling she had gotten over the phone, somehow both calming and incredibly engaging. In person, it was magnified a thousand times.

She glanced up to find his gaze fixed on her, his dark eyes unreadable. The old Alya, the woman who had gotten herself tangled up with Nick Bancroft back in LA, would have looked away. That version of herself had given up her jobs and friends three years ago and fled the country when Nick wouldn't leave her alone, despite the restraining order. But she wasn't that woman anymore, so Alya stared back at him. He was a solid, motionless mountain of a man, with hulking shoulders and thick biceps that stretched the material of his shirt. His power and prowess were controlled but not at all concealed, as if his body was a well-honed tool, ready for use.

The current between them ran hotter, and with every breath, heat coiled inside her. But she couldn't mistake this strong, immediate pull between them for something more than it was—plain sexual interest. She had been down that road of powerful attraction before, and it led to disaster. She searched for something to say. "So...you ever been to Sweden before?"

"Nope."

"Me neither. Cold, dark and snowy this time of the year, I hear."

"Yep."

"Not my favorite conditions, but my agent thinks the photo shoot plus the *Behind the Runway* documentary filming, with its daily YouTube outtakes, is too good of an opportunity to pass up."

"Mmm."

She bit back a sigh. He wasn't giving her any help here but seemed perfectly content to just watch her talk. Thankfully, the click of the conference-room door ended this one-sided conversation.

"Sorry to keep you waiting, Alya," Max said, striding over to the table. "I trust you and Henning introduced yourselves."

That was certainly an understatement. Her former bodyguard seemed oblivious to the tension between Henning and her, but knowing Max, she couldn't be certain.

Wordlessly Henning opened the folder on the table in front of him. The muscles of his forearms rippled and flexed as he sifted through the stack of papers with large, blunt fingers. He pulled out a document and showed it to her.

"Here's the master schedule for the week," he said. "It includes flights, hotel contacts, dinners, photo sessions and interviews."

He walked her through the details of each day as Alya followed along on the pages. His voice was gravelly and deep, as if whatever had scarred his face had roughed up the inside of him too. He was a practical speaker, his sentences short and clipped, his answers no longer than absolutely necessary. Pretty much the exact opposite of Max.

"The chances of Nick Bancroft showing up are very low," said Henning, closing his folder. "It also helps that the Icehotel is in a remote corner of northern Sweden. We have plenty of warning when any-one flies into the tiny Kiruna airport."

She didn't doubt that. What he didn't say was that he had all sorts of connections from his Australian Federal Police days that fed him information when he needed it. And with the kind of details he found, she was pretty sure the routes couldn't all be legal. But she was starting to get the feeling that Henning did things his own way.

"Blackmore Inc. has done an amazing job at keep-ing Nick out of my life. I'm not worried." She sat up straighter in her chair. "I considered going on this trip without security, but if he showed up and I had to deal with him alone, he'd make sure to stir up pub-lic drama. Public displays of personal problems are toxic in my industry, and Nick has already hijacked my career once."

There were models whose lives played out in the tabloids. Drugs, tantrums, drive-through marriages and bitter custody battles—the world had an insa-tiable hunger for these kinds of stories. She had been at the center of one of those stories three years ago when, after Nick wouldn't leave her alone, despite the restraining order, he'd publicly called her emotionally unstable under the guise of worry. She had worked so hard to keep their break-up quiet, but when he twisted her own words into evidence that she was becoming increasingly erratic, just like her mother, the press had been all too ready to pick up that story. Each move to distance herself from Nick became another example of her "irrational" behavior, another incident he used against her in the court of public opinion. All because ultra-rich, ultra-privileged Nick Bancroft had decided he wanted something—her—and he always got what he wanted.

Never again would she let that happen.

Henning was watching her closely. "Nick won't get to you."

The hot intensity in his eyes flared for one, brief moment, and then it was gone. A flush crept up her neck. Five days with Henning next to her—two on a plane and three at the Icehotel in Sweden. Was his effect on her obvious? She glanced at Max to gauge his reaction, but he was looking at the paper in front of him.

"I understand what I'm getting into by taking this job," she said quietly. "Sasha Federov probably wouldn't have given me this chance to represent his brand if my mother didn't still hold her cult-like status in Russia. I'm sure he's expecting me to follow in her footsteps, not just as a model but as an attention magnet. But in my agent's words, I need to grab this chance and hold on to it. Even if it means being followed around by a documentary crew."

Max nodded. "Henning will be connected with the team here if there's anything you need to be aware of. You'll be in good hands." He lifted an eyebrow. "But I think you already know that."

Yeah, she absolutely did. But now that they were in the same room together, the idea of spending the

next five days with this man was getting more…
complicated.

"Have a safe trip," said Max, standing up.

Alya walked over and hugged him. "Thanks for everything."

He had been part of her support system for over three years, and now their professional relationship was over. But the fact that he was at her and Natasha's apartment almost daily meant this was far from goodbye. With one more nod at both of them, Max left.

Alya was alone again with Henning. He stood up and took a couple steps toward her. His gaze swept over her, dark and guarded. They were so close again, and the silence crackled with tension. Alya took a deep breath as the room seemed to heat up a couple degrees. It was too late to close herself to this connection, but she had no idea what to do with it. So she started with the obvious.

"I'm sorry for earlier. When I, um—" she bit her lip "—felt you up. I certainly wouldn't want a guy doing that to me when we met."

Henning's eyes widened a bit, and then he smiled, but the half of his face marred by scars moved only slightly. It was a broken smile, filled with dark humor, and yet his uninjured eye crinkled at the corner, a hint of lightness in him.

"I don't think it's the same, Alya," he said. "At least not for me. Truly, I'm okay with it."

Was there a hint of laughter in his voice? Good

to know. The meeting was over, but somehow, she didn't feel like their conversation had ended. He crossed his arms in front of him, his biceps flexing as he watched her, taking her in.

Finally, Henning spoke again. "We are going to be spending every minute together for the next five days. I want you to feel very comfortable with me."

Alya felt as if he were opening himself to her, just a little. His gaze said *you can trust me*, and she couldn't look away.

"I doubt we'll have any problems," he continued in that low, rumbling voice. "But there is always the possibility that I will need to protect you. Physically."

He paused, swallowing, his Adam's apple bobbing, as the last word sank in. It ran through her body, suggesting much different ways he could physically affect her. Damn, she needed to get this under control. Attraction was about nothing more than sexual interest…which her body was clearly expressing right now. She felt the barely concealed desire in his eyes, and she was almost sure he could see the same in hers. She felt the pain Henning's scars must have caused, and her mind was already at work, connecting that with the intense sense of…protectiveness… she had felt from him over the last three years. Everything else faded as this all fit together, like the final pieces of a puzzle, somewhere deep inside her. She was opening herself to this feeling, she didn't know how to stop it. Or if she wanted to.

"I understand," she said, her voice steady.

He gave her a little nod. Then he rubbed the scar on his neck absently. "I'm aware that with my size and my scars and what Max calls my aversion to conversation, I can come off as a little rough around the edges," he said, cracking a hint of a smile again. It faded quickly. "But I never, ever want to scare you."

Alya frowned. "You don't. Not it all."

She had a strong urge to clear up that misunderstanding, but elaborating would mean wandering into inappropriate territory. Her attraction was raw and very real. Any hints of wariness he had detected were about the intensity of her reaction to him, not fear.

Alya had to make him understand, and words didn't seem to be the right path. So, instead, she raised her hand and slowly reached for his forearm, crossed over his broad chest. She gave him plenty of time to back away, but he didn't, so she touched his skin. The electric spark between them surged once again, and she swallowed a gasp. His muscles twitched under her fingers, and his lips parted. Was he thinking about kissing, too?

"This isn't fear, Henning," she said, her voice steadier than she felt.

His chest rose and fell and she tried—and failed—to read his expression. Finally, he nodded. "You can touch me, do whatever you need during our trip. I don't want to go into this with any hesitancy on your part."

Alya's heart jumped at each image his words conjured. *Touch me. Whatever you need.* The physi-

cal memory of her hands on the hard ridges of his
abs came back, mingling with things she had only
imagined.

There were nights he had watched her through
the security camera in her front hall, making sure
she came home safely. But what about the night she
had come home, half-drunk, with her date, and had
sex against the door in full view of the camera? The
idea that Henning might be watching was a turn-on
at the time. Now her mind wandered further. If he
had watched, had he gotten himself off to it, too?
Damn, that would be hot…

Get your mind out of the gutter, girl. You're in
his workplace.

She lowered her hand, breaking the connection.
Then she smiled up at him. "Is the permission to
touch standard in your Blackmore Inc. contract?"

The hint of a smile returned to Henning's lips,
and he shrugged. "I have no idea. I'm just letting
you know how I work."

"I'm sure you have plenty of satisfied clients,"
she said, laughing.

"There are no other in-person clients for me. Not
now, and not in the future." Henning shook his head.
"Only you."

His eyes were dark flames, flickering, captivating. She was getting used to the way he watched her,
his gaze unwavering. As if every bit of his focus was
on her, as if nothing else in the world existed.

What did it mean to be intensely attracted to her

bodyguard, right from the first moment she crashed into him? She had never felt this way about Max, so his appeal wasn't just the role of protector. Henning awoke a hunger she knew couldn't—shouldn't—be fed...should it?

Maybe this was the wrong approach. She was done running away from her fears. Maybe it was time to take control of the situation, to explore it, to figure out what she was looking for, not just what to avoid.

But Alya didn't know what was going on in Henning's mind. She was almost positive he felt the same intense attraction, but maybe he had reasons he couldn't or wouldn't act on it. Like the obvious ones. What were the Blackmore Inc. rules about personal involvement with clients? Maybe she could just find a way to ask him...somehow. Alya's face flushed as more of that current of sexual interest sizzled between them.

"I'll pick you up at your place tomorrow morning at six," he said.

"I'll be ready for you."

"Alya?" His voice had lowered to almost a whisper. "Please send me a message if you think of anything you need. Or want. Anything."

CHAPTER TWO

THE WORDS WERE out of his mouth before all the reasons not to say them registered. Henning's mind was still stuck on the moment when her slim, tight body brushed against his. When she pressed her hands against his stomach, exploring before either of them seemed to fully register what was happening. Alya was soft. Slim but not frail. So very alive. She smelled of honey and sunshine, and every dark desire Henning had ever had.

But the reason to bury all those thoughts came crashing in seconds later. Her expression when she saw his face. He couldn't forget that for a moment.

Henning took a step away, giving Alya a clear path to the conference-room door, giving himself a little distance from her intoxicating scent. Finally, her bright blue eyes flickered from his.

"I'll walk you to the elevator," he said, heading for the door before she had a chance to respond.

The reception area of the top floor was quiet and bright, the morning sun filtering through the frosted glass and reflecting off the polished wood surfaces.

They headed for the elevators in silence, Henning's body on high alert, fully tuned to her every move. She stopped in front of the heavy metal doors, but she didn't reach for the call button. Instead, she turned to face him again.

"I'm beyond thrilled that Max and my sister found each other. Natasha's happiness means everything to me," she said. "It meant I lost my bodyguard, too, but that's a small price."

Henning could see that this was hard for her to talk about, so he waited, letting her take her time.

"Hiring security is a crutch I've leaned on for a while." She swallowed, the movement sweeping down her long neck. "It used to be necessary all the time, but now it's more often for a peace of mind than actual protection. It's like a little bit of me believed his claims that I was turning into a train wreck, that I doubted myself. And I don't like that feeling of vulnerability."

Henning restrained his urge to react. His deep desire to comfort her, to protect her warred with what he heard in her words: she wanted to stand on her own. So he said nothing, just nodded, storing the information away for later inspection.

"You know a little about what happened with Nick, the way he wouldn't leave me alone and made me out to look unhinged, so I think you might understand why it's been hard to move on. It takes a long time for me to trust anyone. So I wouldn't want any other bodyguard," she added, reaching for the call button. "Only you."

The elevator doors slid open, and she walked in without looking back, vanishing as the cold metal doors closed. Henning took a deep breath, then another, slowing his heartbeat, forcing himself back to the starkness of reality, where she was just a client and this was just a job. Nothing more. He blew out one more long breath and headed for the hall to his office.

The receptionist gave him a neutral smile as he passed and busied herself with something at her desk. When Henning first came to Blackmore Inc., it had taken that woman a few weeks to hide her reaction every time she saw the jagged scars down his face. He remembered the widening of her eyes, the way her gaze drifted over him each time he passed. Not so different from Alya's reaction, really. She was a model, for fuck's sake, paid to live in a world where looks were everything. Of course she'd react to his injuries.

But it had hit him hard. Alya had given him a look that was far too close to the look Corinne had given him five years ago at the hospital, at the very lowest point of his life. Or at least he thought it was similar. Alya had said so convincingly that he didn't scare her, too. Maybe she was one of those women who got turned on by a man who looked more beast than human? That thought alone should have been sobering enough, but the electric current of desire didn't seem to be waning.

Why the hell was he still thinking about this? He had made peace with his scars years ago. He had escaped that disastrous drug bust alive, which was more than his right-hand man got. That one day changed everything, and usually he welcomed the visual reminder of the event he never wanted to forget. Now he was mulling over the way he looked? Damn.

As he headed down the hall to his office, Max caught up with him. His hands were shoved in his pockets, his expression relaxed, like nothing in the world bothered him.

"That went well," Max said lightly. Henning jerked his head in time to see a hint of a smile on his friend's face.

"I'm not sure this is a good idea," muttered Henning.

Max shook his head slowly. "You were the best in the Australian Federal Police force, so I know you're not talking about your ability to protect Alya."

Henning blew out a breath and shook his head. "Most obvious issue, I'm going to attract a lot of unwanted attention, which she doesn't need. It's a fucking fashion shoot, no place for a bloke with a face like this." He rubbed his left cheek, where one of the scars pulled his taut, injured skin tight. "And though I don't track fashion shit, I'm pretty sure this doesn't go with whatever the hell the season's look is."

Max gave a little snort of laughter, then raised an

eyebrow. "You saved a dozen officers from a meth-running gang. You will make sure Alya doesn't spend one minute of this trip worried something unexpected might happen." His mouth curved up into a full smile as he spoke. "Who the fuck cares what this season's look is?"

Henning's mouth twitched until he was smiling, too. Max clapped him on the shoulder. "Seriously, you've been surveilling Alya for over three years now. You know every single thing about her situation and where she might feel vulnerable."

Understatement of the year. But it also meant spending a few days in the cold, which wasn't ideal. The nightmares rarely came these days, and occasionally he took a winter trip to the Blue Mountains with his sister's family and faced the cold without too much trouble. Still…not ideal. But he'd make it work.

There was understanding in Max's easy smile. Had he picked up on the more personal aspects of the job Henning was struggling with? Yeah, that was his problem. Keeping his distance from Alya had been a Herculean effort in the past, but all those hours alone… Henning still wasn't sure how he was going to pull this off. A captivating woman, strong but in a vulnerable place, who needed his help—this scenario was a temptation too strong to resist.

Cameron Blackmore, the company CEO, had offered him dozens of opportunities to work directly with clients since he'd quit the AFP and come to

Blackmore Inc., and he had turned every single one of them down. Henning didn't usually care much about the looks of shock at the wreckage of his face, but it didn't make for the best guard-client relationships. Even before the scars, most people left him alone. Now working surveillance, he was pretty sure he scared most of the IT department shitless.

He and Max came to a stop in front of Henning's office. Henning reached for the handle, but before he turned it, Max quietly cleared his throat, getting his attention.

"I wouldn't have pushed you to do this if I didn't think it was a good option. For both of you."

Henning scowled. "For me? I highly doubt that." He blew out his breath in frustration. "You have no idea."

"Maybe I don't," said Max, his voice almost maddeningly easy and smooth. "Or maybe I can guess why you'd want to stay far away from her. And why you said yes to this job anyway. But I pushed because I think this assignment is different than any other one for you."

Henning grunted in response. That much was true. But it didn't mean he'd survive this week with his sanity intact. Before he could respond, his phone rang. His heart thumped in his chest. It couldn't be Alya, taking him up on his impulsive offer of *anything*...could it? Henning squashed that thought as he pulled out the phone and looked at the screen. *Suzanne.* He sighed.

"It's my sister," he said to Max. "I should take this."

Max nodded and clapped him on the shoulder again before walking away. Henning pressed the button on the screen to answer.

"Hi, Suz," he said, opening his office door. "What's up?"

"Kids melting down, work and an occasional conversation with Kenny," she said dryly. "The usual."

Henning smiled. His older sister's house was pure chaos, but she was happy. She and her husband Kenny had tried for years for a baby, first by themselves and then with some help. Suzanne was at the point of desperation when finally, little Molly came. And then Liam. Growing up, their parents weren't much for outward displays of emotion, and though Henning was close to his sister, neither of them were much for probing conversations. Suzanne had never said a lot about the whole experience with infertility, but just stepping into her house, he knew she was happy. Seeing that was still one of the best things in his life.

Henning headed across his office for his desk and sank into his chair.

"I was calling to see if you have plans this Saturday," said his sister. Dishes clattered in the background. "Molly has a dance recital. Princess themed, of course. And we'll go out to dinner afterward."

Henning took a breath and dropped the bomb as gently as possible. "Thanks, but I'm going out of town tomorrow."

"What?"

The shock in his sister's voice made him roll his eyes.

"You know, on an airplane," he deadpanned. "They even let *me* on those things."

She gave a huff of exasperation. "Stop it. You know I'm just in shock that you're actually going somewhere. Are you..." Her voice turned syrupy, exaggerating the incredulity in her question. "Are you *actually* going on vacation, Henning?"

"Nope," he said curtly. "It's for work."

"You sit in front of a computer for work these days," Suzanne said. "Explain."

"I need to be on the ground for this one."

She was silent for a bit, and the clattering of dishes died down. "You said you'd never do this kind of thing again," she said slowly.

Yeah, he did say that. But the last thing he wanted to do right now was discuss why Alya was the exception to that promise. Suzanne was quiet for a long time, so he leaned back in his chair and propped his feet on his desk, waiting her out.

"Where are you going?"

"Northern Sweden. The Icehotel. Danger level is very low."

More silence. Henning swiped a hand over his face. He knew exactly what his sister was thinking about now, but he didn't want to talk about it. He didn't love the location of the assignment, but he wasn't going to let it be an issue.

"It's cold there," she said quietly.

He frowned. "I've been in the cold since…" Fuck, he really didn't want to talk about this. "It's under control, Suzanne."

"Is there a woman involved?"

Henning choked in his next breath, then disguised it as a cough. "What?"

"You heard me," said Suzanne. "Is there a woman involved?"

He closed his eyes and massaged his temples. "Yes, the assignment involves a woman, but that question makes it sound like something it's not."

"I knew it," she whispered, but he heard it, loud and clear.

He huffed out a breath. "Whatever you're thinking, you're wrong."

"Okay, Henning." Her words had a hint of that syrupy tone again.

"Look up *Behind the Runway* on YouTube. You'll see what I mean."

"I've watched it. The behind-the-scenes show about modeling?" His sister paused, and he was pretty sure understanding was sinking in. He wasn't a fool. There were so many reasons that whatever connection he had felt with Alya in the conference room would die a quick death as soon as they entered that scene, and his scars were just one of them.

When Henning didn't respond, Suzanne finally said, "I see. Do you want me to water your plant while you're gone?"

"My pla—?" He caught himself. Right. The plant his sister's family had given him for Christmas. The dry, brown tangle of leaves in the corner of his living room.

"Don't worry about coming all the way into town," he said quickly. "I'll figure it out."

"You already killed that plant, didn't you?"

"Um, maybe?"

"Henning." She said his name slowly, adding a dramatic pause before continuing. "The kids picked it out for you."

He cringed. "I know. I'll get a new one before they come over here next time."

"That's not the point, and you know it."

He did.

"At least it wasn't a puppy," he grumbled.

A puppy was the kids' first idea, and thank God he had nipped that one in the bud. Judging from how plant ownership had gone, his sister was probably thinking the same thing. Suzanne meant well, but he was the last person a helpless little animal should be dependent on.

"I know you would have done better with a puppy," she said softly.

Henning wasn't sure about that, but he let the statement stand.

"Take care of yourself, Henning," Suzanne added. This time, there was a mix of worry and affection in her voice. "Please."

"I'll call when I get home." He swallowed back his own emotions and ended the call.

Henning set his phone on his desk and ran his hand through his hair, shaking his head. It had taken his sister only one short phone call to uncover all the conflicted feelings for Alya that he was trying to tamp down. Which meant he was going to have a hell of a time putting aside every reaction he had to her the moment he showed up at her door tomorrow morning.

But he'd do it. His job was to watch her every moment of the day. And every long hour of the night. Just the two of them, alone in the darkness, in a remote resort in northern Sweden.

Holy hell.

CHAPTER THREE

HENNING STEERED THE big black SUV over the packed snow that made up the desolate road to the Icehotel, keeping his gaze fixed straight in front of him. The pine forests, covered in white, stretched out along the road on both sides. Alya was looking out the window at the passing landscape, dotted with occasional houses painted bright red and topped with snow. He didn't need to look in her direction to know what she was doing.

He'd been tuned in to her every movement since he'd picked her up at her Sydney apartment. That was expected. What was unexpected was the sense that she was just as tuned in to him. He had kept himself awake half the night going over her response to him yesterday in the Blackmore Inc. conference room. Imagining all the other ways he wanted to end that meeting.

"It's cold here," said Alya, clutching her down jacket tighter around her. "I mean, of course it's cold, but I didn't know it would feel like this."

Henning knew exactly what she meant. When

they'd stepped out of the airport, the wind found its way through his jacket immediately. He had seen snow in person, but nothing like this endless blanket of white. It was fascinating to look at, or at least it should have been. Now, the fascination was tainted by the memory of the ice-cold concrete floor of the warehouse where he had lain, watching his team member die from the shards of glass that had hit them both in the explosion. But he could put that re-action aside for the next few days. Besides, he was Australian for fuck's sake—of course he reacted to the cold.

Henning checked to make sure the seat heater was on max and hiked up the temperature a couple notches. "I thought you were from Russia."

"We left when I was six," she said with a snort of laughter. "And I think my parents did a better job of dressing me for the weather."

Henning smiled. "I should probably call them for some tips."

He glanced over at her. Other than the parka and boots, Alya was dressed for late summer in Austra-lia. She'd walked onto the airplane in tight jeans, a silky top that showed skin, and sunglasses. The look-don't-touch vibe rolled off her. A good thing, as far as Henning was concerned, since the travel portions of the assignment were the most unpredictable—and the most critical for her to feel safe. While he accepted that he could never completely shut down his reaction to her, this cool, polished Alya was easier to separate himself from. But right now, after a day of traveling halfway across the world—hair mussed from fits of sleep, curled up in her puffy down coat with her feet tucked under her—keeping a professional distance was close to impossible. Had he caught her staring at his ass when they were getting off the plane? That didn't help. It triggered a vivid image of her that he'd conjured up in the shower the night before as he came: Alya up against the door, his cock deep inside her as he put his mouth on her soft, slim throat.

Heat flooded to his groin. Fuck. Enough of that.

No encounters with Nick. No scenes that called attention to her personal life. That was his job. Nothing else. Unless she said explicitly that she wanted more. It was this last thought that had kept him up way too late.

Alya yawned and reached into her bag, pulling out the master schedule, scanning the pages.

"Today you have a meeting when you arrive, and then there's drinks in the Icehotel, right?" he asked.

She nodded. "I was just checking to make sure we have time for a nap between those two."

"Can you nap in that igloo?" He had seen photos of the Icehotel rooms, glowing with the tint of ocean blue. They were works of art, really, elaborate beds, chairs and sculptures carved from enormous blocks of ice. Strikingly beautiful but not made for casual napping.

"I could probably nap anywhere at this point,

though I think the frozen portion of the hotel is more like a museum during the day," said Alya, stifling another yawn. "But we're not staying in the part of the hotel with ice rooms tonight. We're scheduled in the regular heated building, right next door, for the first night, so we can use the beds in our room anytime today."

Use the beds. Unfortunate phrasing. As the words left her lips, an image came of using a bed, naked, with Alya riding on top as he fucked her. Henning swallowed back a groan. How long had it been since he'd gotten laid? Too long, clearly.

There were places he could go to fuck, clubs where women got off on having a big, scarred man over them, holding them down, just the way they asked for it. And the women had no problem with his limits either—they had no interest in touching or kissing him anyway. Maybe he should have gone there last night, just to burn off some of this intense want.

But Henning had quit, cold turkey, when he found himself searching for tall, blonde women with endless legs. He had never had a preference before, and he knew exactly why this one was forming. Which was more than enough reason to cut that habit off immediately. What he felt for Alya was so many worlds away from what he wanted from those women. Henning couldn't bear to mix the two worlds.

So it had been a while. Maybe that was why he had thrown caution to the wind and offered Alya anything she needed. Or maybe, after watching those blue eyes come alive under his gaze, he couldn't resist.

During his undercover work with the AFP, he had built a career in part on reading people, looking past what they said and concentrating on what they did. Yesterday, he hadn't missed the way Alya had stepped closer instead of backing away from him, the way she'd licked her lips, the way her breath came faster when she'd touched him. In the days before the disastrous bust that marked the end of his AFP career, he had gotten more than his fair share of attention from women. And he understood his responsibility as a man bigger than most other people, the responsibility of making sure he understood exactly what a woman wanted from him before he touched her. His days of propositions in bars were long over, but he hadn't forgotten how it all worked. He had to be really fucking careful.

The GPS on the car told him they were nearing the place. He pulled off into a little parking lot in front of the unassuming wooden buildings. Tall pine trees rose up on both sides, and Henning assumed the actual Icehotel lay somewhere behind them. He found a parking spot at the far end of the lot, and turned off the car. Then he rested his hands on his legs, ready for whatever came next, but Alya made no move to gather her belongings and climb out. Instead, she turned to face him. He had the feeling she wanted to speak, so he watched her, waiting her out. After her chest rose and fell a few more times, she met his gaze.

"Yesterday, you said you had no other in-person clients," she said. "Why did you take this job?"

Henning swallowed, taking his time to consider his answer.

Because I couldn't say no to you. Because the chance to be next to you for five days was too much to resist.

No, he definitely couldn't go there. Instead, he went for an easier truth. "Because you deserve to feel safe."

She tilted her head to the side. "So does everyone."

"Of course," he said. "But after what happened in the AFP, I won't take an assignment unless I'm sure I understand all the threats and would do whatever it takes to keep that person safe. Anything."

As the words left his mouth, he knew he shouldn't have said them. They hinted at both the past that haunted him and the intensity of his feelings for her, neither of which had any place on this trip. Henning scrubbed his hands over his face. The bristles from his unshaven jaw pricked at his right hand, but under his left hand the scar that pulled at the side of his mouth was unnaturally smooth. A reminder of how wrong things could go.

Alya's expression was completely unreadable. "Henning, I'm going to ask you something I'll probably regret, but here it goes." She took a deep breath.

"If I kissed you right now, would that interfere with our bodyguard-client relationship?"

He stilled. He didn't even breathe, but his cock jolted to life. Did he hear her right? Fuck, he had thought about kissing her so many times it was hard to register this was really happening. In his head, he could imagine the kiss as his old self, before the attack, before the scars. Soft, beautiful before it turned hungry. Perfect.

But deep inside, his past was still an open wound. Lying on that cold warehouse floor, fighting his own pain while trying to save Sanjay, watching the bastard who caused the explosion get away, he had seen his actions for what they were. Selfish. He had been blinded by his own goal, taking a risk to grab the leader, a risk that ended Sanjay's life. *That* was reality, a cold, hard reality he would live with for the rest of his life. Never again would he let his own wants drive his actions. So how could he consider kissing Alya, knowing all this?

Henning blew out a breath. Shit. Why the hell was he thinking about all this right now?

His expression had no doubt grown darker because her smile had faded.

"Sorry," she said, her voice filled with false cheer. "Should have gone with my first instinct to keep my mouth shut. Let's just pretend I didn't say that. I'll find someone else to proposition."

Henning flinched. A storm hit him, a storm of

protectiveness and something else he didn't want to acknowledge, despite the ache of his cock.

"No." The word came out sharp and urgent before he could stop himself. Alya drew in a quick, startled breath, and he winced. But *fuck, no.* The idea of watching her flirt with another man was doing crazy things to his insides. It sent a surge through him, twisting into every long-dormant competitive urge to show her all the ways he could satisfy her better. It was the kind of drive he used to thrive on.

No. Just no. He had sworn to himself when he took this job that it had to be *all about her.* So what the hell was he supposed to do with this situation? Let her go off and find another man, someone who probably wouldn't give a shit about what she needed? If he said yes to this, gave her what she wanted, it would have to be with his sole focus on her, not selfishly chasing his own needs.

He reached for Alya, touching her cheek, coaxing her to look at him. She did, meeting his eyes, and he found traces of embarrassment. Did she think he was rejecting her? Hell, no. *Take it easy.* He swallowed.

"There's nothing in the world I want more than to kiss you right now," he whispered. "I don't want you to ever think otherwise, no matter what happens."

Her eyes widened, and they came alive with unguarded interest. So much better. He pushed on.

"And, to answer your question, no, it wouldn't interfere. Especially not if the doors are locked."

A slow smile spread over her face, a glow of happiness returning. Damn, it was breathtaking. Then she reached for the dashboard and pressed the lock button.

Henning's body jumped to attention, his cock all in, the eager fucker. *Slow the hell down.* He took a deep breath. This was for her. He had to get it right.

"But before we continue, I need to tell you something," he said, keeping his voice quiet. "I haven't kissed anyone since before the attack where I got these scars. It was five years ago."

Her eyes widened. "You've been celibate for five years?"

The uninjured corner of his mouth tugged up. "That's not quite what I said."

Understanding registered in her eyes. "Got it," said Alya, and a hint of amusement twinkled in her eyes. Thank fuck for that.

Henning pressed on. "I'm telling you because I don't even know if I can kiss you the way I want to right now. The way you deserve."

She quirked her eyebrow at him. "And what do I deserve?"

"A kiss promising you that you're the only thing in the world that matters."

She blinked, swallowed, as if his words were sinking in. Good. Because he wasn't fooling around here. Anything that happened with her would get his full attention. She was quiet for a while, and then she straightened up in her seat.

"You know what *I* think I need?" she said with

a little smile. "Something that's hot and fun with someone I can trust. And I'm pretty sure that's what I'll get."

Henning blew out a breath. He could do this as long as he kept his focus on her.

So he looked straight into the endless oceans of her eyes and shut everything else out. "Okay. We can try for that."

Holy shit. Alya took a couple steadying breaths, trying to slow down her runaway heartbeat and jumpstart her brain. Last night, alone in her apartment, this had all sounded way more reasonable. Somewhere around midnight, Alya had decided to simply ask for what she wanted: a few days of sexy fun. Except, the morning after, when Henning showed up at her doorstep, she still hadn't quite figured out what to say.

Are you interested in spending a few of your off-duty hours naked with me?

Maybe a little too direct. Alya had spent a good portion of the seemingly endless procession of flights to Sweden contemplating how to test Henning's interest. His aloofness during the travel had her second-guessing the idea, but once they got into the car, the intense attraction she had felt after yesterday's meeting was back. So, she went with it.

Then came the words she was sure she'd never forget: A *kiss promising you that you're the only thing in the world that matters.* She couldn't resist the intensity in his voice. How did he know this was her personal kryptonite, the thing he could say to send her body into flames? But these were dangerous words, too much like the lies that kept her going back to Nick Bancroft, long after she should have fled for good.

Except Nick was the past, and she wasn't that woman anymore. Just a few days of fun.

Still, the questions kept rolling through her mind. Did the scars around his mouth hurt him? Who had he had sex with for the past five years without kissing? And, most of all, how did she make sure not to get sucked in too deep?

Alya filed her questions away and took off her seat belt. She reached over and unlocked Henning's. He slipped it off his shoulder but made no move to touch her. His eyes were hot but guarded, burning into her. He seemed to be waiting for her, so she unzipped her down parka and shrugged it off.

He smiled a little. "Getting hot already? We haven't even started."

"I was up late thinking about this last night." She winked at him playfully. "Move your chair back a little."

"Anything you want," he said softly, amusement dancing in his eyes. The more they talked this way, close, intimate, the more she could read him. He unzipped his own coat and eased the seat back, tipping it at an angle, making enough room for her to climb on. So she did. The car was big, but so was Henning, so they shuffled and laughed and adjusted until she was facing him, knees tucked on both sides of his thick thighs. His body radiated heat, and God, it felt so good. *He* felt so good.

"Your hands are big," she said, fitting them against her own. His were so much thicker and longer.

"Does that turn you on?"

She laughed. "Maybe?"

Some of the lightness in his eyes faded. "Meaning you wish it didn't?"

She paused. "It's just complicated."

"We can stop anytime."

"I know." She could see he needed that reassurance that she would speak up if she wanted to stop, and he relaxed a little under her touch, his smile slowly returning. But stopping wasn't her worry at all. It was that she really, really liked this—his size, the way he was with her, everything—and she wasn't sure she wanted to know why. But that didn't have to figure into kissing him.

Henning slipped his hands around her waist and cupped her ass, bringing her up against him, closer, until she brushed against the enormous bulge in his pants. His eyes were heavy with humor and lust. Right now, Henning was worlds away from the hard, impassive bodyguard who had traveled next to her all day. For all his big body and muscles, he was... gentle with her. There was no other word for it.

...you're the only thing in the world that matters.

Alya swallowed. He was talking about the kiss, not making some larger declaration. This was sexy fun, just what she had wanted. And she wasn't going to taint it with her past hang-ups. So she pushed all of those ideas out of her mind, and focused on the stunning man in front of her. The man whose heavy cock was currently pressing against her.

"So you want this kind of kiss?" he asked, smiling.

She nodded and moved up and down against his erection, using it to stroke her clit. He flexed his hips and ground against her, sending more sparks of pleasure through her. He did it again, rubbing his cock in every sensitive place, making her moan and shudder.

"Yes," she said, a little breathless. "This is definitely the kind of kiss I want."

He flexed his hips again, and her eyes rolled back as another wave of pleasure coursed through her. *Oh, yes.*

Henning looked like he was enjoying this slow, hot grind just as much as she was, but after hearing about his five-year kissing dry spell, she couldn't help but wonder if he was also distracting her. If it was easier to give her his cock than his mouth.

"Henning?" she whispered.

"Mmm?"

"I want to kiss."

He stilled under her, his fingers tense. Then he nodded. "I do, too."

His gaze was dark, unreadable. She lifted her

hands to his face, and, gently, she cupped his jaw. He closed his eyes as her fingers met his skin. Slowly she ran her thumb over one of the ropy scars by his mouth. A rumble came from deep inside him.

"How does this feel?"

He paused, his breath uneven. "Intense."

"Does it hurt?"

Henning gave a raspy laugh. "Hell, no. Very much the opposite."

"Good." Alya smiled. "Ready?"

He nodded. Alya leaned forward, resting her hands against his biceps. She waited there, looking for hesitation. There was tension, so much tension, as they waited there on the edge of this precipice. But he gave her a little nod, willing to jump. So she brushed her lips against his, testing. His cock throbbed against her, and the muscles of his arms hardened under her fingers. She tested again. His lips felt…different. A good different. She stayed there, not moving, breathing in his warm scent, getting used to this new tentative exploration. Letting him get used to her. More breaths, each uneven rasp stoking heat inside her. She pressed her mouth more firmly against his, and this time he responded. He parted his lips and tasted her. Every brush of his lips, every swipe of his tongue was achingly slow.

Alya tilted her head, learning how their mouths fit together, learning what made him groan. His hands tightened around her, and she slid her fingers along his jaw, the heaviness of each scar line weighing under her hand.

And then something flipped. It was as if he finally let the pent-up want from those five years loose. His kisses turned greedy, and a growl escaped from his chest as he nipped at her lips and sucked on her tongue. All the softness from before was fading, and God, how she loved this new, hungrier side. She moved, letting the stiff, thick ridge of his cock drag along her core, and he responded, tilting his hips, giving them both that exquisite friction. Sighs. Moans. Wordless pleas from her lips for more. Her body was on fire, the pressure building inside as his cock moved against her clit. She kissed the scarred corner of his mouth, his jaw, finding the rough lines, the smooth lines, the stubble. She wanted all of it.

"Fuck, you turn me on." His whisper rasped in her ear. "I want to make you feel good. Can you come like this?"

Alya hadn't thought that far, but now that he mentioned it… "I think so."

"Good." His teeth scraped her neck. "Hang on tight."

She rested her hands on his shoulders and closed her eyes. Damn, just the muscles of his shoulders were enough to send a jolt of pleasure through her. Then, he began lifting her up and down in a slow, steady rhythm that was…oh, God, it was exactly what she wanted.

"Like this?" he whispered. "Does this feel good?"

His voice was a rasp in her ear, a low, rough invitation.

"Yes, Henning," she moaned, her head dropping to his neck as the pleasure built.

The moment his name left her lips, a new rumble came from deep in his chest. Then another. Sounds of raw, insatiable hunger, of contrasts, pleasure and pain, want and fear. And need. So much need. His voice called to something buried inside her, uncovering it. New desires bubbled, still not fully formed. The aching sound grew louder, but it was her own moan that filled the car. She was right there on the edge of coming as he thrusted his hips harder. She searched for his mouth again. The kiss was rough, each aching stroke of his tongue matching the thrust of his cock against her.

Pleasure shot through her as she moved, drawing out the orgasm, losing herself in the heat of their bodies, in the scent of sex, in *him*. Her eyes fluttered closed, and she rested her cheek on his thick shoulder, breathing in his scent. Henning's heart thudded in her ear.

What had just happened? The connection between them was so powerful, almost as if—

Slow down. She wasn't going to mistake pleasure and affection for something else. The ecstasy-induced haze was clouding her brain. So, instead, she took one last, long inhale of turned-on male and put a little distance between them.

"Well, that was certainly a full-service kiss," she said, her voice languid with pleasure.

Henning chuckled, the sound echoing deep in his chest. "It exceeded expectations in every way."

She really should get up, do…something, but he was so warm, and she really didn't want to move. Henning's cock throbbed urgently against her. She peered into his dark brown eyes.

"You didn't come yet," she said with a little smile. "I can help you with that."

He shook his head. "It would be messy, and it's going to get cold in here soon. I'll take care of that later."

"You'll take care of it?" She tilted her head at him. "Alone?"

"I'm good at it," he said, laughter in his voice.

Alya raised her eyebrows. How much lightness and humor did this man have, buried inside him? "I'd like to see that."

His cock pulsed against her, and he groaned. Then a hint of a smile drew at the uninjured side of his mouth. "I bet you would."

CHAPTER FOUR

"TIME TO WAKE UP," said Henning, a little louder.

Alya still didn't stir. As soon as her first meeting had ended, she'd crashed into bed and hadn't moved since. He had let her sleep as long as he could, watching her from the chair by the window of their hotel room. Her long, blond hair was a halo around her face, and her full lips were parted. In another life, he would have woken her up with his lips, but not in this one.

Still, she wasn't waking from his voice alone, so he stood up and crossed the room to her bed. Resting his hand on the bare, white wall, he bent down and brushed his fingers over her cheek.

"Sweetheart? We need to go."

Her eyelashes fluttered, and she drew in a sleepy breath. Henning braced himself against the warmth swelling inside him. For years he had watched her through someone else's lens, in magazines, on billboards, and through the Blackmore Inc. surveillance system. This was so different, so real, so raw. He had no words to understand what was happening inside him now that she had chosen him to be here. To protect her. To satisfy her. He'd devote himself to these tasks, keeping his past at bay, controlling this tightness in his chest, this swelling of *something*, something he wouldn't name.

Alya blinked a couple times, brushing off sleep. Then she met his gaze, parted her lips and...smiled. She fucking smiled, her eyes dancing with lightness as she looked up at him. Coming out of sleep, unguarded, vulnerable, she smiled like he was exactly who she wanted to see when she awoke. The swelling inside him was threatening to burst.

"The time change is disorienting," she said, seemingly unaware that his entire world was tilting. So he took a breath and let her warm voice pull him in. "I was hoping this wasn't a dream."

It was all happening so fast. When she parted her lips, his brain short-circuited. *Kiss her. Kiss her.* The temptation was so sharp and bare that it almost overwhelmed him. He closed his eyes and gritted his teeth. Not happening. This was for her, and *only* her. If they were going to spend the next couple days in close quarters, he needed to get this situation under control.

"Listen, about earlier," he said. "About what happened in the car..."

Her cheeks turned a pale pink, and she propped herself up on her elbow. Her mouth was so temptingly close. "I kinda jumped on you. I'm sorry if I put you in a bad position. Again."

"I didn't mind that particular position at all. I was very into it," he said with a laugh.

Alya smirked at his comment, then gave a sigh. "But we shouldn't? Is that what you're trying to say?"

He shook his head slowly. "I'm happy to do that as many times as you want. Or anything else you're interested in. That's up to you."

"I think I made it clear I'm interested." She blinked at him. "Still, I sense a *but* coming."

He blew out his breath. "The moment we walk out of the room, I'm your bodyguard."

She tilted her head to the side and smiled a little. "You're warning me that we won't be sneaking off to try out one of those ice beds?"

"That sounds really fucking cold."

"I understand." Her smile faded. "Because I'm interfering with your job?"

Henning frowned. To be with someone physically scarred like him would make her—and him—the center of attention. Henning had watched her life in the media enough to see exactly how it would play out: grainy photos of them on the front of all the tabloids. And then what? With Alya's more recent dates, the comments were pettier. But Henning was a big fucker with scars and little patience for people in general. After studying Nick Bancroft for three years, Henning knew how that bastard worked. He was almost sure the guy was a clinical narcissist. Nick still hadn't forgotten that Alya left him, and he might use this chance to make a fresh dig about her unstable mental health or make up some story about how she called him again, begging to take her back, and use it as a reason to show up. Just the idea of it made his blood boil, but how the hell did he talk about this with her?

Henning blew out a breath and tried his best. "Look, you hired me so there was no drama on this trip. And I don't want any...speculations on my watch."

"I spent three years shaping my life around avoiding Nick. I turned down jobs because they required traveling to Los Angeles. I've hired a bodyguard to go to events, even when you were checking to make sure Nick was still across the Pacific. I'm done with that," she said. "It's true that I don't want to attract too much attention to my personal life, but I'm not going to let that mean I can't have one. It just means we need to be careful."

He shook his head. What she was saying made sense. She wasn't making decisions based on fear, and she was willing to take some risks. But what was the point of this risk? So he could hold her hand in the Icebar? Nope, not worth it.

Alya opened her mouth, as if she was going to argue with him, but she hesitated. Then understanding registered in her eyes. "You meant speculations about you," she said softly.

He frowned. "I'm not concerned about that."

"I am." She blinked up at him, her sky-blue eyes clear and unwavering.

Then she bit her lip, and his eyes dropped to her mouth. *Focus.*

"But if you're not by my side, there will be other results, ones you might not like," she said.

Like a hard-on from watching her all day long? He had already reconciled himself with that reality. He gave her a little smirk. "I can handle it."

She raised an eyebrow. "We can talk about it after you see what I mean." She was looking at him, like she was assessing him. He leveled his gaze on her, letting her look her fill. Better if she saw him clearly from the beginning.

At last, she nodded. "Fine. But you're okay with a little fun when it's just the two of us?"

"Anything you want." He touched her cheek. Her skin was so unbearably soft under his fingers.

She covered his hand with hers. "What do *you* want?"

He looked down at her, so close to him on this bed. She was waiting for his answer.

Finally he sighed and told her the truth. "I want you, any way I can have you."

Her breath came out somewhere between a sigh and a moan, and the memory of the kiss in the car came crashing down on him. The memory of the sweet tenderness of her lips that so quickly burst into flames. Alya straddling him, her hands holding him so tight it felt like she'd never let go. And he wanted that again, fuck, how he wanted that. Badly. Just one moment of selfishness, one kiss because *he* wanted it. Henning put his knee on the bed next to her and leaned down, searching her expression. And, oh, that smile as he came close, more than an invitation, with a dizzying lightness that took his breath away.

He closed the last distance between them, his mouth on hers again, and she sighed—*she sighed*. This was too good to be real, but the ache inside was too strong for it to be otherwise. Henning licked the seam of her mouth, and she opened for him. She was here, solid under his hands, all soft lips and hungry explorations. The aching need, the gaping hole inside him opened right back up, and he couldn't contain it. He gave her soft strokes of his tongue, and she matched them with her own. Then she reached up, threading her fingers in his hair, and pulled him down on top of her. They landed on the bed, him over her, laughing, kissing. *God, yes.* He could kiss her all day. Wait. No. She needed to be somewhere right now.

"Your schedule," he murmured, his lips so close to hers. She nodded, her nose brushing against his. So intimate.

Mine. The thought was there before he could shove it back down, and he struggled to bury it, along with the surge of protectiveness that followed. Alya wasn't his. She couldn't be.

Time to turn it off. Time to be the person she needed. He closed his eyes and blew out a breath. *Remember the fucking limits, Henning.* If just kissing her was enough to loosen something inside, he needed to be really careful. Especially in a little hotel room. Where they'd be alone. Together. All. Night. Long.

His dick gave an unhelpful throb, so he pulled back, untangling himself from her arms.

"You're due at the kick-off party in the Icebar," he whispered, straightening up, adjusting himself. "I'll put on my winter gear."

That turned out to be a project. Getting dressed to sit around in freezing conditions took a lot of energy, as did walking around in the gear. The snowsuits the hotel loaned all the guests were warm as hell, which really wasn't working inside, but his discomfort was far outweighed by the knowledge that Alya wouldn't be cold when they sat in the Icebar. Still, by the time they made it out of the hotel room, Henning was burning up—and for once, Alya wasn't the reason.

"I can't wait to see this place," she said as they walked through the quiet hallway, seemingly unfazed by the heat. "Ready to be amazed?"

He shrugged and gave her a hint of a smile. "All I'm thinking right now is that this has *cold as fuck* written all over it."

Alya laughed. "Probably. But I think it'll be more than that."

The farther they walked from their room, the quieter the hallway seemed to get. Every step took them closer to the fashion world, where she was at home and he so clearly didn't belong. Henning frowned as he held open the door for Alya, and they both walked out into the snow.

The cold wind slapped his face, triggering memories that caught him off guard. Everything inside him seized up, and for one, terrible moment, he was back in that warehouse. Lying on the ice-cold concrete floor, with pain everywhere. The shards of glass from the explosion embedded in his skin. Knowing that fucker had triggered the explosion on purpose, just big enough for him to get away.

Shit.

Hell, no. Not going there. Henning swallowed. He had faced the cold a few times in the last five years, but with Alya, every sensation was intensified, including this. How the hell he was going to get through a night in a room made of ice was still a mystery, but he'd do it.

Breathe in, breathe out. Everything was under control. *She* was fine. The tightness in his chest eased a little as he took another deep breath. And he was ready as the next gust hit him. Just one foot in front of the other.

Alya looked up at him. "You okay?"

He gave her a stiff nod. "Thank fuck they loan out winter gear here. Back in Sydney, I couldn't have imagined just how cold a place like this could be. You okay?"

Her long legs and slim waist meant she had a lot less built-in protection. But she didn't seem uncomfortable. She stretched her arms out as the snow fell down on her, welcoming it. "I'm great. Even warm."

So he blew out a breath and concentrated on that.

It was still daytime according to the clock, but there were no traces of the sun. Instead, there was a hazy dusk-like glow near the tops of the trees, the sun having barely scraped the horizon hours ago before sinking out of sight again. Now, the only lights were electric, hung everywhere, sparkling on the blanket of snow that covered everything.

There was no mistaking where they were headed. The arched entrance to the frozen structure that made up the cold half of the Icehotel glowed a mysterious blue at the end of their path, and the enormous white mounds of the snow structure stretched out in all directions, disappearing into the darkness. Little wooden houses stood around the hotel, each with candles in the windows. They walked through the quiet stillness, side by side, together.

"Are those…reindeer parts?" asked Alya, her gaze latched on the doorway.

They came to a stop in front of the entrance to the Icehotel, and Henning studied it. She was right. The door was covered with what looked like reindeer pelts, and the handles were made of…antlers?

Henning chuckled. "I think this is a sign that the accommodations will be on the rustic side."

As he reached for the door handle, Alya sighed and closed her eyes. The snow was falling in large fluffy flakes, and they clung to her dark lashes.

"Still okay?" he asked.

Her eyes fluttered open, and she smiled at him.

"We only get one chance to see this place for the first time," she said. "I just want to make sure I'm paying attention."

Henning nodded slowly. He knew what she meant. Already today, he had felt it more than once: the wish to stop time, to somehow save that first sensation. But for him, that urge had come when he touched her. Kissed her. This wouldn't last forever, not the feeling, and not this intimacy, but the memory might last if he was careful with it.

He rested his heavy glove on the antler. "Here we go."

Henning held the door open for Alya and stepped in behind her. And stopped. The entire interior was ice and snow. Everything. Of course, he had seen it in photos, but to experience it was an entirely different thing. The structure itself was domed, made of snow, with blocks of ice everywhere, clear but with a hint of blue echoing throughout the space. It was nothing like the ice that came out of his freezer. Absolutely incredible. The packed snow of the ceiling and floor reflected the tiny lights set up to make the ice sculptures glow. There was a chandelier hanging in the entrance hall—ice, too, Henning suspected. In the middle of the foyer, there was an enormous ice sculpture of what looked like a Nordic god, bearded and armored, with sword in hand. The bluish cast to the place made him think of the ocean or even the sky.

Alya had come to a stop next to him. There was no one else in the entrance hall, just the two of them, dressed in snowsuits and hats and boots, staring at this miraculous place around them.

"It's breathtaking," she whispered.

"You were right," he said. "Definitely more than just cold."

And then he was inside one more of those moments, the kind he was trying so hard to hold on to. It wasn't just the Icehotel itself, but that they were both standing there, together.

Alya walked across the snowy floor to one of the pillars and pressed her gloved hand against it. "Where did they get all this ice? And how do we know it's not going to crash down on us?"

"I read that the skeleton of the structure is metal, covered with layers of an icier version of snow. The blocks of ice are carved out of the river just outside in the spring, when the ice is the thickest. They're stored in an enormous freezer building until the next winter comes around." Henning had done extensive research, off-hours, to answer all his safety questions. To make sure this place was well-engineered. He walked over to another pillar, running his finger along the seam of the ice blocks as he made his way toward her. "Seems pretty sturdy to me."

Alya looked up at the ceiling, then smiled at him. "Look who did his homework."

He shrugged. "I was a good student."

Her laugh echoed in the open room. The sound

was magical, and *he* was the one who had made her laugh. Fuck, that felt good.

"I bet you were," she said. "You seem very... focused."

Her eyes flickered hotter for a moment, so he took it as a compliment. Corinne had called him many things, long before the disastrous bust. Too intense. Too closed off. But the way Alya said this felt different. He moved closer to her until he was standing right next to her, looking down into her blue eyes, peeking out from under those dark lashes and fluffy hat. His gaze strayed down to her full red lips.

He wanted to kiss her right now, to make these first moments in this ice palace come alive in new ways. Just a kiss, to make this moment everything it could be. Anything intimate in public was supposed to be off the table, but right now, it was hard to remember why. Slowly, he tipped his head down toward hers, and Alya parted her lips. Just one little taste.

But before his mouth reached hers, the door to the Icehotel opened again, filling the room with voices and then people. Henning took a step back, blew out a breath and frowned. Fuck. What the hell was he thinking?

The group of models started through the entrance hall, their voices dying down as they passed. He caught some curious glances and a few nods in Alya's direction. They weren't afraid to stare, and he had almost given them something to stare at.

The group of women continued down the large
ice hallway, but the magic was gone. It didn't stand
a chance when the real world crashed in. Even putting media concerns aside, what did he think this was
between them? Henning could protect and he could
satisfy, and years ago in the hospital, Corinne had
made it clear that those two things were his worth.
He didn't have more to offer, and Corinne left when
he couldn't give them anymore. The idea was hard
enough to swallow as he lay on the hospital bed, his
face a wreckage of stitches and angry red scars. He
never, ever wanted evidence that Alya felt the same.

Henning frowned and nodded in the direction the
models had headed. "Ready to continue?"

Alya nodded.

The hall glowed with dim lights, positioned behind the carved blocks of ice. Henning slowed as
they passed other ice sculptures. Someone had made
each Viking warrior, carved each link of the belt,
each fold of the warrior's tunic. How many people
had worked to imagine and build this monument
of art?

Reindeer pelts hung from the doorways of the
rooms. Alya lifted one to look inside, and Henning
moved in, peering over her shoulder. The scent of
her hair was muted by the sharp bite of reindeer fur.
Yeah, they were definitely the real thing. The room
had the same mystical blue glow as the hallway. In
a twist of irony, the theme seemed to be a tropical
island shipwreck. Ice statues of palm trees stood in

both corners, and at the far end of the room, a grass hut was carved at the shore of a clear, glassy beach. The bed stood alone in the center of the room, the base of it an ice sculpture of a driftwood raft, floating in the sea of snow. Reindeer pelts were spread where the mattress should lie.

Alya sighed. "This is incredible."

Henning was so close to her, her fuzzy white hat tickling his nose. He leaned in for a breath of the sweet scent of her hair, and a rush of lust ran through his body. What would it be like to lie in this bed with her, just the two of them, all alone in this shipwreck? Cold, that's what it would be, unless they worked to keep each other warm. The image was there before he could think better of it: him on top of Alya, looking down into the blue depths of her eyes, heavy with the same want he had seen in the hotel room, his cock ready to sink into sweet, wet heaven.

Henning bit back a groan and frowned. That was a fantasy from another life, before he left the AFP, before the nightmares that meant he should never sleep in a bed with anyone. Fuck. They had two beds in their warm room, so they must have the option of two beds in these ice rooms, right?

"When we stay in one of these tomorrow..." he started.

In his pause, she finished his sentence. "It'll be incredible."

Henning opened his mouth to make it clear that they needed separate beds, but when he looked down, the awe in her expression stopped him. She only got to experience this for the first time once, and he couldn't drag his own shit into that. He could ask her later. This moment was for her, and he wanted it to be good.

So he pushed all those thoughts aside, and went with the next thing that came to mind. "You think there are bathrooms in this place, too?"

"You mean ice toilets? I hope not." Alya gave a little snort of laughter. "I think we passed them in the warm hotel, just before we went out the door. Thank God."

The sound of her laughter was magical, and it melted some of his tension. He could do this. The corners of his mouth tugged up. "Just checking."

Alya let go of the pelt in the doorway, and they continued down the hall. The muted din of voices grew louder. They were approaching the Icebar, and Henning steeled himself for the scene they'd face. He had to wipe his face of all traces of the emotions Alya stirred in him—want, lust, protectiveness and something more he didn't want to name. Something that felt way too close to—

"Henning?" Alya tugged on the sleeve of his coat. She had come to a full stop in the glowing hallway, and she was eying him with a stubborn look on her beautiful face.

So he stopped, turned to her and nodded his head in acknowledgment, waiting for her to tell him what she wanted. Whatever it was, he'd give it to her.

"Sasha Federov, the designer, is a force of nature, but anything you see is about his business, not me personally."

Henning swallowed. "You're letting me know it's going to be intimate between you."

"It's going to *look* intimate," she corrected.

"You're okay with that?"

"It's the way this business works."

Henning swallowed again and kept his expression neutral. Nodded. Put aside that mix of protectiveness and jealousy that crashed down on him. "No pissing contests. I promise."

"Stay with me," she said. "Stay right next to me all night."

Henning stilled. What was this about? He took off a glove and swiped a hand over his face. His skin was cold, and he had the urge to touch her, to see if she was cold. But he didn't.

"Is this in any way about your security?"

She shook her head slowly. "No."

Fuck. He wanted to stay with her for every selfish reason. Because, in some alternate universe, he could see the scene so clearly, walking into the Icebar, touching her, kissing her. Making it clear to everyone that upsetting her in any way would have consequences. But he could never, ever mistake that imaginary universe with the one he lived in.

Henning studied her face, her cheeks pink. The idea of saying no to Alya was causing him physical pain. His hand ached with the need to touch her, but if he did, it would make this even harder. So he put his glove back on.

"I can't," he bit out.

She tilted her head to the side. "Can't or won't?"

"In this case, there's no difference. You don't need me right next to you, and it's not in your best interest."

She rolled her eyes. "Now you're patronizing me. *Why*, Henning?"

Henning looked up and down the empty hallway. She wanted to discuss this, right here? Fine. "Because you're here to spread your wings, not to have your hulking bodyguard next to you, glaring at every man who touches you." He blew out a breath. Shit. Did she hear the jealousy oozing out of that statement?

He could feel himself getting worked up, so the last thing he expected was for her to smile. But that's exactly what she did. It was a beautiful smile, so wide and full of...amusement? That tightness in his chest was easing.

"You're very intense," she said, laughter in her voice. "Anyone ever tell you that?"

"Once or twice," he said dryly.

She chuckled, shaking her head. "Fine. So you're going to brood in the corner while I mingle?"

"Pretty much." He was trying his hardest not to smile. It wasn't working.

"Are you going to be jealous?" Her voice was smoother now, seductive.

Damn. She must have heard it in his voice. He narrowed his eyes at her and frowned. "What I feel when I'm working is irrelevant."

"What about afterward, when we're back in the room?" she said, her voice so soft, tempting. "What if you still feel it then? Will you tell me?"

The question spilled from her red lips, bringing his cock to attention. He scanned the empty hall again, just to make sure they were alone. Then he took a step closer and gazed down at her, letting her see all the want he was keeping tightly leashed inside.

"You want to play with that, baby?" he whispered. "You want to see if that makes you hot?"

She didn't hesitate, despite the warning in his gaze. "I already know the answer. I'm asking if it makes you hot, too."

This could either go very wrong or very, very right. Alya was really hoping for the latter. That don't-fuck-with-her vibe he radiated when he was next to her was a huge turn-on, but she couldn't—wouldn't—use a man as a crutch, just because it felt better than standing on her own. That was her mother's path, and the result was a career and a life that crumbled each time the relationship fell apart. Back in Sydney, she had started to lean on Stewart, her most recent ex, until, finally, she wizened up and decided to take a break from relationships for a while. So Henning was right to turn down her offer, to take a step back when she didn't need him. But...they could play with this set-up a little. Knowing he was watching her across the room, imagining the way he ached for her—that was about desire, not fears.

As long as Henning understood what he was getting himself into. She hadn't missed the sharp flash of heat in his eyes as he sketched the image of a big, ripped bodyguard, there to protect her...and more. He had quickly covered it up with that stoic expression, but now, that sharp mix of heat and intensity shone in his eyes again as he stared down at her.

But he didn't answer. Instead, the uninjured corner of his mouth curved up a little more. It looked like his smile took effort, as if he had forgotten how to do it somewhere along the way. But when he did, his eyes lit up, too, filled with pure, untainted pleasure. It was addictive to watch, to figure out what made him react, and she wanted him to smile a thousand times while they were here. She had some ideas about how to do that.

Henning leaned in, his mouth brushing against her ear.

"You're late," he whispered. "Go in there and do your thing."

He straightened up, wiped the smile from his lips and the desire from his eyes, and nodded toward the Icebar. Game on.

She brushed passed Henning and headed in the direction of the voices. The arched hallway opened into a larger room, even more stunning than the entryway. The Icebar was a work of art. Glittering glassy ice surfaces were everywhere, the walls, the floors, the pillars, the arched ceilings of snow. It was a strange scene, filled with clusters of people, all dressed in the same outerwear. The documentary camera crew added to the vibe, like they were on the set of some futuristic film.

"I feel like we're at the canteen of the rebel base," she said over her shoulder to Henning. "What was that ice planet called?"

His voice was low and intimate. "You mean Hoth?"

"Exactly."

"Definitely an upscale version," he added.

True. Much like in the hallway, everything was ice—the bar, the small, round tables, the benches that lined the walls. Candles burned and torches lit with a flickering haunted beauty. The only other non-ice elements in sight were the pelts that lay on the seating.

Alya wrinkled her nose. "More reindeer? How many had to die to make this place?"

"All so we don't have cold asses," he said, patting the fur on a nearby bench. "Or slide off the bench onto the floor."

She laughed, but this time it was a little too unguarded, a little too free. A dozen heads turned their way. Gazes flicked from Henning to her and back to Henning. And damn, she could see the conclusions in the arches of carefully plucked eyebrows and the parting of pouty lips. She could read those looks.

And if she didn't walk away soon, the documentary camera crew would turn their attention to them, too.

"I'll hang back here," he said, sitting at a table in the corner. He glanced over at the crowd. Heads were still turned in their direction.

Her smile fell, and her heart twisted. *Fuck them all*, she wanted to say. *Come with me.*

But he seemed to know what she was thinking because he shook his head. "I'd rather watch you."

His eyes glittered with…playfulness? Henning? Oh, God, fuck them all indeed.

"You do that," she said, her smile coming back. "Just watch and brood from the corner."

Henning lifted his chin at her and then settled on top of one of those poor reindeer along the bench. He leaned against the snowy wall and crossed his arms, his deep brown eyes fixed on her, intense and guarded. She smiled a little and walked away from him, slowly making her way into the crowd. This was going to be interesting.

Long ago, Alya had come to terms with what it meant to be a model. For so much of this job, she wasn't a real person, just a form for designers to hang their clothes on. But if she really wanted to make it in this industry, she had to be more than that. She had to be the embodiment of other people's desires. These were desires that the magazines and ad campaigns fed into, the desire for happiness, the desire for a life of luxury, and the undercurrent of those desires was sex appeal.

But being this person was a strange thing. From a very young age, she had been told she was exceptionally beautiful, and her mother groomed her for a life with this at the center. She had grown up with an equal mix of both stares and glares because of it. Thank God her parents' marriage didn't explode until after they had their second kid; Alya might have withered up in loneliness without Natasha. Even today, her sister was one of only a few people in the world she was truly close with. Most women kept their distance, as if they assumed beauty somehow made her exempt from more banal desires like conversation and companionship.

The sex appeal part was the most complicated. On the pages of a magazine, she sold the allure of touch, of sex. She wasn't even undressed for these photos, at least not all the way. And yet, as a rule, a stranger off the street was much more likely to approach cute Natasha than they were her. It was as if Alya had some sort of bubble around her with a sign on it: *look, don't touch.* Plus, men's real-life tastes tended toward women with bigger breasts and bigger hips. She elicited a more impersonal kind of desire.

You know you want me. I have what you need.

This was her job, but having Henning here while she did it was...well, different.

She looked over her shoulder and smiled at Henning one more time, focusing her attention on the scene in front of her. Though she had worked in this industry for years, it was hard to call anyone here a

friend. Alya wasn't much of a partier, which ruled
out the easiest way to bond with a good chunk of this
crowd. There were others she might have been more
than just business acquaintances with, but between
her mother's antics and the mess with Nick, she could
imagine why those people had stayed away. Her
mother was known for her off-screen drama as much
as for her on-screen performances, and Alya and Natasha's younger years were filled with Ilana Petrova's
inappropriately young partners, public break-ups,
and accusations of infidelity. And then, just as her
mother finally settled down, Alya's break-up with
Nick turned ugly. For too many years, her life was a
closely followed train wreck, and anyone with good
business sense would have stayed far away. These
days, she kept to herself more out of habit. *Aloof* and
snobbish were much better, reputation-wise, than
train wreck.

A couple models known for partying were settled
up at the bar and clearly past their first drinks, with
a sort of *fuck caring about my image—I'm going to
have fun with this* air to them. Alya understood the
impulse, but it wasn't her path. One of the women
she had worked with before—Brianna?—flagged
her over.

"That guy in the corner," she whispered, *sotto
voce*. "Are you with him?"

Thank God her cheeks were probably already
pink from the cold because she was finding it harder
and harder to hide her attraction. She glanced over

at Henning. His gaze was cool, impassive, but it was fixed on her. Could they see through that hard mask he wore, beyond the scars, to the man who had stood over her in the hallway, whispering in her ear, turning her insides red-hot? That couldn't be it. This was just the usual curiosity.

Alya looked back at Brianna. "He's security."

"I'd hire him," she said, and her tone suggested exactly what services she'd be looking for.

Should Alya be offended for Henning? No, he probably wouldn't care. The fashion industry rested on others' perceptions, but Henning so clearly didn't. She got the feeling that he was a man who only did exactly what he chose to do.

Brianna's gaze drifted back to him, and she smiled. "Yes, I definitely wouldn't mind having him watch me."

Alya bit back a smile. Was she going to ask for Henning's business card next? Alya could see the scene, Brianna sizing Henning up with those bedroom eyes that she was known for. The clench in Alya's gut came out of nowhere, sudden and intense. And completely unexpected.

Oh, this was ripe. Of course other women saw Henning's sex appeal. But when she glanced at him, his eyes were still on her, his gaze unwavering, and his words from that first day in the Blackmore Inc. conference room came back. *There are no other clients for me. Not now, and not in the future.* A hot flame of lust licked through her body, setting it on fire. Oh, now she understood this game she had suggested back in the hallway in a whole new way.

Except she was here for work-related mingling.

"Enjoy the view," she said, smiling at Brianna, and turned to scan the crowd.

The hotel wasn't actually that big, and Sasha Federov's team and the *Behind the Runway* crew had reserved all the rooms in the place, warm and cold, for the next two nights, which meant that everyone here was associated with this campaign. Being at the center of Federov's collection could be a serious career boost, making up for all the time she spent rebuilding her career in a new country after Nick. If she played this right.

She spotted Federov and smiled at him, and he made his way over to her.

"Ahh...you're here," he said, his Russian accent strong and familiar. He kissed her on both cheeks and gestured at the crowd, smiling a little. "Lots of people are asking about you. I know Jean Pierre would love to spend a little time with you."

Right, Jean Pierre Rus. Notorious flirt. The man who would wrap his arms around her in the shoot tomorrow.

"He'll find me," she said.

Federov's eyes were on her, sharp and assessing. Some people would mistake the intensity of his stare for sexual, but she knew what it really was: surveying a part of his empire, an empire that reached beyond the thousand-dollar neckties and one-of-a-kind dresses he created. Everyone in that room was part of it, part of the inventory he handpicked, worshipped, then culled. And right now, he was looking at Alya the way he'd look at his favorite suit, set apart, making sure it was hanging right where he wanted it.

Alya had no illusions about Federov. She was the flavor of the day for a man known for his obsessions that surged and then fell just as quickly. But the artist-muse thing didn't seem to revolve around sex for him—no way she would have signed on to this job if there were hints otherwise. The fucking was optional, though he certainly was known for that, too. In the end, she had taken a good, hard look at this job for what it was: an amazing opportunity to stand on her own and carve out her own path.

"Let me know if you need anything during your stay," Federov said, then leaned in to kiss her cheek. "Though it looks like you have someone else to look after that."

He nodded over her shoulder, and Alya followed Federov's gaze. Henning's expression was stony, his eyes darting from Federov back to her.

"My bodyguard," she said, though her voice might have given away more.

"Interesting." Federov's expression hinted at mild amusement as his gaze flicked back to Henning. "Your mother had many admirers, too."

Her first instinct was to deny the connections he was making, between her and Henning, between her and her mother. But direct responses rarely were taken at face value.

Instead, she gave him a dry smile. "My mother would be the first to say that men were the downfall of her career."

Federov chuckled. "And yet she couldn't resist."

He kissed her again and turned to call Jean Pierre over. She had worked on projects with him before, and she had to admit she kind of liked him, despite his well-deserved reputation as a man-whore. Men like that either seemed to hate women or love them, and he was definitely in the latter category. He was good-natured and laid-back, basically a breath of fresh air in an industry with a few too many divas.

Jean Pierre was also an insufferable seducer, and, from the smile on his face, those efforts were going to be aimed her way. It was actually a good thing in small doses since, tomorrow morning, they would probably be spread out on a bed of smelly reindeer fur, looking into each other's eyes. It was a lot easier to do sultry with someone who actually liked her.

"Alya Petrova." He settled a hand on her back, though the intimacy of this gesture wasn't as effective through the thick coat. "Can I get you a drink? Their signature drinks are *in* ice here."

Alya had no idea what he meant, and she wasn't much of a drinker, but when in an ice bar... "Vodka martini, please."

Jean Pierre raised an eyebrow. "Not my first guess. I would have thought you'd order champagne."

He nodded to the group of models at the bar.

She gave him a little smile. "Family drink."

A preference for vodka was one of the few Russian traditions her mother had maintained after their move to California. One of the many things Illana Petrova, model-turned-actress, was known for.

Jean Pierre flagged down the bartender and ordered, then turned to her as the woman mixed their drinks. He was as good-looking in person as he was on camera, which wasn't a given, with tousled hair, deep blue eyes and a hint of a smirk in his smile that very few guys could pull off. He was assessing her, too, but Alya wasn't sure what his conclusions were, though she was almost sure sex was on the table if she gave any indication she wanted it.

"The last time I saw you, your boyfriend Nick Bancroft was breathing down your neck."

Trust Jean Pierre to get right to the point.

Alya rolled her eyes. "The whole world knows we're not together anymore. He made sure of that, along with implying I was crazy."

Jean Pierre's mouth turned down in a rare frown. "I'm sorry you went through that. That bastard really tried to drag you through the mud."

"Great taste in men, right?" She snorted. "I'm a lot more careful these days."

"And does that bodyguard go everywhere with you now?" asked Jean Pierre in a low voice.

Alya had answered versions of this question, full of insinuation, many times when Max was her bodyguard, and there had never been anything between them. So she answered it the exact same way for Henning.

"Everywhere."

"Huh." That was all Jean Pierre said, but he was definitely registering something.

He looked like he was about to make a comment, but the bartender brought them their drinks. Jean Pierre handed one to her. "Vodka martini in ice."

"Ahh, I see," she said, studying the "glass" made out of ice.

He raised his own ice glass to hers and winked. "To the sexiest winter collection ever."

Alya clinked her glass with his and took a sip of the vodka. It made a cool trail down her throat.

"Want to check out the Viking Room?" he asked. "That's where our first shoot starts tomorrow, no?"

The suggestion itself wasn't out of the ordinary, and the full-on snow gear didn't lend itself to sexy-times. Still, she was getting that vibe in spades.

Alya gave him a hint of a smile. "Not tonight."

"I should have guessed. Someone else has plans for you," he said, his voice filled with amusement.

She shook her head. "He's just doing his job," she said, though she knew Jean Pierre wouldn't believe a word of it.

"Looks like fun."

She followed Jean Pierre's gaze across the room, to Henning. Fun wasn't the first descriptor that came to mind. He definitely didn't belong in this world, and his scars weren't the biggest tell. He was too big, too intense, too guarded, too…everything. He had the presence of a person still in the rough. But what set him apart from this crowd most was that he sat, arms folded, resting against the wall, as if he didn't care how others saw him. Henning didn't seem to care that Jean Pierre was staring at him, assessing him right now, and he answered that stare with a *fuck off, asshole* glance of his own. Damn, she admired his attitude.

Alya took one last gulp of her drink and said good-night to Jean Pierre. Then she started across the room. Henning was watching her like there was nothing else around except her, so she held his gaze, coming to a stop right in front of him.

"Is all that reindeer fur keeping your ass warm?" she asked.

He ignored her question. "Who is that?"

Slowly he stood up until he towered over her, his jaw working, each tense movement, each moment of restraint sending hot bolts of lust through her, making her legs weak. His voice was cool and even, but his eyes blazed down on her. She could think of a handful of answers that were almost sure to stoke this fire hotter. This game was working a little too well for both of them. They were already walking a thin line right here, in front of everyone she worked with. If she taunted him with answers about Jean Pierre, one of them was going to step over the line, and judging from Henning's well-practiced restraint, it would probably be her.

"I'm ready to go back to the room," she said.

His eyes flared with heat, and he glanced once more in Jean Pierre's direction. "You're done with everything here?"

She nodded slowly. Finally he lifted his chin in ascension. "Lead the way."

She brushed by him and headed toward the front entrance. He was right behind her, radiating a hot desire, and his gaze burned into her back. She wanted to turn around, to get a read on what all this tightly reined tension meant, but she wouldn't let herself. Not until they were alone.

She walked out the front door and into the darkness of the night. Henning's boots crunched, so close, but he didn't touch her. Didn't say a word. When they came to the warm building, he held the door open for her, and they stepped in. The hallway was empty, and Alya was ready to continue their conversation right there, but she had enough of her wits about her to ditch that plan and look for a little more privacy. She found a door and pulled it open. An upscale locker room, but at this point she didn't care.

The door closed behind them, and the only sounds were their breaths, fast and ragged. Alya slowed to a stop, and so did Henning, still right behind her. She swallowed. Then slowly, she turned around. *Oh, God.* His eyes were alive and dark, and her entire body exploded with need.

He tugged off his gloves and hat, dropping them on the floor. Next he grabbed the zipper of his snowsuit with his big hand, and she watched, mesmerized, as he unzipped all the way, until the fly of his thermals showed. He adjusted himself so that his thick erection jutted into the V, straining at the material. His chest rose and fell quickly.

"Fuck," he muttered. Then he met her gaze.

When she didn't say anything, he reached for her zipper. He tugged it down, exposing her slowly. His scars twisted as he watched this slow reveal, turning his expression into something darker. Oh, God, this was the sexiest game, and she wanted to play it so very badly. She dropped her gloves on the floor and reached up to his face, touched it, the rough side and the smooth side both under her fingers. He took a ragged breath and stepped toward her, her breasts pressing against his chest. She shuffled back to keep her balance, but he stepped forward again. Step. Step. Slowly, he backed her up against the rough wooden wall. There was nowhere left to go.

Then he slipped his hands into her snowsuit, around her waist and down her ass, cupping it in his enormous hands. He bent down.

"You like to be watched, sweetheart?"

"Yes," she whispered.

"You like knowing that you're the only person I see in that room?" His voice was rougher. "You like knowing I'm hard as hell, wanting you, even while you talk to another man?"

"God, yes."

He had been watching her all day, but it was nothing compared to what she saw in those dark brown eyes right now. It was raw and dirty, twenty-four hours' worth of pent-up lust. Or more.

Then his mouth came down on hers, cutting off all other thoughts as her body burst into flames. They were a tangle of hands and hats and snowsuits, and it was impossible to get close enough. It was a storm, sudden, torrential, drenching everything with its hot, wet downpour. She was so achingly hungry. His teeth caught her lips, his tongue stroked hers with unleashed craving. Alya moaned and kissed him back, showing him what she liked. He was claiming her, not by force or demand but with pledges. The kiss was a string of erotic promises, of all the ways they could be together, of all the ways he wanted to take her. *You know you want to be mine.* His hands had found their way under her sweater, his fingers slipping up her back, pulling his body against hers. She moaned again, and he answered with a deep groan.

And then, as suddenly as it had started, he pulled back, dragging in a harsh breath.

"Holy fuck," he muttered, letting her go.

Alya inhaled deeply, her mind still reeling from kissing, touching, wanting so badly. "The room. Let's go back to the room."

Henning was silent for a moment, and then he nodded. He straightened her clothes and arranged her snowsuit over her shoulders, his touch almost gentle now. He zipped up his own snowsuit a bit, hiding his erection, and then picked up her gloves and the rest of his gear off the floor.

His eyes were filled with that guarded lust he had looked at her with for so much of today. She waited him out, watching him, wondering if he'd speak his thoughts aloud. He swallowed, working his jaw, and he ran his free hand through the short bristles of his hair.

Then he rested it on her face, cradling her cheek with his big palm. He took a ragged breath, and then his mouth was on hers again. His lips stroked hers with more finesse this time, but that edge of longing and need was still there.

"Whatever you want from me," he whispered. "Take it."

CHAPTER FIVE

FOR ONE, HOT KISS, Henning hadn't held back. In that quiet locker room, with Alya up against the wall, her body flush with his, he let himself react, let her feel how deep his want ran. Because the twist in his gut as he watched that man—a man who was everything Henning wasn't—touch her and smile at her? That was a real reminder that she would never really be his. That chasm had opened inside, exposing deep fissures, and all the buried want and need flooded out.

Neither of them had said a word since they left that little locker room. But now, as the door to their hotel room clicked shut and she came to a stop in front of him, they were on again, for real this time. He stepped up close and slid the top of her snowsuit off, guiding it down her body. He got on his knees, easing the material over her ass and down her legs, tracing her curves with his hands.

"Hold on to my shoulders," he said softly.

She held on, balancing herself as he lifted one foot to tug her boot off, then the snowsuit. He moved to the other side to pull off the other boot, her hands warm on his shoulders. God, it felt good to take care of her. He got to his feet and hung up her snowsuit on the hook next to him. Then he stilled as he took her in, dressed in thermals and a soft white sweater. With that searing kiss still licking flames through his body, everything else was fading except the need to give her what she wanted.

He was going to give her a place to let down her guard, to indulge in her own wants. Over the last three years, he had learned a lot about Alya and the way she quietly shouldered the weight of her family. The way she'd supported her sister financially at age eighteen, taking care of Natasha when her mother was too distracted by the drama of her own life. Alya had even sacrificed nursing school so that Natasha could go to college. This was a woman with an enormous heart, and Nick Bancroft had taken advantage of it.

Of all the reasons for Henning to drag himself out of his self-imposed years of seclusion, this was the strongest: he would give her whatever she needed for a few days. And if that meant his cock and his mouth, then hell, yes, he'd give it to her.

He shed his own outer layers and then stood behind her, closer. His thermal layer did nothing to hide his erection. He couldn't resist pressing it between her ass, the urge to have her growing stronger.

Henning brushed her hair to the side and pressed his lips on her neck. "You have the sweetest scent.

I could do this all day long." He caught her earlobe between his lips, and her breath hitched. He took a long inhale and groaned. "You want to know what I've been wondering?"

"Yes." She turned her head toward him, looking over her shoulder, and her blue eyes were electric, shining, alive.

Fuck, he was so hard right now, his cock pushing against the fly of his boxers, hard to ignore. Her voice was a siren's call, so he answered it. "I want to find out if you smell just as good between your legs."

Slowly, Alya turned around, her eyes hot and intense on him, and his body was on fire, overheating in all the layers of clothing. His blood pounded through him, an unrelenting chant. *Mine. Mine. Mine.* Henning swallowed. No matter what he felt, this was a game for her, and he wouldn't forget it.

"Are you at all cold right now?"

She shook her head. Good. He wanted to kiss her, but he held back, knowing how easy it would be to lose himself the moment it began. Not yet.

"You've been watching me all day. Now I want to undress for you," she said, her voice huskier. "And while I take my clothes off, I want you to stroke yourself. Pleasure yourself while you watch."

"Fuck, yes," he groaned as a shudder of pleasure rolled through him. Henning closed his eyes, pulling himself together. Then he slowed his breathing and looked at Alya again.

She smiled and took a step back. Another. Her

eyelids were heavy, her dark lashes falling over the endless blue of her eyes, and her smile transformed into something so clearly seductive.

"You ever look at photos of me?" she said, her voice luring him into this game.

Holy hell. His body was already fully there, but his conscience was pricking at him. They were veering into murky territory, territory he had spent three years trying to resist: his fantasies about her, fantasies he shouldn't have had about a client. So he had pushed them deep down, letting the frustration fuel his determination to protect her from afar. Until now.

She wanted them, and fuck, how he wanted to give her everything she asked for.

"Yeah, I looked," he whispered, testing her reaction. "You like that?"

Her eyes lit up. "A lot."

Oh, fuck, this was hot and dirty and so, so good, and *she* was asking for it. He reached his hand inside his thermals and his boxers and palmed his cock. Her eyes followed his movements, and her pulse ticked hard at the base of her neck.

Alya took the hem of her sweater and pulled it over her head, leaving her in a layer of tight, gray thermals. Her nipples poked out of the material, and she toyed with one. No bra. His cock was leaking, so he spread his precum on his palm and gave himself a stroke as he watched her pleasure herself.

"You ever get off thinking about me?" she whispered.

Shit. He shouldn't admit to it, but this game was too tempting. "I tried not to," he gritted out. "But, fuck, you get me so hard."

She played with the hem of her thermal shirt, then slowly lifted it over her head. Henning braced himself against the wall and stroked himself hard. He was caught in a sea of lust, drowning. Her breasts were small, and her nipples, a delicate pink. He looked down at his hand, rough and big, crassly jacking himself as he watched the most achingly beautiful woman in the world strip. Just for him. Beauty and the beast. The contrast sent a dark swirl of lust and depravity through him. Did it turn her on, too?

"You want this hand on you?" he rasped, pulling down the waistband of his boxers, letting her see each rough jerk of his hand. "The one I use to make myself come when I jack off to you?"

Her mouth fell open a little, and for one long second, he thought he had gone too far. But just as a jolt of fear entered his system, a fear that despite his caution, he had stepped over the line, she smiled. It was a real smile that broke through their game, wide-eyed and full of wonder. Fuck, it was glorious.

Her expression turned seductive. "I like it a little dirty."

The message echoed inside him, urging him on. Yes, she wanted this. She traced the curve of her body down, over her hips, her fingers inside her thermal bottoms. She lowered them, stepping out, and when she stood up, his cock jumped in his hand.

"Nude." The word fell out of his mouth as he stared between her legs.

Alya's real smile peeked through again. "Occupational hazard. Are you into that?"

Henning's chuckle was a gritty rumble. "I'm into *you*, Alya. Everything about you."

A hint of pink colored her cheeks, sending a stab of tenderness through him. It was almost as if she wasn't used to hearing someone tell her how amazing she was. How was that possible? He resolved to tell her as many times as he could.

But right now, he was going to show her. His cock was weeping, as he looked at this beautiful woman in front of him.

"You gonna let me put my dirty mouth on that beautiful pussy?" he whispered, his voice rough. "You gonna give me a taste?"

"Yes," she breathed. "Give me what I need."

Give her what she needs. Don't fuck it up.

Holy hell, that smile was going to bring him to his knees. It was soft, so private, a secret just for him. Now that he knew what it was like to have her all to himself, he could never go back to looking for her in a magazine. Not when he knew *this*.

"Christ, you're lovely," he whispered.

Her eyes fluttered closed, as if hearing these simple words had given her pleasure. Then she turned, glancing over her shoulder as she walked toward the bed. And, fuck, this woman knew how to walk for an audience. She knew how to make each slow sultry step a new promise. And this time, the promise was for him.

She climbed on the bed, her ass arched up to him. But she did this with a kind of effortless grace. It was nothing like the women he had fucked in the club, pretending to be someone else, just for that night. This was part of her. Alya lay down on her side, propping her head on her hand. "You coming?"

Henning nodded, but he didn't move. Not yet. First, he needed to take in every bit of this moment, storing it away in his memory, saving it. In the years to come, he wanted to remember how this felt. When once, for a few short days, he had her all to himself.

There was no hesitancy in the way she lay there looking at him. He loved this confident, hot-as-hell side of her. And after watching her bloom from that dark place Nick had driven her into, he wanted this confidence to fill her until she was bursting at the edges with it. He was going to make sure this was for her.

Henning followed the curves of her body, along her thighs, over her hips, down the dip of her waist and over the curve of her pert tits, up the slim column of her neck, and finally, to her smile. Alya waited, lounging on the bed, watching him, her expression full of lazy desire, like they had all the time in the world. But the flush in her cheeks hinted at other possibilities. That she was aching for him, too.

"You are stunning," said Henning, his voice a little hoarse. "It's *you*, Alya, not just the way you look. It's everything about you."

She blinked at him with a hint of surprise. Her cheeks flushed, and then she smiled. "Then why are you still across the room?"

"I want to enjoy this part. When you look at me like it's my mouth you want, no one else's." His voice dipped lower. "I want to savor it."

Another sharp jolt of urgent lust shot through him, and he palmed his cock and gave that impatient bastard another rough stroke.

It had been so long since he had gone down on a woman. Years, despite how much he got off on it. Since that first kiss with Alya, he had been thinking about it. What would she like best? What would she sound like? Now, finally, *finally*, he would find out. And oh, God, how he ached to know.

He took one slow step, then another, watching each reaction from her, the parting of her lips, the quickening of her pulse as he came closer, closer. Henning pulled off his top and bottoms, but he left his boxers on. Then he knelt on the bed, one knee on one side of her, one knee on the other. She rolled onto her back, and he lowered himself onto his fore-arms until he could feel the heat of her skin under him. Until her quick breaths warmed his cheeks. Because beneath all this beauty was so much emo-tion. She had been burned. Nick had used her emo-tions against her, trying to manipulate her, to drive her back to him. What Henning could give her right now, on this bed, was a safe place to let that guard down and simply feel. And fuck, he had so many plans for how to make her feel.

He bent his head and pressed his lips to her pale, slim neck, exposed just for him. Heaven. He kissed her jaw and then her lips.

"You smell so fucking good," he murmured, looking down at her.

"You do, too," she whispered.

Then she wove her fingers into his hair, tugging his head down, guiding his lips to hers. The onslaught of sensations took over, washing through him as her lips melted onto his. Hungry strokes and sucks and nips...he couldn't get enough. He was drowning again, lost in the drive to press his skin against hers, move his hard body against her soft curves, drive his cock into the heaven of her wet, tight pussy. To never let this end.

This last thought jolted him back to reality, and Henning pulled away.

"You're distracting me," he said with a heavy, low laugh. "I have other plans."

"Plans that don't involve kissing?" Her eyes were glassy, unfocused, and her voice, husky.

"Oh, baby." Henning groaned. "There will definitely be kissing. Everywhere."

He started with her collarbone. "Here," he whispered, his mouth on her salty-sweet skin. He kissed a line down her chest, up the rise of her breast. "And here." Her nipple was hard under his tongue, and she hissed out a breath as he took it between his lips. He cupped one breast with his hand and fit it in his mouth, sucking. His cock gave a kick, and he groaned and sucked harder. Oh, fuck, why did her perky little tits turn him on like they did? If he kept this up, he was going to come before she did. He ran his tongue over her nipple one more time and moved lower.

"You wet, baby?" he rasped, his lips on the soft skin of her belly.

"For you," she whispered, sending another jolt to his cock.

Those two words made his heart stutter. *For him.* The scent of sex was everywhere, pulling him down her body, over her naked mound until finally, finally he was there. How many times had he imagined this, never once thinking that it could really happen? His cock was begging for attention, the insistent fucker, used to getting its share when he played through this scenario, but there was no way he was focusing on that. Because this was so achingly real. So he took another deep inhale and tasted.

Oh, God, his mouth. He was covering her with his mouth, worshipping her with it. Swirls of his tongue, little scrapes of his teeth, all working some kind of magic spell on her. He was a man of few words, but he definitely knew how to use his mouth when he wanted to. Never had she felt a man so intensely focused on her experience. It was as if this was the ulti-

mate turn-on, the moment he had waited for, which...
couldn't be right, could it? But, ooooh, he certainly
seemed intent on proving her wrong. He licked and
groaned and licked again, like going down on her
was getting him just as worked up as she was. With
each grunt, coarse and guttural, he went in for more.

"You like my mouth?" he said, his lips, his breath
teasing her.

"I love it," she whimpered.

"You taste so fucking good."

He sucked on her clit, sending her dangerously
close to the edge. Her moans were loud, scraping
her throat as they poured out, and they seemed to
pour fuel on his fire.

"Christ," he muttered, and one hand left her hip
while the other slid between her legs.

She opened her eyes and looked down at him. One
of his enormous hands was inside his boxers, and his
eyes were closed, his teeth bared. Was he jacking
off while going down on her? Holy hell, she didn't
realize this could get any hotter, but it just did. She
shifted to get a better look at this quiet, restrained
man as he gave himself over to a moment of pleasure.

But when she moved, his eyes snapped open, and
a dark smile tugged at his mouth. "You like seeing
me like this? All strung out on the taste of you, on
the feel of you under my hands and my mouth?"

"God, yes." The answer slipped off her lips. For
once, she wasn't worried about why she loved this
or what it meant. She simply let go.

Then he pressed his mouth against her clit and slid two fingers inside her, taking over, filling her senses, erasing everything except the vision of him, pleasuring her like it was the only thing he had ever wanted.

Whatever you want from me. Take it.

His words came back as white streaks of heat exploded. Her orgasm rolled through her. It was too much. She was making sounds like a wounded animal, cries, whimpers as she came down. Henning growled, lapping at her, drawing out her pleasure. Just...bliss.

Finally Henning kissed her softly, almost tenderly. Then he rose up on his knees. His face was tight, strained, and his cock twitched in his boxers, leaving a wet circle where his tip pushed at the material. He heaved in breaths, the muscles on his chest rippling, his biceps tense. His hands flexed. And she knew exactly what he was holding himself back from doing.

"Do it," she whispered.

Henning groaned and reached inside his boxers, pulling out his hot, thick erection. *Whoa.* She had felt it against her, but seeing his enormous cock was still a shock. His smile was dark as he gave himself a rough tug. "See how hard you make me?"

The hottest words were coming out of his mouth, and she loved it. Her hand moved to her clit instinctively as she watched his hand sliding up and down his huge erection.

He took her in once more, head to toe, and then he roared. He thrust, pointing his cock at her and came, came, came. A second orgasm ripped through her, her slick body shuddering, as she watched the ecstasy take over his features, his hips pumping. The room was filled with sharp gasps as they both stared, openmouthed, at her stomach, slick with his come. Henning looked even more shocked than she felt.

Alya's mouth dropped open as ripples of pleasure still rolled through her. A burst of laughter bubbled up and came out, loud and sudden, and once it came, it didn't stop. She covered her mouth, but it didn't help. The laughter escaped in snorts. Henning's eyes widened, and he stared at her like she was bat-shit crazy.

"I can't believe that just happened," she said between giggles. "That we did that."

Henning's eyes moved from hers to the ribbons of come and back to hers. He lifted his hand to his face, touching his scars with his fingers absently. Then he frowned. "That got way out of hand."

"No. Don't say that." Alya shook her head quickly. "That was the most amazing thing I've ever done. So don't you dare look at me like you regret it."

He was still staring at her with a stunned look. "You're really okay with it? Because I said a lot of things…"

Alya fell back onto the bed, chuckling. "I loved every one of them." His forehead wrinkled, as if he couldn't quite believe it, so she added, "I trust you, Henning. You have to trust me, too. It goes both ways."

He stared at her some more, so she waited him out. Then, finally, his expression eased. "Okay. You're right. But let me help clean you up."

Something about his offering, the way he was looking at her, tugged at her heart. And she flashed to a scene of him following her into the shower, taking his time to clean her, to explore her body, all that intense focus—

No. Having him care for her like that would cross the line she had drawn for herself when they started. It would take them into more vulnerable territory, areas where she had failed spectacularly. Alya was so much stronger on her own, and with this newfound freedom, she'd traveled across the world for an amazing career opportunity and had just had the best sex of her life. There was no way she was going to tangle this up with her old baggage. She had watched her mother get sucked in by each new boyfriend or husband, and it never ended well. Alya had sworn to herself that she wouldn't be involved with another man until she was sure she could stand on her own. Only then could she find something healthy, something real.

Alya forced herself to smile, to wave his offer off. "I'll just take a shower."

His expression darkened, but she ignored another tug at her heart and climbed off the bed, heading for the bathroom. Once safely inside, she leaned against the door and closed her eyes. This was a game about attraction and wish-fulfillment, with clear boundaries around it. She couldn't let herself cross them, no matter what Henning made her feel.

CHAPTER SIX

WHEN ALYA'S ALARM went off the next day, Henning was already up, showered and working on his laptop. He had been in the same place when she fell into bed. Judging from the last two nights, Henning definitely didn't get enough hours of sleep. Was he always like that, or was it the job? She, on the other hand, had rambled, probably barely coherently, over the dinner he'd brought for her from the restaurant the evening before, and he seemed perfectly content just listening. Okay, she had been a little disappointed that he didn't crawl into the narrow twin bed with her, even if his huge body would have taken up most of it.

Alya rolled over, stretched and sat up. Henning looked up from his laptop. His eyes traveled over her silky nightshirt, his expression impossible to read.

"Sleep okay?" His voice had that gravelly quality to it, contrasts of rough and gentle.

"After the hottest sex of my life, followed by a warm shower and food delivered to the room?" Alya laughed. "Um, yeah. I slept well."

A hint of a smile teased at the right corner of his

mouth. His eyes traveled over her once more, slower this time, heat seeping into his gaze.

"We have less than an hour until your day officially starts," he said. "You want me to bring some breakfast to the room while you get dressed?"

"Mmm, thank you." God, this man was amazing, more than—

Yikes. *Don't make this complicated, girl.* She had hired him to support her...though he was giving her things that had nothing to do with the job. Alya rolled her eyes and told that little voice of doubt to shut up. Time to enjoy herself and the company of her supersexy, brooding bodyguard.

"Any preferences?" His voice was filled with all the ways he'd like to serve her, the seductive promise that he would do anything, *anything* to please her.

She stretched and then slid out of bed. His gaze raked over her from head to toe, pausing at the line where her shirt stopped, right at the tops of her thighs. She had slipped on only the shirt of the pajamas set last night, just to see if she could tempt him into bed, but he hadn't reacted. Now he seemed to have noticed.

His lips parted, and his eyes were heavy with lust. He was definitely watching her right now, but he didn't get up, just looked as she walked across the room and searched through her bag for some clothes, her shirt riding up, giving him a nice show of her ass. Good. He could take a bit of teasing.

Her back was to him, so she pulled off her pajama top and let it fall to the floor, leaving her in only panties. A sharp inhale came from behind her, but she didn't turn around. Just smiled as she slipped on a long-sleeved shirt, then a sweater.

"No bra?" His voice was low.

She looked over her shoulder and shook her head. "Not in a fashion shoot."

"You know I'll be thinking about that all day."

Alya laughed and picked up her favorite pair of leather pants. She made a show of sliding each leg into the soft material with an extra little wiggle of her ass. Henning's groan was quiet. She looked over her shoulder, and found one surly, turned-on man.

"My preferences? I'm willing to try lots of things. I think you'll know what I like." She smiled as his eyes narrowed. "I'm answering your breakfast question, of course."

Before he could react, she slipped into the bathroom and closed the door. Leaning back against the wood, Alya let out a whoosh of a breath. Well, that was a fun start to the day, but now it was time to get herself together.

The plan: have fun on this job without freezing her ass off, make it through the *Behind the Runway* interview without saying anything too revealing, have superhot sex with Henning, which hopefully included a chance to explore his pleasure this time, and then sleep in one of the ice rooms. Five-star day in the making, as long as she could tone down her angst.

By the time Alya came out of the bathroom, Henning had returned, and the little table in their room was set with full breakfast plates for both of them: yogurt, breads, hard-boiled eggs, cheeses, meats, fruits…and a large carafe of coffee, thank God. She poured herself a cup and took a long gulp.

"A delivery came for you, too," said Henning. He raised an eyebrow and pointed across the room, next to her bed.

The box was large and round, like an oversize hat box, sky blue with a card on top.

"Not shipped," she said. "Must be designer samples, swag."

Henning wrinkled his forehead. "Designers just give you stuff? Don't people pay ridiculous amounts of money for these things?"

"It's not out of the goodness of their hearts," she said, taking another sip. "They're hoping I'll wear their clothes, preferably on camera for the documentary filming. Free advertisement."

"Huh. Interesting."

Alya zeroed in on the hard-boiled egg. How long had it been since she'd eaten one of those for breakfast?

"You're not going to open it?"

She took her eyes off the egg and waggled her eyebrows at him. "You think there might be something in there that interests you?"

The corner of his mouth turned up in a slow smile. Even on the scarred side of his face, she saw a hint of lightness. "If it's a lacy thong for you to try on, I'd be into that."

"I bet you would."

Alya took another gulp of coffee and walked over to the box. She pulled off the lid and peered inside. Tissue paper covered the top, soft, light blue. She pulled out the first layer and found a white, silk camisole. She held it up.

"Yeah, I'll wear this," she said. She turned around and shucked her top, smiling over her shoulder at Henning. His eyes were wide. He clearly wasn't used to the unabashed undressing and dressing that took place in her world. She slipped the camisole on and faced him.

"You like it?"

His laugh was low and sensual. "I love it."

"Good," she said, bending down to look through the box. More silky shirts and lacy undergarments. Nice but not very practical for the Arctic Circle. Alya took off the lid of a little box to find a...tiara? She held it up, laughing.

"I can't believe this one," she said, looking at Henning. "Who wears these?"

Henning shrugged. "I know someone who wears them."

"Um, the queen of England?"

"Yeah. And my niece," he said with a smile. "Just about every time I see her, in fact."

Alya stared at him, trying to picture this jaded man with a little girl in a tiara.

"Your niece?" she asked. "How old is she?"

Henning's broken smile was warm. "Five next weekend. She has a dance performance while we're here, and I'm almost positive she'll be wearing one of those."

She was still having trouble fitting this information into her understanding of Henning. At the dance recitals of his little princessy niece? She tried to picture the scene: Henning squatting down to five-year-old height as a little girl in a dress and tiara stood in front of him. She'd be explaining something to him, and he'd focus all his attention on the child. His size, the scars, the quiet intensity of him, everything that kept people at a distance—that he *used* to keep people at a distance—wouldn't matter to his niece.

"You missed her dance recital," she said slowly. "For this job. With me."

He shrugged, like he genuinely wasn't worried. "My sister and her family live over in the Manly Beach area, close to where I grew up. I see them all the time."

She knew so little about him, and she was gobbling up this little peek into his life. He was so much more than the version of himself he presented to the world.

Alya brought the box with the tiara over to the table and placed it in front of him as she sat down. "This is for your niece. If she'd like it."

His crooked smile was full of warmth and indulgence. "Thank you. I'm sure she'd love it."

His gaze stayed on her as his smile faded. All that was left was his intense gaze. The breakfast to her room, his anticipation of everything she needed, the orgasms... He was going to ruin her for the real-life version of boyfriends whenever she started dating again.

Alya swallowed and scanned the breakfast spread again. She picked up a little tube, turning it over in her hand. All the writing was in Swedish, of course. "What's this?"

"I think the server said it's caviar paste for the boiled egg." He gave her that little twitch of a smile. "Because you said you were up for anything."

She lifted an eyebrow at him. "I might actually like it. My mother used to eat stuff like this when I was a kid. I think it's a Russian thing, too."

She got to work peeling her egg, and the room was quiet again. Alya peeked up at him, that stoic expression back on his face. What was he thinking about? He wasn't regretting last night, was he?

"We're okay, right?"

He blinked at her, his gaze filled with...irritation? Confusion? She pressed on.

"I mean, after last night, I just want to make sure—"

"Of course we are," he said, his voice gruff.

Of course they were. Sex didn't have to be followed with the avalanche of drama that came with her mother's boyfriends or Nick or any of the other unhealthy relationships that had blanketed her life.

It could just be sex. She bit her lip and focused on her egg.

But before she got a bite into her mouth, Henning had stood up and was making his way around the table. He tapped the front of her chair, and she scooted it out to face him. Then he knelt in front of her, between her legs. He was a big man, big enough so that down on his knees, they were the same height. He settled his hands on her thighs. The gesture was warm and possessive and everything her mind needed to read too much into it.

"I'm not good at this, Alya," he said, gesturing between them. "Even before I…" He looked away, retreating. She lifted her hand to his left cheek, running her fingers down his scars, letting him know she understood, that he didn't need to say it if he didn't want to. He let out a long breath, swallowed, and looked back at her. "I'm sorry if I've done something that makes you feel anything less than incredible. Because that's what you deserve."

She blinked at him, stunned. For someone who didn't like talking, he really struck gold when he chose to speak. His statement was so direct, so opposite of what she had come to expect. Maybe it was that newly found space to simply think and feel for a bit, without distractions, or maybe it was all the orgasms, but when Alya found Henning's steady gaze on her, his dark eyes so clearly telling her he was there for her, all her worries just flowed out.

"The short interviews they're doing for the documentary—at some point, it's not going to be fun," she said. "I know the woman is going to ask me about all the things Nick said about me, especially about leaving Los Angeles because I was buckling under pressure. Maybe she'll ask today, maybe tomorrow. And I have to decide how much to say about it."

Henning's jaw clenched at the sound of her ex-boyfriend's name, but he nodded and waited for her to continue.

"I've worked so hard to get to this point, where I'm not steering my life around him, even from across the Pacific." She blew out a breath. "But if I'm not careful, he can still get to me. With the film crew here and the publicity this is getting, I start to worry he'll do something to get attention. And he may do that." She frowned. "But I have to learn how to shift my own focus."

God, she never talked about this kind of thing with anyone except Natasha. And these days, Natasha was too busy to talk much. But now that she was saying this aloud, she could feel how much these worries were weighing on her. But, ugh, this was not the sexy fling he'd signed up for.

"Sorry for the overshare," she said, rolling her eyes. "I'm just a little nervous."

"Don't apologize," he said, and he sounded almost angry. But he winced as soon as the words left his mouth, and grumbled something under his breath. Henning's eyes were stormy, though she was almost sure it had everything to do with Nick, not her. His voice was softer when he continued. "You're an incredible woman, so strong. But that doesn't mean you can't voice your worries. I'm listening."

He blew out a breath and looked down at his own fingers, now pressing into her thighs. He loosened them, stroking gently up and down. "So if that interviewer catches you off guard, you're worried you'll say something that will trigger harassment from Nick."

She smiled a little. "Yeah, basically. But in my head it doesn't sound nearly as reasonable."

He opened his mouth as if to speak, then shook his head. He started again. "You want me to come with you to the interview? Glare at the woman if she asks about your private life?"

He was joking, but Alya was trying to ignore how good that idea sounded. She shook her head. "I can handle it."

"I know you can handle it," he said, his voice serious. "I'm just asking if you want someone to share that burden, just for a little while."

She lifted her hand to his cheek. "I think that's just about the nicest offer any guy has given me."

"Sounds like you need to check your taste in men," he grumbled. "You should be hearing that every day."

She smiled a little and tilted her head, considering his words. "You must keep your girlfriends very happy."

"There are no girlfriends for me," he said flatly.

"Never?"

"Not anymore."

She wanted to kiss him so badly. Henning watched her lips as she spoke, like he, too was thinking about kissing. So she did it, leaning forward, brushing her lips over his. His hands moved up her thighs, around her hips to cup her ass. A smile tugged at the corners of her mouth, and the relief flowed through her. She kissed him again, and his lips were full of aching desire, like he was giving her a glimpse at just how happy he was making her right now.

CHAPTER SEVEN

"THE LOCATION IS going to make this shoot a little crazy," said Alya as they headed down the hall of the warm portion of the hotel to the lobby, where they'd meet the rest of the crew. "There's a lot of running between the warm and cold parts of the hotel to change, and the ice means that the lights can't be on for too long, so we don't melt the place down. Each shoot needs to happen quickly...you get the picture."

"And then there's keeping you warm," grumbled Henning. He sized her up. Hot, as usual, but the skintight pants and thin fluffy sweater barely looked warm enough for the heated portion of the hotel, let alone in the fancy igloo where they were headed. "How long are you supposed to lie on that bed without a coat?"

Alya shrugged. "They have saunas to warm us after we're done."

"You mean those hot rooms where a bunch of people sit around naked together?" he said, lifting an eyebrow.

She laughed. "Yeah, those. You interested?"

"Sitting in a room watching other people look at you naked?" He shook his head. "I'm pretty sure that would cross my limits."

This morning was already pushing up against the limits of his restraint. And as they walked down the hallway, watching men pass, their gazes lingering on her, he could see those limits were going to be further tested. Nothing about this scene had changed from yesterday; if anything, it should be easier to stomach these looks, knowing he had spent the previous night doing the kinds of things with her he hadn't even let himself dream of. He should be relaxed, especially given the way he had come more intensely than he ever had last night. But he wasn't anywhere near relaxed.

They had come to the lobby, and she slowed to a stop. Various models and staff wandered in and out of the area, speaking different languages, throwing glances at them, their eyes darting from Alya to him and back again to Alya.

To some degree, this was inevitable. He was a big motherfucker, and his scars upped the intimidation factor enough that people tended to give him a wide berth under any circumstance. But here, he stuck out even more. This was an industry designed to make people forget how brutal life could be. Henning was a snarling beast of a reminder that even for someone of his stature, life never turned out like one of the glossy magazine spreads.

Alya tilted her head, studying him, but she didn't

say anything. Maybe she did understand all of this better than he was giving her credit for.

"You ready?" he asked, nodding across the room, where a woman with blue hair and a tablet was waving her over.

"You can stay with me, you know. Watch me get ready." Her smile turned intimate, her voice soft. "You might enjoy it."

Henning gave a rough laugh. "I'm sure there are plenty of things to enjoy about it," he said, letting his gaze travel down her body.

But that would mean watching someone else touch her, dress her, brush her hair, knowing that there were hours before the next time he would be alone with. Hell no.

"I have some catching up to do." He held up his laptop. "I'll be out here waiting for you."

Her eyes stayed on him, clear, assessing, making everything else fade away. So he rested his hand on her lower back. Such a small thing, too subtle for anyone else to notice. Henning hadn't even fully thought it through before his hand was there. They were only a few paces away from the others, a short distance, but as they walked those steps, Henning let his guard down momentarily. He let himself imagine that this amazing woman could be his, really his. He let himself pretend that he wasn't too broken to be the kind of man who would make her feel safe and strong at the same time. Both independent and owned. Always cherished. Everything she deserved to feel. And he let himself forget that he had so much shit buried inside that would destroy this raw, new connection the moment he let her in for real.

None of these things he imagined were truly possible, so he simply let himself have those few steps. And when they ended, he didn't bother looking around. He didn't want to see the stares this time. He didn't welcome the reminder that he had lived and Sanjay had died, the way he usually did. This time, what he felt was the deep chasm between the person that Alya needed and the person that he was. And for the first time since he had been carried off the cold floor of the warehouse, he wanted those deep wounds to heal. But he had no idea how the hell to do that.

So, instead, he took one last whiff of her warm, honey scent, wiped the emotion off his face and walked away.

Alya came out of the makeshift dressing room laughing, all wrapped in a sweater and scarf, her hair artfully piled on her head, dramatic makeup drawing his gaze to the deep blue depths of her eyes.

Laughing. She was laughing, and that fucker she would be photographed with was the one who was making her laugh. Henning gritted his teeth. Hell no. He was *not* one of those jealous pricks who wanted to control his girl's every move.

P.S. This isn't your girl, so take it down a notch, asshole.

But then Alya turned to look at him, and all the

tension inside turned into something else. The look
was there for only a moment, private, but it was personal. A warm, vulnerable hint of a smile. A reminder of all the holes in his defenses that he had
spent the last hour trying to patch.

He refused to react. Henning closed his laptop
and followed behind Alya, the male model and a few
others, keeping his distance. Watching Alya was no
hardship. When she walked out of that room, her
makeup had surprised him, but seeing her from farther away as she turned her head to talk, he understood the effect. Her blue eyes sparkled, even from a
distance, and her dark red lips were so fucking hot.
His gaze was drawn back to them again and again.
How many men would stare at those lips between the
pages of a magazine, imagining what they would feel
like around their cocks? Fuck, he wanted to protect
her from that…which was the wrong line of thought.
He took a couple deep breaths.

They walked outside into the cold winter morning. Snow sparkled in all directions, and the sky was
clear and dim. Outside the cold part of the Icehotel,
a couple generators hummed, their cords disappearing into the structure.

Henning had gone back to the room to gather the
outerwear the hotel had lent them, but Alya wasn't
wearing hers. Instead, she had on a sleek winter coat
that looked way too thin for the temperature. He
glared at the blue-haired woman's back for leaving
her underprepared for the weather, though he knew

it probably wasn't her call. But, Christ, Alya must be cold. He could have held his tongue about anything else, but not the cold. He caught up to them and opened the door to the Icehotel.

"You warm enough right now?" His voice was rough.

She nodded.

Still, he was dying to test her temperature himself, feel her hands. It was hard as hell to tamp down the bone-deep urge to take care of her, but he forced his hand to the side.

Just relax.

Jean Pierre and Alya followed the assistant down the ice hallway, the model's hand now resting on Alya's back. The way Henning's had been. But the winter jacket meant his hand was nowhere near her skin. Yet. That would change the moment they started the shoot. Henning blew out a breath. He was going to spend the day watching her from the sidelines. How the fuck he was going to survive this was unclear, but he was banking on the belief that he could make it through just about anything as long as Alya didn't get hurt.

The assistant led them past doorway after doorway, each room hidden behind a reindeer pelt. Henning had seen photos of a few rooms online, but they were from past years. Each spring the entire structure melted, and each fall, it was built anew. The walls and beds and sculptures he passed right now were temporary; each room represented so many

hours of work that wouldn't last. There was probably some deeper meaning in all this, but since when
did Henning look for meaning in a world where terrible things happened without reason? And why the
fuck did he keep coming back to his past, letting it
taint this burst of happiness that was his present?
The Icehotel was still and peaceful, the opposite of
the world his memories belonged to, so it was time
to get his head on straight.

As far as Henning understood, the designer had
the models in different rooms for the morning sessions, some in pairs and some in groups. Then, in the
afternoon, there would be a larger session in the Icebar, and that damn documentary crew would be following them everywhere. There was a longer break
in the middle of the day, when Alya would have a
chance to warm up as the crews shifted locations.
At least he wasn't the only one thinking about staying warm.

The assistant led them down the hallway, the stark
beauty of the place cluttered with cords and people
and collapsible tables full of God knows what. With
all these real-world items, some of the magic of this
place disappeared. The blue-haired woman stopped
in front of the last doorway.

"The Viking Room," she said, moving the reindeer pelt to the side.

Alya and Jean Pierre walked in, but when Henning moved to follow them, the assistant narrowed
her eyes at him.

"Security," he muttered to her, not waiting for her answer.

The first thing he saw was the bed. It was an enormous Viking ship carved of ice, with its curved hull and the stern in the shape of a serpent's tail, curled and flourished. At the bow was some sort of sea monster, facing outward, warding away other monsters that lurked under the sparkling depths of the icy sea. The entire boat glowed and sparkled from underneath, though he couldn't see any electricity hooked up to it. The actual bed was yet another cluster of reindeer pelts. There were lights positioned around the scene, some behind screens and some from below, though none of them were on.

Henning's eyes went to Alya. She was wandering around, taking in the snow waves and the mermaid ice sculpture along the opposite wall.

"Beautiful," she whispered.

In the middle of the night, long after Alya had fallen asleep, he had lain in the bed next to hers, trying to imagine today, trying to prepare himself for the worst. But his imagination had gone down an entirely different route, one undoubtedly influenced by scenes he had watched in the club, mixed with porn. He had pictured Jean Pierre and Alya and a lone, horny photographer watching them. The reality was a hell of a lot less sexy. For starters, there were a lot more people than he expected, and the conversation was on logistics. Henning suppressed a growl as he also noted that everyone else was dressed warmer than Alya.

"We'll turn on the lights for five minutes, then let them cool, so we don't melt this place down," the photographer was saying in a thick Russian accent. "We tested it earlier, so that's the last thing we'll do."

He sat down on the bed with a clipboard, and Alya and Jean Pierre joined him. "This is a rundown of what I'm thinking. I want to do as much as we can while you have your jackets on. We're going for sexy, not arctic frozen," he added dryly.

The photographer continued to give directions, and Alya and Jean Pierre asked questions and made comments about power dynamics and seduction like they were all talking about the weather. Henning found himself tuning in more closely as the three of them discussed ideas to so carefully play on people's emotions.

Henning's own line of work required him to suppress his emotions, to see through situations carefully and make decisions based on facts, details. It was a skill that surprisingly few were good at. Did Alya suppress her emotions, too, in order to give the photographer what he wanted, or did she know how to find them, on demand? Would he be able to tell the difference?

There were more directions and positioning, and then it was time to begin. A man came up to mess with Alya's hair, though Henning couldn't see anything that needed fixing. She looked fucking perfect because she was Alya, and anyone who thought otherwise was an idiot. Then again, that had nothing to do with fashion.

Soon it was time for her to take her coat off. Henning shivered as she tugged on the zipper, pulling it down, exposing her body covered in a skintight sweater and pants. He clenched his jaw and reminded himself to settle the fuck down. Alya shrugged off the jacket, oblivious to his reaction, and she looked around for a place to set it...but everything was ice. Henning crossed the room.

"I can hold that for you," he muttered.

When she smiled up at him, a little of the tightness inside loosened. Henning retreated to the corner, leaving some woman to finish fussing with Alya's clothing. He unzipped his own jacket and tucked her coat inside, keeping it warm against his body for when she needed it again.

Then the lights went on and the photo shoot began.

It wasn't quiet or private at all, the way the photos made it look. The photographer gave directions, and Alya and Jean Pierre climbed onto the bed, setting up a wintry seduction scene. He had seen countless photos of her, on sofas or beds, with men or alone, all for background research, of course. He had tried not to step over the line, but sometimes it was so hard. Once he even bought *Tropical Bliss* magazine because there was a photo of her alone, walking out of the water in a tiny bathing suit. He'd jerked off to it. Not one of his finer moments, but that was back when he didn't think he'd ever come face-to-face with her.

There was a series of shots taken standing up, with the bed, covered in the reindeer pelts, in the background. Then, during a quick warm-up break, while he covered her with the coat he had warmed against his body, a red satin sheet was fitted over the mattress that lay on the bed of ice. First Alya was alone, dressed in all white, her hair carefully positioned by the same guy who had messed with it earlier, and then, at her side, Jean Pierre eased down next to her. It was all an act, choreographed by the photographer in his running commentary, and yet, seeing it twisted something deep in Henning's gut. He was watching this other man, a man with the kind of easygoing lightness Henning had never had, looking down at her like he wanted to eat her up. And fuck if he didn't want to shove that asshole right out of the bed and onto the icy floor. That man was the one who lay next to her, even though Henning was the one who had made her come last night. He should be the one lying next to her right now. He was getting hard just thinking about all the things he wanted to do.

Henning took off his glove and swiped a hand over his face. It was going to be a long day.

Alya was shivering by the time Henning opened his coat and pulled hers out again. He was trying not to react, but when she looked up at him, he got the feeling she saw something anyway. Henning wrapped the coat around her shoulders, giving him an excuse to look away. She wouldn't ask questions there, in the middle of the bustle of equipment-hauling and cleanup crews around them.

But he was close enough for one, intoxicating breath of her scent, and it took only that one breath for the sharp ache of want to flare up again. Henning forced it back down. But then Jean Pierre was approaching; he could see him out of the corner of his eye, heading in their direction.

"Feels longer in the cold, doesn't it?" Jean Pierre came up next to Alya, getting all in her space in a way that crawled under Henning's skin. "Heading to lunch?"

Alya shook her head. "I'm having lunch in my room."

Henning frowned. They headed out through the snowy cold, but when they were finally in the warm part of the hotel and alone, Henning stopped, right in the middle of the hallway. He was trying to figure out how to say this without being an asshole. Finally he blew out a breath and gave up. "I hope you're staying back from lunch has nothing to do with me."

"You mean you want me to ignore the way you were glowering at me for the last two hours while Jean Pierre and I lay on the bed?" she asked, leveling him with her gaze. "You want to spend more time watching us together?"

Henning closed his eyes and massaged his temples.

"Or you didn't mean to stare at me like you were thinking of everything you wanted to do with me on that bed?" she said, her voice husky. "Am I mistaken?"

"I didn't mean to—"

Alya burst out laughing, cutting off his grumble.

"Yes, you did," she said, still laughing. The sound was beautiful, soft and musical, and finally, reluctantly, he smiled too. "But I also need a little time to relax." She raised her eyebrows at him. "You want to go back to the room and relax with me?"

She tugged on his arm a little, and he blew out a breath and followed her. He probably would have followed her anywhere if she asked. They walked in silence, into the warm building and down the hallway, the tension from the day building with every step closer to the room. Two models passed, their glances bouncing from Alya to him in open curiosity, and Henning scowled at them. Yeah, it was obvious what was going on, but at this point, he didn't care. All he could think about was Alya in white, lying on that red satin bed, looking at him.

Henning entered the room first, giving it a quick sweep because he would never, ever forget that he was here first and foremost for her protection. But the room was silent, the beds made and the breakfast dishes gone. It was simple, impersonal, so much like a setting from a magazine he'd see her in, and, yet, this was real. And of all the men in the world, she was looking at him right now. No one else. What a lucky bastard he was. For a few short days.

He turned to her and fingered the zipper of her coat.

"Are you warm enough?"

She blinked at him. "You have something about the cold, don't you? You don't like it."

Henning swallowed. "We can talk about that later."

She shrugged. "I'm fine. My jacket was warm when you gave it back."

He stroked her hair, but he wasn't convinced.

"Besides, when I lay there on that bed, I found a way to keep myself warm." Her voice was soft and silky. "Want to know how?"

He tugged on the zipper of her coat, drawing out this moment, drawing out this time before the wave of want and need came crashing in. Slowly, he revealed the elaborate wrap of her sweater, soft and white. It twisted around her body, and he reached in to find the ties that held it together. Her stomach was warm under his hands. "Tell me."

Alya licked her lips. "When I lay on that Viking bed, I was thinking about you last night. Kneeling with your cock in your hand. And what you'd say if you were next to me."

Henning chuckled and took a step back from her. "I'd say let's get the hell out of this ice prison and get you warm."

CHAPTER EIGHT

STEAM CLOUDED THE bathroom mirror as Alya peeled off her pants and camisole. She slipped her fingers under the waistband of her panties but paused when she caught sight of the peach, lacy material.

She wiped a patch of the fog off the mirror and studied her arms, her stomach, her hips. In a world where women bonded over dieting wins and failures, she had gotten this body. Tall, slim but a little curvy, with small, rounded breasts and very little sun damage—that last part thanks to her mother's own aversion to the sun, ensuring that not only her mother but also that she and Natasha were camera-ready. It was a body that brands designed for, before they translated those styles into real-world sizes. If she believed everything the fashion industry had taught her, this body was for show, not for real-world practicalities. But Alya didn't care what the rest of the world thought. Today, she cared about what Henning thought.

Did he see her through the lens of the magazine descriptions? *Ethereal* was one of the words that surfaced, again and again, with its companions, *otherworldly* and *untouchable*. That last one she particularly hated. What kind of person didn't want to be touched? Not her, that was for sure.

God, she hoped Henning didn't see her that way. The electric tension between them yesterday had been very much grounded in the physical world.

She stepped out of her panties and into the hot shower. She stood under the showerhead, letting the warm water seep in as she replayed the morning. Henning on his knees in front of her at breakfast. On the Viking bed, with Jean Pierre stretched along her side as Henning's gaze burned into her. Henning keeping her jacket warm against him.

How many times had other men touched her? Her job required close contact with other models, and not once had any one of those intimate poses awoken feelings this intense. But all it took was Henning's gaze to send bolts of heat through her, fighting the cold.

The way he towered over her left her breathless. And the sound of his breath stuttering as she pressed her hand against his stomach. The strokes of his tongue between her legs. Now she was standing under the falling water, naked and burning up inside that memory. A flush crept up her neck, her body alive, craving more.

Alya climbed out of the shower, towel-dried her hair and then wrapped another towel around her body.

When she finally opened the door again, Henning was sitting on the bed, his forearms resting on his knees, his head hung. A T-shirt stretched over his hard, muscular chest, his biceps ripped and cut from years of physical training. Slowly, he sat up, and heat spread through her body in new waves as she took him in. Any traces of smoothness to him were long gone, if he ever had them. Just barely visible on one side were the ropy scars that lined his neck and disappeared under his shirt, healed but far from gone. Henning Fischer was the most incredible man she had ever seen. He had wanted to give her pleasure yesterday. Now she wanted her turn.

When her gaze finally reached his face again, Henning's eyes were on her. His expression was dark and hot, and the tension between them crackled. He couldn't know about the way she had imagined them together, but it was as if he was thinking about those exact same things.

Alya swallowed. Then, slowly, she walked toward him. His legs were parted, and she continued until she was standing between his knees. Liquid heat rolled from his gaze, turning her insides red-hot. The pull between them sparked, alive, electric. His hands moved to her thighs, touching them, but it felt more like an assessment than seduction.

"You warm now?" he asked softly.

"Yes, thanks." She smiled. "You realize the temperature in our ice room will be zero tonight, right?"

His jaw tightened. "Yeah. I'll deal with it."

Henning wrapped his arms around her legs and urged her to sit on top of him, so she was straddling him much like she had in the car. But this time if felt different. More intimate. She rested her hands on his bare arms and explored the heat, the solid muscle, as her towel loosened from around her chest. Henning leaned in closer, dropping a trail of kisses down her neck. "How do you want to relax? Tell me what you'd like."

Alya pulled back a little and raised a skeptical eyebrow. "What about what you'd like?"

"I'd like anything with you, Alya," he said, his face solemn. "Anything."

She had never met a man who had so seriously professed his interest without asking for something in return, and it still threw her off a little. Nick had been so closed off when they were alone, which was partly why the intensity of his pursuit had surprised her after she broke up with him. And the restraining order she took out only seemed to make him more determined. But now wasn't the time to think about Nick.

She focused on Henning, so close. "How about for everything I tell you I like, I get to take off one piece of your clothing."

Henning laughed. "If that's what you want." He gave her a sexy wink. "I'm willing to get naked in exchange for a peek into your mind." His hands moved up and down her back and slow caresses. He kissed her neck again and then her collarbone. "You first."

"I really like this position right here," she said, running her hands up his biceps and over his shoulders. "You're here right in front of me. I can touch you and explore you and look at you."

"And that's what you want?" His voice was getting a little deeper.

"Yes." She fingered the edge of his T-shirt. "This first."

He chuckled. "Not my socks? You don't have a thing for my feet?"

She shrugged. "Maybe I do."

"Do you?" His dark eyes sparkled.

She shook her finger at him. "Not your turn to ask questions."

Henning's smile was full of warmth and humor. "Fine. Undress me."

Alya took her time, moving her hands over his wide, rounded shoulders, over the broad flat planes of his chest and down his stomach. He was muscle all over, hard, ripped muscles that flexed under her touch. His breath quickened as she moved lower. She lifted the hem of his T-shirt and found the top of his jeans. Slowly, she ran her fingers underneath the material. He drew in a sharp hiss, then gave a harsh bark of a laugh. "Does this all count as undressing?"

"It's the best part," she whispered.

Instead of pulling up his shirt, she placed her hands on his waist and slid them up, exploring, inching the material up.

"Holy fuck," he muttered. "Is this how you plan to take off everything I'm wearing?"

"Hell, yes." Alya laughed.

He shook his head slowly. "You better have some good answers to my questions."

Her hands traveled higher, and when she reached his arms, he lifted them for her to ease off his shirt. She pulled it over his head and dropped it on the floor, then leaned back to take him in.

God, was he magnificent. He seemed to be made of an entirely different substance than she was, his muscles carved and rock-solid even in their resting state. He had very little hair on his chest, just a dusting around his nipples and a dark trail down the center of his abs that disappeared into his jeans. So intimate. So sensual. Slivers of light shimmered from between the curtains, dancing up and down the sculpted muscles of Henning's chest. Damn, this man was ripped. The level of fitness that a body like that required spoke to his determination and persistence, especially considering his job was now entirely behind a desk in the IT department. Yet he kept his body in such incredible condition that Alya couldn't help but wonder if he was still preparing for a night that ended long ago.

Either way he was hot. And real. The tufts of hair under his arms and down his stomach looked soft and inviting, but this was a body meant for action. Alya smiled. And no doubt he used his body for action of all kinds.

Her gaze traveled up to his face, and she found him smiling back at her.

"You like what you see, baby?"

Baby. She had never liked that term of endearment before, but it sounded just right out of his mouth.

"Yes," she whispered, continuing her explorations back up his chest. His scars weren't visible from the front, just a hint of them on his left shoulder was all she could see. Slowly, she moved her hands higher. Closer. She reached his shoulder and let her fingers glide to his neck, tracing his scar down.

That's when she felt more of them. The rise of scars along one side of his back, some long, some shorter. When she looked up at his face again, his smile had faded, and his eyes were dark.

"When glass explodes, it's like a spray of bullets everywhere," said Henning quietly. "We were in a warehouse, where these crazy fuckers were cooking ice on a large scale. One of my team members and I went in first, just to take a look, to see what we were dealing with, to try to contain the danger. Thank God I held back the rest of my team because the gang leader set it off on purpose. He even killed some of his own crew, just so he could escape. I got lucky, no burns, but Sanjay, my team member, he got a piece of glass right in an artery. I stayed with him instead of following the leader, but he bled out before help came. I have these scars to remember him by."

A heaviness squeezed at her chest. He carried this with him every day. "I'm sorry," she whispered. She knew her comment was like putting a Band-Aid on a severed limb, but she said it anyway.

"It was a long time ago," he said, softer, stroking her hair.

"Where is the guy who did this?"

"Prison. I was off the force by the time they caught him. Probably better that way."

She lifted her hand and pressed it against one of the scars. He sucked in a deep breath and stiffened, as if she was causing him pain, so she pulled her hand away. But the moment she did that, the pain in his expression seemed to get worse.

"Don't stop," he said, his voice heavy. "It's just been a long time since anyone has touched me this way."

He took her hand and laid it over his scars again. She had so many questions, but she could see it was a painful subject for him. And this was about making him feel good. She'd ask later...whenever that was.

His hands were back on her legs, slowly caressing, moving higher with each stroke. The pull between them was growing stronger, bringing her attention back to where this was headed.

"Your turn again," he said. "What makes you hot, Alya?"

"The way you're saying my name right now is making me hot."

Henning's crooked smile broadened, but he shook his head. "Doesn't count. I need something to work with."

She wrinkled her nose, searching for a good answer. "Big," she finally said. When Henning chuckled, she added, "I'm not talking about what's between your legs. Regular size gets the job done nicely, too."

He raised his eyebrows. "Lots of things get the job done. We're setting the bar higher than that."

"Gladly," she said. "But I meant this."

She found his hand and lifted it up, matching it with hers so they mirrored each other. But it wasn't a mirror at all. Henning's hand outsized hers in every way. His long fingers stretched above hers, and his hand showed on both sides, so much broader.

"It turns me on. To feel the size of your hand when you touch me. The way you touch me is…" *Protective.* She paused, not sure how far she wanted to go on this topic. But he had taken a risk when he talked about his scars. It was her turn. She laced her fingers with his and continued. "I've been wary of this appeal since Nick. It also makes me feel vulnerable." She took another breath and let the rest come out. "I broke up with him in a restaurant, in public. I guess somewhere inside, I knew he could be dangerous. But when we got in the car afterward, he wouldn't let me out. He just kept driving, and when we finally got to his house in the mountains, he wouldn't take me back. He told me that I didn't get to break up with him. I was scared, but before things took a turn for the worse, I snuck out. And I ran, straight to the police."

He nodded slowly. "But he wouldn't leave you alone."

"Exactly. He came to my work, showed up at our door." That part was common knowledge at Blackmore Inc.

He was quiet for a while. "You're worried that because you're turned on by someone with physical power, something like that could happen again?"

"At first I was really worried about that," she said quietly, "but I know what happened with Nick wasn't my fault. And I would never be with someone who intimidated me again. Now it's more of a wariness about myself. I don't have the best relationship track record. Is my attraction to big, powerful guys part of the problem?"

He wrapped his hands around her waist and pulled away a little, staring at her, as if he was taking in what she had just said. Weighing it. Finally he took a deep breath.

"I was really hot for you the day we finally met," he said. "But I will never, ever make you feel like this is a risk. Protecting you will always come first for me, but I can see why that could make you feel wary. The moment you feel like this isn't working, I'll walk away. It's your call."

His eyes were intense, and she could feel how much he meant it.

"I wouldn't have told you all this if I didn't believe that, too," she said. She moved her hands over the thick muscles of his biceps. "So I'm just going with it for now."

"I'm glad you are," he said. "I'm still getting my head around the fact that this is really happening. All these things I've wished I was doing with you."

Wished. He had been thinking about this for a while...when it was his job to watch her. The question she had asked herself the day before came back to her, when he mentioned getting off to photos of her. He had had all-access permission to her feed, but when she and Stewart, her ex, had messed around in sight, it had been off-hours.

She licked her lips. "Did you ever watch?"

She didn't have to say more than that. The flare of lust in his intense gaze told her he knew exactly what she was talking about.

"Yes."

"Did you get yourself off when you watched?"

His breath was sharp, harsh.

"Right afterward." His answer was half words, half groan. "I thought about all the ways I'd make it better for you." He paused again. "I'm being honest with you because you should know this. And if it doesn't feel good, we should stop."

She shook her head. "I thought about it, too. I wondered if you were watching."

"And you didn't stop?"

She leaned forward and whispered, "It turned me on. I wanted you to watch."

"Fuck," he muttered. "You thought about me while you were fucking your boyfriend?"

"Yes."

His cock was throbbing in his jeans, moving against her clit.

She scooted back on his legs until her feet reached the floor. She took a couple steps back and then fingered the towel wrapped around her. His gaze was fixed on her hands, so she took her time as she opened it, letting one side fall. Henning's lips parted, and he muttered something under his breath.

"You owe me a piece of clothing." She smiled a little. "Stand up."

Slowly, he rose. Her heart thumped in her chest, and her breath caught in her throat. Damn, he really was a big man. Alya laid the towel in front of her and knelt down on the floor, the bulge in his pants at eye level now. He was so close, and tension radiated from him, but he stood absolutely still.

She reached up to find the button of his jeans and unfastened it. His breath was a harsh gasp.

"Did you ever see me suck him off?" she whispered. A rough noise escaped from his mouth as she pulled down his zipper. "Did you think about what it would feel like to have your cock in my mouth?" A string of curses came next, and, damn, it was hot. "You want to find out?"

"Yes," he groaned. "Fuck, yes."

Alya's heart jumped in her chest. Her body was on high alert, in tune with his every movement. This was the ultimate high, the moment when she knew this guarded, dark man let himself want. And he wanted *her*. Henning was staring down at her with rawness that made her come alive.

His jeans hung on his hips, open, his cock pushing at the material of his boxers. She was so close she could smell the heavy scent of sex from him. God, this man turned her on, and she wasn't going to worry about all the reasons why right now. She looked up at him, into this stormy darkness of his eyes, and all she could think about was the ways to make that storm ride higher.

"I think the next piece of clothing I'll take off is your boxers," she said.

"I see." His eyes narrowed, and his smile was dark. "You like to play dirty? I'll remember that."

Alya laughed. "I'm sure you will."

His smile faded as she slid her fingers under the top of his boxers. His cock was moving, straining against the material, but he made no effort to adjust it. What would he taste like? The cut muscles of his stomach tensed and moved every time her fingers brushed over his skin. She traced the trail of hair down his abs, to his boxers. Then, slowly, she lowered them, taking his jeans, too. Lower. His hands flexed and balled by his side, but he didn't move to help or speed it up, just waited for her, letting her take her time.

His boxers came lower, stretching over the enormous erection buried in his jeans, until finally it came free. His cock bobbed up, close to her mouth. She exhaled, and his whole body shuddered.

"Okay, I'll admit it," she said, smiling. "I like how big your cock is."

His laugh was short, and he brushed his hand over her cheek. "I'll use it to make it good for you. Really good."

God, she wanted to taste him right now, but this man was all about restraint. She wanted so badly to test the boundaries of that restraint. So instead she concentrated on his boxers, easing them down his legs until they were in a pile on the floor with his jeans. She nudged his feet, and he stepped out. Then Alya sat back on her heels and sized him up.

His skin was golden bronze, a little darker on his chest and lower legs from the sun, but also around his cock. Lord, that cock. It was thick and long and hard to the point that it looked painful. He had both the disposition and the body of a warrior—stoic, ready, with those thick, well-honed muscles. It was easy to understand why the police force had its appeal, and she wondered where he channeled all that energy now. Another query for another time. If there was one.

She pressed her hands on his legs, tracing the edges of his thigh muscles, exploring the insides with her thumbs, moving higher, getting a feel for him.

"I've never taken my time with the undressing part," she said. "Usually I just jump right in."

Henning let out a bark of laughter. "Yeah, we're certainly taking our time today."

Alya suppressed her smile of satisfaction. His voice was full of growly frustration, but still he didn't rush her. Her hands came higher, higher, until she reached the juncture of his legs.

"I have to ask," she said, looking up at him. "Have you been tested recently?"

He nodded. "I'm clean. You?"

"Me, too. And I'm on birth control."

He reached out and caressed her cheek with so much tenderness. "We can still use condoms." His voice was so low it was barely there.

She shook her head slowly. "No condoms. I want to taste you."

His hand tensed as she said that, but he let it fall away immediately. "Just tell me at any time if you want to do things differently."

"You, too."

His laugh was a sexy rumble. "I'm pretty sure I'm not going to change my mind about your mouth around my bare cock."

His crass comment together with the undercurrent of tenderness each time he touched her was doing crazy things to her insides. Alya leaned forward and pressed her lips against one of his balls. A string of curses toppled from his mouth, so she kissed the other, using her tongue.

"Your mouth is heaven," he rasped. He smoothed her hair back for a better view.

"You like watching me like this?"

"You know I do."

She moved a little higher, pressing her lips against the base of his cock. A shudder ran through him as she moved higher, licking the smooth skin. Drops of precum gathered at his tip, and she flattened her tongue and licked them. He answered with a heavy groan. His taste, his scent, the softness of his tip, his sounds of arousal—each element of this experience made her hotter.

"Did you ever get yourself off, imagining this?"

"Fuck, yeah. Too many times to count," he whispered. "But the real thing is so much better."

She licked him again from base to tip. Then she wrapped her hands around his base and took him into her mouth. He was big, really big. She tilted her head up. His expression was twisted in a silent balance between agony and pleasure, but he made no sound.

Alya took him in again, slowly sucking his thick cock deeper into her mouth and pulling out. She could see his hands fisted, the veins popping out of his forearms, but he didn't touch her. Did he want to? She definitely wouldn't mind if he showed her what he liked most. Was he gentle, or did he like it rougher? She was pretty sure she could get behind just about anything with this man. Well, almost anything. But for right now, he seemed to be leaving her to explore on her own.

She sat back, aching from the kneeling, though she hadn't noticed just a moment ago. She was so into this. Into him. "I want to learn more about what you like. But right now, I want you to make it good for me."

He helped her up, his hands gentle on her, stroking up and down her arms slowly as she stood in front of him.

"Fuck, Alya, I want you," he whispered, moving his hands up her shoulders, stroking her jaw. "Can you feel how much I want you?"

She nodded. "You're very direct," she said with a little smile.

His intense gaze burned into her, telling her just how badly he ached for her. He bowed his head, resting his forehead on hers. His fingers traced the line of her jaw, then moved down. His hand settled at the base of her neck, callused and possessive, though he didn't pull her closer, just looked at her with his dark brown eyes. This was Henning, naked and wanting her, and finally, she would have him. She touched his face, too, his lips, his scars, the creases in his brow. She parted her lips, wanting him, aching for him.

Alya lifted her hands and wove them into his hair, tugging his mouth to meet hers. His kiss started soft, surprised, but it quickly turned hungry. She pressed herself against him, skin to skin, and his fingers tightened around her neck as he took the kiss deeper. She sucked on his bottom lip and then bit down gently. His tongue stroked in and out of her mouth as he let out a deep rumble from his chest. He pulled back, a dazed look in his eyes.

"Holy fuck," he muttered with a laugh.

He took a step back and sank down on the bed, and she climbed on his lap. They had sat this way before, her straddling him, but they hadn't been naked. Now, she pressed her body against him, feeling the way her skin met his, the way his hard muscles felt as they moved against her. And the heat—there was so much heat coming off him. He settled his hands on her hips, gently stroking her, moving his palms down, over her ass and then back up again.

"You're incredible," he whispered, his voice reverent.

His cock throbbed impatiently, so she scooted closer until his erection pressed up against her. She grabbed on to his shoulders and moved herself up, using him to stroke her clit. She was so wet as she slid against his cock. His fingers tightened around her ass, and he flexed his hips as she moved back down. The sounds of raw pleasure came from both of them as they shifted and moved against each other. When she slid down again, he ground his hips against hers, whispering how badly he wanted her, how hot she made him. Still, he wasn't speeding this up, just stroking her. Like he was waiting for her to make the next move.

She lifted herself up again, but this time, she reached between them and positioned his cock right at her entrance. Then she raised her gaze to meet his. He was staring at her as if she were the only thing in the world that mattered. And in that moment, it felt like so much more than sex, so much that it took her breath away. But she had promised herself to enjoy this feeling, not worry about it, so, slowly, she lowered herself. Her body needed time to adjust, so she eased down just a little bit, then pushed up again.

Henning's hands dug into her hips, but he didn't move, just coaxed her on.

"That's it," he whispered. "Just like that, baby. You like that? Do you want to ride my cock?"

It was the kind of talk she had ached for. His words were making her even hotter, reminding her all the time that he was the one fucking her. Like he didn't want her to forget. She sank lower and lower until finally he was deep inside her. They sat that way, looking at each other. She had never done a lot of talking in bed, but Henning was being so open about how he felt that she just said what was going through her mind.

"Rougher." The word slipped out, and she didn't want to take it back.

Henning let out a desperate groan and thrust his hips up, deep. He let her set the pace, his hands over her, his hips flexing when he was deepest. He grunted but didn't say anything, just let her slide up and down his thick cock as the pleasure built. Over and over, he pressed deeper inside her, lighting up her whole body each time, until she was dizzy. His breaths were coming fast and hot, and a sheen of sweat built on his forehead. She knew he wouldn't let himself come until she did, but he sure as hell felt ready. He was waiting for her.

"You want me to touch you?" His voice was a gravely whisper. "You want me to make you come?"

He said the words like making her come was the hottest thing he could imagine. She nodded, too breathless to speak, and Henning reached between their bodies and stroked her clit. The orgasm crashed through her as she slid down his cock again. He grabbed on to her hips and kept up her pace, as pleasure rolled through her. Then a ragged groan tore through him, and he buried his face into her shoulder as his hips bucked under hers, setting off another wave of ecstasy.

Gasps. Pants. Henning fell back onto the bed, taking her with him. His breath was in her ear, and she closed her eyes and let this be her world. The kind where all this pleasure and happiness was so easy. Where the past fell away, and she and Henning could simply exist like this.

"That was intense," she said after a while.

His chest rose and fell under her. "The good kind of intense, I hope."

She smiled. "The amazing kind."

The kind that will disappear after we leave this place. God, she really didn't want it to disappear. That last thought was clear and strong, and she struggled to tamp it back down.

Unless...could this be more? Or was that the op-

posite of standing on her own? Alya swallowed.
Later. She could think about that later.

He lifted his head and pressed his lips into her
hair. She took in the warmth of his body, the brush
of his hair against her stomach, his scent that swirled
around her, paying attention to every detail, memo-
rizing this moment.

CHAPTER NINE

"REINDEER? SMOKED MOOSE?" Alya wrinkled her nose as she scanned the cold buffet. "Not sure about this."

She took some caviar and lox instead.

Henning eyed her. "Your mother didn't feed you this stuff, too?"

She shook her head. He served himself a taste of both along with two kinds of pickled herring.

"You're really going to eat that?"

"When in Sweden…" The right corner of Henning's mouth twitched up as he gestured to the various dishes and breads and cheeses beautifully laid out on the tables. "Besides, if no one eats the reindeer, then these animals died for nothing."

His tone was low and intimate, for her ears only, but by the time she opened her mouth to make another comment, the humor in his expression was gone. It was the first hint of lightness she had seen in him since they had watched members of the film crew walk into the restaurant, cameras in hand. And it disappeared so quickly.

The rest of the day had been full, with a second

photo session in the Icebar and a relatively painless interview. Dinner with the photo shoot crew didn't sound very appealing, but after eating in their room for the last few meals, Alya decided they should venture out for dinner, not just for her job but for Henning and her. To take the little cocoon of intimacy they had found out into the world, just to see what happened. But the cool, distant expression on Henning's face when they headed out of the room and through the snow had her second-guessing this idea. The moment they left the hotel building, crossing through the cold darkness of the Swedish night to the little restaurant, he was back to being the man who sat next to her on the plane, the impassive bodyguard who was there to protect her with his life. Exactly what he was hired for. Except now, she was watching him, too.

It was clear that he hated the fashion scene. Though his expression was flat, hard, she read every one of his tells: the working of his jaw as industry snark hummed from the tables, the flexing of his large hands at every stray gaze that lingered on her, the narrowing of his eyes when gazes lingered on him instead. Was his aversion to this scene worse now than when they arrived, or was she just more able to read it? Yes, it had all led to some amazing sex, but watching him right now was driving home the point that all of this had a cost for him.

Still, she was also sure he walked into this job with no illusions, so why was his reaction bothering her? What had she expected? That a few incredibly intense encounters would somehow change the world they lived in? She shouldn't even care since this was all over as soon as they left the place, and yet she did.

"You okay?" Henning's rough voice cut into her thoughts.

"Of course." She gave him a real smile, and his expression softened.

He gestured to an empty table in the corner. "I'll be in the back if you need anything."

Alya opened her mouth to protest, then closed it. She didn't *need* Henning. But watching him choose to walk away, to sit in the corner instead of next to her made her insides sink.

Alya frowned. She was here for work, not fooling around with her hot, surprisingly tender bodyguard. This was probably what her mother sounded like, right before she followed husband number two to another country, dragging young Alya and Natasha behind her, letting it all play out in public. Alya hadn't expected the public drama Nick tried to stir up after she broke up with him. With the intensity of the last couple days, she couldn't help but wonder if she was getting on yet another emotional rollercoaster that would somehow end badly. That despite all her efforts to avoid her mother's path, she still kept stumbling back onto those tracks.

But she and Henning were just having a few days of fun, nothing more. She could worry about all these complications later, after she was done with this job.

They still had tonight alone in the Icehotel, plus a little time tomorrow before they got back on the plane.

So she straightened up and made her way to an empty chair at the table with Jean Pierre and two of the other models. She sat down and nodded to them, searching her brain for their names... Audrey and Katherine.

"Saw your interview this afternoon," said Audrey, glancing over at the film crew, just a few tables away. "Nice job dodging the question about Nick Bancroft's statements about you."

Alya rolled her eyes. "Thanks. I knew it was coming, and truthfully, I thought she'd press harder. I'm just hoping that being professional and open with the interviewer will be the best answer to anything Nick said about my *instability*." She put air quotes around that last word. "But I'll probably get another form of that question tomorrow."

"You didn't respond when she asked about someone new in your life. And she suspected it was me." Jean Pierre laughed. "Which, of course, I didn't confirm or deny."

"Of course not."

Audrey and Katherine laughed, and Jean Pierre shrugged. "It's what they were looking for. Why not?"

"It could have been worse," said Alya. Like if they had instead turned their eyes to Henning, who was doing his best to stay as far away from the camera as possible. He had left the room entirely when she sat down for the interview.

"Change of subject. I heard from the hotel staff that Daxon Miles is coming tomorrow," said Katherine. "He was on some endurance ski trek in Sweden, and now he's heading here."

Alya wrinkled her brow. "Who's that?"

"The hot guy from that YouTube show, Pure Adrenaline, where he cliff-dives and scales mountains—that kind of thing." Katherine smiled. "Hot, single, with *that* kind of reputation."

Audrey laughed. "In other words, Katherine's staying an extra night here."

"Sounds entertaining," said Alya, taking a bite of smoked fish. "You're probably not the only one staying on."

"I can't believe you've never heard of him." Jean Pierre chuckled. "That bodyguard of yours keeping you occupied?"

Katherine looked over her shoulder at Henning, then back at Alya. "I can see the appeal. That brooding, tortured vibe he has going on can make things interesting in bed."

Alya resisted the urge to look back at Henning. She resisted the urge to contradict this one-dimensional view of him, that his scars were about sex appeal, not him. But saying any of those things was as good as admitting the truth: not only were they sleeping together, but she was starting to want more. So instead, she waved off the comment, like

it was just another half-serious insinuation. Like he
didn't matter to her, one way or another. And it felt
like shit to do that.

Alya stopped in front of the doors to the Icehotel and
turned around, looking at him with those beautiful
blue eyes. The snow was falling in tiny, shimmering
flakes all around her. She was so lovely it hurt, but
Henning couldn't look away. Her eyes glittered, and
her cheeks were flushed from sex after dinner. It had
happened, urgent and wordless, as they changed into
thermals before putting on their snowsuits. Alya still
hadn't spoken more than a handful of words since
they left the restaurant, which was fine in his book,
but now, as she looked up at him, he could feel that
something was on her mind.

"You sure you're okay with sleeping in this
place?"

Oh, that. Henning's half-smile tugged at his lips.
"I'm feeling pretty relaxed right now."

"Me, too. But that's not what I meant."

"I know." He did. Looking down at her, he drank
in the warmth of her expression. "I'm fine."

Surprisingly, he really did feel fine. The shudder
of dread that had run through his body the first time
the cold wind hit his face was gone. Maybe it was
the sex, all that intimacy that was loosening something inside him, or maybe the sharpest edges of
those memories of the explosion were finally dull-
ing, but he felt so much better than fine…as long as

he kept his mind on this moment. Not the past, and not the future.

Alya's gaze stayed on him for an extra beat, and then she nodded. So he reached for the reindeer antler handle and opened the door to the frozen palace in front of them.

All the cords and equipment from the shoot were gone, and the hallway was silent. Inside, away from the gusts of wind, the only sounds were the crunches of their footsteps on the snowy floor. The tiny lights behind the sculptures shone through the blocks of ice, but otherwise, there were no other hints of civilization except this marvelous creation of ice and snow that surrounded them. There were others from the shoot staying the night in the Icehotel, but even they felt far away. He and Alya were alone.

"You know where we're staying, I assume," he said. Henning had been a little distracted on that first day, when the receptionist gave her the details.

She looked up at him. "Um, I changed our room."

He nodded, waiting for whatever was making her hesitate.

"I had originally reserved a room with separate beds, so I changed it."

"I see." Henning swallowed.

She frowned. "Judging from the look on your face, I should have asked first. But I just thought..." Her voice trailed off, and she sighed. "Sorry."

He gritted his teeth. Time to put aside his own

baggage and be what Alya needed for one more night. He could give her that.

"Don't be sorry," he said softly. "There's nothing I'd love more than to spend the night next to you."

She blinked up at him, searching, but if she was looking for hesitation in that statement, she wouldn't find any. He had spoken the truth, full stop, and if she wanted him close one more time, he was going to give that to her. Besides, he rarely had nightmares anymore. And with Alya next to him, her body against his, the scent of her surrounding him—these sensations had slowly carved a little opening of light into the cave where he had buried himself for years. It would be enough to get him through tonight.

She must have found an answer because she smiled. "Good. Because I switched us to the Viking Room."

Henning tipped his head back and laughed. All morning in that room, he had watched as another man touched her. Even lay with her. All for the camera. But tonight, he would be the one to lie with her for real in that bed. Hell, this woman understood how his mind worked.

"I thought you'd like that," she said, chuckling. "I want to be here with you."

She grabbed his hand, glove in glove, and started down the hallway toward the Viking Room. They stopped in front of the reindeer pelt that covered the doorway.

"Not a lot of privacy in this place," he said, holding the fur curtain aside for her to enter. When she passed by, he leaned in to press his mouth against her neck. "You're not very quiet, you know. That's not at all a complaint, by the way, just an observation."

She laughed. "You're not either. Between that and the layers of clothes we'll need to keep on, I think we're going right to sleep tonight."

Yeah, right. No books or TV or anything else to distract him. And just the idea of her body next to his on the Viking bed was making his cock hard. How the hell was he going to fall asleep?

The room felt bare without the people and the equipment that had filled it earlier. The bed itself stood out in the center, its rounded hull and sea dragon bow rising up out of the snow, as if it were floating. Henning walked over to inspect the setup. The pelts had been replaced with two puffy sleeping bags, zipped together, and when he lifted them he found a mattress on top of a short platform. He breathed out a sigh. Thank fuck they weren't sleeping directly on the ice.

Alya followed him over to the bed and started to unzip her snowsuit.

His eyes widened. "What are you doing?"

"We're supposed to stuff everything except our boots at the bottom of the sleeping bag, right?"

"But that sleeping bag is about zero degrees right now. You're going to need some body heat to warm it up," he grumbled. "Let me go first."

Henning shucked his boots and climbed onto the

ice ship, slipping into the sleeping bag. Once he was inside, he shoved his gloves to the bottom and then unzipped his snowsuit, wriggling out of it until it was at his feet.

"Fuck, it's cold," he said, shivering.

The cold was everywhere, and for a moment, his muscles tightened, and his breath stopped. A vision of Sanjay on the floor next to him came without warning, blood gushing out of his neck, dying right in front of him. *Hell, no.* Henning was not going to let this happen tonight. If he just focused on Alya, warm and safe next to him, he could get through this. Just breathe in and out. The warmth of his body began to spread, and his breath came back. *Focus on this moment, nothing else.*

Henning took off his extra fleece and made it into a pillow for them both. Then he rolled onto his side and looked up at her. That flash of dread apparently hadn't shown on his face, or at least she hadn't seen it, so he waggled his eyebrows at her. "Okay, baby. Time to climb in and strip."

Alya pulled off her boots and then slipped into the sleeping bag. It was a tight fit, good for keeping the warmth in but not ideal for undressing. Henning pulled down her zipper, and they moved and shifted until her snowsuit and gloves were at the bottom of the sleeping bag, too. Then, finally, they were facing each other.

"You better hope I don't need to use the bathroom anytime soon," she said, smiling up at him. "It's going to be a project."

Henning chuckled and slipped his arms around her, pulling her close, against the warmth of his body.

"Mmm." She sighed, snuggling in. "Very nice."

It was all so good, her soft body, the sound of her satisfaction, the peace of having her all to himself like this, so, of course, his cocked stirred again.

"Ignore that," he grumbled.

"I'll try, but it's what I'm thinking about, too. We need a distraction." She moved against him, and he groaned. "Let's talk."

"I'm not much of a talker under regular circumstances," he said. "And with the most amazing woman lying next to me? I've got nothing."

Her eyes widened, as if his words had taken her by surprise. Then she brushed her lips against his.

"Let's have an AMA session," she said. "Anything is game, and you have to answer truthfully."

"I can ask you anything?"

"Anything."

Well, that was one way to distract him. There were things he'd rather not talk about, but in exchange for being able to ask her anything? Yeah, he could do this.

"I'll go first," he said. "Tell me about when you moved to Los Angeles."

"I was ten and Natasha was eight," she said. "We still spoke Russian together, so we didn't make a lot of friends. My mother's acting career was taking off, and she was caught up in that. All I had was Natasha for a long time. Probably why we're still so close."

He nodded.

"My turn," she said. "Tell me about your last girl-friend."

"Really?" He raised his eyebrows. "Because I don't want to hear anything about other men you've had sex with."

She rolled her eyes. "I just want a better picture of you."

He shook his head. "I've never been good boy-friend material, not then and not now."

"You sure? You've got that big, protective vibe written all over you," she said, stroking his bicep with her hand. "But no diverting the conversation. Tell me."

"Her name was Corinne, and, looking back, I can see I was a shit boyfriend to her. I worked all the time when I was on the AFP, always canceling dinners because something came up. Even when I wasn't working, that's what I thought about. After a while, the only place we got along was in the bedroom." He glanced over at her, gauging her reaction. Her expression was solemn, like she knew what came next. She nodded for him to continue, but this part was the hardest. Henning took a deep breath. "Then, the explosion happened, and I was in the hospital for a bit. She broke up with me. It sounds harsh, but I can't really blame her. The only thing we had at that point was sex, and that wasn't happening while

I was recovering. Plus, I looked like a monster with my stitched-up scars. Romantic, right?"

"Honest," she said. Worry lines creased her forehead, and she opened her mouth like she wanted to say more, but she didn't. Instead, she reached for his injured cheek to stroke it. Henning blew out a long breath, sinking into the comfort of her hand on his skin, just for a moment. But the room was so cold. He moved her hand to his shoulder, under the covers, as he thought through his next question.

"If you weren't modeling, what would you do instead?"

"That's easy. I'd finish my nursing degree." She brushed her hair out of her face. "I'd like to work in the emergency room, I think. There's a lot that happens there, a lot on the line at those moments."

"Why didn't you finish?"

"It cost a lot, and modeling paid instead of cost. And at the time, Natasha and I needed to support ourselves."

She said all of this so matter-of-factly, without a trace of bitterness at being sidetracked from something she had wanted then and still wanted now.

"Do you have any plans to go back at this point?"

"Someday. Modeling isn't really a forever career." She sighed. "Plus I think nursing school will be better when I'm older. There were comments that made me think people didn't take me seriously, just because of the way I looked. They didn't trust me. And then there were doctors who..."

He must have reacted visibly because she narrowed her eyes at him. "Wait—you just asked more than one question, and now you're scowling." She smiled a little. "New subject. I want to know about five years with no kissing but not celibate."

He frowned. "I'm pretty sure you can guess what that means. You sure you want to know more?"

"I do."

He stroked her shoulder and then rested his hand on her neck, warming it from the cold.

"Fine. For a while I went to this…club. And I met some women there. It was just for sex, nothing more. No kissing, no touching." Henning silently begged her not to ask for more details.

Alya's cheeks were flushed, but she kept her gaze steady on him. "And that's generally your preference? Sex with no kissing or touching?"

"That's not my general preference. But under those circumstances, yes, it was."

She lifted an eyebrow. "Those circumstances meaning at sex clubs?"

He hesitated. But he had promised the truth. "Those circumstances meaning after I left the AFP."

"I see," she said. "But you don't go to that club anymore?"

He shook his head.

"Why not?"

"I realized I wanted something else."

"Did you get it?" Her voice was quiet now.

He had promised her the truth, but every version of the truth left something out. Did she already know that she was what he wanted? Maybe it didn't matter anymore.

Henning kissed her on the forehead and held her closer. "Yes. More than what I had hoped for. So much more." She looked up and stared at him, a little stunned, so he kissed her again. "You've gone way over your question limit. Let's go to sleep."

She nodded, her cheek brushing against his chest, her fluffy hat tickling his nose. He shifted onto his back so she could rest her head on his chest. Alya adjusted and then propped herself on her elbow. The sleeping bag fell off her shoulder, revealing the only layer now between her skin and the cold.

"Careful," he whispered, pulling the fluffy down cover up over her, holding it in place. "I don't want you cold."

"You're like a furnace. You'll keep me warm," she said, running her hand over his chest.

Then she brushed her lips over his. She ran her fingers over the scarred side of his face and kissed him again. The familiar desire was still there, but in the warmth of her mouth he found something more, something he wasn't ready to process.

The memory of the kiss lingered as she lay her head on his chest, and he brought his arm around her, holding her and closing his eyes. Even breaths of icy air didn't matter when Alya was warm, pressed up against him. Safe.

As he drifted off, somewhere in the space between awake and asleep, the last of his defenses fell. But for once, it wasn't visions of death that came. It wasn't the gaping hole inside him that he felt, the piece of him that he had left behind on that warehouse floor. It wasn't even lust for the woman who was nestled against him.

It was hope, dangling its sparkling lure, a tempting escape from the dark pool of the half life he had made for himself these last years. He knew what that shiny lure was attached to, knew its promises weren't what they seemed, but right now, it looked better than the waters he was in.

So, for the first time in years, Henning let himself hope.

CHAPTER TEN

ALYA STARTLED OUT of her sleep. Something had awoken her, and her body was on high alert. She was cold, she realized with a shiver. Somehow, the sleeping bag had moved down, exposing her to the arctic temperatures. She lay sprawled across Henning's body, tense underneath hers. One of his hands held her head against his chest, and the other was clamped around her shoulder.

She took a couple deep breaths as relief rushed through her. She was here, in the Viking Room of the Icehotel with Henning. The room was dark and silent, so what had jolted her out of her sleep? She tugged up the sleeping bag and lifted her head to see him.

He was lying on his back. The shadows hid most of the scars along his cheek, but she could see hints of the taut, smooth skin by his mouth. At some point she had read about scars in nursing school, how they could pull and stretch at the skin. Were his painful?

Alya studied him, his face so serious, even in sleep. She tried to picture Henning as a boyfriend, sitting down for a quiet breakfast, reading the newspaper. Not a chance. Had he ever imagined himself on the path the led to a wife, two kids and a picket fence? She just couldn't see that either. Sex? Definitely, but more than that just didn't seem to fit with him.

As she watched, his face drew up into a tight grimace. She sucked in a gasp as a strangled cry of anger and pain filled the room. It was the same sound that had awoken her—she was sure of it—and it came from deep inside Henning's chest. Her body tensed, as his pain echoed through her.

"Henning?" Nothing. She tried again. "Henning?"

His mouth twisted, like she was making it worse. She had to do something. Alya reached out her hand, touching his cheek. He flinched.

"Henning? It's me." She moved her hand along his jaw, down his neck, over his shoulder to his enormous bicep. Then she shook him a little, trying to wake him up.

It all happened so quickly that she didn't remember how he managed it, but in the next moment she was flat on her back. Henning was on top of her, his forearms holding her arms by her sides, her legs trapped between his heavy thighs. The traces of light from the hallway brought his scars into painful relief. He blinked down at her, his eyes unfocused. He squeezed them shut, and then looked down at her again. His eyes widened in surprise.

"What the fuck?" he whispered, more to himself than to her, it seemed.

It took a moment for her to get her voice back.

"You were dreaming, Henning," she said. "I... I had to wake you up."

He was still staring down at her as if he was trying to fit all the pieces of this moment together.

"Alya?" His voice was thick with sleep and confusion.

"Yes. It's me." If she had her hands free, she would have reached up, stroked his face, reminding him of where they were. Reminding him of *them*. But he was holding her down. She tugged her arms, but he didn't move, just stared down at her. Finally he shifted, loosening her arms.

"Alya." Her name was an answer this time, and he said it as if it were the one answer to everything. "You're not hurt. Thank God."

She leaned up to brush her lips against his, and he shuddered, the hard line of his mouth softening. Between her legs his cock grew fast, pressing against her. Heat rushed to her cheeks and a deep groan rose from Henning's chest. She looked up into his intense brown eyes and found a bottomless well of aching hunger.

Her hands were free now, so she brought them to his shoulders, pressing them against the fabric of his shirt. He hissed out a breath, and his cock throbbed against her, but he didn't move. He just looked down at her with a gaze somewhere between wonder and fear.

"I'm fine, Henning," she said, stroking the thick muscles of his shoulders, so tense and hard under her fingers. The air was cold and his body was hot, even through the material of his shirt.

"It was just so cold in my dream. You were so cold. And…" He closed his eyes, and his breaths were long and deep as he touched her bare skin, tracing the planes of her face, as if he was reminding himself of her. As if he needed to remember she was real. His touch wasn't sexual, at least not in the way she expected. He just seemed to want to touch and breathe, to hold on to this moment.

The cold. He had talked about the warehouse, lying on the cold floor, while he watched another man on his team die after the explosion. She was almost sure that's where his mind had gone, even if he didn't say it. That memory was there between them right now.

His eyes were still closed, the fear in his expression just starting to fade. She lifted her head and pressed her lips to his. He didn't move or even kiss her back, but his lips were soft against hers. She did it again.

"Let me comfort you," she whispered.

He shook his head and lifted himself, like he was going to move off her.

She frowned. "You don't want that?"

Traces of hurt came through in her voice, and Henning froze.

"Oh, baby," he whispered, lowering himself over her again. He brought his hands to her face, cupping her jaw as he looked down at her. "I want you so fucking badly right now."

She shifted so her her legs were around his, his throbbing erection against her. "Then have me," she whispered.

"Oh, hell," he muttered, and he drove his hips against hers. She met his thrusts with a tilt of her hips so his cock slid right along her core. Oh, God, he felt so good, his big, hard body over hers.

He stopped, staring down at her, his eyes blazing with intensity. She moved her hands up and down over his biceps, feeling them as they flexed under his weight. She took in this connection, this man who was so many things to her, and tried to put it into words. "Right now, when you look down at me, it makes me feel like you'd do anything for me."

"I would," he said quietly.

"The way you made me feel when you called to check in with me for the last three years—I know it was part of your job, but I can't tell you how important it's been. I had never met you, and the only time you could see me was when I was in my apartment. But it was enough. That was the support I needed for a while." She slipped her hand under his thermal shirt, the warmth of him filling her. "Tonight, please let me give you that feeling you gave me. I want to be what you need right now."

He was still under her hands, as if he was just taking in what she said, so she moved her hand over his shoulder, tracing his scars, then kissed him again. "Let me."

Some people talked while they were thinking, but he wasn't one of those people, she was almost sure. Words were not what he needed. Henning's cock pressed against her, and she tilted her hips, letting him know exactly how she wanted to help him right now.

He rested his forehead on hers. And despite all that she had said, despite all the evidence that he wanted her, she still had the feeling that he was going to turn her down.

"It will be good for both of us," she whispered. "Let me want you, too. Even now."

His erection jolted against her. A heavy breath. Another.

"Jesus," he finally whispered. "God, yes."

The sleeping bag didn't give them much room, but after some shimmying, they were both naked from the waist down. He didn't seem to be in any hurry, and she got the sense that he needed a little time to wrap his mind around this, so she threaded her hands into his hair and let him explore. He traced her body, first over her clothes, and then inside. His rough hand skimmed over her skin, sending shivers through her.

"Fuck, you're so soft," he rasped.

Lower, teasing lower until finally, finally he reached between her legs. Henning groaned.

"You're so wet," he whispered, his voice was full of awe and wonder. "Even right now, you want me."

She closed the distance between their mouths and kissed him. "I want you, just like this."

As those last words left her lips, he guided his cock inside her in a long slow thrust. *Oh, God.* It was pleasure and grief, longing and relief, all in one push as he sank so deep inside her. Their gasps filled the room, but he didn't move, and neither did she. Then Henning positioned his hands under her shoulders, holding her to him, and he pulled out.

Her voice. It had broken through his half-waking nightmare, slow and sultry, changing all the buried memories and fears into something much, much different. Henning gritted his teeth, resisting the urge to fuck away every last vision of the warehouse and the blood and Sanjay's body on the floor, the body that, for one terrible moment, his dream had transformed into hers.

He needed to get that image out of his mind, and fucking was a way to get his world back under control, to clear the slate. But this wasn't some woman from that club, using him as much as he was using her. This was Alya. And he never, ever wanted to use her like that.

"Oh, fuck," he muttered, and he drove his hips against hers, unable to resist. She met his thrusts with a tilt of her hips so his cock slid right along her core. Oh, God, she felt so sweet, her soft, slim body under his.

Her hands moved inside his shirt, slipping down over his bare skin, leaving a scorching trail of heat. She moved her hands around his ass, and he couldn't resist. He thrust his cock against her, and her moan of pleasure was almost unbearably erotic.

He closed his eyes and gritted his teeth to ease the tension building inside him again. If he didn't stop now, he was going to use her. He was no longer moving, and when he opened his eyes, Alya was looking up at him, glaring.

"I decide what I want, not you," she said, like she knew exactly what was going through his mind right now.

He had endless reasons why they shouldn't continue, but she had just given him the one argument that won over all of his. This was going to happen.

"I want to fuck, Alya," he warned. "That's what this will be."

If she was afraid of him, she didn't give any sign of it. Instead, she brought her hand to his face again, and her face lit up with want. "And I want to be the woman you want to fuck."

Henning closed his eyes, trying to contain the last hold on his self-control. "You're so much more. Don't you know that?"

Her nails dug into his skin, and his self-control snapped. In one, hard thrust, he entered her. His mouth crashed down on hers, and he unleashed all his wants and fears in a kiss. Lips, tongue, teeth, anything to have more of her. More. Her hips met each of his strokes, over and over.

"Do I make you wet?" he growled.

"Yes," she cried. "Yes, yes." Her voice was a mix of lust and frustration.

She closed her eyes and moaned.

Over and over, he thrust in and out, and she whispered, *yes*, again and again.

"Is it my cock you want?" He bit out the question.

"I want y—"

He couldn't bear to hear the answer, not right now. So before she could finish, he pushed in hard. The sound that came from her mouth was so beautiful, so full of desire and satisfaction, and it was for him. Christ, yes, it was for him.

"That's fine, baby," he said, holding on, trying not to break. "I'll give it to you whenever you want." He swallowed, the urge to let go warring with the urge to take it slowly, to be careful with her. No, it was better that this happened now, that she understood this other side of him. So he leaned down, taking a breath of her intoxicating scent and whispered in her ear. "But tonight, you're mine."

Her lips brushed the rim of his ear, sending a shudder of pleasure through him.

"Yes, Henning," she said, her voice a heavy rasp. "I'm yours. And you're mine, too."

He turned his head, and she looked at him, her

long, dark lashes low over her eyes. This was all just for him. So he let go. The urge to be rough and selfish was strong, to show her just how broken he was. And he was sure he wore it on his face, a face more beast than human, and the unleashing of this part of him brought the most primal satisfaction. Her cry filled the room, and her nails dug into his skin.

"Henning."

He closed his eyes, drowning in the clusterfuck of emotions that wouldn't stop coming.

"Oh, fuck," he muttered, and she came around his cock, his hips pumping over and over, deep inside her.

CHAPTER ELEVEN

ALYA SAT DOWN on the couch of the hotel's lobby, smiling at the *Behind the Runway* crew, trying to get her head on straight. One guy tested the lighting, and another swept her hair over one shoulder then the other. All she could think about was last night. It had been intense and so incredibly raw. Alya had seen a part of Henning that she had felt, lurking beneath his restraint this whole time. It was a side he tried to bury.

The sex itself had been out of this world, in a category all by itself. That connection, the desperation with which he clung to her, the way he finally let her give when he needed to take, holding her against him so tightly—it made her heart ache. They didn't speak after it was over, but Henning held her against him as he rolled over on his side, his cock still buried deep inside her until she finally nodded off to sleep.

How long did he stay awake? There were no more nightmares, at least none that she was aware of, but when she woke up, she could feel the shift between them. They had crossed a line that they couldn't un-

cross. Did he regret it? He was gentle with her, so
gentle, and he barely spoke. The connection between
them hadn't disappeared, but all traces of the play-
fulness that had bloomed since they had arrived at
the Icehotel had withered. She could feel he was letting her go.

All these ideas swirled around in her head as she
smiled up at the *Behind the Runway* crew, waiting
for this interview. She should be nervous by now.
She always was when *she* was in the spotlight, not
just a designer's clothing, especially these last few
years. But the stomachache that usually plagued her
before anything where she was supposed to "just be
herself" was absent. In fact, in her interview yesterday, it hadn't been there either.

Alya thought back to Brianna, getting drunk in
the Icebar, laughing so freely, daring anyone to judge
her. The all-night partying wasn't Alya's path, but
maybe another part of it was. She had been groomed
for this role for her whole life, her mother's comments laced with warnings about men, backed up
by her mother's own real-life cautionary tales. So
Alya had carefully constructed her life, her career,
her image, knowing that it had to work for both her
and Natasha.

But somewhere along the way, their situation had
changed. The move to Australia had been a relief, a
chance to start over, and it wasn't just Nick she had
needed some distance from. Here in Sydney, no one

seemed to care who her mother was, and she and Natasha both had found that refreshing.

But still, that fear she dragged around from Los Angeles had clung to her, the fear that she was one public relations disaster away from becoming her mother. She hadn't really understood how much it had guided everything she did.

Before last night, Henning had let Alya lead in the bedroom, so careful around her. Then, last night, the roles had flipped. He hadn't held back, but it didn't just set him free. She felt freedom in it, too, a totally new kind of satisfaction, beyond the pleasure itself. That's what it meant to let go of the past: the space to see Henning more clearly, to understand him, to give to him and to find more in what they could be together. It was the space where all the risks lay, but it was also the space where they could find endless rewards.

Their connection was so strong, right from the moment she'd bumped into him in the Blackmore Inc. office. Was she falling in love with Henning, after just a few days together? Could he love her back? It seemed crazy to ask herself these questions, but she let herself anyway. She glanced at him, across the lobby, his brow furrowed as he jabbed at his laptop. He looked up at her, and his expression softened, but he didn't smile.

The interviewer from *Behind the Runway* signaled her, and the cameras moved in, so Alya turned her focus to them. If there was anything she could say about the documentary crew, they certainly knew how to make her feel comfortable. And talkative. She had no idea how much time passed as the woman led her through topics: the best locations to work, craziest thing someone had said on set and the strangest working conditions. She even talked a little about her childhood, navigating her mother's career as well as her own.

"I was on the path to being a nurse. But…" She hesitated. "There was a lot going on, and it wasn't going to work for both my sister and me to go to college at the same time."

Her mother's career had taken a dive by then. They weren't going hungry by any stretch, but money was tight, even with both Natasha and her working part-time.

"So you took up modeling?"

"I had had some offers before, so I got in touch with an agency."

"You left nursing school behind and quickly became one of the most sought-after models in the industry." The woman added a dramatic pause. "Especially after you got involved with Nick Bancroft."

Alya hated this insinuation the most—the idea, floating out in the press, that her success was somehow hooked to Nick. The insinuation that the relationship could have been a strategic move. Countering that idea was part of the reason she had stayed in that relationship longer than she should have.

She realized she hadn't said anything in a while

because the woman added, "But I'm sure no one wants a rehash of a long-gone relationship here."

The woman sounded like she was hoping otherwise, but Alya just rolled her eyes. "I think that topic has been sufficiently covered in the media."

"You look a lot happier now than in those photos."

She snorted. "That's an understatement. I'm living on my own, traveling again. It's freeing, really."

"And what's next?"

"There are a lot of places I've wanted to visit. I'll be at fashion week this spring, both in New York and in Milan, so I think I'll start there."

As she spoke these words, something loosened inside, something that had been clenched for so long she had forgotten that feeling was there. The worries hadn't disappeared altogether, but she didn't have to let them dictate her life. There were so many things she wanted to do, and she could *do* all of them. She could enjoy all the travel modeling gave her while it still lasted, instead of worry about Nick or how it might affect her career or whatever went through her mind.

And maybe, just maybe, Henning might want to be a part of that life. But if he didn't, she'd still go. That's how she knew she was strong enough to ask him. But first, she had to finish the interview.

Henning had only said a handful of sentences to Alya today, and that was probably for the best. Especially since he had gone from melancholy to mad. Now, he had no idea what he was feeling.

But what the fuck was she thinking in that interview? Laying out her itinerary for anyone to have—including Nick? And then, after Alya had done it, she'd turned to him and smiled the most heartbreakingly beautiful smile, so he shoved all those feelings back down. He had no say in how she conducted her life. He was hired to be her bodyguard, nothing more, and that's what he had to focus on.

Henning had learned to point his laser-like focus at a goal as soon as he grew old enough to understand how things worked for a big man in the world. His body was a tool, whether he wanted it to be or not, and carefully managed, this kind of focus was used for good. But the moment he used it for his own wants and needs, he crossed a line. He had to get through this day without letting out this fierce wave of protectiveness that was threatening to pull him under. He was supposed to be letting her go, and all he could think about was pulling her closer. Especially after last night.

It happened every time he looked at her. Like right now, for example, as she sat in the snow, her cheeks pink from fiddling with her skis. His chest clenched. It hurt just to look at her, knowing this was almost over, so he looked down, fitting his cross-country ski boot into the binding. Then he straightened up, using his poles to balance.

"Need some help?" he asked, glancing in Alya's direction.

She shook her head. "I think I've got it."

"Good. Because I'm not seeing a way to move sideways in these things." He looked down at the long, slim skis attached to his boots. He had surfed and waterskied in his teens, so how hard could cross-country skiing be? It was all on water, more or less.

Alya stood up, lifting her feet, testing the bindings. Then she turned to him and smiled. "I have a feeling this will be a short excursion."

Oh, that smile, tentative but warm, despite how selfish he had been last night.

"I'll follow you," he said, and she started toward the frozen river, leaving him with his increasingly frustrating thoughts.

Somehow, while he slept, she had slipped her hand under his thermal shirt without his notice, and he awoke to find it resting over his heart. It hurt to have it there, hurt that she still reached for him the night before, after the way he had taken, taken from her. But the drive to give her what she wanted was even stronger than the hurt, and so he left it there. Let her wake up like that, let her kiss him wordlessly, all the while knowing that this was the very last time he would lie with her.

Tonight, they'd climb onto one airplane, then another, then another, each taking them farther away from this impossible world, this hotel made of ice— ice, of all things—that had him hoping beyond reason, if only for a night, that a broken man could patch himself together for someone who mattered.

Slowly she reached the enormous river, thick layers of ice covered with snow, and found a set of cross-country ski trails that ran along the near bank, cutting lines through the deep snow. There were four total, probably a set for each direction, but there was no one else in sight for miles, so she made her way onto one set and motioned for Henning to take the other. He fit his skis onto the parallel tracks and came to a stop next to her. His eyes still held heat and intensity when he looked at her—that hadn't changed. But she had seen an edge in that look a few times today, almost as if he was angry at her. And he was really quiet. Even for him.

Henning gestured to the flat, open expanse of snow that covered the enormous river. It was empty and still, and it ran for as far as she could see in either direction. "I don't know about this. We're standing on ice, and I can't stop thinking about what happens if it breaks."

She wrinkled her nose. "Think about how thick the blocks of ice in the hotel were. You said they cut them out of this river. We'll be fine."

His nod was more acknowledgment than agreement. "How far do you want to go?"

"I barely made it here, and it was downhill," she said, gesturing to the river bank. "I'd say I'll last ten minutes on this trail, tops."

Finally, a hint of a smile from him. "Remind me why we're doing this again?"

"Because I wanted to see all this," she said, sweeping her pole out along the broad, white landscape. The move threw her off balance, and she tottered on one ski for a moment before recovering. "At the time, it seemed like the best way to do it, though I'm having doubts."

Henning was definitely smiling now. "Okay. Lead on."

The sky was an ocean of thick, gray clouds, rolling and changing. The heavy darkness of the long winter night had eased into a dim twilight, but the sun was nowhere in sight. Instead, it was the snow that lit this vast world, shimmering and still. The only sound was the wind.

Alya had watched the Olympic version of this sport. The athletes wore some sort of thin bodysuits and raced through the forest. She, on the other hand, was bundled in a bulky snowsuit and moving at walking speed…at best. And she was already panting. She glanced over at Henning, who looked hot as usual and not at all winded, though he looked like he was having as much trouble getting into a rhythm as she was.

Alya stopped, one foot in front of the other, which, of course, threw her off balance again. She clutched her pole, trying to steady herself, but she toppled over into the deep snow between the two sets of tracks.

"You okay?" Henning asked.

"I'm fine," she said, looking up at the sky. "Actually, it's kind of nice down here."

Henning eased himself into the snow right behind her. She looked over her shoulder and found him so close. His gaze dipped to her lips, then back to her eyes, but there was more than just heat in that gaze. So much more.

"We could do this, Henning," she whispered. "For real."

He blinked at her, his brow wrinkling, but then he gave her a wry smile. "I doubt it. I'm a lousy skier, and I'm okay with that."

She shook her head. "I mean us. We could try it."

His eyes widened in surprise, and his smile faded. Then he frowned. She probably should have taken that as a warning, but she didn't. If she just laid it out for him, he'd be able to see how easy it would be to just try. "We'd just do the regular stuff people do when they're dating. We could go out to dinner, go to the beach. I'm going to one of Max's fund-raising events next weekend, and you could come with me, as my date. It would be—"

"No. Stop."

She pulled back and blinked at him. "Why?"

He closed his eyes but said nothing.

"No." Alya gritted her teeth. "You don't get to stay silent. After everything that's happened these last few days, if you don't even want to try, you need to explain. I want you to say it."

"We're both going to regret this conversation." He pulled off his glove and traced her cheek with his warm fingers. Then he swiped a hand over his face, and when he looked down at her, his expression was dark. "This is dangerous, Alya. You saw me last night."

Alya struggled to turn around and face him, but her skis were planted in the snow. She huffed out a breath and pushed herself to something that approximated a sitting position.

"Last night, I wanted you, too. I made that clear."

He waved off her comment, as if it wasn't relevant.

"You want to know what I was feeling when I watched your interview today?" His expression was hard. "I was furious, listening to you list off all the places you'd be next so anyone knows exactly where to find you. All that protectiveness I feel knowing how many men are watching you—maybe I could get used to that. But not you putting yourself at risk. I'm not in any condition to watch you do that."

Goddamn him. They lay there in the snow, dressed in bulky snowsuits in the middle of the frozen river, so they couldn't soften or deflect the conversation with sex. Which was probably better. She had sensed that things were off after the interview, and the more she thought about his reasoning, the more frustrated she was getting.

"You're mad that I wasn't sufficiently scared of Nick to hold back where I'll be traveling this year?"

He hesitated, like he knew this question was a trap but didn't quite see why. "Yes?"

"That conversation was a revelation to me. I've never felt freer," she said. The more she talked about this, the sharper her voice was getting. "But you wanted me to hesitate? To go back to how I felt before? You'd rather I cower?"

"You have to be more careful," he said, anger spilling out.

"So I don't have to worry? Or so you don't?"

Henning's jaw worked, his mouth in a grim line, his scars stark, white against the ruddiness of his skin. "Look how crazy this is making me, after just a couple days. How far will this need to protect you go? Until I smother everything that's good between us?"

God, he had been right. She really regretted starting this conversation. And now she couldn't let it go. "You're already planning out some terrible end for us?"

"It's my job to consider all aspects of a problem, Alya. One of us has to." It was such a low blow, to take her newfound lightness and turn it against her.

"Good news. This problem is about to disappear for you," she snapped back. "I'm officially done with having a bodyguard around."

His face twisted in pain as she said that, and her gut clenched. Shit. She was sinking to new lows, too. What hurt the most was knowing that no matter what came out of her mouth, no matter how terrible it was, he would still protect her with his life.

After that last comment, all the anger seeped out of his expression. He was staring at her with that same, intense gaze, but this time it made her even more frustrated.

"What the hell does that look mean?" she snapped.

At first she thought he wasn't going to answer, but then he whispered, "I'm just looking at you. So I remember."

Alya closed her eyes, pushing away the urge to cry. Because it wouldn't do a thing. So instead, she turned away and tried to get up. Unfortunately, her feet were stuck under her, and she tumbled back into the snow with an undignified plop. Why was she having this conversation with these damn skis on? She rolled around, her skis in the air, until they were pointing in the right direction. Then, using her poles, she managed to get herself upright and standing. Henning was watching the whole time, of course.

"I'll still be there to protect you. That will never change." His voice was soft. "If you change your mind. If you need a bodyguard at that event next weekend. I can…" He paused. "I can come home with you, too, if you want me there."

God, this was torture. He was offering to go back to the way they'd begun this trip. This was his compromise?

"I don't want you as a bodyguard or as a fuck buddy, Henning," she said, looking up at the gray sky. "What makes me angry is that at some point, I know I'll actually be tempted. But I'm making myself hold out for something better. For someone who thinks it's worth the risk to fall in love with me for real."

CHAPTER TWELVE

YOU DESERVE TO be free.

Alya had found the note lying on top of her clothes when she unzipped her suitcase back in her Sydney apartment. Just these five words, written in Henning's blocky script. She had spent an embarrassing amount of time staring down at them for the second day in a row. The painful twist of her gut each time she looked had dulled, leaving room for other emotions churning in her stomach. Warmth. Longing. Desire. But frustration and anger overshadowed all of those.

Why the hell did he write these words to her? Henning Fischer wasn't an impulsive man, so he would have carefully planned these five words, planned the method of delivery, so she wouldn't discover them until after they had parted. She could picture that intense look on his face as he deliberated how to convey what he felt while minimizing his risk. He must have slipped the paper into her baggage when he took it out to the rental car, back at the Icehotel. She could see him, taking off his gloves, exposing them to the cold air he hated so much, just to avoid saying the words to her face.

She had opened the Pandora's box of her heart, and his response was to try to help her shove it all back in. Try to go back to the way she used to be. To the way they used to be. Hell, no. She had had enough of backtracking.

A knock at her bedroom door startled her out of her thoughts.

"It's me," said her sister from the hallway. "Can I come in?"

"Of course." Alya smoothed her hair and checked to see if her cheeks were flushed.

Her sister opened the door, and her eyes went instantly to the paper in Alya's hand. Too late to hide it. "Sulking again?"

Alya sighed. "Maybe."

"I suspected as much. So I brought you the solution to all problems," said Natasha, nodding toward the hall, her eyes sparkling. "Ice cream. Join me?"

Alya's mouth twitched up. "You're making it hard to maintain my sulky frown."

She followed her sister into the kitchen and took a seat at the countertop bar. Natasha took two bowls from the cabinet and headed for the freezer.

"Are you sure you want to go to the fund-raiser alone tonight?" Natasha asked, setting the chocolate ice cream on the countertop between them. "I wish we could all go together, but Max and I have to be there early. One of the many adventures of dating a famous Jensen family member."

Alya narrowed her eyes at her sister. "Did Max get you to ask me about going alone?"

"What?" Natasha frowned. "No. It's just that the event is so public. And after those *Behind the Runway* clips got so much attention...well, you'll be in the spotlight, I'm sure. I know that's not your favorite thing." She pulled out spoons from the drawer and started scooping.

"A week ago, I would have cared." Alya leaned her elbows on the counter and sighed. "Now I'm tired of making my decisions that way, based on my past. I thought it was just about Nick, but it's more than that."

Natasha took a bite off her spoon and nodded. "Explain."

"When we came to Australia, I put my life on hold for three years, shaped it around avoiding Nick." She paused for a mouthful of ice cream. "Staying out of the media, even when it would have benefitted my career, setting up a security camera in our apartment—which, by the way, I took down this morning."

A flush rushed to her cheeks as she thought about the other reason she had taken it down. Knowing that Henning could be watching her—watching but still staying away—was torture.

"Yeah, Max called me about it," said Natasha,

scooping out another bite. "I figured that's what happened."

"And then I let my relationship with Stewart drag out for months, just so I wasn't alone," she said.

Her ex-boyfriend was a male model, not the thin, androgynous type, but bigger, bulkier, with tattoos and scruff. Yes, he was hot, but long before their breakup, Alya had tired of Stewart's endless chatter about protein shakes and bench press maxes. But the lack of connection, the lack of drama had actually been a relief after Nick.

"Well, Henning definitely isn't Stewart."

Alya rolled her eyes. "That's for sure. But I want a different life. One that's not carefully constructed so I can avoid my fears. One where I'm actually living my life."

Natasha smiled. "I approve."

"Aww, thanks," Alya said dryly.

"For the record, I'm in favor of the idea of going alone, as long as you really want that," said Natasha, her spoon clattering in her bowl.

"Me, too," she said. "But the truth is, I miss Henning. A lot. Enough to consider some bad ideas."

"Like what?"

The heat pulsed to Alya's cheeks again. "Last night, I missed him so much that I was actually entertaining the idea of calling him, late at night, for a little pick-me-up. Grabbing at the scraps he offered."

Natasha laughed. "That idea has some pros, you know."

"Yeah, I'm well aware of the benefits." She shook her head. "But I'd be letting him into my life under his conditions. That's been my problem all along. I've been willing to compromise far too much. No. I deserve more than he wants to give. I'm not compromising, just for amazing sex."

Natasha raised her eyebrows, and Alya sighed.

"It was really, really, really good."

Henning stood in front of his sister's door and swiped a hand over his face. Uncles don't miss their nieces' birthdays. If it had been anything else, he would have said no, but he couldn't say no to Molly. Still, Henning stood at the front door of Suzanne and Kenny's quaint suburban home in the sweltering morning heat, unable to get himself together for a five-year-old's birthday party.

Tonight was the fund-raiser, and he wasn't going. He hadn't spoken to Alya since he left her at her doorstep, hadn't even seen her through the security feed. Max was the one who confirmed she had taken down the camera.

The last few days had been hell, alone in his office, sitting at his computer. At Alya's request, he had dismantled other parts of the system he had set in place for her safety over the last three years. He knew it was coming, but he just hadn't expected the camera from her apartment to go away so soon. It was supposed to be the way he could still check in on her, make sure she was okay even if she was keeping her distance.

He thought he would be relieved to get out of the cold, back to the summer heat of Sydney, but he was wrong. Nothing about this week felt like relief.

But nieces still had birthdays, even when the last remnants of his twisted heart were bleeding out. Fuck, he was turning into a sappy bastard. It was time to put himself aside and eat cake and paint his fingernails, or whatever Molly had planned for him.

Henning straightened up and knocked on the front door. Molly opened it immediately.

"Uncle Henning!" The pint-size ball of energy made a running jump into his arms, and he picked her up and swung her around in a circle.

"It's the birthday girl," he said, but his voice came out like it was full of gravel. Christ, how long had it been since he had spoken aloud?

"I saw you standing there in the window," she said. "Mummy said not to disturb you. What were you doing?"

Henning winced. "I was just thinking about…the place I got your birthday present."

It was as close as he could come to the truth.

She was hanging on around his neck, and she pulled back in his arms, her eyes wide. "Can I open it?"

"Of course. It's your day," he said, kissing her on the cheek. He set her down and handed over the present.

"Wait for everyone to see it, Molly." His sister's voice came from somewhere in the house. "Let Uncle Henning come in."

Molly grabbed his hand and tugged him inside. "We're having hotdogs and chips and carrot sticks and marshmallows and apple juice," she said, leading him into the kitchen.

Suzanne was standing at the stove, pulling the hotdogs out of the boiling water. Henning walked over and kissed her on the cheek. "Hotdogs and hot chips. My favorite brunch menu."

"Me, too," said Suzanne, rolling her eyes.

"Me, too," Molly echoed with a little squeal of joy. "I'm going to go tell Daddy and Liam to come downstairs. And then I can open my present, right, Mummy?"

She ran out before the answer came. Suzanne turned around, giving him the older sister assessment. "You okay?"

"Fine," he grumbled, knowing she could see he was so obviously not fine.

Henning sat down at the kitchen table, but Suzanne was still watching him like a hawk. Finally she sighed. "I watched the show."

Henning gritted his teeth. The YouTube snippets from the Icehotel. The footage he had resisted watching all week, knowing there would be glimpses of Alya. Those few days together were captured on film, suspended in time for him to relive, over and over, if he let himself.

"It's Alya Petrova, isn't it?" his sister said softly. "The reason why you went. She's the only one from Sydney, the only one it could be."

Henning pinched the bridge of his nose.

"If that woman did anything to hurt you..."

Henning gave a short bark of laughter. "You'll what? Meet her in the middle of Main Street at high noon?"

Apparently, the role of older sister didn't expire, even into adulthood, because she didn't smile. "She hurt you. I can see it." Suzanne crossed the kitchen and sat in the chair next to him. "I can't believe she did that, not when—"

"Enough," he grumbled. "Not that it's any of your business, but I was the one who messed it all up. Not Alya."

"What?" Suzanne pulled back and stared at him like he was crazy. "What the hell, Henning? You barely leave your apartment for five years, and then you travel across the world just for a woman—and not just any woman but Alya Petrova—and you mess it up?"

So much for the protective sister thing. "Thanks, Suzanne. Great summary of my life."

She shook her head, slowly, her forehead wrinkled. "But why? If you simply weren't into her, then fine, I'd accept that, but I can see that's not the problem."

"*You'd* accept that? Thanks again," he said dryly. "Can we not talk about this, please?"

Thank God Molly ran back in, cutting off their conversation. Kenny followed on her heels, with Liam asleep in his arms. Molly climbed up on Henning's lap and kissed him on the cheek, on his scars. It didn't usually bother him, not from her at least, but the last person to touch him there was Alya.

"Now can I open my presents?"

"You better ask your mum, sweetheart."

The moment Suzanne nodded, Molly grabbed the present, her chubby little fingers tearing at the wrapping paper. She opened the little box and pulled out the tiara. "A princess crown," she whispered, her eyes wide in amazement. "A real one. Mummy, he got me a real princess crown."

Molly put it on her head and scrambled onto her feet, wandering around the kitchen. She turned around and curtsied for her audience. "Did you get it from a castle?"

Henning smiled at her. "No, sweetheart. It's actually from a friend."

"The friend you were with? Mummy showed me on YouTube."

Even his niece knew about Alya? Henning swallowed back a fist-size lump in his throat. "How do you know about YouTube?" he asked, his voice wavering.

"I can do it myself," she said, her eyes shining. "I'll show you."

I can do it myself. Molly's favorite line. He started to protest, but she had already run off. Henning rubbed his temples. Shit. He really did not want to see this video, but how did he explain that to Molly without disappointing her on her birthday? He looked up at Suzanne in a silent plea, but she was giving him a strange look. No, his sister was definitely not going to help him out with this.

Molly returned a moment later with a little tablet, which she laid on the table. She climbed onto his knee and bent over the device, scrolling until she pulled up the video. Damn, the girl could barely read, but she knew how to find videos on YouTube.

"Do you really know how to do that by yourself?" he asked softly.

She smiled brightly, bursting with pride.

And then it was on, and he was back there at the Icehotel. The clip was from inside one of the cold rooms—the beds, the sculptures and even the damn reindeer pelts were all in view. He could see everything, feel everything. He could feel her.

"Mummy and me looked for you, but we didn't see you," she said. "Why not?"

Henning searched for an answer that a five-year-old could understand, but he was coming up with nothing.

Molly had already turned back to the screen. "Here she is, here she is. Mummy said she thought this was your friend."

And then Alya was there. On the screen. It was the day of the photo shoot, and the Viking bed was in the background. The clip started with her laughing at something that was said off camera. God, she was lovely. After spending all those days with her, it shouldn't have caught him off guard, but seeing her took his breath away.

The sound of her laughter hit him hard. The weight of the last few days without her crashed down on him, and his body felt so heavy, too heavy to even move. He was in love with Alya, and he couldn't have found a less suitable match if he had chosen deliberately. This amazing woman was everything he wasn't. Everything he didn't deserve, especially after that last day together.

Molly was expertly skimming through the video until she found a little snippet from an interview. It was from the last day, and he had waited in the lobby instead of following her into where they had set up a makeshift studio. Alya was answering a question about Federov's style, but Henning barely heard a word of what she said. All he saw were those big, blue eyes, those lips, her skin—so soft, he could still feel it under his fingers. He would never stop aching for this woman.

"Is she really a princess?" asked Molly, interrupting this downhill train of thought. "Is she magical?"

Henning felt the uninjured corner of his mouth tug up, despite everything. "Are princesses magical?"

Molly nodded eagerly, her eyes wide.

"Disney," Suzanne muttered, rolling her eyes.

"Is she?" Molly asked again.

Henning nodded solemnly at his niece. "She's not a princess, but I guess you could say she's magical."

"Can I meet her the next time you see her?"

He swallowed another lump in his throat and gave Molly a kiss on the top of her head. "I don't think there is a next time, sweetheart." The words were so painful to say, and he braced himself as the heaviness came back. "But if there is, you can definitely meet her."

Suzanne was staring at him, her lips parted, her eyes wide in shock. Shit, he had to pull himself together. Alya's interview was still playing, and Henning couldn't bring himself to tell Molly to turn it off.

"It must be difficult to have a private life in such a high-profile role," said the interviewer.

"Yes, though my 'private' life hasn't been that private, right?" said Alya with a little chuckle. Damn, she was amazing. She looked so confident, even as the interviewer asked about one of the hardest times of her life. "It's my experience that we don't choose who we fall in love with."

"So how do you manage that balance, the personal and the public?"

She shook her head, smiling. "I don't have any good advice in this department. I tend to fall in love with the wrong person, and it's never a secret for long. But each time, I still hope that we'll get it right."

Suzanne's voice broke into the interview. "Molly, put that tablet back upstairs, please. Uncle Henning has seen enough of that."

His niece frowned in confusion, and she looked like she was going to protest, but Suzanne added, "Now. Please."

As soon as Molly left the room, Suzanne put her hands on her hips. "That woman is in love, and now I'm almost sure it's with you. I saw it. You've got that look on your face like you're going to lose it soon. Explain to me what the hell is going on?"

"It's complicated," he muttered. "It's for the best. Really."

Except it didn't feel that way at all. It didn't even feel complicated anymore. It just felt like shit.

It felt like shit as he ate his hotdog and his pink cupcake and as he played Molly's favorite princess card game, and he felt even worse as he sat in his black Audi on the drive back to his empty apartment. Suzanne and her family were the most important people in his life, and he was spreading his brooding misery to them, too. At least Molly hadn't seemed to notice.

But Henning just couldn't let go of it. Somehow, in this unfair world full of death and sadness, the most beautiful, most amazing woman in the world had wanted him. And he had shoved the invitation to stand by her side tonight at the fund-raiser back in her face out of fear for her. He'd overreacted outside the Icehotel out of fear. Henning sat in his car long after he had turned off the engine, gripping the steering wheel, trying like hell to figure out why he had sabotaged the most beautiful week of his life. Why was he clinging to this fear, even after the threat had faded, still letting it guide him? For the first time in five years, he let himself examine the part of him he had tried so hard to bury.

He hadn't felt fear when he walked into that warehouse with Sanjay; it was one of the reasons he had quit the AFP. Instead, he had calculated the risk of going in early, just the two of them, and assessed it as the best option. If he had held them back, acted out of fear, would that have saved his teammate? Maybe, or maybe the explosion would have happened when the whole team came into the building. Maybe even more of his team would have died. Still, lying in the hospital bed in the days after the explosion, he had wondered if that absence of fear meant something was wrong with him, if years of seeing the very worst of people had turned off something fundamentally human about him.

But at Blackmore Inc. he had felt fear for Alya. It was the reason he had been so drawn to her, long before their days at the Icehotel, and the reason he had gone so far beyond the parameters of his job. It wasn't just about making her feel safe. His fear for her had let in a sliver of hope that his years on the AFP hadn't permanently damaged him, that there was a chance he could be whole again.

Which made him feel even more messed up about his blow-up at her about giving away her schedule. Had his reaction been so fucking selfish? He didn't truly want her to cower, just so he could get another hit of that deep-seeded need to protect her, to remind himself that he was not just a cold strategist in a man's body. And, yet, out on that frozen river, that's exactly what he did. He had dumped all her fears back on her.

As Henning closed the door to his apartment, he couldn't shake the sound of Alya's voice. He leaned back against the door as whispers of her fingers played across his skin, over and over, setting him on fire. His willpower was slipping at the memory of how she looked at him when she touched him, her breaths teasing him.

That memory led to others, taking him down the road he was trying so hard to resist. Now that it was here, he didn't stop it. Just once more. Just one moment of weakness, so he could remember what it felt like. The sounds she made as he thrust deep inside her, his cock unbearably hard and aching, holding on until she came.

Fuck. It was too much. This was why he shouldn't even see her, despite the way Suzanne had stared at him like he had his head up his ass. Because as soon as she came close, he wouldn't want to let her go again. And he shouldn't take another step into her life unless he was sure he could give her what she deserved: love, not fear.

Still, she was alone tonight, and he needed to know if she was all right. Maybe Max would be willing to send him an update. Just to make sure.

Henning swiped a hand over his face, picked up his phone and dialed Max's number.

CHAPTER THIRTEEN

"WE'RE HERE, MA'AM," said the driver, peering at Alya through the rearview mirror.

She swallowed. "Just give me a minute."

He nodded. "Of course."

Alya took a few yoga breaths, her usual preparation for stepping out of the car before an event, preparing to face looks or judgments or whatever came her way.

But just like at the Icehotel, when she waited for the interview, the usual twist-in-the-gut feeling was conspicuously absent. In fact, that little flutter of nerves in her stomach was surprisingly invigorating. It was refreshing to step out knowing that whatever went through the minds of everyone who was watching, it didn't change anything, not really. All along she had thought that not worrying about what others said about her meant the kind of recklessness that really had never been her style. But for her, it was something else. It was putting aside all her fears and looking forward. Not backward, not to the side.

Anything involving Max Jensen and his family—

who were like royalty here—attracted the Australian press, and this fund-raiser was no exception, which made it a great place to test her resolution to just relax and look forward. She was ready to enjoy the night with her sister and Max and the rest of the Blackmore Inc. group, off duty. Alya took out her compact mirror and checked her lipstick once more. Cherry red, as Natasha had called it, to match her dress.

Her lipstick was in place. Her hair was woven into an intricate knot on her head, exposing her neck. The pearl earrings and necklace gave the whole outfit a classy look, and all the red said sexy. It was the kind of look designers might dress her up in, but she never picked it out herself. Until today. Let the fun begin.

"I'm ready," she said to the driver. He climbed out and walked around the car to open the door for her.

Sydney's hot summer air poured into the car, along with a cacophony of voices and music. Bulbs flashed and the crowd moved as she stepped out into the late-afternoon sun and onto the red carpet. Alya hesitated, even looked back for a moment, instinctually searching for someone's hand to grab, someone who would make her feel less exposed. No. She was doing this on her own. The first times would tug on her vulnerabilities, but she'd learn. There was no way to move forward without risk. She had condemned Henning for not being willing to take risks, so it was time for her to step up her own game, too.

Alya held her head high and walked forward, ignoring the questions that were coming from all sides.

"Everyone has been talking about your *Behind the Runway* interview. Can you comment on who is the source of your thoughts on falling in love?"

"Who are you hoping to get it right with?" called another voice.

"You were seen talking intimately to Jean Pierre Rus. Can you comment?"

"Nick Bancroft posted about the flowers he sent you on social media. Are you two back together?"

She almost rolled her eyes at that last one. Of course Nick was going to find a way to make this about him. She took long strides to the circular part of the carpet, pausing there, turning for the cameras.

"No matter what I say, you'll probably come to your own conclusions," she said, smiling mischievously. "So, no comment."

Was it really so easy? Of course, she had answered questions with *no comment* for years, but still, the insinuations had lingered, each a new bite of insecurity that tore at her, deep inside. All this time, she had cared what they thought. But today? It was...fine. The speculations were so far from the truth, and if she told anyone the real story of her and Henning they wouldn't believe her. She had taken a risk for a man, he had offered her less and she had decided she wouldn't settle. So simple, and yet it was everything.

Alya smiled at the cameras one more time, and then walked into the entryway. The first portion of the event was an open-aired affair, on an enormous patio right on the harbour, lined with colorful flowers. Giant sails sheltered portions of the patio from the sun, and the guests gathered around standing tables under them. A passing server offered her a glass of champagne, and she took it, scanning the place for familiar faces. Max and Natasha were here somewhere, maybe talking with donors. The rest of the Blackmore Inc. team, whom Alya had met over the years, would show up with their partners at some point, but at the moment, Alya didn't see any of them.

She did see the society columnist for *Luxury*, one of the many magazines where Alya's private life occasionally had entertained the readership, despite all her efforts to avoid it. Nathaniel Woods. Over the past three years, she and Natasha had come up with coordinated plans to avoid him at events like this, but tonight, she walked straight up to him.

His eyes showed a hint of surprise, but he kissed her cheek and smiled. "Alya Petrova. You're voluntarily talking to me?"

Alya laughed. "I know. Can you believe it?"

"You look lovely," he said, and his smile was warm. He asked about the Icehotel, Federov's collection and her plans for the spring, and they chatted about other Sydney events. The more they talked, the more she felt her confidence growing. Whatever he ended up writing, she could handle it.

But just as he was leaning in to kiss her on the cheek again, Nathaniel froze.

"Just FYI…" He cleared his throat. "There's a

very...distinct-looking man staring at you intensely. He's quite large."

Alya's heart jumped. No. It couldn't be. Probably another one of the Blackmore Inc. guys. Henning had probably checked in with someone in the office to make sure they'd be there, just to make sure she was safe.

Still, she hoped. Damn, Alya had spent the week hoping. Wasn't she done with it? If she turned around now and it wasn't Henning, that was probably the one thing she couldn't handle in front of a crowd.

"Aaaaand he's coming this way," added Nathaniel. "I don't suppose you know who this is."

"I might."

Okay, she could do this. Just hold it all in. She had years of practice controlling her feelings, and it was time to put that experience to use. Her heart pounded harder in her chest, and she took another yoga breath, this one completely useless. Then, slowly, she turned.

"Henning?" She whispered his name as he stalked across the patio. She blinked, taking him in. He'd gotten a haircut, and he was wearing...a suit? In fact, he looked a lot closer to the cadet photo she'd found of him online, the one before the attack.

"I'm getting the *time-to-leave-us-the-fuck-alone* vibe from him," said Nathaniel quietly. "Strongly."

"That's about right."

Was this real? Henning took a few last steps and stopped in front of her. Alya's heart was pounding so hard she was sure everyone around them could hear it. She reached out to touch him but pulled her hand back as her mind kicked into gear. This was the man who had shot her down, and now he just showed up? Did he expect her to welcome him, just because he changed his mind?

She swallowed a lump in her throat and straightened up. "What are you doing here?"

"I'm here to say I'm sorry," he said softly, his voice was raw, vulnerable.

Her heart stuttered. Oh, damn. She was so in love with this man. And he had the power to hurt her. She looked around, and sure enough, no one was hiding their curiosity.

She gestured to Nathaniel. "Henning, meet Nathaniel Woods, columnist for *Luxury* magazine."

Henning tipped his chin in Nathaniel's direction. "I'll be reading your column for the next six months to make sure this moment doesn't end up there."

Alya raised an eyebrow. "Unless that's what I want."

"Unless that's what she wants," echoed Henning in a low grumble.

Nathaniel smiled a little. "Well, I think that's my cue to duck out of this conversation."

He kissed Alya on the cheek and walked away.

For a moment that impenetrable mask was back on Henning's face, but then he took a deep breath, relaxing, letting her see the longing in his eyes. It was painful to see. He looked like he'd been just as miserable as she had been since they returned from

Sweden. His fingers flexed. Did he want to touch her as much as she wanted to touch him? If so, he held back.

"I messed up," he said, his voice rough, "and I don't know how to make it right. I have no experience with this. But I promise I'll figure it out."

Alya scanned the patio, taking in the other guests who surrounded them. The closest were in listening distance, and she caught a few more furtive glances their way.

She looked back at Henning and frowned. "You want to do this right here, in front of everyone?"

His jaw was clenched, and he looked like he was in the middle of some sort of internal debate. Then he closed his eyes and swallowed. "I don't. I'll leave if you ask me to."

Alya blew out a frustrated sigh. She was still so mad at him, but, Lord, she had missed him. Tearing out the security cameras had felt like tearing out a whole piece of her, the last connection between them, forged during the most difficult years of her life. He had been there all along for her, and she had gotten over her fear slowly, so slowly, with so many missteps. Yes, he was allowed to have missteps, too, but this one seemed to scrape against her rawest wound. She knew all of these things, and yet Alya wasn't ready to ask him to leave. At least not yet.

The longer she mulled this over, the more that look of intense determination settled into Henning's expression. He opened his mouth to speak again, but she held up her hand. "Wait. Let's go somewhere else."

He nodded, looking a little brighter. Had he expected her to turn him away today? And he still came?

She scanned the area, looking for someplace with a little more privacy. There weren't a lot of options completely out of sight, but the guests were mostly clustered in the shade of the enormous sails, so she nodded over to the sunniest corner, where at least they would be out of ear range at the far end of the patio. It was lined with a white pillared railing that looked out onto Sydney Harbour, decorated with a few large plants in terra-cotta pots. Alya headed for the shade of a planted palm. Henning's hand brushed the small of her back as she walked, and for a moment, it felt as if they had rewound a week. They were so close. But his hand dropped almost immediately. They weren't at the Icehotel anymore.

Alya found a little nook behind the fronds of the tree. She hadn't spotted her sister yet, but if Natasha was watching, she was probably trying to get a better view. Max, too, and maybe even the whole Blackmore Inc. group. But right now, she needed a little space from the world.

She turned around to face Henning. He had wedged himself between the plant and the railing, and one leafy frond batted at his head. He brushed it away and looked down at her, the dark intensity of his eyes heavy. No one in the world looked at her like this, like he would get down on his knees for her, give her anything. The ache of their separation echoed between them, back and forth, turning her insides molten-hot, but she resisted reaching for him. Instead, she crossed her arms.

"I still haven't decided whether you should stay or go," she said. "You have five minutes to explain to me why letting you stay would lead to anything else besides heartbreak. For both of us."

He nodded, then drew in a deep breath. "I hurt you, and I'm so sorry. I've spent the last week thinking about it. You pulled security, taking me out of your life. And it's been hell."

She could hear this was painful for him, too, and she had to resist the strong urge to comfort him.

"It wasn't about you, Henning." Well, that wasn't quite true. She swallowed, pushing herself to continue. "Okay, maybe it was a little about you, but mostly it was about letting go of a past that I have to put behind me. All the way."

He didn't speak, but she could feel he was completely tuned in to everything she said, each movement of her lips.

"I need more than a protector, Henning. I need someone who will support me as I change my life to something that I want. Something that I love."

"You deserve that, Alya," he said roughly. "You deserve everything."

His words quaked through her, filled with emotion. He brought his hand to her cheek and traced her lips.

"I've spent the last five years with Sanjay's death

hanging over me," he continued. "What would happen if I lost you? Just that thought makes me want to hold you so tight, to make sure nothing ever happens to you." He closed his eyes and let out a long breath. "There's a part of me that's always going to want to protect you. But I need to deal with it in another way. This is my shit that I need to address, and I'm willing to do it. And if you need to wait for that change before we see each other again, then I respect that. I just wanted you to know that I'm choosing love over fear, starting right now."

Oh, God, this man. Just seeing him again felt so good, so right. He was promising her he'd work on this.

"I don't want to wait, Henning," she said quietly.

The intensity of his expression didn't waver. "There are parts of me that are broken, that might never get fixed."

She lifted her hand to trace the jagged scars down the left side of his face.

"That's what I thought about myself for so long," she whispered.

Henning smiled, really smiled with all the warmth and tenderness she had missed. His scars pulled on the left side of his mouth, making the smile all that more vulnerable.

"Can we please figure this out together?" he whispered.

God, she wanted that. Alya took a deep breath and nodded. His arms came around her, and he held her close as she slipped her hands under his jacket, against the hard muscles of his back. She wanted to stay here, just like this, resting her cheek against his chest, and she probably always would. But they needed to finish this conversation.

"Staying here with me means we'll both be in the spotlight, starting now," she said, pulling back a little. "Everyone watched us walk over here, and if you hold me like this and look at me like this, people will take photos and write about us and make all sorts of speculations about why we're together. They'll dig up the story of your scars and lay it out for everyone to comment on. If you stay, we're saying yes to all of that. Even if we go our separate ways in the future, you won't be able to take that back. Are you willing to do that?"

His broken smile was full of hope. "You're worth that risk. You're worth everything. I'm willing to show you that, again and again. Tonight or any other night." Then he raised an eyebrow. "And if I have my say in this, we're definitely not going our separate ways. You're the only one I've wanted for so long now, and that's not going to change."

She closed her eyes and let the words sink in. He was here. This was real. She looked up into his deep brown eyes, and she had the strong urge to kiss him, to remember all the things she had learned about him back at the Icehotel. Was he right, that what they had between them wouldn't change? God, she hoped this would last forever.

She threaded her fingers into his hair and tugged a little, urging his mouth down to hers. It was a soft, slow kiss, making her insides melt and her heart skitter in her chest. There was nothing hesitant about it. She put aside the cameras and the whispers and everything else, and she kissed him again and again. It was so freeing to simply kiss this man she was in love with, right here, for the world to see.

"I don't think the palm is hiding much," she said with a little laugh. "By the way, how did you get into this event?"

Henning smiled. "It started with a call to Max. I asked if he'd check in on you and to get back to me. But he told me no, straight up. If I wanted to know, I had to come myself. So I told him you didn't want security, and he said, 'looks like you've got a problem on your hands.' Next thing I knew, a courier delivered a ticket to my house."

She could picture his expression as he opened that envelope, struggling with what to do. "How long did you sulk at home before you decided to come?"

"Only five hours or so," he said with a grin. "Half that time was spent going through scenarios if you had brought a date, figuring out how to deal with that."

"What did you come up with?"

"Nothing you want to hear about."

She laughed. "Lucky for you, I came alone."

"Lucky for me," he echoed.

Alya found Henning's hand and laced her fingers with his. "You ready to get out from behind this tree?"

"I'm willing to try just about anything, as long as it's with you." His voice was soft, that gruff, gentle rumble she had missed so much this week, so she squeezed his hand, and together, they walked into the crowd.

Henning looked down at the loveliest, most amazing woman in the world. Somehow, he was the one holding her hand right now. Love, not fear. It was the answer to everything, really. "Where are we going?"

"To find Max and Natasha. And I think the rest of the Blackmore Inc. crew is here, too," she added with a mischievous smile.

Henning raised his eyebrows, and then started to laugh. He just let himself go, laughing and shaking his head. "Is this a test? Right in front of all the guys I work with."

"No backing out, right?" She kissed his hand. "But no, it's not a test. I told Natasha I'd come find her right away when I arrived. She's been a little worried about me this week."

Her sister had been worried about her. His smiled faded. "It was a hard week?"

She nodded, and, fuck, it was painful to see it all over her face.

"I hurt you," he whispered. "I'm so sorry."

She bit her lip and nodded.

He slowed to a stop and lifted his hand to her face,

resting it on her cheek. "It was an awful week for me, too, if that's any consolation."

"Maybe a little bit." Her lips twitched in a hint of a smile. "But I guessed it would be. I just didn't think you'd do anything about it."

He slipped his hand to the base of her neck and pressed his lips against hers. "But I did."

He wanted to stay like that, holding her, kissing her, but there would be time for that later. So he let her go, and they walked across the patio, decorated with flowers, toward the French doors that led inside. There was plenty of open staring at him as he and Alya wove their way through the crowd hand in hand. He could feel the gazes that traced his scars, then dropped to his hand that covered hers. It would probably always be like this, but as long as it didn't hurt Alya, he didn't care.

They were about to go inside when Natasha walked out alone. Her mouth fell open the moment she caught sight of them.

"I can't believe it," she said, her brow wrinkled.

Henning cringed. Shit. Alya told her sister everything, which probably meant Natasha hated him at this point. The last thing he wanted was to upset either one of them again. But Alya squeezed his hand, reminding him that he wasn't alone, that they were in this together.

Then Natasha broke into a smile. "I've got to go tell Max I lost the bet." Natasha wrapped her arms around her sister's waist and kissed her cheek. "But you look so much happier than you did all week, so I guess I'll get over losing it."

A little relief flooded in, and Henning let out his breath. It was going to be okay.

Natasha gave him an assessing look. "Henning Fischer?"

He nodded, kissing Alya's sister on the cheek.

She smiled. "Come on. We're all inside, out of the sun."

Natasha led the way across the open room, to a lounge area on the far side. But Alya slowed to a stop at the entrance, letting Natasha go ahead. The voices of the other Blackmore Inc. men echoed in the room. Henning squeezed Alya's hand.

"You okay?" he whispered.

But when Alya turned around, her face was lit with a smile of pure happiness. "I'm so much better than okay." Her blue eyes sparkled and danced as she looked at him.

"Only you, Alya," he whispered, brushing his lips over hers. "That's all that matters."

She stood on her toes and kissed him back, her mouth soft and warm. After days apart, the fire between them sparked and sizzled, almost irresistible. But this was so much more than attraction. This moment was a dream he had never allowed himself to hope for.

"Thank you for coming, Henning," she said, her voice serious.

"I'll always come for you."

Always. A word he hadn't believed in for so long. Until Alya.

Then, slowly, they entered the lounge. All the Blackmore Inc. principals were seated around a low glass table. Derek Latu and his wife, Laurie, were on one side of a long sofa. Derek and he grew up together, and he was the reason Henning had come to Blackmore, Inc. after he left the AFP. Right now, his friend's gaze moved between Alya and him, and his smile was wide. Jackson McAllister leaned against Cameron Blackmore's chest on the other side of the sofa. When Henning started at Blackmore Inc., if anyone had told him the CEO would fall head-over-heels in love, enough to chase a woman halfway around the world, he would have laughed. Then again, the same could probably be said about Henning. But seeing Cameron and Jackson gave him another surge of happiness. Cameron had made mistakes, and they were still together. Marianna Ruiz and Simon Rodriguez were there, too, squashed together on an oversize chair, Simon's arm draped over his fiancé's shoulder, holding her close. Their story began years ago, back in Miami, and it was another testament to the resiliency of love.

"I told you he'd step up," Max said from the far sofa, tugging Natasha onto the cushion next to him.

"You bet on my relationship with Alya?" grumbled Henning, but he couldn't hold back his smile.

Max smirked. "Hey, I bet *for* you. Natasha was the one who bet that Alya would turn you down."

Natasha turned around and swatted at him. Then she turned back to Henning. "I was just looking out for her. Nothing personal."

"I appreciate that," he said. "I messed up."

"See why I bet on him?" said Max. Natasha rolled her eyes as she shifted closer to him.

"Come sit down for a bit," said Simon, gesturing to the open spots on the far sofa. "You two need a drink?"

Alya looked up at him, and he shook his head. They had just found each other again, and he wasn't quite ready to share her. But if that's what she wanted...

"Not yet," she said. "I think I want to go down to the beach for a bit before dinner."

She winked at him, and Henning slipped his arm around Alya, breathing in the scent he had ached for all week long. Alya chatted with the others for a few more minutes, but he wasn't following the conversation anymore. The air was warm, and the breeze blew gently through the open windows. And Alya was there, so close. It was a heaven Henning had never believed in, but tonight, for the first time, he knew it existed for real. This was all he needed.

* * * * *

LET'S TALK
Romance

For exclusive extracts, competitions and special offers, find us online:

f MillsandBoon

🐦 @MillsandBoon

📷 @MillsandBoonUK

♪ @MillsandBoonUK

Get in touch on 01413 063 232